SWEET ADDICTION

Barbara Diamond

Shrubs Publishing

Contents

SWEET ADDICTION

Chapter One

Our sun-tanned bodies shimmered in the sun. The water splashing gently on the boats bow was soothing and totally relaxing. Maddy, Max and I were having a great time on my daddy's big boat which Daddy had kindly offered to us. So, we all could have a break. The week after Stefano left was terrible. I was lost and confused; I didn't understand why he wanted me as a mistress.

"No strings attached?" I thought. I was unhappy and I knew I missed him. Jaine' could see I was unhappy and lonely and she suggested I take a break.

"Go, Tassy, go and relax and get some girl time." I hugged her.

"Thank you so much I really could do with a break and from men" I said as I kissed her on the cheek. From there it all happened.

Daddy organized a crew and I got the girls together.

"Oh, Tas we would love too" they both said.

Everything was arranged and we were to have 10 days cruising the Islands. The Boat was a luxury boat with 3 crew and everything was supplied and done for us. We felt like Queens.

"This is amazing!" Max said as she floated on her back in the water.

I lay there on my sofa bed and sipped my Vodka Sunrise.

"Yes this is just what I needed." I said to myself.

I had told no-one of my encounter with Stefano and about his proposal. I still didn't know how I felt about it. There was no denying I wanted him and I missed him but I wasn't sure if I could give up my other casual lovers. I decided not to ring him and just have a break from everyone and their demands. Maddy looked gorgeous in her bikini, her long legs had certainly got the attention of the crew.

"Well, this is the life" she said with a smile.

"Sure is," I replied as I finished my second Vodka sunrise.

"Want a drink Maddy?"   I peered at her through my sunglasses.

"I'll have what you're having" she said

"Max, how about you?" I asked as she sat down on her sofa bed.

"Love one" she said.

I got up and went to the bar. I could have just yelled out to our waiter to get them for us but I needed to stretch my legs. Our waiter was a 30-year-old quite handsome man suntanned, dark hair and cute body named Peter.

"Hey Peter" I said as I approached the bar.

"Hello, Tasmin." he answered with a smile.

I noticed he was staring at my breasts in my bikini. I blushed as I haven't had much male attention for a while.

"Can I have 3 Vodka Sunrises please" I said looking into his eyes.

"With pleasure."

"I'll bring them over with some snacks ok?"

"Thanks." I said noticing how his eyes twinkled in the sun.

"Drinks are coming girls." I said as I sat down.

Peter arrived with the drinks and snacks and put them on the table.

"Anything else ladies?" he purred.

Well, I could think of few things like bringing me to an orgasm and sucking my tits with that tongue. I thought to myself and feeling little horny. Maddy and Max also noticed this tanned hunk and our eyes looked at him with wicked thoughts.

"Mmm, I could definitely screw that one" she said as he walked away.

Max agreed "He's hot."

Actually, daddy had thought of everything. The crew of three men were all very nice to look at and be pampered by. It was hard not to fantasize about what wicked things I could do to all three. And I'm guessing Max and Maddy were thinking the same thing. Dave was our Captain and he was a blonde blue-eyed hunk with big bronzed muscles. He could jump my bones any day. Jamie was the Chef and he also was a brown-haired hunk with beautiful eyes and smile.

"Did my dad set us up with three handsome men for a reason?" I couldn't help giggle out loud.

"What's funny?" Max asked as she sipped her drink.

"I was just thinking of our three hunky crewmen and what naughty things we could do to them."   I said with a cheeky grin.

"Yeh, I have noticed them." said Maddy with a smile.

"Why don't we give them a show?" I suggested,

"What like"? Maddy replied.

"Take our tops off and sun bake"? I looked at them both.

"Sounds good to me." Max said already taking her top off.

So, we all did the same and put more oil on our bodies and laid back on our sofa's. Peter was watching from the bar and couldn't take his eyes of them. His erection already straining in his shorts. Dave was up top and saw the whole show.

"Well, this is interesting" he thought as he licked his lips.

We lay there unaware of horny eyes watching us we were in our own little fantasies. The afternoon drifted into Vodka Sunsets and we went for a siesta and shower before dinner. One my way to my room I went into the kitchen and talk to Jamie. He was preparing the nights meal. He looked up when I entered.

"Hi, Tasmin, how is everything?" He asked with a smile.

"Everything is great Jamie"

"You are spoiling us."

"Good that's what your father wanted us to do" I smiled at him and then thought why not?

"Jamie, I thought tonight maybe you and the other crew would like to join us for dinner and company?"

"Though you would have to cook?"

"That would be my pleasure I will whip up a seafood feast and a surprise for dessert?"

"You and your mates on a platter with chocolate baileys sauce would be just delicious thanks." I thought to myself with a wicked smile.

So, it was all arranged and dinner would be at 7 with drinks at 6 on the deck looking at the sunset. He said he would let the others know. I half skipped to my bedroom on the way telling Maddy and Max our dinner plans.

"Oooh sounds exciting" Max said as lack of men and sex had been on her schedule for the last month or so.

Maddy informed us that her and Mitch were taking a break as he was doing a surfing tournament trip with some of the guys and would I be ok if we saw other people casually? So, the three of us were not committed to any man. Single, Sexy, and horny in the secluded islands with three hunks on board.

"Well, it could be fun," said Maddy.

"Which one do you fancy Tas?" she asked

"All three I thought"

"I don't mind there all cute" I answered.

"Max how about you?"

I looked at her and she spoke.

"Well let's have some fun and see what happens."

We all agreed planning a seduction was definitely a hot mission one we all wanted to explore further.

"Dress light" I teased them as I went to lie down for half an hour.

One hour later after my energy nap and shower, I looked at my selection for tonight's seduction.

"Mmm, the white see through lace dress would be hot." I thought to myself.

"G/string and white lace bra or maybe no bra?"

"Yep, that should knock them out."

Max and Maddy had also dressed to the occasion. Max in a very short black strapless mini dress. That showed her beautiful tanned body which was glowing. She said she did have g/string on. Maddy was in a Red short tight dress that showed her breasts and legs.

"God girls hope these men can handle us." I laughed as we did look goddamn hot.

"I hope these sailors are hungry."

Chapter Two

The guys were waiting for us on deck with drinks made and ready. Their eyes bulging when we came on deck.

"Ladies you all look ravishing" Dave beamed at us.

"Come take a drink and sit down."

He winked at me and I nearly melted. I suppose because he is the captain he gets first pick, I thought to myself thinking I hope it's me. We all chatted comfortably with these charming men.

"Was this meant to be?" I thought.

Peter got the wine ready for dinner and Jamie went into the kitchen to serve entrée Max followed. Dave was very charming listening to me and smiling those sensual eyes that look like they're saying,

"I'm saving you for sweets."

We ate a delicious meal of seafood chicken and salad. Jamie sure knows how to cook and the flavors were divine. We watched the sun go down and the boat now was glowing and twinkling with the fairy lights. It was very romantic. Peter and Maddy were starting to dance to a slow salsa and Max helped Jamie clear the table. I looked at Dave who had not taken his eyes off me.

"You like what you see?" I asked with a sexy smile.

"Like"

"I want to hold you in my arms." He pulled me close.

I could smell his breath of wine, his male scent and those strong arms wrapped around me.

"Oh God," I missed this closeness.

My body was betraying me again and I could not think about Stefano or any man at the moment. I was lost in those eyes and that mouth.   The way he talked watching his tongue and every move. Jamie and Max brought back dessert. Jamie had created a strawberry chocolate tart which the strawberries had been soaked in Grand Marnier. It looked delicious. I put some on a spoon and tasted and rolled my tongue around all the flavors. Dave was watching with interest and I could see I had him in my spell. I then put some more on a spoon and lifted it to his mouth to receive. He opened without protest and also teased me with his tongue.

"Oh my! this is fun".

My body tingling all over. Peter and Maddy had adjourned in the lounge room to get better acquainted with their tongues. Jamie and Max obviously were playing in the kitchen and not just with the dishes. Dave's hand was gently pinching my nipples through my dress and nuzzling my neck,

"Oh, that's feels nice" I realized how I missed a man's touch.

Our lips met and I accepted his tongue and gave in to submission. He was holding me close and I could feel his erection through his pants. His other hand had found my favorite spot and I didn't resist. I wanted him and my body was again lost at sea. I laid there on the sofa with the stars glowing in the night sky and let go of my release as Dave did magic tricks with his tongue and fingers. He kissed me then and pulled me up,

"Let's go somewhere more private?" He said with glowing eyes.

"Sounded great to me"

"I'm a no strings attached girl just having a good time"

We went to my bedroom as staff quarters are smaller. My bedroom was huge with an ensuite. He pulled me into his arms,

"Tasmin you are very appealing and sexy."

"I want to make love to you my sweet mermaid."

I let him peel my lace dress off to expose my g/string. He picked me up and laid me on the bed. He undressed and was standing naked before me. I looked at him and his manhood that was fully erect, willing and waiting. I sat on my knees as he stood by the bed and looked up at him with my big seductive eyes that were saying to him.

"Let me suck you honey."

I teased him with my tongue and had him in submission in little time. I handed him some tissues just when he was about to blow. He spat out his juice with a groan from deep down.

"Mission one completed" I thought to myself.

Dave got us some drinks and we got ready for round two. The gentle rocking of the boat and our rocking collided and once again I was lost at sea. He lay beside me and got his breath back.

"That was fantastic baby. You're sure know how to love a man." I laughed and gave him a passionate kiss and cuddled into him.

"Will we get dressed and go up deck?" he asked looking into my eyes.

"We could have a spa under the stars?" He looked at me for an answer.

"Why not the nights not over and maybe there's round 3." I thought.

"Yes, that would be lovely." I said taking his hand.

We got dressed which was only my g and dress and he put only his boxers and pants on. We got up on deck and Maddy and Max were there drinking and cuddling up to Peter and Jamie.

"Everyone having a good night." I asked with a big smile. Our eyes all met and we all laughed.

"Just beautiful and perfect" said Jamie who obliviously had just had the best sex in a while.

"Yeah," said Pete.

"How lucky are we?" He looked at Dave and Jamie.

"You Ladies sure know how to show a guy a great time." Said Pete looking at me with hot eyes.

Was I seeing things or did he just make a pass at me? I said to the girls, "Let's do a bathroom break," and they followed me downstairs. We freshened up and the I asked them,

"Are we swapping or staying with the same?"

"I can see Pete has the hots for you" Maddy said looking at me.

"Is that ok?" I asked her.

"Yes, lets screw them all!" she said with a big smile.

"Max, what do you think?" Maddy and I both looked at her.

"What an orgy"? she said with big eyes.

"Yes," replied Maddy.

"Ok," said Max.

"They're all cute."

"Why don't we do a striptease for them as a treat and a little lap dancing?" Maddy said as she put more red lipstick on. We looked at her with smiles on our faces.

Chapter Three

We came back on deck and Maddy put some sexy salsa music on. Maddy told the boys to get comfortable and sit back and enjoy the show. They sat there their eyes growing big and not to mention what's growing in their pants. We started swaying to the music and Maddy peeled my dress off touching my breasts as she did so. I then did the same to Maddy and then Maddy and I did the same to Max. It was all very erotic and sexy. The boys were entranced and watched every move. We were dancing just in our g/strings and let the music take control. Our breasts jiggling to the beat. We then picked a man and did a little lap dancing on them. I went to Pete and Max went over to Captain Dave and Maddy went up to Jamie.

"No hands" I slapped Pete's hand away from my boobs.

"You boys will have to good if you want to touch?" I said it with a smile.

They all laughed and promised to be good. We knew we were playing with fire and it wasn't long before we were groped and kissed. We had some more drinks and decided to have a spa. We climbed in it was warm and inviting. Pete didn't waste any time he was already touching my sensitive spot and feeling my breasts with the other. I found his huge erection and pulled along his shaft. Our lips met and our tongues were dancing in each other's mouths. The others were also heavily into foreplay and it was getting very heated. The spa only lasted half an hour as we all knew what we wanted, and it wasn't just foreplay. We all found our private sofa's and proceeded to play some more. Pete was different to Dave; Pete was a little gentler and more submissive whereas Dave was like a Jack Rabbit. We took our time and I teased him with my tongue and then he took me out to sea and back again. He mounted me gently and took me to great heights under the stars. We lay exhausted in each other's arms and had a little laugh.

"I hope you don't mind that us girls seduced you all?" I said cheekily.

"No not at all."

"It's been very pleasurable and interesting getting to know each of you."   He looked at me and smiled.

"Oh no you think were sluts now?" I said ashamed

"No baby I don't think that."

"You're beautiful women who want a little attention and love?"

"So, what's wrong with that?" he looked at me

"As long as we don't lose our jobs because of this."

"We can enjoy this tropical romance holiday and spoil you ladies" I looked at him.

"That's how I see it too."

"I'm glad we understand each other and that this is purely casual?" He hugged me then and kissed my lips with softness and teasing.

"Let's get drinks?" I said getting up and putting my dress on I couldn't find my g so my dress would have to do. Well, my nipples poked out of the lace and you could see my bum and my pussy.

"Very nice" Pete grabbed me around the waist.

"I think I'II pass on the drink I'm busy now"

"Ooh he's got second fire." I groaned as my knees buckled when he sucked my nipples through the lace.

He pulled me back down on the sofa and I fell into his strong arms and huge erection. His hand already up my dress to my favorite spot and his tongue and lips doing magical things to my nipples through the lace. He left my dress on and rolled me on my knees. He entered me gently and held me around my hips and we thrusted together we made love again under the stars and once again my body betrayed me to lust and desire. We lay there exhausted and after regaining my breath and was able to talk I said

"Ok that was hot but now I really need a drink." He laughed and said he knows a good waiter who can look after my needs.

"What would you like?" he got up and put his boxers on and went to the bar.

"Jack Daniels and Coke" I replied just as Maddy and Jamie appeared looking all flustered and sweaty.

"I would love a drink"? Maddy asked with a shy smile. I looked at her and laughed.

"Too late to be shy honey." She came over and hugged me. We sat there and enjoyed our drinks and listening to the Ocean, so calm, and peaceful.

"This is beautiful Tas" Maddy squeezed my arm while I looked at her and smiled.

"You're my best friend and I love you" I said as I touched her hand.

Max finally arrived back on deck looking like she had been put through the washing machine. Her hair was a mess and she had this dreamy look about her. We laughed and Max sat down to join us.

"That was totally wicked," she said with excitement.

"He wouldn't stop" she added with a grin.

"I know it's amazing." I said smiling at her.

Maddy also couldn't deny she also had a great time.

"I think it's the thrill of each man and how different their techniques are" she said with a big smile on her face.

"Well, we have one more to go haven't we"? I said looking at them.

"Yes, they agreed" and this one would stay all night.

"Ok let's do it!" I said as we giggled again. The boys had got our attention because of our giggling and asked what's so funny.

"Well, we have been a bit wicked" I said with a smile.

"We thought we have to finish this night with another bang and spend the night together."

"So, what do you think?" I said looking at them.

"Fine by us." Dave talked for them.

"Ok by me," said Jamie looking straight at me with a sexy look in his eyes.

"This will be interesting." I thought to myself with a sexual urge to seduce him beyond submission, there was something about him that really turned me on and attracted me to him. I felt my juices starting flow and my pussy was pulsating just thinking about this man was teasing me. Jamie got up and held his hand out to me,

"Tasmin, coming?"

"Did he say coming?" I think I just did.

We all said goodnight and went to our rooms. Jamie did not disappoint. He brought me to climax with such skill and I felt like I was floating. We made passionate love throughout the night and finally fell asleep in his arms.

Chapter Four

We woke to another beautiful day in Paradise. Jamie had got up early and prepared a feast on deck for us all.

"I think we all need energy after last night," he said with a smile.

We all agreed and ate like Kings and Queens. We spent the morning sun baking and swimming. It was glorious. Even the boys joined us for a swim to cool off.

"Well, this is great!" I said as I sipped my Vodka Sunrise.

"No doubt about it." answered Max.

"I want to stay here forever" said Maddy.

"So, what are we going to do tonight, girls?" I looked at them with excitement.

"Well, we could play some games," said Max with a smile.

"Oooh that sounds interesting like twister only naked?" replied Maddy.

"Girls, that's a bit naughty." I said giggling.

"Ok well what about Strip Jack Poker?" said Max.

"Yeh, that sounds good." I replied with a big smile.

"And when you lose, you not only lose a piece of clothing but you have a shot as well?" Maddy said.

We all giggled again and started planning our night. I would wear the whole lingered get up and that will take a while to be stark naked in front of every one plus I was a good poker player. Jamie announced we would be having dinner on deck and pre drinks would be at 5pm. We lay there enjoying the day. We swam, snorkeled, fished and sunbathed till

4pm. The boys had caught some fish for dinner as well. We went to our rooms to get ready.

"See you in an hour." I said to the girls.

"Remember to wear a lot of lingerie tonight. We'll have them stark naked before us."

I showered and loved the smell of a coconut mango body wash. I let the loofa slide up and down my legs and around my favorite spot. I got dressed in my peek a boo red corset matching g/string, stockings, suspenders and stilettos and a tight black mini dress which showed my suspenders a little bit.

"Mmm, just a little tease" I thought to myself.

Put my hair up and went to put jewelry on and spotted my diamond earrings that I had brought with me. My thoughts immediately went to Stefano and I sat down on the bed and held the earrings in my hands.

"I love you Stefano, but I don't know if I can be faithful to you."

All these thoughts were in my head and I felt a little guilty about what we were doing. I looked at myself in the mirror and I liked what I see.

"I am a no strings attached girl with a huge sexual appetite?"

"I wasn't ready to settle down to one man yet."

"There's no harm in having a bit of fun." I reassured myself as I put on my earrings and they looked incredible.

"Yes, why not be spoiled." I went up on deck and the boys were there but not the girls.

"Wow" Dave whistled.

"You look gorgeous Tasmin" Jamie said with a smile.

"Honey I could eat you" Pete drooled.

The girls came up on deck just as I was blushing like my red corset. They looked hot. They went all out and looked very sexy. The men were aroused now and clearly could see a good night coming on. We ate a wonderful dinner and the seafood melted in our mouths. Jamie could really cook and he said,

"Sweets are a surprise?"

"Oooh, I love surprises." I said with a giggle.

"So, do we?" the girls echoed behind me.

We asked the boys if they wanted to play a game.

"We thought Strip Jack Poker"? said Max.

"But it has a twist"? added Maddy.

"You have to take a shot when you lose as well as your

Clothing"? she said with a big smile.

"Ok" said Pete.

"I had better set up the shots."

"Great I love Poker"? Dave said looking at me and winked. I blushed again and looked back at him with a look of, "Oh, you do, do you?"

We all got comfortable for our game. We sat boy/girl boy/girl and giggled about how funny it was. The game started a bit slow as everyone didn't know the rules. So, we played a couple of hands to get the hang of it. Max lost the first game and she skulled her shot and slipped off her dress to reveal a black see-through corset. She looked hot. The men stared and licked their lips. Next game Maddy lost and she also had her shot and stripped off her dress to reveal a purple hot lace corset.

"She looked stunning"

The boys were in a trance, and were obviously hoping the girls lost another game. Next game I thought I lost so I bluffed Pete and I won that hand. Pete stripped his shirt off and took his shot. The next game and the game after that, Max and Maddy had lost and had stripped their stockings off. The next game I think the boys ganged up on me and I lost. Off came my dress to expose my red corset with the peek a boo.

"Oh, honey gorgeous" Dave went to pinch one.

"No"

"No hands" I gave him a gentle whack.

We kept playing cards and Maddy and Max kept losing. They were topless and had their g/strings still on. We were all getting quite drunk and the boys finally lost a game. Dave took off his shirt, his muscles gleamed in the light. His eyes kept looking at my peek a boo and I knew he wanted to touch me. I lost the next hand so I took off my stockings.

"Who wants Sweets"? Jamie asked.

"We do." we all answered.

He left and then returned with chocolate mousse and strawberries. It was delicious. The chocolate mousse melted in your mouth it was divine. We played another round of cards and this time Pete lost his pants. It was getting naughty now, Maddy and Jamie were already kissing and fondling. They excused themselves for the night. Max was wasted so I helped her to bed. She couldn't even open her eyes and I left a bucket by the bed in case she got sea sick. Pete and Dave were still on deck with another drink.

"Want a night cap?" Pete asked.

"Yes, thank you I'll have an orgasm cocktail.(baileys, cognac and ice)." Pete looked me and smiled wickedly,

"Want a double?" I laughed and said.

"Surprise me." I sat on the sofa and Dave followed.

"How about 2 me spoil you at the same time?" He looked at me with big eyes. I wasn't sure, I was pretty tipsy,

"Well, if you are both gentle with me." I said with a shy look.

"Baby, come here" he grabbed me and pulled me into his arms. His head bent down to suckle my nipples.

"Oh, my he sure has a way with words?" I was lost in the moment. Pete returned with drinks and sat down on the sofa with us.

"So, you're ok with this?" he asked as his fingers traced around my face and mouth.

"Yes, I trust you both and if you both are gentle with me its ok." I said and looked at them both one on either side of me.

Dave kissed me first his tongue probing my mouth open and searching for my tongue. His fingers playing with my nipple. Pete went down to my favorite spot and spread my legs, his finger finding the entry through my slit in my g/string.

"Oh, baby you're wet." He said as his tongue entered.

Dave had his erection near my face for attention so I gave him a real spanking with my mouth. He told me to slow down otherwise he would put cream all over my face.

"Oooh there's the cream now, where's the strawberries?"

Pete now had entered me with his penis and was thrusting me to a nice rhythm. Dave and Pete took turns and, in the end, I had two at the same time. It was very erotic and the orgasm was out of this world. They were both gentlemen and I lay there in their arms until I said

"I must go to bed to sleep."

They thanked me for a wonderful night of lust and passion.

"I said, any time." with a wicked smile.

After a long kiss from both men, I retired to my room, checking on Max on my way. She was snoring and was out to it. Too much alcohol for her I thought. I showered and got into my silk pjs and snuggled into bed. I felt wonderful. I just had the best orgasm with two hot men.

"God I'm becoming a little slut" I thought to myself,

"Must try to control my lust and naughty thoughts" I said to myself.

I drifted off to sleep and dreamed of paradise and a lot of men with tanned bodies and huge muscles.

Chapter Five

Max looked terrible in the morning; she came up on to the deck and hid behind her sunglasses.

"How are you honey?" I looked at her and smiled.

"I've felt better" she said softly.

"Have some juice?" I handed her a glass.

"Thanks that's very refreshing." she smiled through her sunglasses.

Maddy appeared looking gorgeous as normal and sat down and smiled at Max and Me.

"What happened to you last night Max?" she asked.

"I think I drank too many shots?" she replied.
"Oh sweetie you'll be fine just don't drink too many shots that's what does it" Maddy said as she poured herself some juice.

Jamie appeared with breakfast which Max refused. Maddy and I were hungry especially after our sexual appetite soaked our energy. Pete and Dave arrived they had been out fishing and caught some lovely bream. They both gave me a smile and I blushed thinking how wicked our night was. We were sailing to another Island today and helped the boys to prepare for this. Dave took me to the steering of the boat and I was amazed of how many gadgets there were. There were buttons for everything. He let me steer the boat and wrapped his arms around me and nuzzled my neck at the same time.

"Don't distract the driver" I said laughing.

"I could fuck you right here"? he said huskily. His hand found the slit in my sarong and went in to feel my bum cheeks. His finger slipped into my pussy and slowly played with by bud. His erection was pressing into me and I knew it wouldn't be long until I was seduced. I heard him sheath himself. He entered me and held me around my waist to take my weight. He felt so good and I clung onto the steering wheel while he thrusted and pumped me.

"Oh Baby" he moaned. My legs were crumbling beneath me and my climax was coming.

"That's it honey give it to me?" he urged me on. I felt that beautiful sensation and collapsed against his chest. He came too his groans exploding with mine and held me tightly.

"Are we on course Captain?" I stared in front of me and all I saw was the sea. He laughed and nuzzled my neck with kisses. We cleaned ourselves up and continued our sailing lesson. Maddy was also having her own sailing lesson while watching Pete do all the ropes.

"I might tie you up and have my way with you." he said

"Oooh' said Maddy with excitement.

Max was in the kitchen with Jamie getting a cooking lesson. I think he screwed her on the kitchen table and feasted on her. Once the boat was under way the girls and I relaxed on deck. We lay there in our bikinis until we took our tops off. Pete gave us some non-alcoholic cocktails.

"Thanks Pete oh how yummy?" I smiled at him.

"You know what's yummy?" he said looking at all three of us licking his lips, his eyes hot and gleaming. Our breasts oiled up and perky waiting to be touched and sucked.   He wanted to play with all three. There so hot.   He had a good perv and we giggled as we knew what he meant. Lunch was served and we all ate together on deck. We anchored at the next Island and we went for a swim. The boys were very frisky and took our bikini tops off.

"Hey give that back?" I said to Pete.

"No way come and get it" he said with a wicked grin. I swam over to him and he grabbed me around my waist. He kissed me and I tried to get my top back.

"Later?" he sexily said and then let me go. After our swim we all lay on the deck and dried off. Pete organized drinks and we lounged in the shade. I looked over at Maddy. Dave was sucking Maddy's nipples and she was feeling his erection. Max and Jamie were also kissing and feeling each other. Pete smiled at me and asked if I wanted my bikini top back?

"No could you rub some suntan lotion on me"? I said with cheeky eyes.

"My pleasure Baby" he replied as he straddled me to rub lotion over my breasts. He rubbed cream all over me and the pinched my nipples.

"Come honey lets go downstairs"? he said holding my hand. We went to my room and had a shower. So much for the suntan oil, that was wasted.

We soaped each other up and his erection was jutting out and waiting for my touch. I squatted down and took him in my mouth and teased him with my tongue. He groaned in lust and pleasure. I sucked him and licked him. He was losing control and I knew I was playing with fire. He quickly pulled out and slowed down the pace. When he had recovered and controlled himself, he slid into me. I leant forward and let him pound me. He pulled out again.

"Baby can I give you more pleasure." he asked as his finger played around my forbidden hole.

"If you are gentle." I said.

He entered me slowly and his fingers pinched my nipples at the same time. His other hand was in my sensual spot and I went with it. I felt myself coming and there's no denying it is such a release and a complete orgasm. I clung to him as he washed me again. We fell on the bed and laughed.

"You're very easy to be with Tasmin." Pete said with a smile.

"You are too Pete" I answered with a smile. We fell asleep for an hour and woke up in each other's arms.

"That was beautiful Baby" he nuzzled my neck.

"Mmm sure was" I said sleeply.

"Let's go up deck for drinks"? Pete got dressed.

"I wash up and be with you soon" I said as I rolled over. He fell back on the bed and kissed me tenderly   Feeling my breasts and pushing his erection into me.

"Oooh are you going to take me again"? I asked with big eyes.

"If you want me to"? he said with those beautiful eyes. Pete got undressed and I found myself feasting on him

"Oh Honey" he groaned.

He then did magical things with his tongue and I climaxed. again. He mounted me after putting on a condom and pounded me Lifting my bottom to get him deeper.

"Oh god" I could feel myself floating and that beautiful feeling getting stronger. Pete was going for it now and his need was urgent.

"Come Baby"

"Come with me"? he groaned huskily.

We both went out to sea and back again. Pete once again got up and dressed and I said I would be up soon. I snuggled in and fell into a deep sleep. I woke to Maddy knocking at my door.

"Tas are you awake"? she said opening the door.

"Hi" I said sitting up and stretching.

"I just needed a little rest before tonight."

"The boys want to know if we want to go onshore to a restaurant and nightclub tonight?" she asked.

"Yes, that would be great" I replied thinking do I have the energy.

"What do you think." I looked at her.

"Ye,s Max and I think it will be fun."

"Ok, I'll get dressed and meet on deck." I said getting out of bed.

"Are we going soon?" I asked as I had lost track of time.

"In about an hour." Maddy replied.

I showered, dressed in a hot red dress that showed a lot of cleavage and the back showed my lovely tan. Put my hair up and my twinkling earrings on.

"Very nice" I remarked looking at myself in the mirror. Grabbed my black clutch bag and joined everyone on deck.

The girls as usual looked hot, Maddy wore a black mini dress with a split nearly to her knickers that's if she had any on. Max wore a camel strapless tight dress that looked gorgeous on her. The back was not there and it dipped down to her bum crack. I don't think she had knickers on either.

"Maybe I was over dressed?" I thought to myself.

The boys also looked very handsome, black pants, and crisp white shirts and a tie. We all got into the cruiser to go ashore. The restaurant was stunning, great atmosphere and the different food smells were enticing. They seated us at the round table and brought over the menus. We ordered nearly everything and said we would all share each other's plate. The seafood was out of this world and it melted in your mouth. We drank a crisp white wine which complemented the seafood. We chatted and laughed. We all got on so well and it was very relaxed and easygoing. We left the restaurant and went to the club which was two doors up. The music was pumping and the vibe was intoxicating. We found a table and ordered drinks and then hit the dance floor. The boys said they would watch for a while and the girls and I went and did some sexy moves on the dance floor. We danced so well and a lot of people were watching us with interest. A few other women joined us and then we did The Nut Bush song by Tina Turner. Everybody clapped when we had finished. The boys said it looked great all these hot women bouncing up and down on the dance floor. It was quite an eye stopper. We ordered more drinks and then the boys took us to the dance floor. We did dirty dancing with them and got the attention of other men in the club. One man approached Maddy to ask her to dance she declined saying.

"Sorry sweetie I'm taken tonight" He smiled at her and said another time maybe? Don't think so though Maddy unless you're going to chase me around the islands. After another round of drinks, we called a quits as Jamie announced.

"Sweets" is back on the boat.

Dave who hasn't been drinking as he has to drive the Cruiser back escorted us giggling girls to the cruiser. He helped each one on board with a little smack on our bottoms as we climbed in.

"You girls are very naughty and you all need to be spanked."   He said with a big smile.

Well, we all knew what he meant by that. It only made us giggle more. Pete and Jamie were also quite drunk and cuddled up to us as we sped along the water. Pete had his hand up Max's dress and no I don't think she had knickers on. Jamie also had his hand up Maddy's dress right up to where her split stopped. She didn't look like she had knickers on either. Naughty girls, I thought to myself. I sat near Dave and watched him drive the cruiser with such skill. It was a real turn-on. He looked at me and winked.

"Like what you see?" he said cheekily.

"Sure do." I said.

"I can't wait for "Sweets." he licked his lips.

Mmm Dave covered in cream and chocolate would be quite delicious. We got back to the boat and the girls rearranged their dresses, looking a little flustered. Dave once again helped us on board giving each of us a little squeeze on our bums as he got an eye full as we climbed onboard. Pete got drinks ready and Jamie got "Sweets". Dave grabbed me for a quick kiss and cuddle.

"Baby you look hot tonight." he said in a sexy voice.

"I want you later."

"Do you want me later?" I mimicked him

"That will get you a smack on your bum with my dick." He said with big eyes.

"Oooh, I'm worried." I said cheekily. He kissed me again probing my mouth open to receive his tongue.

"Wait till I get you alone I'm going to do wicked things with my tongue." he whispered in my ear. I felt tingles throughout my body and my pussy was pulsating. Jamie appeared on deck with a chocolate torte with chocolate sauce and chocolate swirl on top.

"Oh, my it looked amazing" We sat down and he cut a piece for us all. "Small for us" we girls chirped.

"Were watching what we eat." I said looking at Dave licking my lips seductively.

He smiled and said "so am I" looking at me and licking his lips. I blushed at the color of my dress. We all enjoyed our cake.

"Jamie that was incredible."

"Could you come to my work and cook that for us." I asked.

"Yes! I could do that when I'm in your town," he said with a smile.

Everybody was getting pretty drunk and we danced and laughed and kissed whoever's lips teased us. Before we knew it an orgy was happening and the boys were randy as hell. Pete and Jamie wanted to have Max at the same time,

"I haven't had two men at once" she said shyly.

"It's ok you will love it" I assured her. So, Maddy, Dave, and I cuddled on the sofa and started kissing and fondling.

"I'm one lucky guy with two hot chicks to suck my dick." he said in a cheeky voice. Maddy and I obliged and had Dave in our spell and before long he was groaning and begging us to stop.

"Do you want us to stop?" I asked as I rolled my tongue around his knob.

He pulled us off him and flipped me on back and said it was his turn. He started with my breasts and then his tongue trailed down to my favorite spot. He licked and finger fucked me. His finger circled my clit and made me cry out. Maddy was getting excited at watching Dave have all the fun. Maddy wanted to lick me and Dave mounted her from behind while she did naughty things to me with her tongue. He was in his element and did not disappoint either of us to bring us to orgasm. We swapped around and Maddy straddled Dave's face while I bounced up and down on his dick.

"Wow it was explosive" Maddy and I both had big smiles on our faces.

We could hear Max groaning and she was enjoying herself. After that sexual interlude, we took a break and had some drinks. Max was amazed how two men could bring her to such intimate orgasm and back again.

"That was so hot." she said as she sipped her drink.

"Do you both have done that before?" she looked at us both. We both nodded with big smiles.

It was Maddy's turn to be seduced by two men and Dave and Jamie obliged. I could hear her little squeals of delight and the boys were grunting and groaning. It was very hot. Pete and I enjoyed our drinks and I was quite happy just to talk and cuddle. He kissed me passionately and played with my nipples and I knew he wanted more. I let him fuck me and again my body felt that beautiful feeling. Now it was my turn for a wild ride with two men. Dave wanted to fuck me again, and so did Pete so I let them seduce me, lick me, suck me, kiss me, and fuck me. My legs were like jelly I couldn't move. Dave carried me to bed and laid me down.

"Stay the night with me." I said grabbing his arm.

"If you want me too." he said smiling.

"I might shower first." Dave went into the bathroom.

I could hear the water running and it sounded wonderful. I wanted the water on me so I went into the shower and joined Dave. He soaped me up and I did the same to him except for getting sidetracked when I dropped the soap. Of course, I couldn't resist the throbbing cock in my hands and then in my mouth. We then had incredible sex in the shower and once again my legs failed me. Dave carried me to bed and held me till I fell asleep.

Chapter Six

The next week was filled with relaxing days of swimming, sunbathing, screwing, sucking and generally having a great time. Our last night on the boat was a party to end all parties.

"What shall we do"? I asked the girls.

"Well we have to make a night of it" replied Maddy

"Lets have a romantic dinner party"? said Max

"We will get the boys to dine, wine and seduce us" answered Maddy.

"You mean dress formal and little underneath?" I asked.

"Yes" said Maddy.

"Ok by me," said Max.

"I'll go and talk to Jamie and see what he can organize." I said as I got up from my sofa. I went into the kitchen and Jamie was there preparing the menu for tonight.

"Hey Jamie"

"Do you want a Dinner Party tonight"

"I was thinking the same thing" he said with a smile.

"You were"? I looked at him how did he know?

"Yes, I thought as it is our last night, I should do something special" he answered

"Is that ok"? he went on.

"That would be great if it's no trouble" I said with a smile.

"Oh and by the way we thought we would come formal"?

"Perfect" Jamie said with a grin. So, everything was arranged drinks at five and dinner at Six. Jamie said he would let the others know. I went to the girls and told them.

"I don't a long dress to wear." said Max looking in her wardrobe.

"I have a long red one if you like" said Maddy. Max looked at her.

"I love you Maddy" she said excitedly.

We all went to our rooms to get ready. I had a shower and shaved any hair and moisturized my body and put shimmer on. I had brought my silver strapless gown from France so I decided to wear that only with a g/string and of course my twinkling earrings. I looked at myself in the mirror.

"God! I look elegant and sexy"

I dabbed some perfume in all the right places and went up on deck. Maddy and Max were already there and they looked elegant and sexy as well. Maddy in a long Black strapless gown which showed a lot of cleavage and leg through the slit up the leg. Max wore Maddy's' Red strapless gown which showed a lot of boob and also had a slit up the leg.

"Well girls you look amazing and very sexy" I kissed them both on the cheeks.

"So do you" Said Maddy with big eyes.

"Where did you get that dress"? she continued.

"Janie' brought it for me in Paris to go to the Ritz" I replied smiling.

"It's gorgeous"? she remarked with a big smile.

"Can I borrow it sometime"? she added cheekily.

"Of course, honey anytime"? I replied smiling.

We sat at the bar and waited for our hosts. They arrived with nothing much on except a black vest black bow tie and black pants. Their muscles bulging out from their vests. They looked hot!! They had oiled themselves and their vests were open. Well this is interesting I thought to myself and Maddy and Max also were speechless. Pete had made strawberry daiquiris and they were delicious.

The boys took our hands and seated us at the table which Jamie had set up very formal with big white candlesticks and flowers in the centre. Dave seated me and nuzzled my neck and shivers went down my spine. His male scent was intoxicating. Jamie appeared with entrée of Scallops. It was so yummy and the scallops were so fresh. The boys took our hands and led us to dance floor so they could seduce us some more. Dave held me close and his hand pushed my bum and back into his groin.

"God I don't think I'II make main course if he keeps doing this" I thought to myself.

The song finished and we were seated once again. Jamie appeared again with fillet migon and appagus and puree parnsip.

"When did you have time to prepare this"?

"You're amazing" I said with a warm smile.

"Thank you Tasmin"

"I have really enjoyed cooking for you all on this trip" he replied with big beautiful hot eyes.

We enjoyed every mouthful and sipped a red-light wine and talked about what reality will face us when we get home. We all agreed that going back to reality was looking a little boring after our tropical adventure in paradise. We would treasure these memories forever. We all toasted to that. Jamie said "Sweets will be served in half an hour so we all danced together. I danced with Dave and then Pete cut in and swirled me around. Dave then grabbed Max in his strong arms and swept her off her feet. It was very romantic and we were all having a great time. We sat down giggling and had another drink. Jamie appeared with sweets. It was a big platter of strawberries, cream and chocolate fountain.

"Oh my god" I nearly fainted.

"My favorite "Sweets" ever!!

Jamie put in on the coffee table by the sofa's and the men took our hands. Dave took my hand and I accepted and he led me to the sofa. Pete and Max and Maddy and Jamie followed. Dave teased me with a strawberry and cream and I lashed at it with my tongue. He then let me eat it. Watching my eyes as I did it. The Seduction was there and I was hooked like "An Addict" His lips proceeded to follow the strawberry.

"Oh My" his tongue devouring mine and the strawberry.

I dipped a strawberry in chocolate and let it cool. Then went to lick it but just holding my tongue just enough to touch and looked into Dave's eyes. He was in a trance! He pulled me close and his lips were upon mine again with the chocolate and strawberry. He was devouring me and the sweets. He helped me with my zipper and slipped me out of my dress. My nipples were hard and ached to be touched. I only had a silver g/string on. It shimmered in the light of the moon and fairy lights. He pulled me down on the sofa and laid me on my back.

He put some chocolate on a spoon and dripped it on my nipples, "Oh My" it was warm not hot and he then bent his head to suckle the sweetness. I arched my back as he sucked and teased with his tongue. Then he dripped more sauce and feasted again. I glanced over at the other girls who were getting the same treatment. Dave was getting more chocolate to sauce to drizzle on my pussy. I took my g off and I spread my legs and let him feast.

"Honey, you taste so sweet" he slurred as he continued to bring me to climax. I was lying there in paradise and my body once again went out to sea and back again.

"Let's go downstairs" Dave said pulling me up.

He grabbed a bowl of strawberries, cream and chocolate sauce and led me downstairs. I went to the bathroom and cleaned up the chocolate around my breasts ready for feast two. He was lying on the bed and his manhood was erect and ready. I got some sauce and straddled him dripping sauce over his knob.

"Oh! I made a mess. I'll have clean it up" I said with a cheeky sexy smile.

I teased him like he was a long lolly pop and sucked him hard and teased him with my tongue.

"Enough Wildcat" he said huskily and rolled me underneath him. He spread my legs and entered me with urgency and firmness. He sucked and pinched my nipples and thrust into me with his chiseled hard bum which I had full hold of.

"Oh honey!" I cried as he pumped me higher and higher.

He lifted my legs and put them on his shoulders to give greater success in hitting my g-spot as I moved with him.

"That's it, baby" he groaned.

I was lost in the whole rhythm of grunting and groaning. My world exploded inside me and I let out a huge cry.
"Dave I screamed" as my climax heightened.

I clung to him and breathed the same heartbeat. We came together and collapsed on our backs breathing hard.

"I will miss this and you" he kissed my hand and looked into my eyes.

"Yes I 've certainly had a great time and you are very easy going to be with and not to mention hot in bed!" I grabbed his penis and gave it a gentle squeeze.

"Maybe we could hook up sometime"? he asked looking into my eyes.

"Well if you are ever in LA give me a call I live in hills and its very nice you can visit anytime" I said with a smile.

We kissed and he pulled me into his arms. I felt very safe and warm. It was the same feeling all my lovers gave to me. His erection was noticed and I smiled at him.

" Again now?" I smiled.

"Again" he grabbed me and rolled on top of me.

He got a strawberry dipped in cream and teased my lips with it.

"Eat my love you need your strength" he smiled a cheeky look.

We played and teased and made passionate lust as the boat gently rocked.

"Want a drink"? Dave asked.

"Love one" I replied putting on my silk robe and g/string.

We went on deck and the others were there drinking and laughing.

"Wondered when you too would surface?" said Pete with a smile.

I blushed again the colour of strawberries! We drank cocktails under the stars and snuggled up to each other on the sofa's. We had changed partners again and Jamie and I were sitting together and Max and Dave, Maddy and Pete. The cocktails were intoxicating and we were all giggling and quite relaxed. The night ended with another orgy of desire and lust. We all gave in to be seduced by not two but three men at one time.

"Oh My" that was a first and I must say quite amazing and sensual.

They were very gentle and attended to all my needs and my orgasm came from deep down and I cried out to the sea. Maddy and Max also enjoyed it saying it was the most sensual experience they ever had and one they would never forget. The night ended and we took our partners for the last night of comfort and cuddling all night till morning. There's nothing quite like it than waking up with a man beside you.

Truly the best feeling. Jamie and I spent our last night together and we showered first and of course Jamie took me in the shower and made my knees tremble. I buckled when he entered my forbidden place. He rocked me gently he took me out to sea. We washed again and Jamie wrapped me in a big fluffy towel and carried me to bed.

"Sleep my angel and I will love you again in the morning" he said softly in my ear.

I closed my eyes and drifted into a deep sleep as the boat sung me a lullaby as it gently rocked. I woke early morning to Jamie kissing my breasts and nuzzling my neck.

"Oh" what a way to wake up"? I thought to myself.

I greeted him with a kiss and he greeted me with an erection. We held each other close and pumped away as our bodies clung together with sweat. Jamie was groaning now and I knew his need was urgent we thrust together and that beautiful feeling became stronger and stronger.

"Oh Baby" he cried as his orgasm exploded.

I clung to him and wrapped my legs around his bum and thrusted until I could feel no more and once again I was lost.

We were arriving in Port in 2 hours so we got up and got ready. Jamie went and started breakfast and I showered got dressed in a white silk sundress and sandals. Packed my suitcase and went up on deck. The Girls were already there and we all hugged each other.
"Good Morning" they chirped.

"Good morning to you both" I hugged them back.

"We have had the best time ever Tas" said Maddy.

"Yeh" Max said with a big smile.

"We should do this more often?"

We all laughed and sat down to breakfast. The boys joined us and we all had a lovely breakfast. We all exchanged ph nos and kissed each man passionately.

"Thankyou for the great time I will never forget you" Dave said with a sad look in his eyes.

"Me either" I replied.

"Goodbye Pete its been really nice to meet you and fuck you"! I said with a big smile.

"Likewise honey its been a wild ride" he said with a big grin.

"I will visit you when I'm in your neck of the woods" he said.

"Goodbye Jamie I would like to see you again and talk about your cooking?" I said with interest.

"Sure I would love to" he said excited.

"I will be in your area in about 2 months as my sister lives not far from you" he continued.

The men helped us with our bags and escorted us to the waiting limo Daddy had arranged to greet us. Thanks Daddy you've thought of everything.

"Goodbye Goodluck" we all yelled out the windows.

The limo drove away and 3 men stood on the jetty wondering if it had all been a dream or "Had they just been seduced by 3 beautiful mermaids?"

Chapter Seven

Life went back normal. The girls and I had said we would not tell anyone about our tropical orgy in paradise. One we would always remember and keep a secret. Jaine was pleased to see me and she looked me up and down and agreed that a tropical break was what I had needed.

"Tassy you are glowing and looking radiant?"

"Your holiday went well I see?"

She smiled at me and I knew she could read my thoughts.

"Oh by the way that charming man Stefano has called nearly every day. He wanted to know where you were and who you were with"? she said looking at me.

"Ok I'II call him and let him know I'm home" I replied.

Thinking how demanding of Stefano to want to know everything. I still felt an addicted desire when I thought of him and knew I still needed him, wanted him, lusted for him, I couldn't let him go. I will have to think of a compromise with him that suits both of us I thought to myself.

I got home from work and I unpacked and ran a bath. The smell of jasmine and rose oil was relaxing. I needed to think and work out what to do.

"Can I give up my lovers?" I said out loud.

I thought of Sam and how comfortable I felt around him.

"I'm not ready to give him up"? I said to myself.

I let the steam and franrance entwine my body and daydreamed Sam and Stefano both fucking me at the same time.

"Oooh" I felt tingles all over my body.

I let the sponge slide over my body and my finger found my sensual spot.

My other hand pinching my nipples imagining it was Sam's tongue and Stefano playing with my clit. I climaxed and called out their names

"No I definitely cannot give up Sam."

"Was I obsessed or addicted to men?"

"Was it normal to have so many sexual desires and fantasies with different men?"

"Does that make me a slut or whore"?

"No a whore is for money" I said to myself.

"So isn't a Mistress a Whore"?

I now realized the connection and wondered if that's what Stefano thinks of me? I lay there in the bath and thought more about Stefano. There was something about him that was intoxicating and exciting that I knew I couldn't let go. I wanted more sexual encounters and pampering from this man.

I got out of the bath and dried off and put on my fluffy dressing gown and slippers. I went downstairs and the machine was flashing,

"Tasmin I know you are there please ring me" Stefano sounded a little abrupt.

I made a Jack Daniels and rang Stefano.

"Hi Baby" I said coolly.

"Hi Baby is that all you have to say?"

"Where the fuck have you been?" he was quite angry.

"I've been on Daddy's Boat with the girls and had a relaxing tropical holiday?" I said in a matter-of-fact kind of voice.

"And what no men?" he asked.

"The crew were old men who were not interested in us" I lied.

"Well good just as well then" he continued.

"How are you honey I've missed you Baby" he sounded so sexy and desperate.

"I'm great thank you and yes I've missed you too" I lied again.

"I'm in town tomorrow and I want to see you?" he asked with urgency.

"I would love to?" I replied.

"Where?"

"I'II pick you up at 6pm at your house?"

"ok cant wait" I answered.

"Either can I" he said in that sexy European voice.

I danced around the the lounge room in my dressing gown and nothing else. I was seeing Stefano!

Chapter Eight

The next day went quickly and Jaine said go early and get ready to go on your date. I hugged her and she gave me a wink.

"Enjoy Tassy youre so young Enjoy"

I got home and had a shower and sat on my bed and planned my seduction. The peek a boos is his favorite I thought to myself as I picked out my lingere. I wore the peek a boos and fishnets and a new black lace mini dress that had a around the shoulder cut. I put on my earrings and necklace and bracelet. I looked at myself in the mirror,

"Oh Wow"
I looked a knock out! How could Stefano say no to me now I thought to myself. I was ready at quarter to six so I skulled a glass of white wine to settle the nerves. Retouched my lip gloss and heard the roar of the Audi speed up my drive. He came to my door with beautiful Roses and Lillies and I accepted them graciously.

"Come in" I stepped aside for him to pass.

He passed and paused and his lips met mine. I hadn't even closed the door!!

He strong arms pulled me in and I was once again lost in love or lust or both? I managed to shut the door and escape Stefano's grip and I got a vase for the flowers.   I reached up to the cupboard and Stefano could see my bum cheeks and suspenders.   I heard him take a groan as he watched me.

"There beautiful" I said smiling at him.

"A beautiful flower for a beautiful woman" he said sexily.

"Where have I heard that before?" I said to myself .

Oh yeh Sam said that, I smiled to myself and thought if only Stefano knew how many lovers I had here. I placed the flowers on the table and we left to go.

"Not so fast honey" he said grabbing me around my waist.

His lips met mine and I accepted his tongue and his hands pushing into my back to feel his manhood through his pants.

"Were got time" he held me tight.

He picked me up before I could resist he climbed the stairs to my bedroom. He pushed open the door with his foot and threw me on the bed. He hurriedly undressed down to his boxers. I just lay there in a trance or shock of his abrupt urgency to have me.

He did miss me I thought to myself. He peeled my mini dress off to expose me peek a boos and he smiled.

"Oh baby have you dressed for the occasion"? he asked huskily. He came to me and sucked my nipples like he was starving. His finger already found my favorite spot through my slit in my panties.

"Honey you are very juicy?"

His head bent to my thighs and gained entry to a pulsating hot pussy. His manhood was straining through his boxers and so I released his weapon. He gave it to me in my mouth and I also feasted on him. He mounted me gently and then withdrew and put me on my knees. He gave me a slap not hard but not soft "ouch" I said looking around at him.

"What was that for"? I asked.

"I think you have been naughty on your holiday?" he said as he bit my left bum cheek.

"Ouch" I said again.

"I haven't and I don't know what your talking about?" I lied again.

"You have been sunbaking in a g/string" ? he said as his hand felt my bum cheek.

I didn't say anything, I jiggled my cheeks to tease him and waited. He entered me and thrust his manhood into me. He was a little forceful. He was jealous that I exposed myself without him there. I think I have touched his ego? He was urgent now and he pumped and thrusted. My climax was not far away and I went with the rhythm.

"Oh Baby" he groaned as he grabbed my hips.

"Stefano" I cried when my body exploded and he pumped harder groaning and finally collapsed on my back.

"Honey are you alright youre not going to have a heart attack are you"? I was a little concerned.

His breathing came back to normal and I relaxed after that.

"Sorry I have missed you and I got a bit frantic" he apologized. He kissed me and held me in his strong arms.

"Lets go and have dinner I've worked up an appetite?"

Chapter Nine

We went to a gorgeous French Resturant which I had never been too.   I had heard about it and always wanted to go. We were seated in a private table in the corner.

"Mmmm no private room tonight"? I asked looking at him.

"I shall have you all to myself all night and very soon" he answered with a grin.

Stefano ordered a scallop entrée, Roast Duck, and Sweets was a surprise.

"Oooh I love surprises?"

We ate and enjoyed every mouthful, our legs were touching under the tablecloth. His hand between my legs trying to gain entry. I slapped his hand.

"NO touching" I said with a wicked smile.

"Oh Honey I just want a taste"? his eyes glowing.

We danced and he held me close and I clung to him as he swayed around the dance floor.

"Lets go and have sweets"? he whispered in my ear.

We returned to our table and Stefano took my shawl and clutch bag and held his hand out for me.

"I thought we are having

"Sweets"? I asked confused.

"We are come" he held my hand and led me to the door.

"Did he day come"? I think I already did.

We drove to a Hotel I didn't know and we went up to the Penthouse of course.
Everything was there flowers, champagne. strawberries, cream and a bottle of my Sweet Obsession chocolate Sauce Bailey's flavour sitting on the trolley.

"How did you get that"? I went over and picked it up.

"Jaine kindly gave me one" he smiled.

"Oooh you naughty boy" I teased.

He pulled me close and he nuzzled my neck and his tongue went around my earlobe.

"Oh God I felt my knees tremble"

"Champagne Baby"? he asked licking his lips.

I nodded as I was in his spell. A spell of lust and desire. He handed me my drink and I sipped the liquid silk and watched his eyes bore down on me. He pulled me towards him and I floated into his arms. I finished my champagne and he took the glass from me. He unzipped my dress to reveal my peek a boos, suspenders and fishnets.

"Oh honey you look so delicious"?

"I'm going to eat you?" he said huskily.

I just stood there my pussy pulsating in my panties. He carried me to the bed and then got the "Sweets Trolley". He dipped strawberries in champayne and made me suck the juice out and then he would devourer the strawberry. Next cream on my nipples and on my clit. I lay there in a spell letting him feast on me.

He dripped chocolate sauce on my nipples and left a drizzle line all the way down to my pussy. I watched him with big eyes. He licked, sucked and ate all the chocolate sauce off my body and all those intimate places. I once again felt that incredible feeling that no woman can deny its "Heaven".

Once I got my breath back and regained mental awareness, I pushed him down on his back.

"My turn"? I snatched the bottle from the trolley.
He dispensed with his boxers and his erection was needing my attention.
I dripped sauce on his nipples and on his knob and I teased him. I gave
him no mercy and punished him with my tongue and lips. Stefano
groaned and gently thrust his cock more in my mouth. I was like a
wildcat feasting and out of control. I then made him come in my mouth
with the Bailey's chocolate exploding together.

"Mmm"

"salty and sweet"?

"Oh honey that was great".

"You wild sexy thing" he rolled on top of me and pinned me down.

"Now its my turn to watch you to scream out to beg"?

He held both my hands above my head with one hand and I could
only wriggle my hips and legs. But not for long. He pinned me down
with his body. I was in his submission.

"Oh I loved it"!!

He started with my neck then lips and then my breasts. He lightly sucked
and pinched my nipples and teased me. He saw my robe sash on the bed
rail and proceeded to tie my hands to the bed post.

"Not tight" I panicked.

"Ssshh its alright baby I wont hurt you just pleasure YOU?" He
said in that sexy calm voice.

"Trust me" he looked into my eyes and then kissed me.

"Yes I trust you will be gentle with me"?. I looked into his blue
crystal eyes that were full of need and desire. I melted into them.

"One more surprise"?   he said as he pulled out a black silk tie out
of his pants.

"Oooh" I was in a spell.

He blindfolded me and said he wanted me to feel his touch.
I lay there exposed but I felt incredibly safe and my sexual desire to have this man was intoxicating. He licked my nipples with more cream and his tongue Trailed down to my favorite spot. His hands were everywhere and they were caressing and tickling.

"Open your mouth Tasmin" he commanded in a husky voice. I opened and his finger had cream on it.

"Suck it Baby" he teased

I sucked the cream off his finger. He took his finger out and said keep your mouth open I obeyed his command as a game

"I mumbled yes Sir"

I recognized it as soon as it hit my lips his cock with baileys on it and it was tantalizing. I did what he wanted and continued to play the naughty girl who needed big cock. I feasted and sucked like a vaccum and he was groaning And putting more in my mouth. I could see nothing I could not touch him only with my mouth. It was explosive and and the anticipation of whats next?

He held my head and guided me and before long I felt that Groan come from deep down his throat and his muscles Tighten and then relax. Stefano had a towel there this time so I didn't have much "Salty and Sweet".

He cleaned me up as I couldn't move

"Are you going to untie me now"? I asked with a cheeky smile.

He took off my blindfold and I blinked at him.

"Not yet honey one more surprise"? he laughed at me.

"You look very vunderable lying there baby" he stared at me lying tied to the posts with my peek a boos and still feeling very horny in this position.

It was exciting and I knew that just lying there tied up was taunting him. He gave me a drink of champayne and some strawberries

"Eat you need your strength" he winked at me.
I blushed and he came in for the kiss. He then put my blindfold on and kissed me again and down to my peek a boos. I arched up with pleasurable pain and   begged him to stop!

"You want me to stop we've just starting" he said laughing.

I heard him unwrap something and I was waiting for the Thrill of what was going to come. His fingers had oil on them and he massaged all around My pussy and forbidden place.

"Oooh was he" I was a little scared but still excited

"I'm going to make love to you everywhere" he said

"Baby please no I mean be gentle" I said softly

He kissed me on the lips and reassured me everything will be alright and that he would give me great pleasure. He played with me with his finger and then I heard a buzzing sound.

"I recognise that sound" I thought to myself

He teased me with the vibrator and then I felt his big erection slowly gaining entry to my forbidden place. He fucked me with the vibrator and his cock and I was in bliss.

"I was crying out begging him to stop"

Though I didn't want him to stop. He kept going and going   and I gave in to him. My orgasm was loud and I felt his orgasm at the same time. We clung to each other and couldn't move.

He took off my blindfold and untied me and carried me to the shower. We washed each other and let the water drown our bodies. He wrapped me in a fluffy towel and carried me to bed.

"A girl could get used to this" I thought to myself.

Tucked me in and asked what I would like to eat?

"You Baby"

"Just you" I said looking at him with dreamy eyes.
He ordered coffee and chocolate cake and came back to bed. He lay next to me only in his boxers and black pants. His sculptured upper body overpowered me and desire was once again there.

"Room service will be here in a minute" he said taking my

Hand away from his crutch. He got up because I think he didn't trust himself and didn't want to be caught with a hard on. Hurry room service I thought. There was a knock at the door

"Thank Fuck" I groaned to myself

Stefano brought the trolley back to the bedroom and I sat up in bed like I was a Sex Goddess ready for the next feast.

"Coffee and Congac Madam" Stefano rolled it off smoothly from his tongue.

"Thankyou Sir" I answered giggling

The congac was warm and my body was tingling all over. Stefano reached in for a kiss and I accepted his tongue and lips. The taste of congac on them was delicious and I wanted more.

I licked my lips waiting for more congac kisses. Stefano smiled at me and kissed me again. I was lost in his arms and he held me tight. His hand already pulling my towel off. He spoon fed me chocolate torte and I seduced him with my tongue and lips. He watched me closely.

"You'll get in trouble if you keep doing that" He said firmly.

I kept doing it rolling my tongue around and my eyes focused on him.

"Little Witch" he grabbed me and straddled me.

"Now I've got ya" he said with a big smile.

I lay there unable to move but only my tongue just to tease him more. He kissed me then hard and urgent sucking my tongue pinching my nipples

"Stop I begged"!!

"Never" he said in between breaths.
He spread my legs and entered me with his throbbing penis and pumped
me, lifting my bum cheeks up to give him more penatration.

"Baby honey" I cried out as he pumped faster and harder

He groans were loud now and I was already lost in my own orgasm which
took me to over the moon and back again.

Chapter Ten

Two days after my Stefano's sex romp he phoned to say he had to go back home something urgent has come up. Could he see me tonight and we will talk then. He arranged for me to come to his hotel and go to work from there tomorrow.

"Ok see you around 5" I replied.

The next morning I packed more fresh clothes for work the next day and threw in my short red mini and my lingere was still there in the penthouse. I had a busy day at work and Jaine' thanked me for the hard work I had done.

"Everything looks perfect" she said smiling.

"Have tomorrow off and see Stefano off"? she said not sure if I was going to get upset again.

"You know Tassy its not my business but you need to sort out that arrangement espesically if you get hurt and lonely when he leaves"? she hugged me and kissed my cheeks.

"You are so young do not get tied down to anyone yet"?

"Explore your possibilities before you settle"? Qui I looked at her and she was right and I knew I could not give up Stefano or anyone.

They were my "addiction" I had to have them. I arrived at Stefano's hotel at 5pm and he was waiting for me in the foyer.

"Tasmin honey" he embraced me

He took me up to his room and we only got in the door and he practically rapcd mc.

"Slow down Baby"

"we have all night" I nuzzled in his ear.

"That's not long enough" he growled.

Oh was he tense and upset about something? I thought

"Honey whats wrong"? I   looked into his eyes

"It is nothing just family business" he said with a sad look in his eyes.

I hugged him and did not pressure him to tell me more. As much as I wanted to know I knew he was hurting. We stripped off and had a shower and Stefano did not disappoint bringing me to an amazing orgasm that made my knees tremble.

I got dressed after regaining   feeling in my knees into my lingere and red tight mini and killer red stilettos.

"Oh baby you look hot"?

I put my hands on my hips and teased him

"You want to feel how hot"? I challenged him in two strides he was holding me and kissing me with that tongue and lips.

"Very hot I might have to take you back to the shower" he teased

We kissed and I clung to his big shoulders and he picked me up with my legs straddled around him. My mini was right above thighs and he held my bum cheeks.

"I could take you right now"? he said as his hand unipped his pants/

His cock was hard and he slipped on a condom and slid into me.   He walked with me attached to the bed and sat down he thrusted me up and down and hard

"Oh Honey" I cried as his manhood was hitting my g/spot.

He kept going and I climaxed in his arms as his climax took his breath away. He withdrew and threw the condom in the bin and reshipped. He helped me off the bed and I arranged my mini.

"Now I'm hungry" he said with a smile.

Dinner was organized in a private function room I would have been happy to stay in our room but Stefano said its good to get out and also safer for me.

"Oooh" I thought he's totally wicked.

We ate a beautiful dinner and the wine was really Yummy.

"Whats this one" ? I asked as I licked my lips.

"A chablis from France" he answered with a smile

"Its delicious" I said handing my glass for more.

"Don't drink too much or you might get drunk" He said with a grin.

"And then I can have my wicked way with you" I smiled back and said I could handle anything he gives.

"I'II hold you to that" he said with enticing eyes.

We danced and he held me close and I could smell his manly frangrance and desire stirred within me.

"Do you want to go"? he asked

"yes I'm a little tired and I would like to take my heels off" I replied

"And everything else" he added with a grin

Our car took us back to our hotel and he halfed carried me. He laid me on the bed and took off my stilettos and stockings and suspenders. He then unzipped my dress and peeled it off me. I lay there in my peek a boos and panties. That felt better.

"Cocktail in bed"? he asked cheekily

"Mmm a Baileys, contreau and ice would be nice" I replied.

"You mean an orgasm"? he smiled

"Yes and make it a double"!!! I answered with a sexy smile

"Coming up Madam" he said in a Waiter's voice.

"Ooooh an orgasm coming up" the thought appealed to me.

Stefano brought drinks to the bed and undressed down to boxers.

"Your orgasm Madam" he teased me with my drink

"Give it to me" I tried reaching for it.

"Oh Baby I 'm planning to" he replied with a big grin

He finally gave me my drink and I swirled it around to mix the flavors. It was strong but yummy. I put some on my finger and put my finger in his mouth. He obliged and sucked me. I did it again and he repeated the game then I took a swig and kissed him and oh the flavors and passion of our tongues mixed it together. His lips left mine and went to my nipples and he licked and sucked gently.

"Oh Baby" he cooed

"I could feast on you 24/7"

I was entranced in his tongue skills and my head was light headed.   That was a strong drink. His tongue had found my sensitive spot and it felt wonderful. He took his time and teased and teased me with his tongue his finger gaining entry and teasing me there too. I arched my back and that beautiful feeling stirred in my body and once again I was lost in paradise. He rolled me over and put me on my knees And then he entered me gently. We thrust together and he was riding me like a bucking bull.

"Take it Baby" he groaned

I bucked and thrusted like a wild filly and lost all control.

He held my hips and thrusted harder as his climax took over his body and he rolled me on my side and spooned me. We lay together for awhile and our breathing returned to normal.

"that was out of this world" he kissed me on the lips

"Sure was it was pure bliss" I replied dreamily.

We slept in each other's arms and woke early morning. Stefano was nuzzling my breasts and kissing my neck. I giggled

"Good morning honey" I kissed him on his cheek

"You can do better than that"? he rolled ontop of me and pressed his lips to mine.

His tongue urgent and wanting. I could feel his erection and my own desire was stirring inside me. He took my corset off and my knickers.

"that's better stark naked" he slapped my bum gently

He put a condom on and put me on top of him

"I want to see your eyes while you fuck me"? he said huskily.

I slid up and down and twisted and teased with my hips and I played with my breasts to tease him more.

"Oh honey you look so sexy and hot"? he leant up to suckle my breasts.

He grabbed me under my bum and pumped me up and down. Hard and forceful but pleasurable. He had me where he wanted me. I needed him and I wanted him always. Our orgasms came loud and together and we lay exhausted my heartbeat beating with his. We showered and once again made love like there was no tomorrow. He would be gone soon and once again I will miss

His strong arms and sexual encounters like it was an addition. I will have withdraw symptoms from not having my Stefano Fix!! I didn't want to think about it just enjoy the last moments with him. We got dressed and had breakfast overlooking the city and bay.

"Your'e very quiet Tasmin" he asked as he poured the coffee

"Oh just thinking when I will see you again"? I looked At him with sad eyes.

"Don't cry" I said to myself.

"Baby I ''m sorry I have to go home, My wife Anna is Very ill with a virius and the doctor's arent sure if She will make it" he held my face in his hands.

"I love you Tasmin but I have to go to my wife"

"You understand don't you"? he said with sad eyes

I felt the tears swell in my eyes and I nodded

"Yes I do, you have a duty to her and you love her?" I answered

"Yes I do"

"But I also love you" he added

"You have thought about my proposal havent you?" He asked with curious eyes.

"Yes and No" I replied not sure whether to lie or not

"You want to be with me"

"don't you" he continued

"you are my life Tasmin I need you in it" he kissed me on the lips and held me close.

"I want to be with you too" I replied with a smile

"Good then I will arrange everything" he said firmly

"You will get an apartment in town, a new car and bank account" he continued on

"Wait Wait" I said loudly wanting to be heard
"I don't need or want anything from you"?

"I just want you"! I said firmly

"No I insist you will accept my gifts and do what you
Are told"! he repeated himself

"Stefano no I cannot" I insisted back

He held my shoulders and looked into my eyes

"honey you are mine and mine only and I want to spoil you" he said arguing.

"Shit whats the point he's won this one" I thought to myself

"Ok I said only I keep this cottage and my car" I challenged him.

"Alright you can but when I 'm in town you must be At the apartment" he said with a smile.

We cuddled some more and I didn't want to think About losing Sam, Jake or other lovers. His flight was in 2 hours so we said our goodbyes and He promised he would ring me tomorrow.Tomorrow seems so faraway.

Chapter Eleven

James had been watching Tasmin's house for two weeks and was getting pretty pissed off because he didn't know where she was. He even went to her work and went inside and brought a yummy cake from a lovely French Blonde woman with big tits. Oh he did like big boobs!

"Where was she"? he fumed

He sat outside Maddy's house and that also was quiet. She must have gone away with Maddy he thought to himself. He was angry and frustrated now he needed to see her he went home to his private bedroom and looked at the photo of Tasmin that he had stolen from her house and masturbated.
Stefano rang me the next day and I asked him how it was going?

"Is Annie alright"? I tried to sound sincere

"The doctor's don't know yet its still touch and go" he answered quietly.

"Oh honey I wish I could be there to comfort you"? I replied

"Well maybe you can soon"?

"I will let you know" he said sounding a bit more cheerful

"I miss you" I said softly in the phone hoping the tears wont start.

"I miss you too" he answered quietly"

"I will ring you in the two days" he said and then he was gone I went to say

"I Love You" but he was gone.

I stared at the phone and started crying, Pull yourself together I said to myself You can keep busy seeing other people Just as I started to prepare dinner the phone rang.

"Sam I cried"

"How are you"? my heart skipped a beat

"Good honey" " I'm good"

"I have missed you" he continued

"how's your Dad"? I asked concerned

"He's doing ok a bit tired" he replied

"What are doing tonight"? he continued

"Well I'm just making dinner" I said

"What are you having"? he asked cheekily
You on a plate with chocolate sauce all over I thought To myself

"Oh arr anything you want"? I invited him to dinner

"Whatever you whip up Baby is delicious" he said huskily

"I'II see you soon then" I said hurriedly as I wanted to get dressed
for the occasion.

"Ok" he hung up

I put lamb racks in the oven, potatoes and pumpkin in Roasting dish And
went upstairs to get ready. I put on my white virginal outfit and a white
chiffon short Dress which was sleeky and see through.

"Mmm nice very pure" I looked at myself in the mirror

Hair half up and a little lip gloss. I dabbled some perfume in all right
places and went Downstairs. Checked dinner and put some beans on. The
doorbell rang and I went to open the door. Sam stood there handsome as
anything and smelling so good

"Hello Honey" he said with a big smile

"Those eyes, I've missed those eyes" I melted looking into them.

He had wine and gorgeous lilies (white) in his hands.

"For you" he handed me the flowers

"Thankyou there beautiful" I replied with a smile

"come in and make yourself at home" I smiled again

I turned and walked to the kitchen and as I did I made Sure my dress swished enough for him to get a glimpse Of my suspenders. I reached up to get a vase out of the cupboard and this Time my bum cheeks were exposed. He was right behind me his hands already around my waist And pulling up my dress more.

"Oh honey I've missed you" he nuzzled my neck

I could feel his erection in my back and my sexual Appetite was stirring
        "Baby please let me get the vase"? I asked as his hand Was between my legs.

"Oh baby youre wet for me" he said huskily

I gave up on the vase and turned to kiss him His lips found mine and his tongue beckoned me to battle His finger was inside me now and he was playing with My clit.

"Oh God my body was betraying me again but it felt So good" I couldn't let him stop I wanted more.

I tuned off Dinner and he carried me to the sofa He undressed down to his tight boxers

"Mmm very nice showed his huge bulge" I thought to myself. I licked my lips and took off my white dress to reveal my white virgin corset and suspenders.

"I going to take you my little virgin" he grabbed me and laid me on the sofa.

He got a condom out of his jeans and placed it on the coffee table

"I've brought more" he teased

He unbuttoned my corset and my breasts spilled out. He sucked my nipples and teased me with his tongue

"Oh it was heaven" I laid there in bliss

IIc took his boxers off and his erection was begging me to take him in my mouth. I teased and taunted him with my tongue and lips.

"Oh Baby he cried"

"Stop or you'II wear cream"? I said huskily

"ooh salty now wheres the sweet"? I

Laughed in my head. I eased off so he wouldn't blow and slowed the pace down.

He head had gone between my legs and he told me to lye Back and enjoy. That beautiful feeling was happening and I arched my back And he pinched my nipples at the same time my orgasm Exploded inside me. He sheathed himself and mounted me putting my legs On his shoulders and he pumped and pumped and We were lost in our groans and cries of escasty. Sam stayed the night and we made passionate love Again in the morning.

It was Saturday so we didn't have To rush away for work. I got up and made breakfast and took it out on the patio. We sat and chatted easily and laughed at each other's jokes. Sam was quite funny and I felt totally relaxed around him we spent the morning in each other's arms and went for a walk in the gardens.

"It's looks great Tasmin everything is trimmed and pruned".

"yes thanks to you" I squeezed his arm.

We went inside and ended up stairs to my bedroom we fell on the bed laughing and he kissed me passionately.

"Baby you make me feel great" he said between kisses.

"Good you make me feel horny" I said laughing

He was tickling me all over and I was wriggling and he was wrestling me on the bed.

"Got ya" he held me down.

I tried to move but he was so strong. He kissed me then and was already unbuttoning my shirt to gain access to my breasts.

"again I said"

"yes again my love" he said with that sexy voice

I gave in to submission and let him take control of me. My orgasm was once again out of this world. Sam was definitely a great lover one I couldn't let go. He was like an addiction I needed him like my morning coffee. All smooth, silky and warm. We showered after our sweaty excerise and didn't hear the Phone ring.

We were having too much fun in the shower. Stefano was not happy that Tasmin did not pick up But left a short message anyway,

"Tasmin where are you"?

"I'II will call later"

"Miss you Baby" he hung up

After a long eposide in the shower that made my knees Tremble I dried off and dressed again. I saw the machine flashing and pressed the button I listened to Stefano's message and didn't realise Sam heard it too.

"Who's that"? he asked looking into my eyes

"A man I met in Paris" I replied not trying to show any emotion.

"One of your lovers"? he raised his eyebrows at me

"Yes if you want to know he is"! I said with pride.

"Do you love him"? he asked

"I like him a lot and we are friends" I replied

"So do you love me"? Sam grabbed me around the waist and pulled me in.

"Ooh those strong shoulders, those eyes bearing down on me

His breath close to me and his lips wanting to taste.

"Sam you are a very special friend" I said sincerely and

"I love spending time with you" I added

"I like spending time with you too" he kissed me then.

Our lips met and I parted to accept his tongue. He kiss was tender and soft and he pulled away and said

"One day you will have to give up your lovers if I want You all to myself"? he said with serious eyes.
"oh Shit here we go everyone wants me to give up my sexual desires or were they Addictions"? I thought

"Honey lets not rush things lets just have fun"? I said thinking

No strings attached remember that's what we both wanted. Just casual comfortable hot sex!! And of course friendship I thought to myself. Sam stayed the whole day and I said stay another night As I did get lonely not to mention a bit scared after the Jame's encounter. I could not tell Sam or Stefano or anyone about it.

James had threatened them and James is a sicko who knows what he might do?. I made a light dinner Pasta Bolognaise and garlic bread. We ate by the fire and drank a lovely shiraz red. We sat there and watched the flames flicker and our hands were on each other's leg.

"I might go and put something more comfortable on"?

I said getting up. I went to clear our dishes but Sam stopped me.

"You change and I'II clean up" he gave me a gentle whack on my bum

"go" he pointed.

I changed into a black silk baby doll nightie and black G/string I came downstairs and Sam had put some music on and Had stoked the fire.   He had moved the coffee table and Had put cushions and the throw rug from the sofa on the rug by the fire.

The lights were down low and I entered the room like a Sleek black cat purring waiting to pounce. He was sitting on the rug with fresh drinks in hand. He took one look at me and his eyes and smile said it all

"Honey come here" he put the drinks down on the hearth and held his hand for mine. He pulled me close and then kissed my neck and down to my breasts.

"You look so hot and sexy I want to eat you" he said smiling

He lay on his back and he beckoned me to straddle his face.

"Oooh he held my bum cheeks and just feasted"
He then turned me around so we were in a 69 position and Gave me his erection. His finger was inside me and his tongue was licking My clit. I bobbed up and down on his manhood giving Him no mercy. Our orgasms exploded in each other's mouth's and we Were Satified with our feast. Besides "Sweets" were yet to come

We drank some more wine and I got a cheese platter, some strawberries and of course my chocolate sauce Hazelnut This time. We talked about our futures and dreams and   I realized we were both very in tune wanting similar things in life.

"Could Sam be the only one for me"? I thought to myself as I stared into the fire.

Sam was tracing my nipple through my silk and pinching it to poke out, he did the same to the other one. Our lips touched and the passion heated up and before long our bodies were entwined and sweaty. I cried out when I climaxed as Sam pumped me and Pumped me until a deep groan came from his throat. We caught our breath and Sam stoked the fire again. We lay there and finished our wine and cheese platter.

"Lets go upstairs"? I said holding his hand

I grabbed the sauce and we went upstairs.

"Shower Honey" he stripped his boxers off

"Coming" I said following him into the shower

"you will be soon" he said with a cheeky smile

"is that so"? I challenged him with my hands on my hips.

He picked me up and lifted me into the shower black nightie and all.

"Oh Baby" he looked at my breasts as I had a wet silk nightie that showed my breasts and nipples sticking out.

He fondled them gently teasing me pinching my nipples and his other hand in my g/string' He ripped it down my legs and I stepped out of it. He took off my wet nightie but when he got to head he covered my face and sucked my nipples hard but pleasurable.

I cried out for him to stop and he took the nightie from my head.

"Oh my how eroctic" my body tingled all over.

He soaped me up and dipped some soap around my forbidden place.   I knew he liked doing this in the shower. Oh what the hell as long as he was gentle I would go with it. He sat on the floor and he pulled me down to receive him. He gently and slowly entered me and my back was against. His chest and he fondled my breasts.

"that's it honey nice and slow" he urged me on

"Oh Baby I cried" the build up was happening

His finger entered my pussy and once again I had the most amazing clitoral, vaginal and anal orgasm. We went back to bed I was too tired for "Sweets" though I think I had that in the Shower and I fell asleep in his arms. I woke to the early sun streaks coming in the bedroom I looked at Sam he was still asleep. God he looked good. His face soft and peaceful. He opened his eyes to meet mine.

"Good morning honey" he kissed me gently

"Good morning baby" I replied kissing him back. He stretched "looks like a beautiful day" he said as he looked outside.

"Lets go for a drive up to the mountains and take a walk" He looked at me for approval.

" Ok Why not" I answered.

"later I'm busy for now" he said with a smile.

He rolled on top of me and kissed my breasts and nipples.

" Oh my this is a great way to wake up"? I said with tingles

"Sure is" he said between sucking, his erection pushing into me

He put a condom on and entered me slowly and then built up pace. He put my legs on his shoulders and thrusted harder and harder.

My orgasm was close and he played with my clit at the same time.

"Oh baby" I cried out as my body shattered around me.

He was groaning and emptied himself inside me with the protection of a condom. Our breathing was ragged and raw and finally we got our breath back.

"Shower honey"? I asked teasing him with my tongue.

I jumped up to run to the shower but he caught me with his big arms grabbing for me.

"You little witch"?

"are you going to be naughty"? he nibbled my ear.

"Maybe" I replied with a wicked look in my eyes.

"You might get more than you bargined for"? he smiled sexily.

"OOh I' m scared" I teased him

He held my bum cheeks firmly and pressed his growing Erection into me.

"you might be sorry"? he teased back

He lifted me in the shower and we held each other under The steam. I dropped the soap and picked it up getting sidetracked on the way. His big erection waiting for me. I tormented him with my tongue and lips. He groaned and held my head and played with my hair.

"Honey you had better stop or you will have a face mask"? he said with urgency.

I knew I was playing with fire so I slowed down and let him take control. He turned me around and entered my bottom gently

"Told you, you would get more than you bargained for"? he said huskily.

He was fucking me in my vagina and my anus and it was very pleasurable and orgasmic. We got dressed and went for a drive we would get breakfast on the way to the hiking trail. We found a lovely café at the foothills and ordered pancakes, bacon and eggs.   Juice and coffee. Sam also asked the waitress could she organize A picinc lunch packed in paper bags so we could Carry it.

"Sure Honey" she flashed a smile at him.

After our breakfast we headed up to the mountains. It was beautiful and a little cold as it was Autumn. We had brought jackets and I brought a scarve And beanie. We parked in the car park and set out on our way. The air was cool but the sunlight was glorious. We hiked to the waterfall and sat there and took in The view. It was very magical. After we rested we went to the next trail that led Up further up the mountain. The trail was easy and we took our time as We walked up a steady incline.

One hour later we got to the top and sat On the picinc table and bench seat There also was a fireplace so Sam lit a fire and we Sat there and got warm.   The wind up there was Quite cool. We ate our lunch of chicken salad rolls with Orange juice. The view was spectatular and you could see For miles and miles.

"Theres the ocean" Sam pointed at the horizon.

We cuddled up by the fire and kissed tenderly. His hand inside my jacket to gain entry to my breasts.

"Sam what are doing"? I asked looking at him.

"Havent you ever done it on top of a mountain?" He asked with a smile.

"No I cant say I have" I looked at him

"theres even a table for us" he pulled me towards it

He laid me down on top of the table and opened my Jacket. He then lifted up my jumper and teeshirt To expose my bra. His thumb and finger found what they were looking for.

"Oh honey" I cried outloud

It truly was bliss noone around and the cool air On my breasts was tingling. He unzipped his fly and pulled his penis out. I grabbed at him and found what I was looking for. His erection was huge and I tried to pull my jeans down. He helped me and then put a condom on

"you came prepared"? I stared at him

"Always I have a few"? he said with a big grin

I then straddled him on the picinc bench. He entered me and I bounced up and down while he held my hips. I could cry out and scream his name and no one could Hear it, only the wildlife and mountains. We were coming together on top of a mountain and it Was heaven. We got our breath back and got dressed.

It was time to go so Sam put out the fire and we Started the decent back down the mountain. It took us 2 hours to get down but we did take it slow. Even stopping at the waterfall and resting

"You want to fuck under the waterfall"? Sam asked

"I have more condoms"? he looked at me cheekily

"I think you have had enough" I said looking at him

"never enough with you" he pulled me in to kiss.

We arrived back at the car and were glad to get in and rest. Sam drove us home and I snuggled into his shoulder while he drove. It was just dark when we arrived home and I didn't want to be alone.

"You will stay wont you"? I asked with big eyes

"yes honey if you want me to"? he said smiling

"Good lets go inside and light the fire" I said

Sam lit the fire and I made coffee and congac to Warm us up. The congac warmed us up and we were totally relaxed watching the flames dancing around.

I finished my drink and I went upstairs to get changed in to something more comfortable I put on a white silky nightie and silk robe.
Did my hair and put some perfume on in all right places. Tonight we will have "Sweets" I thought to myself With a smile.

"Are you hungry"? I asked Sam as I came into the lounge Room.

His eyes beamed at me and I blushed thinking of wicked thoughts.

"I'm hungry honey for you"? he grabbed me and pulled me On the sofa.

His lips met mine and his strong arms were around me pulling me close and on his lap. He made me straddle him and he slid his hands up and down my silk nightie over my breasts, down to my navel and back up again.

It felt amazing and so sexy!! He bent to kiss my nipples through my silk and bit one gently

"Honey gentle" I scolded

"you might get bitten too if   your'c not careful"? I added with a smile

"Baby you wouldn't"? he said biting the other nipple

"Ouch" I said pretending it hurt.

"I'm sorry honey did I hurt you"? he looked worried

I had better put him out of his misery now I laughed and kissed him hungrily.

"You little wildcat" he tossed me underneath him

He held my hands above my head and said now I'm In for a rough ride. I wasn't scared I knew he was teasing.

"Baby let me go" I wriggled underneath him

He liked this and started nipping at my breasts and nipples. Just gentle nips with his lips. He lifted my nightie and his head hid under the silk he sucked and teased with his finger and my nipples could take no more

"Stop Stop" I begged

"No Baby take it theres more to come" he continued his mission.

His finger went to my sensitive spot and I looked into his eyes and they were talking to me.

"Sam theres hazelnut sauce on the table if you want some"?

"God what a question"? I thought to myself.

He took off my nightie and knickers and got a towel from the cupboard and laid me down on it.

"Don't want to mess up your sofa"? he smiled wickly

He drizzled sauce over my nipples and a trail down to my pussy. He started his journey and I lay there absorbed in lust and submission. My body submitted to his sexual demands and we feasted on each other like wildcats. We both looked at each other and laughed. We both showed the remains of chocolate and come

"Sweet n Salty" on our faces.

I got up and got warm flannels and handed one to Sam.

"Thanks honey though you do taste good" he wiped his face.

I put my robe and knickers on and made up some soup and herb bread. We sat by the fire and enjoyed pumpkin soup and bread our appetite for sex and food was fulfilled. Sam put the fire down and we adjorned upstairs. I lay on the bed and watched Sam undress. He had the best muscles and his tight butt was such a turn on

"What are you staring at"? he put his hands on his hips I giggled his muscular frame and his erection jutting up

"You and your big cock"? I said licking my lips

"is that so"? he jumped on the bed and pulled me in to receive his lips and tongue.

He pulled my sash loose and my robe opened to expose my breasts.

"oh honey" his hand brushed against them

His lips kissing them gently as I think he thought they were Tender. Which they were. We kissed and fondled each other until we knew we were ready. He put me on my knees and took me from behind. He thrusted and pounded me like I was a filly and he was the stallion. Our orgasms exploded together and he collapsed beside me We fell asleep spooning each other and woke early morning.

A morning quicki was in order, shower and get dressed. We both had to go to work so there was no time to be passionate. We said our goodbyes and drove off in different directions.

Work was busy as it was Monday and all the orders came in. Wedding Cakes to make, icing flowers, and chocolate tortes. Jaine made the sponges and white chocolate fudge cakes. I made icing flowers and got the chocolate ready for the tortes. When the sponges were cooled I prepared to asemble them they looked fantastic when finished.

I asked jaine' if she had heard from Jean-Paul and she said "I have and he is well"

"He is coming over in a few weeks"

"And I think he is bringing Phillipe' with him"

She looked at me for a reaction.

"Oh ok that will be nice" I said not showing any emotion.

"Did I want to complicant my life with more lovers?" I thought to myself.

Though Phillipe' was quite breathtaking and not to mention an Italian Stallion.

"We should all go out together when they are here" she said

"Yes let me know" I answered still dreaming of the Italian Stallion.

We finished our work and left for the day.
"See you tomorrow Tassy" Jaine' hugged me.

I drove off and put on my favorite cd.

"At last she's back" James watched from his car.

"I will see you soon Tasmin my love"? he said with a smile.

I got home and my answering machine was flashing. It was Stefano and he was furious.

"Why havent you rung me back" he roared in the phone.

"Oh shit I forgot to ring him back" I kicked myself

I dialed his number and he answered on the third ring

"Where have been"? he asked sternly

"Hi Baby sorry went out with the girls got home late"

I lied but it sounded better than telling him I was seducing And fucking another man for two days in my bed.

"well I was worried you should have rung me"? he replied sounding a little softer in the voice.

"How is Anna"? I asked politely

"She is the same" he said quietly

"I miss you Tasmin"? he said huskily

I could feel his erection through the phone.

"Honey where are you in the house"? I asked cheekily

"I,m in the study"? he replied   not understanding.

"Can anybody see you"? I asked again

"No its very private" he sounded excited

I think he knows what I'm hinting at.

"Honey I havent much on" as I took the cordless

Upstairs and quickly stripped down to my bra and knickers.

"Ooh what havent you got on"? he asked in anticipation.

"My Black Bra and Black knickers" I lay back on the

Pillows and listened to his breathing through the phone.

"I'm imaging your cock in my mouth and you licking and Teasing my pussy"? I said in a sexy husky voice.

"Oh honey youre driving me wild" he breathed

"Take your cock in your hand and imagine that's Me sucking and touching you" I said seductly. I heard him unzip his fly and I waited with anticipation

"Oh baby my nipples are so hard they need to be sucked"? I cooed in the phone.

"I'm so wet and juicy baby Mmm I taste good" I continued

"Honey I want you" he groaned through the phone

"I have my vibrator and I imaging it to be you Honey" I egged him
on.

"OOh that's feels so good" I kept him going .

"I bet your cock is so hard and throbbing for my mouth" I drew him
in

"Oh Baby" he groaned

Stefano had his manhood in his hand and was giving himself A serve.
Just listening to Tasmin and her dirty talk drove him wild and
uncontrollable.

"that's it baby give it to me" he groaned more
"Fuck me Baby I'm so wet and hot for you" I replied

I heard the groan and I lay there feeling very horny and happy that I could
seduce a man to desire and lust over the phone.

"We need to get Skype" he said after a few moments. I laughed not
a bad idea I thought.

"That was great honey I needed that" he said in that sexy Euopean
voice that melted me every time.

"Did you come"? he asked

"No not quite" I replied still feeling horny.

"Well get your vibrator and I will talk dirty to you"?

I lay there waiting for instructions and took off my bra and panties.

"Are you naked Honey"? he asked huskily

Just the sound of his voice nearly made me come.

"Yes" I breathed

"let the vibrator tingle your nipples and imagine that is my tongue Baby" he instructed

I did what he said and let the vibrator buzz over my nipples and closed my eyes and imagined Stefano was sucking my nipples.

"That good baby I think youre very juicy for me"? he continued

"Now vibrate your clit" he commanded

I did what he said and imagined it was him there teasing me

"Come Baby Come"

"Give it to me" he kept going

"Stick it up your pussy and fuck yourself hard" he added

I let the vibrator go in and out and god it felt great.

"Oh honey I 'm going to come" I breathed into the phone

"that's it honey   you feel so good" he urged me on.

I came then loudly in the phone and I heard him groan as well.

"Did you come again"? I asked surprised

"Oh baby I couldn't help it you were so hot"? he said

I could tell he was smiling through the phone. We talked more about when we would see each other

"I cant leave here for awhile" he said

"ok we might have to meet half way"? I asked

"No you will come here and I will put you up in hotel and we will have privacy" he answered

"I cant it wouldn't be right" ?

"Your wife in the same town people might find out"? I was a little worried.

"People know I have women and we can be distreet. I wasn't sure I said I would think about it.

"I love you baby" he said through the phone.

"I love you too" I answered not sure if it was love or lust.

I just knew I couldn't live without him, he was my obsession and my Addiction, I needed him. We ended our call and I went to bed dreaming of Stefano making love to me in everyway.

Chapter Twelve

Work was busy all week so when Maddy rang and said

"Let's catch up at the nightclub on   Sat night"

"sounds great see you at yours at 6pm"? I asked smiling through the phone.

"ok great I will tee it up with Max" she answered

"Cant wait to catch up and goss"? she added excited.

"Me either see you then" I replied excited too.

Saturday came quickly and Stefano had rung everyday to talk and of course phone Sex!!

It was quite hot and naughty lying there with your lover's voice so sexy and horny In your ear and your hands are his hands gliding over your body and doing wicked things to yourself. He rang just when I got out of the shower and I picked up

"Hi honey guess where I've been"? I said cheekily

"Where" he laughed

"In the hot shower with the sponge and soap" I said seductly.

"Honey Mmm I'm imagining it your tits and those tight Little buds to suck" he answered back huskily

I lay on the bed and opened my legs got vinny out and Stefano whispered hot things in my ear. I did what he wanted and came loudly over phone. He also was wanking and pulling his throbbing cock in IIis hands, tissues ready for the explosion.

"Baby that was great but enough is enough I need you for real in the Flesh"? he growled softly and playfully.

"I know baby it will be soon ok"? I answered gently

Stefano wanted to know where I was going and what I was doing pretty much 24/7 and I didn't like lying to him.

"The girls and I are having a quiet night in dvd's Popcorn and pizza" I said as I put a slinky black lace mini dress on that showed my cleavage and it was short.

"ok have fun then" he replied

"and I will ring you tomorrow for more sweet loving"?

"Can you download Skype and then I   can see your tits and Pussy"? he added

"ok I will tomorrow" I said smiling thinking cheeky sexy

Hot man that cant do without and either can I. I hung up and looked in the mirror

"Am I fooling myself"? I questioned myself

"Do I really love him or is it lust and desire"?

"I do look hot"? I looked again

"Have a little fun no strings attached girl remember" I talked to myself.

I did my hair down with light curls and applied a makeup, smokey eyes and pink gloss. I put on some jewellery not Stefano's gifts though as I didn't want to lose them. Locked up and drove to Maddy's house. Max was there and Maddy fixed some drinks,

"To a good night of whatever"? she skulled her glass

"Whoa"? I said

"Slow down"

"Whats wrong"? I said looking at her

"Well Mitch is extending his holiday with his mates and wont be back for maybe another month"? she said Pissed off.
"Oh well don't dwell on him" replied Max

"plenty more in   the bar and sea"? she laughed

We all laughed and agreed that our holiday was the best. We called a taxi and went to the club it was crowded but we got a table. We ate light and ordered more drinks.

"Cheers to us" we giggled and glinked our glasses

The music was calling us so we hit the dance floor. We all could dance quite well and soon got the attention of four men who then approached us on the dance floor.

"Can we join you"? a cute one asked,

"Sure" said Maddy and we danced with four hunky men who we didn't know.

They joined us at our table and we all introduced ourselves. Rick, Jay, David and Scott were their names and we all Talked and giggled when they said something funny. Rick got the next round and we toasted our new friends.

"Here's to a good night" said Maddy looking at Scott.

They were all about our age or a bit older and we found we had some things in common. They all loved sailing and all water sports. David and Jay actually were competing in a yaght race next weekend and said we all should come and make a day of it.

"We'll see" replied Max looking at David

He was quite cute with broad shoulders and acute smile. Jay was also handsome and kept looking at me and checking out my cleavage.

"Lets dance" jay said as he held his hands out to Maddy and I.

Scott joined us and so did David. Rick and Max were talking about something and said they would join us in a minute. We danced and the boys took turns in holding us close and swinging us around.

Jay held me close and complimented my dress

"you look hot in that dress Baby" he whispered in my ear.

I felt tingles all over my body. I looked up at him and smiled and he smiled back. David cut in and held me close and he danced quite well. He pushed my back into his groin and I could feel a big bulge.

"Oooh that feels bigger than I've had before" I thought to myself

I danced easily with David. Jay was dancing with Maddy and Scott and Max and Rick were dancing also. My arms were around David's broad neck and I felt his big shoulders and continued to feel all the way down to his waist and buttocks which were very firm. His arm around my waist and his other pulling me in at the back of my neck. I knew he wanted to kiss my lips met his and he practically held me off the floor. His tongue searching for mine. I looked into his brown deep eyes, my he was handsome, and my heart skipped a beat.

"God here comes that feeling again"? I thought to myself

"Should I fuck him or not"? I battled for the answer in my head.

"no strings attached girl" was my answer in my head.

"Lets get a drink"? David   led me to the bar.

"What would you like"? he asked with a glint in his eyes.

"YOU on the bar and me bouncing on you" I thought

"Jack Daniels and Coke" thanks I replied

We drank our drinks and chatted comfortably and then returned to our table. Everybody was there laughing and drinking. I sat down next to Jay as he was next to Max and then Scott, Maddy and Rick sat. David slid in beside me and his hand went between my upper leg near my suspenders which he could clearly see.

"Very Nice" he whispered

"I would like to see the rest"? he winked at me licking his lips.

My pussy was pulsating just thinking of jumping this hulk. He would have to be the biggest man in height, size, muscle broad shoulders that I ever had. His hand was going further up my dress thigh and I tried to smack him away under the table. I looked at him and smiled

"Behave or I will have to spank you later"? I whispered

His smile said it all and I knew we were definitely going to fuck each other later.

"What shall we do now"? Scott asked everybody

"We could all come to my house"? replied Maddy

"Its not far from here"? she added

The boys all looked at each why not they all nodded. I excused the girls and I for a bathroom break.

"What are we doing girls"? Maddy asked us

"What do you mean"? replied Max

"Gee Max do I have to spell it out for you"? Maddy said mpatiently and a bit drunk,

"they want to have an orgy don't they"? Max caught on Maddy looked at Max and hugged her

"that's right baby girl"

"you just have a great time and relax and oh don't drink too much, or Tas and I will have to fuck Four of them" she added touching up her lip gloss.

"So which one do you want first"? she asked me

"Mmm David is certainly big"? I said with a smile

"Yes he is big ooh that could be very exciting" Maddy was checking herself out in the mirror.

"Ok well theres four of them and three of us"? I said looking at them both for an answer.

"Well the fourth one out joins one couple"?

"Simple" Maddy had it all figured out.

"Max are you ok with this"? Maddy asked her again

"Yes why the hell not they seem very nice men I supposre we can trust them"? Max fixed her hair and lip gloss.

So it was agreed I would have David first, Maddy would have Scott and Rick and Max would have Jay. And then we would all swap and I would then have Jay And Scott. Maddy said she wanted David next and Max Would have Rick. Seemed like a great seduction.

We met the boys by the bar and we all went outside to Get taxi's. Rick and Jay had stocked up on the alcohol and we were Set for the night. We bundled into two taxi's and headed to Maddy's. I was in the back seat with David on one side and Rick on The other. The both had their arms around the back of seat. I definitely was the meat between the sandwich.

David put his hand on my cheek and pulled me to receive His kiss. Rick had his hand going up my thigh to my Suspenders and David had left my lips and was nuzzling My neck and his hand was in my corset pinching my nipple I had to control myself and not groan out loud. The taxi driver unaware of what was going on in The back seat.

I turned to kiss Rick and he obliged and opened his mouth And his tongue went down my throat.

"Oooh he has a long tongue" I thought trying not to giggle

David meanwhile was teasing my nipples and had his tongue In my ear. Rick's hand was inside my g/string now and his Finger was inside me.

"Ooh" I groaned to myself and spread my legs for him To get further access.

I knew Maddy's was about 5 mins away and tried to stop The men continuing more.

"We will be there in 5 mins" I said adjusting my dress

They both had huge smiles and huge erections. We finally arrived and paid the taxi driver, he winked at Me. Oh shit did he see everything. I blushed!

Chapter Thirteen

We all got drinks and Maddy put some music on. Max, Jay, Maddy and Scott were dancing and I whispered In Maddy's ear

"Do you mind if Rick joins David and me first"? I asked

"Why what happened in the taxi"? she asked with a smile

"Lets just say he has a long tongue" I replied my eyes Big and glowing.

"Go for it honey" I'II have them later.

We both hugged as we danced and Maddy peeled my dress Off to expose my black corset, suspenders and g/string The boys mouths were open and they just watched, Their eyes growing big. I did the same to Maddy and revealed her black lace teddy We turned to Max and took her top off first then her skirt. She was wearing a red corset and suspenders. We both commented

"Very nice Max"

"Thanks I purchased them recently and have been wanting To try them out".

The men came in for the kill David grabbing me and picking me up to take me to the bedroom.

"David put me down we   to share as there is 4 of you"?

"Yeh ok" we can handle that" he said still holding me.
I looked at Rick and said for him to come too. We went to the spare room and they undressed stark naked. David's erection was huge and I wasn't so sure now that maybe He is too big.   Rick's erection was big but not as big as David's.

I sat on the bed and they stood in front of me and I took Them both in each hand and began to play and tease. I would suck one hard for 5 and pull the other one hard. They lay me down on my back and David put his fingers Inside me and teased. He then bent his head and ate me his tongue swishing Around and around my clit. I clung to him my legs on his shoulders. Rick was beside me and his cock was calling me to suck him.

"Oh god this is great" I thought to myself as I sucked and Groaned.

David wanted me to sit on him and so I did while Rick Got more sucking treatment. David slid into me and god he was big. I groaned when he thrusted his huge weapon deeper. We continued this for a while and then swapped Around. I sucked David hard and gave him no Mercy.

Rick was taking me on all fours while I straddled David and was sucking him dry. I knew I was playing with fire and that it was not Long that they would both be inside me. My body was betraying me and that beautiful feeling Was stirring inside me. David was kissing my breasts and he asked if I wanted To take both of them.

"I said yes if youre both gentle"

David pulled me ontop of him and his strong Legs spread my legs to have more of him inside me. Rick came from behind and teased and put spit on and Around my forbidden hole. He gently massaged and teased and then eased his Cock into me gently and slowly. David moved his hips to thrust more and Rick thrusted from Behind. I was in bliss with two men. My body going with the rythum and their hands everywhere Was driving me wild.

"Oh I'm coming I grabbed David's biceps for support

And he gave me more and so did Rick. My orgasm took over my whole body and I shook with Excasty. The boys had withdrew and were spilling their Juice over my tits. I lashed out with my tongue and got a droplet.

"Ooh salty now where's my sweet" I giggled to myself.
A shower was in order so we went into the ensuite and Got in. David said he would go first then Rick. Rick sat on the bed and had a smoke and drink to wait for His turn. David kissed me passionately and soaped me all over and in All those places they had just been. His erection jutting out My mouth closed over his knob and he held my head and Guided me. He pulled me up and turned me with my back to him. I knew what he

wanted to do. He entered me slowly and my legs were trembling under me. He picked me up and held me on his cock while he pumped Away.

"Oh God" I screamed   when he thrusted harder and my Insides tearing apart.

He was groaning and I was lost in lust and our bodies moved With each other.

"That's it honey give it to me" he urged me on.

I was floating now and my climax numbed my whole Body I couldn't move. He held me and washed me again and then kissed me. He left and Rick entered. I was struggling to stand and Rick took me in his arms And cradled me.

"Are you alright Baby"? he asked as his finger traced my Nipple.

"Yes just a little shakey" I answered hanging on to him.

"I'II be gentle honey" he said kissing my nipple.

His erection was pushing into my navel and I dropped the Soap and my mouth found what it was looking for. I gave him a serve and he pulled me off

"I want to save the rest" he said huskily.

He turned me to the wall and spread my legs for easy access. His finger in my pussy going in and out and his Throbbing cock entering my forbidden hole. He was gentle and his finger played with my clit, While his other finger was inside me and his cock Was fucking me from behind. My knees went weak and I could feel that beautiful feeling Happening again.

"I cried out" when I climaxed and he let his orgasm out too.

We both clung to each other and then he washed me again. He wrapped in a bed robe and carried me to bed. My legs were so weak that I couldn't walk.

"Would you like a drink Baby"? he asked smiling

"love a Jack" I replied.

"Give me ten and I will be out and ready to rock n roll" I said smiling.

He left and I lay there to get my strength back. I put on my corset and G/string and found a black silk Robe in the cupboard and went out to the lounge room. Everybody was there drinking and laughing and had Obiviously had a great time too. Scott had rolled a couple of joints so we starting smoking And drinking. Scott sat beside me and put his hand on my leg and came In for the kiss. I was stoned and a little drunk and his tongue was begging Me to fight him Maddy had gone with Jay and David to the bedroom

"Good luck with that" I thought to myself

Max was with Rick and she was giving him a blow job. Scott took my hand and we went to the spare room And smoked the rest of the joint. He lay me on my back and spread my legs to feast. He did that for 10 minutes I thought I would explode He then put me in a 69 position with me on his face While I sucked and teased him. He rolled me over when he had enough and put a condom On. He mounted me and he felt so good. He pounded and thrusted and lifted my bum cheeks to Go further.

I clung to him and dug my nails into his back when he Hit my g/spot. My climax was coming fast now and I could not stop it. He kept going and I clenched my legs around his buttocks And thrust with him. He groaned loudly and collapsed on top of my breasts.

"oh honey" he said when he got his breath back

"that was amazing"

I smiled at him and he smiled back. We lay there and cuddled and kissed passionately. We got up and went into the shower and once again the Water soothed my body.
Scott soaped me up and dipped the soap in my bum And I knew he wanted more shower sex as well. I let him take me to great heights and he was very gentle in every way. We washed again and my legs were giving up on me. He carried me to bed and lay beside me.

"You want to join the other's"? he asked looking into my Eyes.

He was very handsome with his big hazel eyes and olive Skin.   He kissed my lips and got up and dressed.

"I'II be there in a minute" I said as I snuggled in for a rest.

I must of dozed off and woke 1 hour later to music pumping And a lot of laughing. I got dressed in my robe and g and went and joined the party.

"Hi guys" I said with a big smile

"Where have you been"? Maddy asked

"I had a little power nap" I replied getting a drink

Maddy had a big smile on her face and I could tell she Had a totally wicked time. We smoked some more joints and my head was spinning. We all giggled and asked the guys if they wanted lap dancers.

"Hell Yes" they all said

We did a strip tease and teased every one of them. I was with Jay this time and I put my tits in his face and straddled him in the chair. He grabbed me around my bum cheeks and bounced me up And down on his jeans. Max had gone with Scott and Rick to the bedroom. Maddy said why don't we have a foursome. We all agreed it would be fun and the boys said they wanted

To see a little girl on girl action and would we oblige them. The boys sat on the sofa and I sat in the middle of them That was Maddy's instructions. She sat between my legs and started playing with my pussy. Her hand pinching my nipple at the same time. She then kissed me on the lips and then on my breasts.

The boys were excited watching us and already had their huge dicks in their hands. Maddy then produced a dildo and starting teasing me with it.

"Oh god" she was getting me wild.

David guided me to his erection and I teased him with my Tongue and lips. Jay was playing with Maddy from behind while she performed amazing things to me with the dildo. We were all coming together and we cried out when our orgasms exploded around us. We lay there on the sofa exhausted. None of us could move. My head was on David's belly, Maddy was buried in my pussy and legs and Jay was resting on Maddy's Back. We must have looked a sight. I was exhausted. We all went to bed on the lounge rm floor. The boys put two mattresses on the floor and we all played there and smoked more joints and had a cognac. I was floating and my body was lost in a sea of bodies. Hands were everywhere you didn't know whose it was. Someone's dick entered me, I knew it wasn't David. We went with the music and our bodies danced and we all cried out for more I think it was at that point I passed out!

Chapter Fourteen

I woke a few hours later and I needed water. I tried to move and looked around at everybody sleeping. David was on my left with his hand on my waist Rick was on my right with his leg over mine. I slowly tried to move and managed to get Rick's leg off me and David's arm from my waist. I climbed out and put on my robe after finding it and went into the kitchen. I went to the sink and poured myself some water. I gazed out the window and I dropped the glass and screamed!! "James Fucking James" was staring through the window at me. He looked at me with those scary mean eyes and ran off, David arrived at the kitchen door first and took one look at me and told me not to move. I was shaking all over. There was glass on the floor and I had blood dripping from my hand. Everybody was in the kitchen now all stark-naked staring at me and asking what happened? I was still shaking and I tried to talk but nothing came out.

"She's in shock." said David who obviously knew first aid.

"Don't move honey" he said softly.

"Rick hand me my shoes" David asked

He put his shoes on and walked towards me moving glass out the way and then he picked me up in those strong arms and took me into the bathroom. The other's cleaned up the glass and blood on the floor. He got a big fluffy robe off the hook and wrapped it around me. He took my hand and looked at the cut.

"Mm it's deep honey" he said inspecting it.

It was still bleeding so he wrapped it up and held it above my heart so the bleeding would stop. I was numb it didn't hurt. I just couldn't believe I saw James at the window or did I imagine it? I thought

"Tasmin, Tasmin, are you listening to me?" he was saying. I looked at him and started crying. He held me close and comforted.

"What happened Baby can you tell me?" he said kissing my tears.

"I, I saw a man at the window and I dropped the glass" I stammered out.

"What" David was concerned now.

"Maddy! Can you come here"? he yelled. Maddy appeared wearing a dressing gown and hugged me.

"Honey are you alright?" she kissed me on my cheek.

"Stay here with her" David said firmly.

"What's wrong?" replied Maddy

"Nothing, I'll be back in a minute" he said leaving the room. I just sat there numb and then heard the boys talking and a lot of footsteps running around.

"What's going on?" asked Maddy looking at me.

"Tell me Tas" she beckoned

"I saw James at the window" I said scared

"What James friend of Mitch's that James"? she looked at me confused.

"Yes" I said softly

"Why would he be here?" she asked trying to work it out.

"I don't know" I stuttered looking away so I wouldn't see her glare.

"Have you seen him again after Tony's?" she looked at me

"No not really" I lied and she could see right through me

"Tas tell the truth."

"What happened?" she continued

"I think he's following me" I said looking at her

"Why is he stalking you?" she was concerned

"I don't know." I lied again

"Something happened didn't it"? she would make a great detective. She just didn't stop with the questions.

"Ok, but if I tell you, you must not tell anyone" I trusted her

"Ok I promise" she waited for what I had to say.

I thought I wouldn't tell her everything just enough to let her know I'm worried and it will be alright.

"He came to my home and took advantage of me" I said quietly.

"He raped you?" Maddy was on her feet now

"No, no, I was drunk and he was drunk and he screwed me and now he won't leave me alone" there I said it.

"He's pissed at me for not ringing him for another date." I continued, Maddy wrapped her arms around me.

"It's ok! We'll go to the police." she said.

"No, we can't"

"I haven't a leg to stand on"

"I let him in got pissed and had consensual sex" I said looking at her to see if she believed me,

"Ok, I won't say anything"

"Yet" she added

Maddy looked at my wound which had stopped bleeding and wrapped some gauze and a bandage around it. She went to the kitchen and made me a hot chocolate. Max hugged me when I came back to the lounge room.

"Are you alright sweetie." she looked worried

"I'm ok just dropped the glass" I lied

The boys came back in and said someone had been outside as there were footprints on the lawn and outside the window.

"We've checked everything and we will stay with you all night" David announced. The others nodded.

We all went back to bed and David asked if he could join me. Maddy had put me in the other spare room and told me to sleep. David didn't want me to be alone. Everyone would be safe tonight. He followed me to the bedroom and we lay together in bed. I lay in his arms and he comforted me.

"Sssh it's alright baby." he stroked my hair

I fell into a deep sleep and dreamt of Stefano and that I was in Switzerland and that we were together at last. We were making love in a beautiful Swiss house by the fire and Stefano was kissing me everywhere. I returned the kisses and looked at him and it wasn't Stefano it was James. He was kissing me and laughing and holding me down. "I'm going to take you Tasmin." he said Roughly and "you will love me back." I screamed and struggled with him and he would not let me go.

"Tasmin Honey wake up" David was shaking me I was clinging to him and hitting his chest and saying

"No no."

"Tasmin you're dreaming wake up" he said softly I opened my eyes and David was there holding me.

"Sorry I had a bad dream" I said shakily

"It's ok honey lie here in my arms and I will keep you safe." he kissed my lips gently.

"I can't sleep I'm too scared I might have another bad dream" I said quietly. He kissed my lips and gave his tongue to me.

"I will get you tired" he said with a smile. He kissed my nipples and his finger went to my favourite spot.

"Lay back and go with it" he said huskily.

I did what he said and tried to relax and not think about James. He was slow and gentle and made me climax with ease. I cried out and clung to him and he knew I was ready for him. He put a condom on and entered me gently. I groaned as he was big and he knew it. He pumped me gently and kissed my lips and teased my nipples. We were both dancing now and our breathing was becoming raggered and loud. We both climaxed at the same time and lay entwined in each other's arms. I woke in the morning and felt much better, David was sleeping still so I went to get out of bed quietly.

"Not so quick" he was awake. His arm already pulling me back into bed.

"Come here baby" he kissed my neck. I lay down and we kissed passionately and I could feel his manhood erect straining into me.

"I want you honey before we get up" he said huskily. He teased my nipples and went to my clit and had breakfast.

"What a great way to start the day" he said with a grin when I climaxed and cried out.

He mounted me and fucked me like there was no tomorrow. I thrusted with him and orgasms came together and loudly. Maddy was making pancakes and coffee and it smelt great.

"Coffee honey?" she handed me a cup.

"Thanks" I said and sat down at the kitchen table.

"How did you sleep?" she asked concerned.

"Ok in the end" I said smiling as she knew why.

"How did you sleep?" I asked her.

"Just bloody fantastic" she said smiling and I smiled back.

"I'm sorry about last night." I said changing the subject.

"It's not your fault." Maddy replied as she flipped pancakes.

"I know but it's James and he is obviously obsessed with me." I said looking at her

"It will be alright I think you should stay with me for a while." she said firmly

"I don't know I have things to do at home."

"No, you will stay here until everything calms down." She said this time quite firm. Like there is no more discussion. She has made up her mind.

"Ok I'll go home and get clothes for the week." I said agreeing with her.

"And not by yourself." she added. I looked at her.

"I will not be made a prisoner by this man." I said quite angry.

"We will take precautions and watch our backs." she said all police like. God she should have been a cop or social worker?

It was a beautiful morning and Maddy had laid out breakfast on the patio. We all sat there and talked about last night and how wicked it was.

"We all should do this again." said David with a huge smile winking at me. Everybody agreed it was fun and no strings attached.

It was decided that David and Scott would drive me home to get my things. Max, Jay, Rick and Maddy were going to go for a walk and then do some shopping.

"How about we meet up for dinner at 6?" she looked at us.

We nodded and then I got in to David's car which he had picked up earlier. It was a big car for a big man, black SUV with big shining mags, sunroof and tinted windows. I felt like I was in the FBI car being taken somewhere to hide.

We drove easily up the freeway, David's beast roared along and we listened to music. I was in the front and David kept his hand on my leg. He would smile and wink at me.

"God, I hope he hasn't fallen for me." I thought to myself.

I don't want any more demands of male ego of wanting to own me and restrict me. He is very handsome though and that cock I could get addicted to that! Tingles magically appeared in my body just thinking of his big muscles. David glanced over at me and smiled.

God, I hope he doesn't know what I'm thinking. I smiled back. Well, I'm one hell of a lucky bitch, hot guy in front and a hot guy in the back I thought as we were getting closer to home. What would Stefano say to that? I thought to myself.

"Just up here turn right then second on left." I said.

David followed my instructions and I pointed my house to him. He drove up my driveway to my cottage.

"Very nice" David was impressed. Even Scott commented on the view and gardens.

"It's a great view and I like your statues" he said looking at me with a cute smile.

The statues were mostly of women naked so of course he would like them. I opened up Fort Knox and the boys were impressed.

"My Daddy" I exclaimed

"Make yourself a drink. Bar's in the lounge"

"I'll have vodka and orange juice please." I added

I checked my answering machine as it was flashing 4 messages all from Stefano. I would listen to them later. My cell was flat so I put that on charge. Scott handed me a drink.

"Cheers" he said smiling. Nice eyes I thought and took the drink.

"thanks" I smiled back at him

"Come out to the patio and see the view"? I said. Opening the French doors. We sat on my comfortable outdoor chairs, listened to silence and gazed at the view

"Peaceful up here" David commented.

"Yes, that's why I like it" I replied.

"I can see why" he looked at me.

"Your gardens are beautiful"

"Do you do them"? Scott enquired

"No, I have a gardener who tends to my lawns" I said smiling. Thinking how he tends to other things too! We finished our drinks and I said I was going upstairs to pack a few things.

"Make yourselves at home" I said as I climbed the stairs.

I went into my room and Oh home sweet home.

I loved my bedroom it was my room of luxury and pampering and not to mention Seduction I pulled a small suitcase from the cupboard and put it on my bed. I put some clothes, knickers, bra's, nighties, slippers and my silk dressing gown packed neatly in the case.

I decided to have a shower, freshen up and get changed out jeans and top. The water was glorious and soothing, I lathered myself in mango, coconut body wash. I heard a noise and I looked up and Scott was standing there.

"Are you perving"? I asked cheekily

"Yeh and I like what I see" he smiled back his erection straining in his jeans.

"Would you like me to wash your back"? he looked at me with horny eyes.

"Yes, that would good" I said flashing a sexy smile. He took his jeans off and boxers and his weapon were set free.

"Oh, my very nice" I smiled to myself thinking of wicked things.

"Where's David"? I asked

"He's in the bedroom waiting" he answered looking at me to see if that's ok.

"Oh, I see" I said back to him smiling shyly.

"We will be both gentle like last night" he whispered in my ear and nuzzled my neck.

"David said for me to have some time with you first" Scott continued as he kissed my neck down to my nipples.

"Ok" I replied not really caring as my body was responding to his caresses and kisses.

His hands were everywhere and were teasing and torturing me to take him in my mouth. I went down on my knees and sucked, licked and tormented him back. I would give him no mercy. It was very dangerous I knew I was playing with fire. His hips were jerking and thrusting gently and I took more of him. He groaned and pulled my head up so I wouldn't wear cream. I managed to get some and thought "Mmm there's my salty now where's my Sweet" I giggled to myself.

He pulled me up and held me and we continued our journey of lust and need. His erection growing again and his was finger fucking me to get me ready for what was to come. He turned me and held me around my hips while I leant forward for support of the wall and he hacked me up and plunged into me.

"Oh my" he was forceful but gentle and teased me with cock plunging in and then withdrawing and kept doing it to tease me more. Finally, he kept it in and he thrusted and pumped me.

"God it felt good" I let go and let him take me everywhere and my orgasm exploded inside me. Once again, my body succumbed to lust and desire. We washed again and kissed.

"Beautiful baby" he gave me a bum squeeze. I giggled.

"Yeh it was great" I stared at him with dreamy eyes.

I dried off and put my black silk short dressing gown on which I always hung in the bathroom. Did my hair and applied a little perfume to all the right places as the seduction was not finished yet. David was lying on my bed in his boxers and he looked like the hulk but gorgeous. I felt like I was a black wildcat about to pounce. I did and jumped on him and straddled him and held his arms above his head, well tried to. He laughed.

"Yeh what are you going to do?" he said huskily.

"I'm going to get you to beg." I said sexily.

He pulled my sash open to expose my naked body. My breasts perky and my pussy pulsating. Wanting him but taking my time to seduce and cast a spell on him. I let go of his hands and told him to be good and not move.

"Not likely" David replied.

I gave his nipple a pinch and got his attention "ouch" he said his eyes of a lion about to pounce in for the kill. I slid down to his huge erection and unleased his weapon. I rolled my tongue around his knob and looked up at him with big eyes. He was in my spell and his eyes said what he wanted. I kept eye contact with him as I teased his knob not putting his penis in my mouth yet. He was trying to get me to take more but I got out of his grasp.

"Soon Baby Soon" I scolded him and then sucked his knob again.

His hands in my hair and holding my head. I looked at him to say I have you now and now I will show you no mercy. He looked at me with eager eyes. I took him then putting as much of him as possible in my mouth. I sucked and pulled him hard and feasted on him like a wildcat. He was groaning.

"Oh, baby give it to me" he was close now.

I grabbed the hand towel I had brought with me and kept sucking like a hoover. He was jerking his hips up and he was building up steam.

"Here it comes" the taste of salty hit my mouth and damn I forgot the chocolate bailey's sauce. I put the towel over his manhood and let him clean up. I licked my lips like a contented wildcat and adjusted my robe.

"That was yummy" I said giggling. He grabbed me and flipped me on my back.

"Whoa" you wouldn't want to mess with him in a dark alley.

"Yummy I'm going to eat you"? he said licking his lips.

He kissed me and our tongues played together in our mouths. His lips left mine and trailed to my breasts and nipples. I arched up when he sucked me, he held my hands. So, I couldn't push his head away. He was torturing me with pleasure. It wasn't like James and how rough and horrible he was, he was gentle but firm but you still felt safe.

His head went to my sensitive spot and he let go off my hands and spread my legs. He picked my bum up and lifted my pussy into his mouth. He also was a lion feasting on his prey. His tongue and fingers were everywhere and his hand was playing with my nipples.

"Oh honey I cried" my orgasm happening.

"Give to me baby" he urged me on.

His tongue and finger playing with my clit and hole. I let out a groan my release shuddering around me and David just lapping it up and giving me more. I lay exhausted after that my body took a little time to recover. I cuddled into David's strong arms and chest

"Mmm a girl could get used to this"

Scott came in with drinks and what great timing. I was thirsty and a vodka was perfect. We sat on the bed and drank our drinks a man on either side. Scott kissed me and looked into my eyes.

"Two of us now." he had puppy dog eyes.

"Yes, if you're both gentle." I said looking at them both.

Somehow, I don't think David can be gentle he is a gentle giant.
We kissed and fondled and David wanted to fuck me while Scott came
from behind. I sat on top of David and put his huge cock inside me. I
gently slid and slithered, his hands on my hips.

"Oh honey" he jerked his hips and made me take more.

"Oh I cried" I clung to his biceps.

Scott was preparing me and he gently entered me as well. It was
very erotic and both men took me to great heights of ecstasy.

Chapter Fifteen

We all showered separately as time was getting on and we still had to drive back to Maddy's. David carried my suitcase downstairs to the car before I came downstairs, I listened to Stefano's messages. I was to ring him straight away and why didn't I answer my cell. I rang him quickly as the boys were downstairs and out of ear shot.

"Hi Honey" I said casually.

"Where have you been?" he asked not angry but curious.

"Sorry baby I was at Maddy's and I didn't have my charger with me" I said hoping he didn't read anything into it.

"I miss you Baby" he said huskily.

I knew he wanted phone sex and I didn't have the time. I can't tell the boys to wait while I have it off with my phone lover.

"Honey, I have to ring you back later when my cell is charged." I said looking at the time.

"Why are you going somewhere?" he sounded a little pissed off.

"I'm going to stay with Maddy for the week as she is going through a rough time because Mitch is gone."

I lied thinking that sounded better than telling him a phsyco stalker was following me and by the way he raped me. Yeh, I think I will not tell him the truth. There was no other way.

"Ok but ring me tonight cause I want to talk to you." More like fuck me over the phone I thought.

"Sure honey I will"

"Ring you later" I hung up and went downstairs.

I left some censor lights on put security on and Fort Knox was secure. The boys were in the car and I climbed in the front seat and looked sadly at my Home Sweet Home. I loved living here I didn't want to go. I was suddenly very angry and pissed at James for intruding in my life and how dare he threaten me or any of my friends.

"Are you alright honey"? David asked me.

"Yeh sorry just in a day dream" I replied looking out the window.

We headed back to Maddy's and I didn't see the white pickup truck parked up the road. James had watched everything he could see two men going into Tasmin's house and he was in a rage.

"What the fuck?" he screamed in his head.

"What are they doing there?"

He had tried to see through the window and at one stage he saw them in the lounge room. Then he didn't see them and knew they must be upstairs. He wanted to go in and kill them all except Tasmin. He would never hurt her he just wanted to love her. He went back to his car and waited angrily thinking; "Soon Tasmin we will be together again" and he laid back and imagined she was naked and giving him a blowjob.

As soon as he saw the Black SVU he followed from a distance. We sped down the freeway and I just gazed out the window. I didn't feel like talking. James kept the SVU in sight and sped along the freeway behind us. We arrived at Maddy's and went inside. So she is at Maddy's good. He had a wicked look in his eyes as he sat back and waited. He had all the time in the world. Maddy and Max had prepared a great dinner of Apricot Chicken, Scallop potatoes and beans. They also had dressed up the dining room table and it looked very elegant.

"Nice job girls" I hugged them.

"How did you go home?" Maddy asked looking at me.

"Good, it was nice to go home" I said smiling

"But it will be nice here too" I added

"Let's get dressed up and have some fun" said Maddy

"I don't know about you but I'm exhausted and my nipples are a bit tender" I added

They both laughed and we said what the hell one more night. We asked the men what they wanted to do and if they could stay the night as we were still a little nervous. The guys said no problem but Rick said he had to go as he drove trucks and his shift started at 4am. We thanked Rick for a great weekend of lust and he left with a big smile after we smothered him with kisses. We went inside and asked the boys to make drinks as we wanted to change for dinner.

"Let's have some fun." said Maddy with a smile.

"What like?" I asked intrigued.

"Well, no knickers for one and we will dress really skimpy and sexy" she said excitedly.

"Come on I have heaps of skimpy and sexy clothes." She said again as she dragged us to her bedroom.

"Ok let's do it" I said smiling at Maddy and Max.

I hadn't brought lingerie so Maddy lent me hers and a tight black dress with lace down the sides. You also could see my suspenders as the dress was short.

"Hot smoking Hot" Maddy exclaimed

"Not bad looking at myself in the mirror"

Max liked the red lace mini dress with black lingerie underneath. Maddy went for a tight pink dress that showed her suspenders and could just see her bum cheeks.

"Ok, let's eat I'm hungry" she said as she fixed her lip gloss.

"Yes me too but not for food" I said giggling and they both giggled too.

We went into the lounge room and the boys greeted us. With big smiles and our drinks were waiting. They all hugged us and kissed our necks

"You all look so hot" Scott said checking out how short our dresses were. His hand slid up my dress to caress my bum cheeks.

"Scott behave." I slapped his hand away.

"Oh, honey you look good enough to eat." he pulled me in and held me tight with one arm.

"Mmm no knickers?" he smiled at me and his finger went straight in. He withdrew it and sucked.

"Mmm you do taste mighty good" he winked at me and I was blushing and the others were also getting seduced. Oh, what did we except wearing no knickers I thought to myself.

"Should we skip dinner and go to straight to Sweets." David said with a hard on.

"No boys we have made dinner and now we will eat"

Maddy went to the kitchen and Max followed. David grabbed me and came in for the kiss. His hand was already up my dress to have a feel. Jay and Scott not far behind their hands groping.

"Easy Boys" I said trying to push them away. They were like a pack of wolves about to strike their prey and devour it.

"Now boys let's eat first, have a few drinks and then we'll play" trying to stop all three about to make me their meal. Maddy and Max appeared with dinner. Thank god or I would have been dinner on the table. We ate and enjoyed some white wine. Hands were touching everywhere and the boys were randy as anything.

"Sweets can wait till later." said David as he pulled me close to kiss.

Everybody was kissing and fondling. We adjourned to the lounge room where the boys told us to sit down. We did as they asked and they told us they had a little game to play. We sat there excited when they produced scarves to blindfold us.

"Oooh" I said with big eyes

The other girls agreed also with big eyes. They blindfolded us and we didn't know what was going to happen. I felt something touch my lips and his erection was wanting entry. I smiled as I knew it wasn't David it was Scott or Jay? No words were spoken as it would have given it away. You would only know if it was David as his is huge. I giggled. He made me open to accept his gift and obliged him in teasing and sucking, we weren't allowed to use our hands so my tongue guided me. I heard him groan and was trying to figure out who it was? I think was it, Jay? I thought to myself. I was close now his hips were jerking; he was pinching my nipples hard and he pulled out suddenly with a groan. Jay, I thought. I heard more groans as the others climaxed. David said do not take our blindfolds off and we all giggled. They gave us a drink and then told us to go on our knees on the sofa's. It was rather exciting and not knowing who?

The build up was intoxicating my pussy was pulsating with the anticipation. I knew Maddy and Max would be feeling the same. I felt a finger playing with my clit and then a tongue and a finger entered me

"Oh that's feels good" I said in a sexy voice.

No answer gee the boys were definitely playing the game. His other hand had pulled my dress off to reveal Maddy's black lace corset and suspenders, stockings but no knickers. I heard an intake of breath and he plunged his finger in further. His tongue followed. I groaned and wriggled but he held me tight. I think it is Scott now it's not David and I'm pretty sure it was Jay before. I giggled and he smacked me gently on my bum.

"Oh my" I giggled again

He then plunged into me and held my hips and thrust me back and forth. He was spanking me with his cock? My juices were starting to flow and my body was totally lost in his spell. His finger was on my clit and his cock was trying to get my g/spot. I was groaning now and moving with his hips and my climax was close. He kept on and urged me on groaning and letting out a moan when he came. My climax took me over the edge and my body tingled all over, I felt my release and once again I was lost in his arms. He took my blindfold off and I was right it was Scott. We kissed and laughed about what just happened. I looked over at Maddy and Jay was with her and Max was with David. We all had drinks after our orgy and were all exhausted.

"I need to go to bed and get sleep before work." I announced.

Everybody agreed they were all wiped out and needed to rest before our week of work. It was agreed that David and Scott would stay but Jay had a big drive home and said he should go. We said goodbye to Jay and kissed him and said hope we would see him again. He assured us we would. James was sitting in his white truck watching the goodbye thing and nearly puked.

"Who is that jerk?" he said angrily to himself.

"And who are the other two jerks?" he continued to sit there and get more agitated.

It was getting late and I said goodnight to everyone. David wanted to stay with me but I said would he mind if we do it another time. He said ok and that he understood, anyway he had Maddy or Max. I went to my room and got my clothes ready for work. My cell rang and Stefano was there and didn't sound happy.

"Why didn't you call me back?" he asked sounding a little put out.

"Sorry Baby we were busy and I ran out of time"? I answered. He accepted my answer and we chatted about what is happening.

"Annie is the same in a coma and the doctors don't know if she will wake up." he said quietly.

I tried to comfort him and before I knew it, he was hinting for phone sex. I knew he missed me and so I gave him a tease over the phone. It wasn't the same as being together but it was some kind of relief for him.

"When will you come?" he asked impatiently.

"Soon honey I will ask Janie' tomorrow." I answered.

"Ok baby miss you" he hung up.

What am I going to do I thought to myself. I can't just leave Jaine'
and take off to Europe. I fell asleep unaware of James waiting outside
and watching.

Chapter Sixteen

I got up early and got ready for work. I went into the kitchen and the boys were there having breakfast.

"Morning" I said as I made a coffee.

"Morning Tasmin" David and Scott replied. I sat down and drank my coffee, Mmm it was good.

"Thanks for staying guys we should be ok now" I said looking at them both.

"Are you sure that creep is not coming back?" David said concerned.

"Yes, I'm sure it will be alright." I assured them both.

"Well, we are a phone call away" David said looking at me not sure if he was comfortable with this.

"Look we will ring you every night and check in OK?" I answered with confidence.

"Ok if you're sure" Scott said looking at David and then at me. Maddy and Max came in then and we all hugged.

"Sleep well?" I asked them both. They both blushed and grabbed their cuppa's.

"I was just telling David and Scott that we love having them as bodyguards but life has to go back to normal?" I said looking at the girls.

"We will be alright and we will ring and check in." I continued looking at Maddy for support.

"Yes, we will" she looked at the boys.

"Ok only if you feel ok about it." Scott answered, David nodded.

We said our goodbyes and I headed off to work. I didn't see James sitting in the street and drove to work. Jaine' was as bubbly as ever and told me Jean-Paul was coming later in the week. No wonder she was bubbly I thought to myself.

"That's great Jaine" I said smiling.

"He's bringing Phillipe with him" she continued looking at me.

"Mmm ok" I replied not trying to look excited.

I would like to see Phillipe again, he was intriguing and not to mention an Italian Stallion. We got busy with the orders of the week and I also had to make more chocolate sauce and labels. I got the icing flowers made and started the chocolate sauce. Jaine' was busy making the sponges, tortes and white chocolate mud cakes. We took a breather at lunch time and enjoyed a coffee and sandwich.

"Jaine' can I ask you something?" I said as I sipped my coffee.

"Yes, Tassy what is it?" she replied.

"I need a little time off to go to Europe"? I said slowly.

"Why?" she asked

"Stefano is going through a bad time and he needs me" I answered truthfully.

"How long would you want?" she asked.

"Probably a week if not more." I replied thinking I've just had 2 weeks off.

"How about you go next week for two weeks as I can manage here and Jean- Paul will be staying for a month." She replied looking at me for my reaction.

"Are you sure you want to go Tassy?" she asked again.

"Yes, I do want to go and be with him and help him through this" I answered.

"Ok then that's settled." she replied pouring another coffee.

"Only on one condition." she added.

"What's that?" I asked.

"That you see Phillipe when he is here." She answered smiling.

"Yes, I suppose I can do that" I replied smiling back at her. We went back to work and got everything ready for tomorrow.

"Have a good night, Tassy" Jaine' hugged me.

"I will and you too" I hugged her back.

I drove back to Maddy's unaware that James was waiting outside my work. Maddy wasn't home yet so I made a Jack Daniels and relaxed on the sofa. I heard a noise outside sounded like the rubbish bin had fallen over. I went to the back door to investigate and I got the shock of my life. James was standing there; I went to scream but he grabbed me and pulled me inside and closed the door.

"James what the hell?" I stammered.

"Hello Tasmin" he held me tight.

"What are you doing here?" I asked pissed off.

"To see you my love" he replied looking at me with greedy eyes.

"I must warn you Maddy and her boyfriend will be home any minute" I said trying to sound convincing.

"Good then we can have a fun time together." he said smiling.

"What do you mean by that?" I asked angrily.

"You like a few men don't you Tasmin?" he said as his hand grabbed my bum.

"I don't know what you mean." I snapped at him.

"I've seen the men coming and going here and there and I think you and your girlfriends are little sluts." He said pushing me into his erection.

"James you've got the wrong idea of me I'm a simple girl who goes to work and comes home." I answered. Thinking this man knows everything about me.

"No Baby you like men to fuck you everywhere, don't you?" He said licking his lips.

"James, you have to go Maddy will be mad if you are here." I said again hoping he would take the hint.

"I've missed you Tasmin and I want you" he looked into my eyes with an evil look.

"Let's go to your room." he said just as the phone rang. I went to pick it up but James stopped me.

"Let the answering machine get it." he said as his hand was trying to pull up my skirt. It was Maddy saying she would be late as she had a meeting at work.

"Good" James said "now where is your room?"

"James, I beg you to go." I pleaded with him.

"Baby I've missed you" he replied not listening to me.

"Which room is yours?" he asked again.

I pointed to the middle room and he half dragged me there. I thought maybe I should just give in to him and then he would leave me alone. We entered the room and he closed the door with his foot.

"Baby" he started kissing my neck

"Mmm you smell so good" he kept nuzzling

"James if I let you have me will you be gentle and not tie me up?" I asked thinking of what he did last time.

"Love me Tasmin and I will not hurt you" he said between kisses on my neck.

Oh, what the hell just do it and get the fuck out I thought to myself. He started taking my clothes off and I tried to think. He was David or Scott and not James.

"oh Honey your tits are so beautiful" he said sucking my nipples.

I must get through this and give him what he wants I thought to myself as his hand was pulling my knickers down. He picked me up and carried me to the bed and laid me down. I was now naked and he smiled at me and licked his lips.

"You're so beautiful Baby I 'm going to have fun with you." He said as he undressed.

I lay there motionless thinking is this really happening. Should I struggle and fight, no just play along and you won't get hurt I thought. His erection was huge and he wanted me to suck so I did. He groaned and jerked more in my mouth making me take more of him. He was pinching my nipples and he groaned more until he spewed his semen in my mouth. I nearly gaged. It was Not like my salty and sweet. He got a towel and cleaned me up.

"That was incredible" he said with a smile.

I just lay there and said nothing as I knew there was more to come. He sucked my nipples and his tongue continued down to my favorite spot only this time I didn't want it. He licked, put his fingers everywhere and then mounted me. He was forceful and thrust into me with no respect. I didn't move just tried to think of one of my other lover's doing what he was doing. It was over very quickly and I thought thank god.

"Come baby and shower with me." he said pulling me off the bed.

Oh no I thought not again. He soaped me all over dipping the sponge in my forbidden place. I knew it wouldn't be long before he did the deed. He entered me and pumped me I thought god this is not like the others. The others are gentle he is so urgent and rough. It was over. I got out and dried off and put my fluffy robe on. James was right behind me and grabbed me around my waist.

"Not so fast Honey" he said huskily

"I haven't finished yet" he added.

"James, I have given you what you want so can you please go away now?" I said trying be calm.

"Soon Baby when I have finished." he kissed my neck and his hand pulled my sash undone. His erection was firm again and I thought is there no stopping this animal. He pulled me back to bed and put me on my knees. His finger went in and then his tongue and he kept going and going.

"Come for me Baby" he urged me. No, I will not give him that pleasure I thought.

"Come on Baby give it to me." he said again.

"I will not go until you give me your sweet juice" he plunged his finger in and out and his other hand played with my breasts.

Get it over with, I thought. I had to imagine it was Stefano there fucking and licking and bringing me to a climax. I did what he asked and he licked up my juices and commented how yummy I was and that I was very sweet. He then entered me and put his finger in my bum at the same time.

"You like that honey" he moaned as he thrusted more.

"Yes yes" I lied hoping it will be over soon. Don't cry I said to myself, I tried to imagine it was Stefano. He moaned loudly and withdrew and came over my back.

"Oh, Baby that's so good!" he groaned. Thank fucking god he's done I thought my body repulsed by his actions. He took me back to the shower and washed me again.

"James you must go now." I said softly

"Yes, I will kiss me first." he pulled my face to his.

I let him kiss me and I accepted his tongue even though I was repulsed by it. When it was over, he left the shower and got dressed. He came back in the bathroom and told me to be a good girl and that he would see me soon.

"I love you Tasmin" and then he was gone.

I sank to the shower floor and cried and cried. How can I get rid of this horrible man? After I had washed off James's smell and I got into my silk pj's and robe I felt better. Maddy had just got home and I made some soup and toast for us. We sat on the sofa and chatted and I tried not to look at her as she can read minds.

"Are you ok Tas? You look a little pale." she asked

"Yeh just a busy day at work" I replied thinking thank god she doesn't suspect a thing.

"I'm a bit tired I might go to bed" I hugged her.

"Ok sweetie sweet dreams see you in the morning" She hugged me back.

I went to bed and snuggled into my donna. I grabbed my cell on the way to bed and I thought I would ring Stefano.

"Hello Baby" I said when he answered.

"Hello Honey" he replied

"How are you?" he asked

"Good really good" I lied.

"You sound tired baby." he said softly.

"Yes, I had a big day at work." I replied lying again.

"Anyway, guess what I can come next week for two weeks." I said suddenly excited.

"Really that's fantastic." he replied grinning over the phone.

"Ok I will finalize everything and fly you out on the weekend."

"Ok, does that sound alright for you?" he said sounding excited.

"Yes, it does Oh I can't wait" I replied feeling a little bit horny thinking about him.

"Are you in bed?" he asked huskily.

"Yes, I am" I said thinking naughty thoughts,

"Good because I want to have some fun" he said sexily.

"I want you to get your play toy out and imagine it is me" he ordered

"Ok' I giggled. I got my friend out of my drawer.

"Now what?" I asked knowing full well of what is going to happen next.

"Play with your nipples and imagine I'm sucking them" he said in that sexy voice.

I did what he said and then he said to play with my clit and bring myself to orgasm. I knew he had his manhood in his hand and was masturbating to the sound of me groaning and playing. I could feel that beautiful feeling happening and Stefano urged me on.

"That's it baby come for me" he huskily said. He was groaning now so I knew he was close.

"Oh honey I want to suck you" I groaned in the phone that took him over the edge and I heard a groan and knew he had come. My orgasm was nearly there.

"Keep going baby let me fuck you" he said excitedly.

I plunged my friend into my pussy and fucked myself thinking it was Stefano. I came loudly and Stefano soothed me over the phone.

"Oh, Baby I love you and can't wait to see you?" he said. I was tired now and we said goodnight and Stefano said we must get Skype and a web cam so he can see me fucking myself.

"Ok Baby I will organize it tomorrow" I said yawning. We hung up then and I fell into a deep sleep.

Chapter Seventeen

The week dragged on and we got all the orders done by Thursday. Jean-Paul and Phillipe arrived Thursday afternoon and we greeted them with smiles and kisses.

"How are you Tasmin?" Phillip enquired.

"Good and you?" I asked

"Yes, good and busy at work so it's nice to relax." He replied with a smile.

"We will have to catch up." I said smiling at him.

"Well, I thought tonight would be good?" he asked

"Ok' I answered.

"Good I will pick you up or will we meet?" he asked.

"We could meet in town at a restaurant." I said. Thinking that might be safer.

"Ok say 6pm at the French restaurant?" he replied

"Yes that would be fine" I answered

"Good, good see you then" he said with excitement.

I drove home to Maddy's and this time locked all the doors when I got inside. Must be more careful. I went to my room, showered changed into a sexy black lingerie number and my hot red tight dress with stilettos. I wore my hair out and of course put on my dazzling earrings. Mmm Hot I thought as I looked in the mirror. Maddy came home, I could hear the rustle of keys in the lock.

"Oh, Tas you're home." she sounded surprised.

"Sorry I locked the door and I didn't hear you come in." I answered.

"You going out?" she eyed me up and down

"Yes, with Phillipe he's over from France." I replied

"You look hot are you going to have fun tonight?" She enquired with a cheeky smile.

"We will see what happens." I answered with a smile.

"Have fun and will I see you later tonight?" she asked

"Not sure. I will ring you and let you know." I said

"Yes please, so I don't worry." she replied sounding like my mother. We hugged each other and my taxi arrived.

I arrived at the restaurant and Phillipe was waiting looking very handsome. I must control myself I thought. We were seated in a private corner and Phillip was the perfect gentleman. We chatted easily and laughed together. We ate a delicious menu of seafood, duck and chocolate mousse. The champagne was so yummy I was getting quite tipsy. Must slow down I thought. Phillipe stood up I thought he was going to ask me to dance but he got on one knee and took my hand. What was he doing Oh shit his not, is he? I tried not to laugh and be serious.

"Tasmin you're a beautiful, sensual and kind woman any man would be proud to have you as his own. Will you marry me? I love you and have not stopped thinking about you." he looked at me with those puppy dog eyes.

He produced a ring box and opened it. Oh god it was beautiful, a huge diamond with little cluster of diamonds around it. It was amazing. My tongue was caught in my throat and I didn't know what to say.

"I, I don't know what to say" I stammered

"Say yes my love" he kissed my hand and then slid the ring on my finger, it fitted perfectly.

"Oh Phillipe its gorgeous I can't accept this." I said shaking my head. This is too soon I thought, I'm seeing Stefano in three days and I can't let go of Sam yet?

"You are very special to me Tasmin I can't stop thinking about you" he continued on

"Phillipe I can't I don't love you" I said truthfully.

"We had such a great time in France, I thought you had feelings for me" he asked with sad eyes.

"Oh I do and yes we did have a great time but I'm not ready for marriage yet" I replied looking into his eyes.

"It doesn't mean we can't have a bit of fun" I said smiling at him trying to cheer him up.

"Do you want to come back to my hotel" he looked at me.

"Yes, I would as long as you realize I can't marry you" I said trying to reassure him.

"Marry me yet" he said with a smile

"I want you to think about it and let me know in a while for your answer"? he came in for a kiss.

I accepted his lips and tongue and his hands pulling me close. Oh my that tongue and lips he sure knows how to kiss. He paid the bill and tipped the waiter and got a taxi to his hotel. I haven't been to this one I thought its very elegant. His room was very nice and he had ordered champagne, strawberries and cream. Oh, my favorite. He pulled me in and closed his arms around me. He felt so good and I could feel myself swaying in his arms.

"Champagne Baby?" he asked

"Love some" though I knew I probably shouldn't. He handed me a glass and proposed a toast

"To us and our future" he said looking into my eyes.

"To us" I said but not the future I thought.

Not yet it's too soon I can't be tied down to one man I'm a no strings attached girl. Oh god what's happening to me?

"Strawberry" he asked,

I snapped out of my thoughts. I accepted the strawberry as he teased it near my lips and then dipped it in the champagne and back to my lips. Oh, yum I ate it all. He gave me another one and I devoured that one also. I did the same to him and he teased me with his tongue Around the strawberry and then ate it. He led me to the bedroom where he peeled my dress off and went down to nuzzle my breasts.

"Oh, Baby you're so beautiful I could eat you up"? he said huskily.

He teased me with his tongue and kissed my nipples. He pulled my corset down and put some cream on my nipples and began to feast. I arched my back and lay there and let him seduce me. I wanted him and I wanted to suck and tease him. He undressed down to his boxers and his huge manhood was unleashed.

"Mmm very nice" I commented trying to touch him.

He helped me with his manhood and I put some cream on his knob and feasted like a wildcat. He was groaning and telling me to slow down or I will wear more cream. I took the hint and let him play with me for a while. His tongue took over my body and he feasted on my clit and pussy. Oh, my I was in Bliss! He put a condom on and put me on my knees and entered me. He was gentle but forceful. I moved with him my hips meeting his and his breathing becoming raggered. We were urgent now and we both climaxed together. Once we got our breaths back, we lay there and held each other.

"That was great" he said in my ear

"Yes, it sure was" I replied still buzzing from my orgasm.

"More champagne?" he asked as he got my glass

"Thank you" I said as he handed me my glass.

I sipped the liquid silk and looked at this gorgeous man, should I consider marrying him or should I keep him as a lover? I thought. He smiled at me and I smiled back.

"Shower?" he asked as he got up

“Yeh ok” I replied

I stripped off my corset and entered the shower. Once again, he made passionate love to me and once again I was lost.

Chapter Eighteen

Phillipe said to think about his proposal and not be too hasty in deciding.

"I would make you happy and look after you." He said wrapping his arms around me.

We said our goodbyes and I said I would talk to him soon. I told him I had to go to Europe on Business and that I would have an answer when I returned. I got at taxi back to Maddy's and she had already left for the day. I got ready for work and daydreamed about Stefano and that I would see him in two days. I couldn't wait, I missed him, and I knew he was like an addiction, I had to have him. I arrived at work and Jaine' was bubbly as ever.

"I'm so happy Tassy"

"I think I'm in love" she danced around the kitchen.

"Oh Jaine' that's great" I said smiling at her.

Why shouldn't she be happy, she deserved it. We got all the orders finished and sat back with our coffee and admired our work.

"When do you leave?" she asked

"Sunday morning early" I replied sipping my coffee.

"I hope it all goes well for you and that you and Stefano can have some peace together" she said looking at me concerned.

"Thanks, Jaine' it will be alright" I said not sure myself what is going to happen. We finished early and we both locked up and hugged each other.

"Take Care Tassy" she kissed my cheeks

"See you soon" I drove back to Maddy's and she was home from work.

"Hi honey" I smiled at her

"Hi yourself" she laughed. I told Maddy my plans and she listened and sighed.

"You know Tas you don't owe this man anything." she said cautiously. Not wanting to get me upset.

"I know but there's something about him I can't let go." I looked at her.

"I just don't want to see you get hurt." she held my hand.

"I know and I won't, I will see him and spend some time with him and then I will say goodbye."

I said lying because I knew I couldn't say goodbye. He was in my life and I wanted more of him, we weren't finished yet? Our lives had just begun. I packed my things hugged Maddy and drove home.

"Oh, home sweet home!"

I entered my house and it seemed empty and cold. It was a sunny day and I opened windows and let the fresh breeze through. I rang my parents and let them know I was going to Europe and that I would be back in 2 weeks. I also rang Sam and told him.

"I was coming out today to see you" he said disappointed.

"Well, I don't leave till tomorrow you can still come" I said thinking is that wise I will probably end up in bed with him.

"I would love to see you before you go"? he said sounding excited.

"Ok see you soon" I said and hung up.

The phone rang and it was Stefano.

"Hi Baby" he said excitedly

"Hi honey" I returned the excitement

"Can't wait to see you"? he said

"Me either" I replied.

"What are you doing now"? he enquired

"Just packing" I lied

"I miss you Tasmin" he cooed in the phone huskily, oh shit he wants phone sex now!

"Did you get the webcam?" he asked

"Oh, shit sorry I forgot I was so busy at work." I lied again thinking I can't tell him I was having sex with an Italian Stallion who asked me to marry him?

"Oh, Baby play with yourself" he said softly Oh, what the hell I have time and I just can't say no to this man.

"Ok sweetie just gives a minute to get ready" I said trying to take my clothes off.

"Leave your bra and knickers on"

"I want to imagine those sexy legs in black silk knickers and your tits in silk as well"? he said as he also was getting ready to play with himself.

"Ok baby" I laughed thinking he's so naughty.

"Get your sex toy out and tease your nipples with it" he said sexily.

"Ok" I got my friend out and proceeded to tease my nipples.

"Oh, baby that's feels so good" I slurred into the phone.

"I want to suck them" he teased.

"I want to roll my tongue around then go to your sensitive spot and lick you there" he urged me on.

"Baby I like that your tongue doing all those naughty things to me"
I said as that beautiful feeling started to happen

"That's it honeys you're so wet"

"Let me taste you" his voice was sounding raggered, he was close
now.

"Pull your knickers off and fuck yourself" he said firmly. I did what
he said and I groaned into the phone and he groaned as well. After our
sexual phone interlude, I lay there and talked to him.

"Can't wait to have you in the flesh?" I said huskily

"Oh, Baby wait till I get my hands on you I'm going to fuck you all
night long" he said cheekily

"Stop you're making me horny again" I said laughing

"Good that's what I like" he answered in a sexy voice. I said I had
to go and pack and he said to ring before boarding.

"See you in Zurich honey can't wait" he replied happily.

We hung up and I starting packing. I looked at the time shit Sam
would be here soon! I thought maybe I shouldn't have asked Sam to
come, I still like him a lot too and I wasn't sure I could give him up either
he also was like a sweet addiction. I just had to have him. Well, I can't
back out now he will be soon. I quickly showered and put on a new red
see through lace bodysuit with buttons at the crutch with no bra or
knickers. How wicked I thought. I teamed it with a black mini and a
black silk blouse which showed the red lace underneath. I didn't wear
stockings tonight just some red stilettos. Hot, Hot, Hot I thought as I
looked in the mirror. I hope he likes this? I thought. I put my hair up in
a pony tail and applied lip gloss and natural makeup. I went downstairs
put a cute white apron on and started preparing lunch for later and of
course some "Sweets" strawberries dipped in chocolate and white
chocolate. The doorbell rang and I looked at the monitor it was Sam.
Mmm he looks handsome standing there and of course he had red roses
and a bottle of wine or champagne very nice I thought. I checked myself
out in the hallway mirror and yes, I looked a knockout! I opened the door
to the warmest smiles and those eyes!

"Hi honey" he grinned at me,

"Hi honey yourself" I grinned back

"Come in" I moved aside and he lingered past touching

My face and came in for the kiss. His tongue found mine and he wrapped his spare arm around me and pulled me in. He kicked the door softly with his foot.

"You look gorgeous and I've missed you" he kissed me again. I hardly could get my breath.

"You look good Sam." I looked at him when he stopped kissing me.

"I feel great and now that I see you, I feel even better" he said smiling.

"For you" handing me the roses and yes it was champagne.

I went to the kitchen but didn't get a vase down from the cupboard as I remembered what happened last time, I did that. Sam smiled at me

"Here let me" he opened the cupboard and reached up and got a long vase for the roses.

"Though I should have let you do it." he turned to me and smiled again. I blushed the colour of the roses.

"Mmm something smells good." he whiffed the air.

"Something special for lunch I whipped up" I replied smiling.

"I'm hungry but not for food." he grabbed me around my waist and pulled me close.

"His lips went to mine and his hands pulled me up to his body, lucky I had stilettos on or I wouldn't been off the floor. He untied my apron and his hands went under my mini and up around my bum.

"Ooh you feel nice" he said as he felt the lace with nothing under it only skin. He unbuttoned my blouse to reveal my red lace with my breasts and nipples very visible.

"Oh honey are you trying to seduce me?" his head went to nuzzle my breasts. He gently bit my nipple through the lace.

"Sam, I cried" and clung to his big arms.

"Actually, I'm not hungry I'm starving." he picked me up and carried me upstairs.

"Sam put me down I have to turn off the oven." I said trying to struggle out of his arms.

He took me back to the kitchen still carrying me and bent down with me and I turned off the oven. He then turned and carried me back up the stairs. God this man is fit. Enjoy I thought to myself. He laid me on the bed and unzipped my mini and peeled it off.

"Baby you're beautiful" he looked at me.

I lay there in my red lace body suit and stilettos. He came down for the kiss and I accepted his tongue and lips. His need seemed urgent and I battled with his tongue and then he trailed his lips to my nipples. He gently bit and sucked my nipples through the lace.

"Oh, honey I cried softly" it felt so good.

His head then trailed to my pussy and he bit through the lace and nipped me and then put his finger under the lace and entered me. His finger pressing my clit and his other finger inside me. I spread my legs to receive him further and I was in bliss! His tongue was trying to gain access so in the end he popped the press studs to expose me. He feasted and thrusted his finger in and out. I could feel my whole body react and it wasn't long before I was coming.

"Oh Sam don't stop." I pleaded with him

He licked and fingered me harder and I groaned and clung to his head and shoulders. My climax took me to the top of the mountain and back again. He looked up at me and smiled

"You sure taste good honey" he grinned from ear to ear.

"I want some" I tried to pull him up.

"You want what?" he teased

"You know what." I teased back

"This?" he undressed quickly to expose his huge erection.

"Yes that" I replied huskily reaching for it

"You have to wait" he grabbed my hands above my head.

He then half straddled me and teased his cock near my mouth. I lashed out with my tongue and he directed it to my mouth. I opened to accept and he slid it into my mouth. I licked, sucked, teased and looked at him with big eyes. He still wouldn't let my hands go. He was pinching my nipples while I sucked him like a hoover.

"Oh, Baby you're going to wear cream." he said with a raggered voice.

"Oooh there's my cream now where's my strawberries?" Oh, that's right there in the fridge for later? I thought to myself. He withdrew and had grabbed some tissues before and shoved his spurting cock into them.

"You're a naughty girl." he looked at me and smiled.

"I might have to spank you with my big dick." he said wickedly.

He removed my body suit and stilettos and put a condom on the side table and then kissed me with gentle passion. His manhood getting ready for action again. He sheathed himself and entered me slowly. Oh, he felt so good and I moved with his hips to a gentle Rocking rhythm, I wrapped my legs around his bum as he pumped and thrusted harder and harder. He lifted my bum and plunged deeper and I groaned with ecstasy, it definitely was the ultimate climax hitting my gspot at the same time. I cried out his name just as my climax happened and he groaned as well. We were moving together as one and we were both lost in each other's bodies. Our breathing returned to normal and I lay there thinking our naughty I am. I'm fucking one lover now and leaving to fuck another in Europe. This has to stop I thought to myself. But who do I give up? How do I decide? I love them both. I decided to stop torturing myself with guilty thoughts and just enjoy.

"Remember Tas you are a no strings attached girl" I thought yes, I am.

"Are you hungry for food now?" I asked rolling on to his side and looking at him.

He looked at me with big puppy dog eyes and said not quite. Oh, what now I thought smiling,

"Shower" he pulled me up and held my hand to the shower.

He soaped me all over and turned me towards the shower wall, I knew what he wanted and I knew I had to give in to him. He entered me gently and his hand played with my pussy. I groaned and he held my hips and moved them with his rocking motion.

"Oh Baby" he moaned huskily and I knew he was close.

I moved with him, gently going with his thrusts until I could feel no more. He held me as my knees buckled and I put my hands on the wall to steady myself.

"Oh, Sam stop I can't take anymore" I pleaded with him

He came then and everything else was a blur. He washed me again and wrapped me in a big fluffy towel and carried me back to bed. I snuggled in and got warm and gazed dreamily at him. Mmm a girl could get used to this I thought as I watched him get dressed, his muscles gleamed with water droplets. I can't let him go he's in my heart and head. When I got warm, I got up and got dressed back into my red lace bodysuit and skirt and top. I didn't put on my stilettos but my black flats. We went downstairs and I finished heating lunch. I dished up and we ate and drank the champagne he had brought.

"This is delicious" Sam said as he handed me his plate for seconds. I put more chicken pasta bake on his plate and handed it to him.

"Thanks honey" he said and winked at me.

We had a lovely time and I felt very comfortable around Sam. He was very easy going and always flashing that beautiful smile at me. His eyes would light up and I would get goosebumps. Maybe he is the one? I can't let him go yet, I have to think about everything and of course, Stefano's proposal which I had not given him an answer yet. I knew he would be wanting that when I went to see him. We lay on the sofa after lunch and my head nestled in his chest. My head rising and falling with his breathing. We both snoozed for an hour and I woke out of my dream of Sam and Stefano and them tugging at me and my heart and who was I going to say goodbye too. I could honestly say to myself that out of all my lovers Sam and Stefano have been my favorite. One of them is my soul mate but which one? Will I regret the decision I make and will I be able to be faithful to one man? I struggled in my head with these choices and I was starting to get anxious.

"Are you alright Babe?" Sam asked as he sensed my stress.

"Sorry I'm a bit distracted and stressed about flying." I said hoping he would believe me. He held me and rocked me like a baby,

"I wish you weren't going." he looked into my eyes.

"You know Tasmin you are very special to me." he continued.

"I might soon want you all to myself and not share you with anyone." he touched my face as he looked at me.

I stared into his eyes, was I dreaming or was this real. He was beautiful, calm, and desirable. He was everything a woman could ever want. He was my addiction.

"Sam, aren't you seeing that girl still?" I asked softly

"No, she has met a man now and we are just friends with no benefits." he said looking at me.

"She wants to settle down and have kids" he added.

"I told her I understood as I have been having the same feeling but with someone else"? he looked into my eyes and held my trance like I were in his spell. I looked back at him.

"Those eyes you could melt in them" I leaned forward

To kiss him, his lips and tongue accepting mine.

He held my head in his hands as we kissed passionately. My head was spinning and I tried not to think about all these men (addictions) putting demands and decisions on me. A voice was saying in my head

"Tas you're 25 you're ready to settle and have a family." Another voice was saying.

"I like my carefree life of no commitment, no strings attached girl." Sam was nuzzling my breasts and he knew I was anxious and stressed.

"What's wrong honey?" he asked looking up at me taking his lips from my nipple.

"I was just thinking of what you said before about settling down." I said softly still in a dream.

"You mean me, don't you?" I looked into those eyes.

"Yes, baby I mean you, you have captivated my heart and my thoughts" he kissed me again his tongue searching for mine. I pulled away after the kiss,

"Sam I'm not sure if I'm ready to settle down yet." I said gently and calmly looking into his eyes.

"Honey I'II wait for when you're ready, you're worth waiting for." he answered softly and touching my face.

"Sam that would mean I wouldn't be tied to you and this is still special friends with benefits." I looked at him for his reply.

"Well, I suppose so, does that mean you will other lovers?" He answered slowly not sure himself what he was saying.

"Yes" I whispered. I looked at him and he had sad puppy dog eyes, I smiled at him and reassured him.

"Sam you are special to me I just need some time to work out what I want."

"But you will the first to know" I added. He looked at me trying to figure out something.

"Do you have another special friend with benefits?" he asked looking deep into my eyes, I knew I couldn't lie!

"Yes" I breathed.

"Is he here or in Europe?" he quizzed me again. Shit what's with all the questions I thought.

"Europe" I said softly.

"So you're going over there to see him?" he sounded a bit hurt now.

"Yes" I breathed again.

"Shit!" he exclaimed and turned away from me.

I jumped; he had never raised his voice to me before it gave me a fright. He realized this and grabbed my shoulders.

"Baby I'm sorry I didn't mean to shout" he said softly

"I love you Tasmin and I don't think I want to share you with anyone."

"Is that so wrong?" he looked at me with glazed eyes. A tear rolled down my cheek and he caught it with his lips.

"Honey please believe me I'm sorry I didn't mean to make you cry." he held me close. He released me and looked at me.

"Have some time, I will give you that, but remember I will always be here for you when you need me and hopefully one day forever." he went down on one knee.

Oh my god what is he doing? I thought, I started shaking. He pulled a ring box out of his pocket and flipped it open. It was beautiful, very delicate and fine, different to Phillipe's ring.

"Oh, it's beautiful" I exclaimed it was the most gorgeous ring I have ever seen.

"Tasmin, I love you and I want you to be mine forever."

He held my hand and slipped the ring on. It fitted perfectly. I looked at it on my finger and I didn't know what to say.

"Sam" I stuttered, "I can't accept this yet I need some time." I looked into his eyes hoping he would understand.

"Ok baby we will do it your way, for now anyway." He said holding my hand. I took the ring off and gave it back to him,

"Keep this safe and I will think about it." I said.

"Make it one day soon" he answered looking into my eyes. We held each other and then he pulled me up.

"I want to make love to you before you go." he said in a deep sexy voice.

I followed him upstairs and thought to myself that I at least owe him a good time after the effort with the ring. God it was beautiful!! He peeled off my mini and I stood there in my red lace bodysuit which showed everything. I did look hot. He looked at my nipples and licked his lips keeping his sexy gaze on me. He was like a mountain lion about to pounce! His big arms wrapped around me and his lips covering mine. His hand pushing my bum into his erection straining in his pants. His hand at the back of my head holding me in his kiss and embrace. He stopped and gave me some air and I looked at him and smiled.

"You're so handsome, strong, sincere, sexy should I go on?" I smiled again.

"I have deep feelings for you but I don't know what to do." I said honestly and softly.

"You have to trust me that I can give you the world and much happiness" he said tenderly.

"I will always be faithful and never hurt you" he also added. I nodded.

"I know you would be all those things and more." I replied holding his hand and stroking it. He nuzzled my neck.

"Love me baby."

He breathed and his lips went to my breasts and starting biting my nipples through the lace. I arched my back and cried out. My hands in his hair. He picked me up and placed me on the bed. He popped the press studs and pulled my lace suit over my head. His hands caressed all over my body.

"You're delicious, I want to lick you all over."

He said huskily as his tongue trailed to my nipples. He got up and undressed unleashing his manhood which was standing to attention! I grabbed him and pulled his torso into my face where I wrapped my hand around his shaft and caressed softly. My tongue rolled around his knob and I sucked it gently.

"You little wildcat" he moaned. I sucked harder and teased him with my tongue.

"You'll pay for that" he teased. He rolled me underneath him and he held my hands above my head.

"Are you going to be a good girl?" he asked.

"Maybe." I giggled. He reached out for the condom and put it on. He spread my legs and entered me with forceful passion. He gave a big thrust.

"Say you will be a good girl." he asked again.

"Ok I'll be good" I teased.

He kissed me then and pumped me, lifting my bum and thrusting into me. He then rolled me onto my knees and took me like a wild stallion bucking and fucking me.

"Let go honey." he urged me on. I let go and I was lost in his rhythm and he took me to great heights of ecstasy. We lay together and our breathing returned to normal.

"What time is your flight tomorrow?" he asked.

"8am" I answered.

"I will drive you to the airport and see you off. Is that, ok?" he asked as he played with my hair.

"Yes, if that's ok with you?" I replied not wanting to think about leaving him.

"Are you hungry?" I asked as I played with his chest hairs.

"A little bit but manly for you not food?" he replied with a big smile.

"Well, I have a bit more packing and then I will make an omelet for dinner." I said getting up and putting on my robe.

He lay on the bed and watched me. I packed my suitcase and jewelry case and shut the suitcase up. I picked out my black silk pant suit and a lavender lace blouse and also took my leather jacket. I placed them on the chair ready to wear for the plane. I packed my high heels and flats which I would wear on the plane and then change into heels when I arrived. I grabbed my makeup case and went into the bathroom to pack it.

"They're all done" as I put all my cases together at the bedroom door. I got my Christian Dior handbag and put my flats and heels in, some lip gloss, wallet, passport, tissues, sunglasses and a book in. I nearly forgot my charger for my cell and grabbed that and put it in my handbag.

"All finished." Sam had been watching me.

"Yes, now I'm all yours" I said as I jumped on the bed.

"Good" and he grabbed me around my waist and kissed me passionately on my lips.

"Don't forget me Tasmin." he murmured in my ear.

"I won't Sam I won't" I said looking into his eyes. We went downstairs and I made a light dinner and we sat by the fire and relaxed.

"Let's go to bed." he kissed my neck.

"Yeh, I suppose we should. We have an early start." I replied getting up to fix the fire.

"What time should we leave?" he looked at me.

"I have to be there 2 hours before the flight." I answered.

"So, we would have to leave around 5am." I said yawning.

"Ok let's get some sleep." he grabbed my hand and led me upstairs.

We lay in each other's arms and caressed each other. Once again Sam made passionate love to me and it was making my decision that much harder. He was so good to be with. He made me feel whole and happy. How can I choose? I fell asleep and woke to the alarm at 4.30am.

Chapter Nineteen

I got up and showered and dressed. Sam had made coffee and handed it to me when I entered the kitchen. He had put all my bags by the door ready to put in the car. I went around and did a last-minute check, put the security system on and we were on our way. At the airport Sam got out and got me a trolley for my bags and then loaded it up. He turned to me and held me with his big arms.

"Come back to me Tasmin I love you." he whispered in my ear.

We kissed passionately and then we said our goodbyes.

I watched him drive away and tried not to let the

Tears fall. Goodbye Sam, I will miss you and one day I will come back! I rang Stefano just before boarding and he said he would meet me at Zurich.

"Have a good flight" he said. I boarded the plane which when I picked up my ticket that he had brought me it was first class.

"Wow" I've never been in first class. It was an eye opener.

Champagne on arrival, comfortable recliners and charming hostesses. This should be a good flight? I thought to myself. We got under way and after we were above the clouds and we could walk around they served breakfast. Bacon, eggs, croissants, mushrooms, tomatoes, juice and brewed coffee. I dozed after breakfast and day dreamed of Stefano and Sam and how I could make any decision about them. They were both different and both very appealing and desirable. I must of fell asleep and the hostess woke me for lunch. I thought we just had breakfast. Well, it was actually midday so I must have slept. Lunch was served and it was delicious chicken dish. I looked around at the other passengers and there were all types of people. An older couple sat opposite to me and a younger man and woman probably in their twenties sat across from me. We all nodded at each other and enjoyed our lunch topped off with a white sparkling wine. I sat there and thought about Phillipe and his proposal and Sam's and Stefano's proposal, how do I tell them I can't marry them, it's not because I don't love them, I do, but it's the attachment thing and the settling down part I'm not ready for. The young couple looked across at me and smiled, I smiled back.

"Travelling to Europe?" the man asked.

"Yes" I answered and smiled again.

"We are off to France and Italy" he continued

"Lovely just beautiful there" I replied not really wanting to have a inadept conversation with strangers.

"Where are you going?" the man said looking at me. He was quite attractive, brown hair and lovely eyes. His partner was a small blonde girl, a little plain Jane type. She smiled at me shyly and I returned the smile.

"I'm going to Zurich on business." I replied not wanting to go into detail about my trip?

"Zurich nice" he replied with a glint in his eye.

I thought to myself what does he mean by that? He introduced himself Danny and Julia and I told them my name.

"Are you traveling alone?" he asked looking at me and stopping too long to gaze at my lace top as I had taken my jacket off but my lace top was not see through as it had lining underneath. I didn't like his questions?

"I'm meeting my girlfriend there and we are traveling around Europe" I lied as it sounded better than saying I'm meeting my older man who wants me as his Mistress!

"We should meet up in Italy or somewhere and get to know each other." he said with a grin.

Julia just looked at me, she would do anything he said. I didn't want to offend him as I have to travel the next 10 hours with him.

"I'm not sure if I have time, I have a few conferences to attend but give me your number and I will ring you if I can organize something" I lied again thinking I wish he would piss off!

And now I'm struck on a fucking plane with him. I flashed him a cute smile, there take that you bloody sleash and I hope you get an erection! Deal with that! I thought. I giggled in my head and ignored him and asked the waitress for a Jack Daniels, might as well it's going to be a long flight! After two Jacks I felt better, I was relaxed and floating in the air. Literally. I got up and went to the toilet. God they were luxury as well. Beautiful soaps and towels. I freshened up and looked in the mirror. I looked fresh, pretty and carefree. I smiled at myself. Go get them Girl! I giggled to myself. I went to go out the door and Danny was standing right in the way.

"Excuse me" I tried to get past. He blocked me and leaned in to whisper in my ear,

"Ever done it on a plane before?" he said huskily looking down my top as he said it. I looked up at him,

"No, I haven't." I replied trying to push past again.

The door was open behind me and he pushed me back in and closed the door. No one even noticed. I was in shock and I didn't think I should start screaming on the plane.

"What are you doing?" I said quietly as I didn't want anyone to hear.

"You're very pretty and I've got a hard on just looking at you." his arms went to engulf me.

"Danny, you can't just have your way with me on a plane in a toilet." I said trying to make it sound like a joke and besides

"I don't even know you, I don't just screw anyone, anytime." I added firmly.

"I suggest Danny that you wank yourself stupid and think of your beautiful girlfriend." I said unlocking the door and walking out. He didn't have time to react.

His mouth was wide open in shock! He came out 10 mins later looking rather sheepish. He obviously had wanked. I giggled to myself and tried not to look at him. I gazed up and he was looking right at me saying with those eyes.

"That was great!"

"You missed out."

I ordered another Jack and settled down to my drink and book. I would occasionally glance at Danny and Julia. She was asleep and he was lying back reading a car magazine. He looked over at me and smiled.

"Sure you don't want a rain check?" he asked cheekily.

I laughed and ignored him. I dozed off and woke late afternoon, we weren't arriving till 7am in the morning so we still had a long way to go. I went to the toilet and freshened up. I looked at the girl in the mirror she stared back. Is this the right thing to do? Am I making the right decision. Remember Tass you're a no strings attached girl. I'm free. I'm just having fun exploring possibilities. I love Stefano. I love Sam. I have feelings for other men also. Is this normal to feel these feelings.

Chapter Twenty

I came out of the toilet and the older couple were sleeping and I snuck back to my seat. The hostess came up to me, She was around 25 my age and she was very attractive. Beautiful blonde hair in a bun and her Eyes were very appealing. I couldn't stop looking at Them.

"Would you like something to drink"? she asked with A smile

"Yes please I think I need one"? I smiled back at her.

She looked like an Angel.

"Where are you going to"? she asked

"To Zurich" I replied

"I live just outside of Zurich she said smiling

"Sorry what drink would you like"? she asked again

"Mmm let me think a Vodka Sunset I asked smiling

She came back with my drink and a little antipasto Platter and said that if I ever need anything over there To ring her, I thanked her, She handed me her number

"Monique" she squeezed my hand gently.

"Tasmin" I touched her hand back.

"Its very nice to meet you"? she said in a European Accent.

"Are you Swiss"? I asked intrigued by this woman.

"Yes" she replied.

We exchanged smiles and she left to attend to other people. I needed time to think of all my own problems. Dinner was served at 6pm and it was fish or steak.

I said steak, I felt like some meat, I must be craving Men and the animal in me. Monique smiled as she gave me my dinner and She said please come and see me if you have time. I feel we have some kind of connection, I know it sounds Silly cause we don't even know each other, she had said. I agreed there was something there and she intrigued me.

"Ok if I have time"? I said smiling at her.

The night turned into late night and I slept peacefully Till 5am. I dreamt of Stefano and his big arms around me. His hands doing wicked things to me and I to him. I think I slept with a smile on my face. We were landing in 2 hours so I wanted to freshen up before Then. I gazed around everyone was asleep. I got up and went to the ladies. Monquie was coming out as I went to open the door.

"Good Morning" she looked at me smiling

"Good Morning"

"That's a lovely perfume" I commented

"yes its Channel no 5" she repli

"Thanks" as she held the door for me.

I fixed my hair applied some makeup and changed my flats Danny and Julia were awake now and said good morning to Me.

"Good morning" I answered smiling at them.

Monique brought juice and coffee around and I thanked Her when she handed me a mug. We drank our coffee and then the mugs were collected, Our plane starting to make a desccent. I was nervous now and I'm sccing Stcfano. Yes I have missed him. I sat there and did my breathing as I hate decending and My ears always hurt.

I was relieved when the tyres hit the tarmack. I waited for the other's to leave first and then Monique Said goodbye to me, saying I hope to see you again.

"I hope so too" I said as we hugged

Danny and Julia were not too far away and they Turned and said goodbye and safe travels, I wished them the same.

Chapter Twenty- One

I got out of the first class lounge and there he was. God he looked so handsome waiting there, our eyes Met and he came quickly to me and hugged me.

"Hello beautiful" he kissed me passionately.

A few people were staring I didn't care I had Stefano In my arms.

"its so good to see you" I said as I wrapped my arms Around him.

"Come lets get out of here"? he held my hand and led Me to the exit where customs is and my bags.

We got through customs easily and quickly. He took me outside to where his BMW was waiting. It was black, sleek and fast. Stefano told me he had booked me into a hotel not far From his house so he could come and go home Quickly If needed. He drove along the Auto Barn easily and had his Hand on my leg just nearly between.

"Cant wait to get you alone"? he said huskily

"Me either" I said smiling at him.

We arrived at this gorgeous hotel chalet and it had Little flower boxes with red roses spilling over. Stefano got my bags and we checked in. An old lady With a charming smile greeted us warmly. Her English was very good.

"Come this way let me show you your room"? she Led the way to our room.

It was a beautiful room with a lounge room, and Bedroom and bathroom. Very cosy and the décor looked expensive.

"If there is anything else you just ring"? she pointed To the phone.

She smiled at me and said something in Swiss to Stefano and He laughed and handed her a tip.

"What did she say"? I asked him

"She said beautiful wife you have" he looked at me and grinned.

"So she doesn't know you"? I asked relieved.

"No that's why I booked here"? he answered as He went to the bar.

He poured some freshly brewed coffee for us and Picked up a plate of croissants and fruit and brought Them to the sofa.

"Thankyou" I said as he handed me the cup.

I took a crossiant and bit into it, it melted in my mouth. I kicked off my heels and curled my legs up on the Sofa. We finished our coffee and croissants. Stefano was Impatient to get me undressed and naked. He held my hand and led me to the bedroom. We lay on the bed and we passionately kissed. His tongue searching for mine, his hand trying to Gain access to my breasts. He took my top off and pulled my silk pants off.

I lay there in my Bra and knickers. He undressed down to his boxers and put some Condoms on the bedside table. His erection jutting upward ready and willing. He came down to kiss me again and his hands Unclipping my bra so he could release my horny Boobs.

"Oh honey I've missed you"? he said as he nuzzled My breasts. His tongue licking my nipples and gently Biting them with his teeth.

His other hand pulling my knickers off and his finger Entering my favorite place. I lay there in ecasty and let him feast on me. I climaxed loudly and clung to his shoulders. He could wait no longer and he put his condom on and Entered me.   His thrusting and pumping urgent as He obviously has missed me. He moved to a steady rythum and I moved with him. We both groaned loudly when we climaxed and lay There together breathless.

"Oh I needed that"? he rolled onto my side.

He grabbed me around my waist and pulled me ontop Of him.

"Baby youre so hot and horny" he said as he played with Nipples.

He got rid of the old condom and it wasn't long before He was inside me
again.   This time I was on top of him. I bounced up and down and he
held my hips and Pumped away not giving me any mercy. I was close
now and he was fucking me like a Jack Rabbit.   He let out a groan and
I felt my release At the same time. I lay there ontop of him and my body
rose with his Breathing.

"Shower" he smacked my bum gently.

We went into the shower and of course we had more Hot sex! He carried
back to bed and said rest. He got dressed into some clothes he had
brought With him. Jeans and a white silk shirt which he left Unbuttoned.
He looked godam hot and sexy. Yes a girl can sure get used to this?   But
which man? How do I decide, I love them both and they both Make me
happy.

I lay there and dozed off for awhile. I woke to Stefano nuzzling my neck
and I rolled over So my back was to him.   He lay there and spooned me
His hands around my breasts teasing. I could feel his erection pressing
into my bottom. He had slipped his jeans off and I already was naked
from Our previous sex romp.

His hand playing with my favorite spot and his other Hand teasing my
nipples. He was naked now and condom on he entered me   When he
knew my clitoral orgasm was close, He plunged into me and fucked me
with no mercy Whispering in my ear that you are mine Tasmin and I will
take whats mine?

"You belong to me"? he said louder

As he thrusted harder into me to make a point. Point taken I thought to
myself as my orgasm Collided with his. I lay in his arms and was
somewhere between Heaven and Earth.   It took me a good while before
my Body returned to its senses.

"Stefano honey that was incredible"? I said looking into His eyes.

He looked back into mine and I melted, I knew I was lost, I knew I was
in love. We kissed passionately and he got up and went to The bathroom.

I heard the water running and temptation was calling Me. I moved like a wildcat sleek and sexy, I'm coming for my feast. I entered quietly and came up behind him. I wrapped my hands around his manhood and Squeezed gently.

"Let me wash it Baby" I cooed in his ear as my tongue

Licked his neck and then nibbled his ear. He turned around and I was already swatting ready for Playtime. I picked up the sponge and put body wash on it and Soaped him up and down, slid down each leg and Then back up to his balls and bum.

I rinsed him off and wrapped my mouth around his Throbbing penis, my tongue rolling around his knob Inside my mouth and gently sucked and teased. I made my move and sucked harder and took more Of him in. His hips jerking begging for more. I gave him no mercy and he was in my spell of Seduction. I probably could ask for just about anything at this Point of time as he was mine.

He wanted more and I had him in my control. What a power trip I thought to myself. To have a man under your submission and they cant Control themselves and their need is urgent and you Control when to strike and feast like a wildcat. I knew I was playing with fire and his need is close I fastened the pace and sucked harder, his groaning And hip jerking indicating he was about to blow!

"Baby do you want it"? he breathed

"Yes honey give it to me" I tried to spit out with His cock in my mouth.

I continued my mission and 15 seconds later I had a mouthful and a face full of come.

"Ooh theres my salty nows wheres my sweets"? I thought to myself.

I washed my face and he pulled me up into his arms.

"Youre beautiful honey you suck so good" he kissed me on The lips.

Our bodies clung to each other wet and hot. He turned me around so he was behind me and spread My legs and made me bend over. He entered my pussy And slid up and down, his finger on my clit at the Same time.

"Honey" he said huskily

"That feel good Baby" he gave a little plunge as He said it.

"Yes its so good" I breathed back

He put his thumb in my bum hole and played there too.

"You like that honey"? he said softly and sexy.

"Yes Yes" as my orgasm was close, my knees Buckling under me.

He pumped harder and faster and I was already gone. My orgasm exploding on impact. His exploding with me. He supported my body as I couldn't feel anything but Utter ecasty. He washed me and carried me back to bed. I snuggled in to keep warm and watched as Stefano Got dressed.

"Having a good look"? he asked cheekily.

"Mmm" I purred.

"Maybe its time for presents"? he got my attention now.

I sat up and said all excitedly

"Presents what Presents"? I clapped my hands Like an excited child.

He went to the cupboard and pulled out a big white Box with a red sash and bow on it.

"For you honey" he handed me the box.

I fumbled with the lid and opened it to reveal under the Tissue paper a long red gown with a split up the leg, It was strapless and had diamantes on the breast line. There also was a shawl. It was exquisite.

"Ohh" I breathed

"Its gorgeous" I lifted it out of the box.

There was more tissue paper underneath and I   Looked inside and there was a gorgeous red lace Short baby doll dress with suspenders, stockings, And g/string.   Beside that was some knockout Red stilettos that also had diamantes on the toes.

"Keep going" he urged

"What more"? I realized there was more tissue paper

And underneath that was a red silk robe with diamantes On it. Beside that was a red clutch bag with diamantes On it.

"Honey there gorgeous and I love the diamantes"

I said my face glowing He smiled and said

"Baby there not diamantes there diamonds" he Looked at me.

"What"? I looked back at him.   They must have cost A fortune.

"I cant, you cant, its too generous"? I said looking at The beautiful and exquisite collection in front of me.

"Yes I can" he pulled my face to his and kissed me. His tongue looking for mine.

"They might come off"? I said worried.

"it doesn't matter if they do but they wont as they are Stuck on with special glue" he reassured me.

I lightly touched the diamonds and ran my finger Around them. They were small and it wasn't like a lot Of them, just a few on each item. It really was the most gorgeous items I've ever seen. Or ever dreamed of, they were twinkling at me.

"How will I get these through Customs"? I suddenly Panicked.

"Its ok baby I'II take care of it"? he answered gently And he came in for a kiss. His lips and tongue said

Everything and I accepted his gift. His hands already in my blanket
exploring and I was Trying to push him away as I didn't want to damage
my New preisous gifts. He packed them neatly back in the box and put
the box On the table. He removed the red gown and shawl and hung it
up in The closet.

"For tonight my love"? he looked at me with those hot Sexy eyes
bearing into mine.

I could hardly wait. The lovely old lady whose name was Hannah had
Prepared a small feast for us.

"Put on your lace dress with your robe with no Knickers on" he
said firmly and then added

"Your stilettos too"

"Yes Sir" I sat up and saluted him.

He laughed and said hurry up and get dressed.

"I'm hungry" he added looking at me licking his lips.

I got up quickly and put on the lace dress it was low in   The cleavage
and it just covered My bum, it was tight, it was gorgeous. Put on my robe
and stilettos. Fixed my hair and put a little red lipstck. Hot! as I looked
in the mirror. I entered the lounge room and Stefano just stood and Stared
with those come fuck me eyes!

"Honey you look gorgeous."

"Come here"

I sleeked over to him and he grabbed me around My waist and pulled me
close. His hand under my robe to feel my bum cheeks. He pulled the sash
loose and he exposed more of me. His lips trailing my breasts and nipples
down to my navel.

"Honey" I tried to pull him up

"Aren't we going to eat?" I was struggling to talk as his finger and
tongue had entered me.

"I am" he purred

He came for air, thank goodness otherwise I would be On the table as the food. I got out of his grip and strode over to the table. The view was beautiful with its green mountains and You could see some glaciers on top. There was a Church in the distance and shaggy cows Grazing in the distance.

"Its breathtaking"? I admired the view and came up Behind me and put his arms around me.

He pointed in the towards a road and said he lived along There about 20kms away. I gazed in that direction and my thoughts drifted back to His Wife.

"How is she"? I asked softly

"She is doing better, she is awake, but doesn't Recognise anything or anyone"? he answered

I could feel his body tighten around me he was really Stressed and tense. I turned around to look into his eyes, He had tears in them and I held him tight.

"Don't worry it will be alright"? I said tenderly not Sure myself if it would be.

We didn't speak anymore about it as I could see and Feel his sadness and pain This is not like Stefano I thought to myself Stefano is strong, stubborn and always right. I must distract him and cheer him up I thought as I sat down and poured the coffee. The sun was streaming in the windows and I felt like I was the wife and my husband was about to join me For lunch after our lovemaking.

We ate and chatted calmly and with no demands on Each other. We didn't talk anymore of his wife or situation. I knew I was here to help him through this crisis in his life. Emotionally and physically. After lunch he pulled me up and on to his lap. My dress too tight to straddle him so I sat side on. He kissed me on my lips and I took him in and played with his tongue. He strong arms holding me. I started to get tingles of desire going through my body. I was horny and hot again. I got off his lap and unlashed my robe and hitched up My lace dress to expose my pussy and then sat back Down straddling him and the chair. His head nuzzling my breasts and nipping at my nipples. His hard on pressing into through his pants. His finger went to my sensitive spot and he gently teased my clit and hole. I was in ecstasy. He teased and teased till I could take no more. I wanted his tongue and lips. He picked me up with me still straddling him and he cleared half of the table and lay me down.

"Baby on the bed." I said giggling

"No, I'm still hungry I want to eat." he licked his lips. He grabbed the maple syrup and drizzled some on my pussy.

"Don't get any on my robe" I half yelled at him. He smiled and shook his head then removed my robe.

"Happy now?" he asked with that sexy smile.

He got a cushion for my head and spread my legs for him to feast. His hands underneath my bum cheeks picking me up and eating me like I was a Big Burger. His tongue going in and out and his teeth giving little gentle nips to give me a bit of pleasurable pain.

"You taste so sweet" he said grinning. I wriggled and giggled and he held me firm.

"You're not going anywhere."

His big arm holding me across my boobs. His other hand now playing with my pussy while he licked and sucked. His fingers pinching my nipples and I could not resist. I lay back and enjoyed, I was his, and I gave in to desire and lust. I think I called out his name when I came and my body shattered inside me. His jeans were off and he was already to go. His erection eager and throbbing. He slid me down to the edge of the table and picked up my bum cheeks and spread me wide with his body as he slid into my wet pussy. He pumped and thrusted, our bodies moving together in a rocking motion. The more I moved he moved more and harder. His orgasm was close and his breathing was becoming raggered. He pumped me faster and plunged harder and harder.

"Oh baby" I cried out when he took me over the edge. He groaned and slowed down until he had emptied. He was half leaning on my chest and supporting his weight with his other hand on the table. He was still inside me and I clenched my inner pelvic muscles to show him I could see feel him. He looked at me and smiled and said;

"You want more do you?" he teased as he gave a little thrust.

I laughed and our eyes twinkled together. He withdrew then and helped me up and off the table. I went to the bathroom to freshen up. I came out of the bathroom and Stefano was on the bed.

"Are we going out?" I asked looking at him lying on his side, his long muscley physic just so hot to look at.

"No, not till later" he said smiling

"Come here." he patted the bed.

"I think we have had enough for now."

I challenged him putting my hands on my hips standing there looking hot in a tight red lace dress that didn't hide much. My legs looked longer with the stilettos on.

"Is that so?" he jumped up so fast and grabbed me around the waist and put me over his shoulder, like a fireman hold. He then gently smacked my bum and his finger even went in.

"Naughty girls need to be punished" he walked towards the bed.

Before he put me down though he said he liked his position as he could finger fuck me and I couldn't resist. Sure, I could hit his back but it would be no use. He played for a while and sat on the bed with me still over his shoulder. He then lay down and got me to straddle his face in a 69 position. I sucked and bobbed up and down while he licked and finger fucked me. Oh god it was so tantalizing and I attacked him like a wildcat on heat. We both gave each other no Mercy! We both climaxed loudly, semen hitting my mouth and my juices hitting his. He handed me some tissues and I cleaned up. I took off my stilettos as I thought I would stab him.

"Don't take them off" he pleaded

"I'll put them on later."

"My feet hurt" I added. He came down to rub my feet and that felt better.

"I will run you a bath" he got up and put the water on.

154

Chapter Twenty-Two

The of smell Jasmine was enticing and calling me. I got up and carefully took off my lace dress. Stefano was sitting on the side of the tub swirling the bubbles around.

"Madam" he took my hand and helped me in. The water was hot and refreshing. I lay back and let the bubbles work their magic on me.

"Mmm this is great" I looked at him as he gazed dreamily at me. His eyes talking to me.

"You want more baby?" he said huskily

His eyes telling me what he wants. He took off his boxers and slid in the bath up the other end. Thank goodness it was a huge claw bath that was big enough for us. Our toes touching and teasing each other under water. He grabbed my legs and pulled me up to him. Water went everywhere spilling over the edge.

"Baby look what you have done?" worried what Hannah would say.

"It's ok, the floor has a drain hole and the cleaners will mop it up" he said calmly. He wiped the bubbles from my breasts and gently sucked and licked my nipples.

"Oh, Baby that feels so good" I jiggled my breasts to tease him.

I could feel his erection under me and I knew he wanted more. He washed me and prepared me for our next sexual act of lust and desire. He turned me so I was sitting in front of him with my back towards him. He entered my forbidden place gently and his finger went to my favorite spot and teased. He held my hips and guided me up and down slowly and gently. His finger fucking me and my clit at the same time.

"Oh honey" I groaned.

His own groaning was ragged and rough, he was close too. He pumped me a little faster and harder just enough for me to bear. His finger going 100 miles an hour on my clit and his other finger inside me. He's very talented. I thought to myself. My orgasm collided with his and he didn't withdraw he emptied himself inside me. I thought I'm on the pill so everything is safe and I can't get pregnant if we are careful. He slid out of me and I lay exhausted in his legs his arms around me.

"That was so hot." he whispered his fingers squeezing my nipple.

"Mmm" I was still in dreamland. The water was going cold and I shivered.

"You cold honey?" he rubbed my arms

"Yes, a little bit" I replied as my body was regaining feeling.

"Come on" he got up and grabbed me under my arms and pulled me up.

I was a bit unsteady on my feet. We nearly both slipped in the water. He big arms caught me and he lifted me out of the bath. He got a towel for himself and grabbed a big fluffy towel and wrapped me up and carried me to bed. Put me under the donna and kissed my lips.

"I'll make you a warm drink." he went to the bar. He made me a hot baileys and chocolate drink. It was delicious. It warmed me up in no time.

"You spoil me" I said with a big smile.

"I could spoil you more." he looked at me and as if to say you haven't given me an answer yet?

"Where not talking about that now are we?" I said to him

"Why not?" he challenged me

"You know how I feel about you Tasmin and I want to give you the world." he added.

"But I can't really have you." I looked back at him and thought maybe I shouldn't have said that.

"Baby we've been through this and I can't marry you."

"You know that"? he said gently so he wouldn't hurt my feelings.

He sat on the bed and took my hand,

"My wife cannot ever give me a child but you can Tasmin." he looked me in the eyes.

"You want me to have your children but not marry you?" I stared at him in disbelief.

"One day when Anna is gone, I will marry you." he said softly and kissed my hand.

"I love you honey and you are my world" he kept going.

"I have to think about that." I said still in shock. He kissed me then on the lips and I kissed him back. I'm not sure of anything anymore. That's just made it more confusing. More decisions.

"Where are we going to tonight?" I asked as he was getting distracted with my breasts.

"To this very nice prestigious hotel for the night." He replied as he went for the dive to suck my nipples.

"But we are here for the night." I answered back not understanding.

"No this is our base camp and we do little trips from here." he answered me looking at me to see if I understood. I nodded I get it now. We got up and got dressed. Stefano said to wear my lace dress and wear the other lingerie with the gown tonight.

"Pack a small suitcase for our casual clothes." he said.

I packed first and made sure I had what I needed. I then got into my lingerie and stepped into my gown and put on my stilettos. Stefano zipped me up and wolf whistled.

"You look incredible just gorgeous." he exclaimed.

My hair was up and I teamed it with my dazzling earrings, shawl and clutch bag. I looked in the mirror. My dress fitted perfectly. My breasts spilling out of my bodice, maybe a bit tight there, but otherwise gorgeous. The split in the leg went right up nearly to my g/string. It was tight and showed all my curves. We went downstairs and informed Hannah that we would not be back for two days.

"Two days? I thought you said one." I panicked as I haven't enough clothes.

"We'll go shopping." he smiled at me.

"Ok" I felt relieved now.

Hannah said something in Swiss to Stefano and he smiled at her and replied back something. I didn't ask what she had said. He led me to her car and helped in. We drove for half an hour through little villages and winding roads. We arrived in Zurich at 6pm and we escorted to our hotel room. The Valet parked Stefano's BMW. Our room was the Penthouse and it was magnificent. The view was incredible and the room spared no expense. Everything was first class and I felt like a princess. There was a lounge room, spa room bedroom and bathroom. There also was a kitchen and bar and a big dining room table. Stefano whispered in my ear,

"I'll fuck you on that later." he said huskily smiling at me. He pulled me close and I was lost in his embrace. He held me tightly and kissed my neck and wanted to go further down.

"Baby slow down" I tried to squeeze out of his grip.

"I want you now honey." he held me firm.

"But dinner." I said trying to get his hands off me.

"Dinner can wait" he said huskily

"Somebody might come in." I looked around.

"No honey no one will come in" he reassured me.

He unzipped my gown and I climbed out of it. He draped it over the chair. I stood there topless with my g/string, suspenders, stockings and stilettos. He picked me up and took me to the bedroom and laid me on the bed. He undressed down to boxers and put a condom on the bedside table.

"Soon we won't need these." he said to me

I haven't decided yet I thought. He started with my lips, then my neck and trailed down to my breasts. He licked them and teased me with his tongue. His trail continuing down to my navel. His tongue swirling around and giving me little nips with his teeth.

"Oooh that tickles" I wriggled.

He took my g/string off and continued his mission. He brought me to a climax and then rolled me on my knees and put a condom on and entered me. We pumped together until our bodies were coming and we were crying out each other's names. We lay in each other's arms and waited for our bodies to return to normal. We got up and Stefano helped me back into my gown. I fixed my hair and lip gloss and put on my g/string and stilettos. He also got dressed and held his hand to me.

"Come with me honey." he grabbed my hand and led me to the lift.

We went down some 10 floors to a private dining room. He opened the door and the room was full of fairy lights and a round table set for 2. It was very romantic. He held my chair for me and then a knock at the door startled me.

"Come in" he said firmly.

The waiter was there with a trolley full of food. He served us and left us alone. We had scallops for entrée, and for main we had pork belly and cranberry sauce. It was very delicious. Sweets was later Stefano informed me. We drank champagne and he asked me to dance. We danced slow and sexy, Stefano holding me tight. He unzipped my gown and let it slide down by body. I stood there in my g/string, suspenders, stockings, and stilettos.

"Someone might come in." I said as I covered my breasts.

Stefano went and locked the door. I felt better then. We danced some more and then he took me to the table. He cleared the table and laid me on it.

"Sweets" he said sexily. He kissed my breasts and his tongue slid down my navel and then to my favorite spot.

"Oooh that felt good"! I lay back and relaxed.

He brought me to a climax and once again I was lost in his arms. He helped me with my gown and we had some more champagne.

"This is beautiful Stefano." I looked at him and smiled.

"You're beautiful Tasmin" he smiled back.

We left then and went back upstairs to the Penthouse. Stefano once again unzipped my gown and I slid out of it.

"Put on your lace dress and no knickers" he said with a glint in his eyes.

I did what he said and came back to the lounge room Where he waiting with cognac and the fire was blazing. He handed me my glass and we sat by the fire and watched the flames dance around. He leaned to kiss me and I accepted his lips and tongue. His arms pulling me close as we kissed passionately. His hand slid up my dress to caress my bum cheeks and my intimate spot.

"Oh honey you're wet for me." he said huskily. He took a swig of cognac and he laid me on my back and spread my legs.

"I'm going to have my 2nd Sweets now." he told me as his head went to my wet pussy. His finger dipped in and his tongue did the most amazing tricks.

"Baby" I cried as I clung to his hair. His other hand pinching my nipples through my lace dress.

"Give it to me Baby let go." he urged me on.

I arched my back as that incredible feeling that no woman can deny filled my body. I lay there panting waiting for him to pounce and finish his mission. It wasn't long and he was inside me, pumping and thrusting like no tomorrow. I moved with his hips and our breathing became one.

He groaned as he spilled his seed into me and I didn't realize he had not put a condom on. He did not withdraw either and his sticky juice was inside me. Then he pulled his weapon out and undressed me and carried me to the shower. He washed me all over and dipped the sponge around my bum and sensitive spot. He was ready for round 2 and he turned me towards the wall and bent me over and then gently entered my forbidden place. His hand playing with my clit and hole while he gently pumped my anus.

"Oh Stefano" I cried as my knees buckled under me.

"That's it baby keep going." he said as he groaned and pumped more.

He came then and I was struggling to stand up. He held me as he washed me again and then wrapped me in a huge towel and carried me to bed.

"Sleep my Angel" he kissed my lips. I fell into a deep sleep and don't remember anything else till I woke in the morning.

Chapter Twenty-Three

"Good morning honey" he nuzzled my neck. I curled up against him and felt his huge erection straining into me.

"Good morning, Baby" I replied smiling to myself.

What a way to wake up I thought. His hands were playing with my breasts and his erection was wanting entry to my pussy. He slipped his manhood in and fucked me hard and fast. God he certainly was urgent this morning. He came inside me groaning my name as he did.

"Shower" he said as he withdrew and went to the bathroom.

I followed him with his stickiness between my legs. I got in the shower and Stefano washed me all over making sure I was clean in all those places he had just been.

"Stefano you didn't wear a condom?" I asked him as I washed my hair.

"No, I didn't. You are on the pill so I thought it would be ok." he replied as he wiped the shampoo from my face.

"Yes, I suppose so" I answered trying to remember when I last took my pill.

I finished washing my hair and got out of the shower and dried off. I wrapped my hair in a towel and put on a complimentary robe that hung in the bathroom. I went to my dresser and applied moisturizer and a little makeup. I went to get my pill packet out of my makeup bag and it wasn't there. I searched everywhere, in my handbag and suitcase.

"What are you looking for?" Stefano asked when I looked a little frantic.

"My pill packet is missing." I replied still looking for it.

"When did you take it last?" he asked

"Umm I think on the plane." I replied as I was making a mental note in my head of trying to remember.

"Oh, Shit! I think I left it in the toilet on the plane." I said remembering now.

Monique was there with me and I remember her going down on me but the rest is a blur I thought to myself. Did I take it then?

"Don't worry honey a few days won't matter." he said calmly as he didn't seem worry.

"Do you think its ok?" I asked him as I looked into his gorgeous come fuck me eyes.

"Yes, baby don't worry we will get more today." He reassured me.

"Ok" I replied thinking it will be ok.

I got dressed into a casual black mini, red silk blouse and black flats. Breakfast had been laid out on the balcony and the view was amazing. The city below and the mountains in the distance. Stefano poured the coffee and I helped myself to a croissant and fruit.

"Honey have some bacon and eggs?" he asked

"No, I don't feel like it today." I replied

"Coffee and croissant are enough" I added.

He helped himself to bacon, eggs, tomatoes, and mushrooms. Well, I suppose he has a big appetite and he needs his strength I thought. After breakfast we went for a walk-in town and did some shopping. Stefano wanted to buy me everything I saw and I told him no, I don't need anything.

"Let me spoil you." he said with a smile

Oh, what the hell let him spoil me I thought. He brought me a new black silk suit with a gorgeous silk lavender blouse. It was exquisite and the silk was tantalizing on my skin.

"It looks gorgeous on you." he said huskily with a cheeky look in his eyes.

He grabbed me around my waist and came in for the kiss. His hand pushing my bum into his groin. I slapped his hand away.

"Baby not here." I said as I tried to get free.

"Why not in the dressing room?" he asked with a cheeky grin.

"Out" I commanded

He left sulking and sat on the couch outside waiting. The saleslady gave him a smile and he smiled back. I came out showing him another skirt and top which was gorgeous. It was beige and to the knee with a slit up the leg. The blouse was cream and beige flowers in a soft silk material. The sales lady gave me some cream stilettos with a little bow on top, they were gorgeous. Stefano wolf whistled when I came out.

"Absolutely beautiful" he said huskily.

I blushed as the sales lady was watching and probably a little bit jealous. She put all my purchases in a bag and Stefano paid for everything.

"Thank you honey I love them" I kissed him on the lips.

"More to come we're not finished yet." He held my hand and led me to a lingerie shop. We entered and two sales ladies approached us.

"Good morning, Madam and Sir" one of them said.

"Good morning" we both said.

"What would you like?" she said looking at me.

Stefano talked for me and said we would like a black number with the whole trimmings and also a couple of silk nighties and silk pjs. They both got to work and brought in the most gorgeous numbers. I didn't know which one they were all lovely. Stefano liked the black peekaboos and the black nightie and pjs. I couldn't decide they were all to die for.

"Get them all." Stefano said with a smile.

"I can't honey it's too much." I shook my head.

"No, it's not." he said and then said to the sales lady to wrap them up.

The sales lady smiled at me and I smiled back. We left there with bags and bags. Stefano hailed a taxi and we piled in. The taxi took us to our hotel and Stefano paid the fare with a tip. We fell on the bed exhausted from our morning shopping spree and I kissed Stefano Passionately and thanked him again for all his treats. He grabbed me around my waist and pulled me onto of him.

"You can thank me personally." he said cheekily.

"Is that right?" I answered with a smile. He unbuttoned my blouse and his hand slid into my bra.

"Mmm you feel hot and ready for me." he said trying to take off my bra. He finally got it off and slid my mini down leaving me only in my black lacey knickers.

"I could rip them off." he looked at me with a grin.

"Then you would have to buy me more." I said.

"No problem I love shopping especially lingerie" he replied as his lips went to my breasts.

He teased me and before long I was in his submission. We made love tenderly and once again I knew I had deep feelings for this man. Lunch was served on the balcony and we sat there and chatted about our mornings venture.

"I have to go out for a while later." Stefano said after lunch.

"Ok where?" I asked looking at him.

"I have to go home and check in." he replied looking at me.

"Oh" I answered feeling a little sad he is leaving me.

"I will be back before dinner" he said cupping my face in his hands.

"Tasmin, I have to go you know that." he pleaded with me.

"I know" I replied not wanting to look into his eyes.

"It will be alright I will be back soon." he said kissing my lips.

"It's ok, I might go for a walk." I said.

"Good that will be nice for you" he kissed me again and left.

I left the Chalet and walked up the street to some shops, and a quaint hotel. It certainly was very beautiful here; the mountains surrounded the village and it was a lovely view. I went into one shop and looked at all the souvenirs. The woman in there was friendly and asked where I was from and where I am staying. There were a few other customers in the shop, but I didn't notice one woman glaring at me. I brought some souvenirs for the girls and a little Cuckoo Clock Magnet that you could stick on the fridge. As I was leaving the woman who was glaring at me stopped me at the door and grabbed my arm.

"We know all about you and you are not welcome here." She gruffly said.

I looked at her and didn't understand at first and then realized she knew about me and Stefano.

"Leave and go back to where you belong, you do not belong here." she continued in an angry voice.

"I'm sorry I don't know what you're talking about." I decided to act dumb and innocent.

"You know what I mean you whore, slut!" she spoke with disgust.

I was in shock and I didn't know what to say. By this time everybody in the shop had heard and were all staring at me.

"He will never marry you or give you anything you slut, marriage breaker whore!" she spat at me. Tears were swelling in my eyes and I wanted to run away.

"I'm sorry you feel like that, but Stefano and I are just friends." I said quietly.

"Liar you're his whore." she spat again.

"Leave our country and do not return you are not welcome here"
she said again angrily.

She let go off my arm and I fled. I rang back to the hotel and locked
myself in my room. My head was spinning and I didn't know what to do.
I have to get out of here I thought I cannot stay here. I sat there and cried
and thought about everything the woman had said and it was true. How
could I deny it. I remembered Monique had said to ring if I need her so
I did.

"Tasmin how are you?" Monique asked

"I'm a little bit upset and I don't know what to do." I answered with
a sniffle.

"Are you crying sweetie?" she asked concerned.

"I'm just having a moment." I answered trying not to cry.

"Where are you?" she asked.

"I'm at the Radisson in Zurich." I replied

"But I'm also staying at Wintergarten as well." I added

"Ok do you want me to pick you up and you can come here and
stay with me so you can sort it out." she said in her sexy European voice.

"Is that alright with you?" I asked

"Of course, I will be there in about 30 mins depending on traffic".

"Ok" I answered feeling a little better.

We hung up and I went and packed. I packed everything, only
leaving the lingerie. I took the two outfits from today's shopping but left
the lingerie. I folded them neatly on the bed. I then wrote a note and left
it for Stefano.

"Stefano,

I have decided to leave I do not belong here and people have made it quite clear. You will forever be in my heart. I love you more than anything and I will always remember you. You need to be with your wife and see it through. She needs you and so do I but that would make me selfish. Do not follow me or contact me again. Goodbye my love. I will love you forever.

-Tasmin.

The tears were streaming down my cheeks and I grabbed a tissue and wiped them away. I left the note on the bed with the lingerie. I touched them one last time and whispered Goodbye my Addiction, my love. I got my suitcase and bag and went downstairs.   Monique arrived 5mins later and hugged me.

"Tasmin are you ok?" she kissed my cheeks.

"I will be." I replied hugging her back.

"Come let's go"? she opened the door to her black sports car. Very nice I thought.

We drove off and she told me she lived not far from here. I told her that we were staying at Wintergarten Chalet and I had some luggage there to pick up.

"No problem we will go and get it." she had said with a smile.

Her eyes twinkling in the sun. Gee she was beautiful. We arrived 40 mins later at the Chalet and I said to Monique to wait in the car. I would be 5 minutes. I went to my room and quickly packed. I left the red gown, and lingerie folded neatly on the bed. I touched them they were beautiful, silky and sexy. Hot!! And those diamonds. Was I crazy to give this all up? I thought to myself. Yes, probably but I have a conscious and I can't do what I'm doing. I did one more sweep of the bathroom, bedroom and lounge, I had packed everything. I felt sad but I knew this was the right thing to do. I thanked the lady and told her Stefano would be back to pay. She asked where I was going and I told her home. I got in Monique's car we drove away. My tears begun to swell again. I glanced out the window and thought only of Stefano, my love, my sweet obsession and my addiction. One I would have to give up forever.

Chapter Twenty-Four

We drove in silence and we got to Monique's house who she shared with a friend.

"Does she mind?" I asked worried.

"No, not at all she out on a flight." she replied.

"Oh" I said

Monique helped me with my bags and we went inside. It was a beautiful modern and light house with French windows that opened to a fantastic view across to the mountains.

"This is simply gorgeous" I said as I looked out the windows.

"It's great, isn't it?" she looked at me and smiled.

"Would you like a drink?" she asked

"I would love a Jack Daniels if you've got it?" I asked

"Yes, I have it" she went to the bar.

"Ice" she glanced at me.

"Yes please" I answered with a smile.

We sat there and gazed out the window not talking much just thinking and dreaming.

"Do you want to talk about it?" Monique asked as she put her arm around me.

"I'm not sure where to start." I replied looking at her.

"Why don't you start from the beginning?" she said

"Ok, but maybe we should have another drink." I replied

"Ok I'II get them and some snacks." she got up and went to the kitchen. I followed to give her hand and also to use the bathroom. We got settled again on the sofa and I took a swig of my drink which was a bit stronger this time.

"Well, I met a man and he is from Switzerland and he wants me to be in his life but he has family commitments and he can't be with me full time." I shortened my version and didn't say any names. Monique didn't have to know the nitty gritty details just the outline of my situation. She nodded as she listened.

"Do you love him?" she asked tenderly

"Yes, I do but I also love someone else." I replied looking at her to get her reaction.

"What you love two men at once?" she asked in disbelief.

"Yes, and I can't decide which one to be with." I replied honestly.

"You know love is never easy." she sighed

"There are always complications." she added

"Are you in love?" I asked her

"No, not at the moment I'm in between love." she replied looking at me.

"What do you mean in between?" I asked

"Tasmin I'm bi-sexual you must have realized that." She said looking at me.

"Well, I knew you liked women." I blushed thinking of our episode on the plane.

"Yes, women are less complicated than men." she replied

"You got that right sister." I laughed. She looked at my empty glass.

"Another?" she asked as she got up.

"Yeh why not get drunk and drown my sorrows." I said with a smile. Monique got up and brought more drinks back to the lounge. She sat down on the sofa and said tenderly to me,

"Tasmin, I like you and I think you like me." she said as she touched my face.

"I would like to know you better." she said as she trailed her finger down to my breasts and circled my nipple.

"Oooh" I giggled.

She kissed me and her tongue prompting my tongue to play. I was relaxed as the Jack had kicked in and I responded to her. Her hand unbuttoning my blouse to reveal my bra. She lifted my bra up and pinched my nipples and then bent her head to suck them. I arched my back as it felt so good. Her hand went up my skirt to my juicy pulsating pussy. Her finger feeling my clit and slipping into me and out again. She continued to suckle my breasts as she did this and I could feel my whole body respond to her touch. I'm not lesbian, I thought why am I attracted to her. She grabbed my hand and pulled me up and led me to her bedroom. I was intrigued and interested by her and felt very relaxed. She took my clothes off only leaving my knickers on and made me lie on the bed. She undressed to her knickers and lay beside me. We kissed and fondled each other, it was magical. I never have been with just a woman there's always been a man with a hot cock there as well. She pulled off my knickers and spread my legs and put her head between them and licked me like a wildcat like it was licking up cream. Her finger fucking me at the same time. I was groaning now and I moved my pelvis with her finger. She stopped and produced a dildo from her bedside table and put a condom on it and slid it into me. I groaned again as she went in and out with this buzzing dick. Her finger still playing with my clit as she fucked me. That beautiful feeling was happening and I couldn't stop it. I groaned more and she kissed me, then left my lips to feast on my pussy while I was coming. I lay there panting waiting for what was next, my body totally in her submission. She then straddled my face in a 69 position and I too feasted. Her pussy sweet and sticky. She handed me the vibrator which she had taken the condom off and asked me to oblige her. Well, I suppose I couldn't say no. I brought her to a climax and she groaned and begged me for mercy, which I didn't give her any. She was

so hot and horny I had to satisfy her. We both lay in each other's arms
and I drifted off to sleep.

Chapter Twenty-Five

Stefano arrived back at the Penthouse at 6pm and was surprised that Tasmin was not there. He saw the note on the bed and sat down and read it. He had to read it twice. He did not understand it. Where was she? Why did she leave? He was pacing around the penthouse trying to work out what had happened. We had spent a lovely morning of love making, breakfast and shopping and now she is gone, why? He was at a loss? He tried to ring Tasmin's cell but it went to message bank.

"Tasmin Honey if you there pick up or ring me." he said. Stefano then ran downstairs and asked the front desk if they had seen me.

"No sorry Sir we haven't." the lady replied.

Stefano was pissed now and went and poured himself a large whiskey straight and drank it quickly. His head spinning with questions with no answers.

"Damn it Tasmin where are you?" he yelled into the air.

He then rang the airport and asked if she had boarded a plane and they told him no. He poured himself another and then another until he had drunk the whole bottle and passed out on the bed.

I saw my cell flashing as I got dressed and knew it would be Stefano. He would be furious with me for leaving. I must be strong and not answer it. It is the only way.

"Are you going to get that or just stare at it?" Monique enquired looking at me.

"It's not important." I replied turning away from her so she couldn't see my tears.

"Let's go out for dinner." she said clapping her hands.

"Oh, I don't know I'm not really in the mood for socializing." I answered hoping I wouldn't offend her.

"Come on it will be fun and you need a distraction." She said with a cheeky smile.

"What kind of distraction?" I asked a little intrigued.

"Well, there's a world of Italian, Swiss, French and Austrian men waiting out there and they're very hot." she laughed trying to make me laugh. I couldn't help but laugh she had that Aura about her.

"I know a great night club we could go to." she smiled at me again.

"Ok, ok."

I knew I was defeated. What the hell I do need a distraction. One from Stefano. I couldn't get him out of my head. His eyes following me everywhere. Stop it I thought to myself.

"Let's get glammed up." she grabbed my hand and went to her bedroom.

"What are you going to wear?" she looked at me.

"Mmm" she was eyeing her wardrobe and then me. She was about my size and I just stood there letting her take control.

"Mmm something that screams 'come fuck me as my boyfriend is a bastard."

She said as she flicked through her dresses. She pulled out this smoking hot black lace mini dress with sequence on the breast line. It was gorgeous!

"Have you got lingerie?" she asked me.

"Well, I have this red peek a boo one." I said seeking her approval.

"Oooh show me, no wait put it on." she was excited now.

"Surprise me." she clapped her hands and went and lay on the bed waiting.

I went to my bedroom and undressed and put on my peek a boos. God, it did look sexy with my nipples sticking out. It was hard not to resist pinching them. I had brought my black stilettos on with suspenders and stockings. I dabbed some perfume in all the right places and I went back to her bedroom. Monique had also changed into some lingerie, a black number it was very seductive. Her eyes big and wide when I entered the room.

"Oh My God you look so beautiful, an American goddess." she breathed.

I must be honest I was really turned on by the seduction. She herself looked like a Swiss Goddess with flowing blonde hair and a hot body, and those eyes saying "I want you" It was like I was in a fantasy. It didn't feel wrong with being with a woman but I wasn't so sure I could live without a man? I came to her on the bed and kneeled on the bed in front of her. She touched my nipples gently pinching them then sucking her finger and then touching my nipples again.

"Gorgeous so hot." she couldn't take her eyes of my peek a boos.

Her head came in to suckle me and tease me with her tongue. She would kiss my lips and slip her tongue in to play and then go back to suckling. My hand was playing with her breasts and I was in another world of lust and desire. I wanted more and she was hungry too. She wanted me to 69 her so this time I straddled her face and she spread her legs for me to feast like a wildcat. We brought each other to climax and we groaned and licked and went with the amazing feeling of desire and contentment. It was nothing like I have experienced before. There was no demands or manly physical presence. It was different to climaxing to a man orally fucking you. with a woman it was inner spiritual sexual healing of emotions and physical stress. We lay there in pure bliss and when our senses came back to normal, we got up and went and got ready. I took the dress Monique had leant me and went and showered. I put my peek a boos back on and slipped the dress on. It clung to my curves and it fitted perfectly. I wore my hair down and put light curls into it. Put a smokey look eye makeup on and some lip gloss. Put my stilettos on and grabbed a clutch bag and light black short jacket. I might be cool outside I thought. I went into the lounge room and Monique was dressed and looking stunning in a black tight mini and silver lace top revealing her black corset underneath. Very sexy and tantalizing. She also had her hair down with light curls, she looked beautiful. She had made a drink for us both and also had rung a taxi. We drank our drinks and toasted to a great night of surprises and put our jackets on when we heard the taxi honk. We giggled like school girls and held each hand to the taxi. The driver was outside the car with the door open for us. His eyes bulging at the sight of us and having a good look.

"Good evening, ladies" he spoke excellent English. We flashed a cute smile at him and got in the back seat.

"Where to?" he asked

Monique answered in German and he said something and nodded. She smiled at me and held my hand.

"Now be careful of the Men tonight some might be too sleezy, we have to be patient and very fussy." she said to me.

"They will eat you alive." she laughed looking at me and pinching my nipple through my dress.

"You look very hot and sexy like a black cat on heat." She said with a smile. I blushed and smiled back.

The taxi driver was watching everything and was very turned on by these two women. He smiled to Monique in the mirror. She smiled back. God what I wouldn't give to fuck those two? He thought to himself trying not to get a hard on while he was driving. Monique had noticed the handsome driver with his horny eyes and thought she would have a little fun as she knew they were 20minutes at least before they got there. Monique leaned into my ear and asked;

"Do you want to have some fun here in the back seat and give the driver a thrill?" I looked at her and giggled.

"Are you sure?" I whispered back.

"You just let me play with you for a bit." she whispered

"ok" what the hell she knows what she's doing.

Monique caught the driver's eye and placed her hand down my top. He nearly ran off the road. I wasn't sure this was a good idea. She then pulled up my dress to reveal my g/string and suspenders and slipped her finger inside the material. She pulled down my dress so my breasts could come out. She then leant in to lick and tease my nipples as her hand was in my crotch. He was trying to drive and look at the same time. She then slipped my g off and spread my legs and exposed my pussy to him. He was frantic now and pulled off the road to a side area that was not in view of the road.

"Ladies do you want some help?" he purred from the front seat.

Monique looked at me and I nodded in approval and he got out of his seat and got in the back in the middle of us. His erection straining in his pants. He starting kissing Monique so I played with his erection through his pants. He pulled his jeans off and unleased his huge manhood. I got on my knees on the seat and bent down to suck him. Then Monique would come down to suck him too. We both teased him with our tongues and he finger fucked us on our knees. He was groaning and we sucked harder. Each taking turns of sucking his cock and balls. His hips thrusting upward for us to take him further, which we did. He grabbed a hanky out of his jeans just at the right moment and spurted his semen into it and gave a deep groan. We looked at each other and smiled and thought quietly. Job well done! He kissed us both and got back in the front seat and we continued our journey, luckily, he had turned off the meter. We arrived at the club 10 mins later and he thanked us for the great ride.

"No charge it's on me." he smiled at both of us and held the door open for us.

"Thank you it was our pleasure." we both smiled at him.

"If you need a ride home here is my number." he gave Monique his card.

"Thankyou" she said. We entered the club and went to the eating area and the waiter got us a table.

"For two ladies?" he asked with a smile.

"Yes, thank you" Monique answered. Heads were turning our way and I looked around at all. The handsome faces and smiles coming from everywhere.

"Told ya, they're going to eat us alive." she said excitedly.

We ordered a light meal and some white wine as well. I couldn't help think of Stefano and what he would be thinking now. He would be furious. To see me now dressed to kill and out without him. I could see it now. He would be livid. I giggled to myself Monique was doing a lot of checking out men and seeing which ones would be potential victims.

"What do you think?" she asked but I was a million miles away.

"Tasmin, are you paying attention?" she asked looking at me as if I was in a trance.

"Sorry I was somewhere else for a second there." I spluttered out meeting her eyes.

"You're not thinking of your man are you?" she asked firmly. I looked at her and tried to smile and I didn't want to cry in public.

"Come on let's have fun and forget about worries for a while." she said touching my hand and squeezing it.

She was right, have some innocent fun and live life. Our meals arrived and our wine and we enjoyed our food. We went to the dancing part of the club after a stop to the bathroom to freshen up. We both checked each other in the mirror and commented on how hot we both looked. We went back out and the waiter got us a table by the dance floor. He brought our drinks over and smiled at us. We thanked him and sweetly smiled back. The music was playing a sexy beat and Monique said let's dance. We moved to the music seductively and sexy, we knew eyes were on us, undressing us. We danced another dance when two men approached us on the dance floor. They were both attractive, blonde and muscley.

"May we.?" one of them asked.

Monique nodded and he took my hand and pulled me around in a little spin to his big strong arms. He was very nice. The other blonde had taken Monique in his arms. They were both Austrian and here working in another town. We found out later when we stopped for drinks and chatted. They were carpenters and they were here on a working contract. We danced again this time swapping partners. His name was Hans and his friend was Karlos. They both were charming and very attentive. Monique winked at me to give her approval and that we should go for it.

I winked back and smiled. God she was beautiful and carefree. She reminded me of someone.

"No strings attached girl?" I thought that person is me.

We danced some more and did a slow waltz. I was with Karlos this time and he also was so nice to be in those strong arms. He pressed his groin into me and looked deep into my eyes. His eyes talking to me and I felt tingles go through my body. He came in for the kiss and I accepted his lips and tongue. We swayed to the slow beat and kissed passionately. I glanced over at Monique and she also had her tongue in Han's mouth. The song finished and we went back to our table.

"More drinks ladies?" Karlos asked flashing his huge smile.

"Yes please" we both smiled sweetly at him.

"So, what are you both doing after the club?" Hans asked looking at us both. We both looked at each other and Monique said we are not sure.

"Well Karlos and I stay in very flash accommodation and if you like we could go back there and party?" he asked with his eyes dancing.

Monique said we had to go to the bathroom to freshen up and that we would be back in a minute. He stood up when we stood and we tattled off to the Ladies. It would give him time to talk to Karlos and us girls to talk as well.

"Well, what do you think?" Monique asked as she applied lip gloss.

"I think they are perfect gentlemen with hot bodies." I replied back looking at her.

"Do we have an orgy with them?" she asked me

"If you think it's alright." I trusted her.

We returned back to our table and they both stood when we approached. Gee it was charming. They pulled our chairs out and helped us sit. So nice to be pampered. We chatted easily and drank our drinks. When we had finished Karlos called a Taxi and we went to the entrance. He opened the door and we climbed in with Hans in the middle. Karlos rode in the front and directed the Taxi driver to our destination. Hans had his hand in Monique's crotch and his other hand was caressing my breasts. He kissed Monique and then he would kiss me. It was very erotic. We arrived at their apartment and they hurried us inside. It was a bachelor pad with open plan, big windows and a big tv screen, with a huge spa at one end with the bar.

"Wow" we both said as we entered. It's the companies and we all share it.

"How many share it?" Monique's eyes were wide.

"Well at the moment there is about 6 of us here" Karlos answered.

"What now?" Monique breathed

"And they all look like you both?" I think she just came in her g/string.

"Well, they probably are still out partying" Hans replied as he went to the bar.

I looked at Monique and thought are we getting over our heads, Are we playing with fire if more men come home and find us fucking. Because I knew we would definitely screw this two and probably swap. They were hot and the alcohol was starting to affect me. Hans had got our drinks in plastic cups and put them by the spa.

"Ladies would you like a spa?" he grinned at us both.

"Why don't we give you a lap dance first and then we can have a spa?" Monique said sweetly and seductively.

They both agreed as they wanted to undress us slowly. Karlos put on some sexy salsa and we danced and wriggled our hips and bum around them. I went up to Karlos and urged him to unzip me and peel off my dress. His eyes lit up when he saw my peek a boos and he grabbed each nipple and twisted them gently. His head following his hands. His lips were hot and his tongue lashed out at them. I turned around and bent over in front of him and his finger followed my g/string and then gained entry to my favorite place. He was kissing my bum cheeks and then he spread my cheeks and went in for the dive and licked and teased me. It was very sensual. He then took off my corset and my suspenders. Peeled each stocking off with his mouth including my g/string. He then carried me to the spa and put me in. Monique was also put beside me. We both giggled and watched with big eyes as the men undressed. Their hot bodies revealed under their clothing. God they were muscled and hot, hot, hot! I licked my lips when I saw their huge throbbing cocks and I knew I wanted them. They got in the spa and sat on either side of us. Karlos on my side and Hans on Monique's. Karlos handed our drinks to us and we all cheered and made a toast.

"To Life and all the great things it has to offer." Hans raised his glass and we all raised ours and cheered.

Karlos had his hand underwater playing with my breasts and I think Monique was getting the same affection. I giggled, then Monique would giggle and the boys would laugh too. Hans got out and refilled our drinks and made them a little stronger. I took a swig and nearly choked. Hans patting my back while I had a coughing fit.

"That's a bit strong." I splattered out eventually.

"Sorry do you want me to soften it down for you?" Hans went to get up.

"No, it's ok I'll get used to it" I answered smiling at him.

"Are you trying to get us drunk?" I asked smiling again at him.

"Yeah, I want to have my wicked way with you." he replied huskily.

"Mmm maybe I'll make you suffer now that I know you've been naughty." I teased him with my smile and ryes.

"I reckon if you don't stop being cheeky I'll put you over my knee." he said in his sexy accent and then grinned at me.

I smiled sweetly back and I knew we were going to have an interesting and hot night. Karlos and Monique had started kissing and fondling each other. Hans was sitting next to me and he pulled me on to his legs and I lay back in his big arms and let him seduce me. After coming in the spa Hans helped me out and gave me a big towel to wrap around me. Hans made another round of drinks, this time however he didn't make mine too strong. I smiled at him when I sipped it. His eyes watching every move I made.

"Don't want you to pass out, do we?" he said with a big grin.

I laughed and he came in for the killer kiss. His lips warm and inviting. His tongue searching for mine. I responded with my tongue battling with his. His hand playing with my breasts and squeezing my nipples. His lips trailed down my neck to my breasts to play. He sucked and teased hard till I begged him to stop.

"Do you want me to stop?" he looked up at me with big blue eyes and a cheeky smile. He was very handsome and probably was about 30.

"Yes No" I cried out as he sucked my nipples hard again.

I lay back on the sofa by the spa and let him seduce me. His finger had plunged into me at the same time and he was tormenting me, going in and out with his thumb on my clit. My body wanting more and I let go and let him take me over the edge. His tongue doing magical tricks to my clit as he licked and finger fucked me. I wanted him and I wanted to taste him. His erection was throbbing for my touch and I reached out a touched his knob with my wet finger. Then I put my finger back in my mouth and continued to touch his knob. Our eyes met full of desire and lust. I went on my knees and teased him with my tongue and sucked him hard and gave him no mercy. I knew I was playing with fire.

"Slow down Baby." he groaned as his hips rose upwards to take him more.

I couldn't stop I was like a wildcat hungry for the thrill of taking a man to the edge and he can't resist. He was mine and, in my control, and spell. He was getting close now and his groaning was making me suck harder. He grabbed the towel right at the last minute and shoved his spurting cock into it. I just watched in my own spell and fantasy as he cleaned himself up. I licked my lips like a cat cleaning her whiskers.

"You want more?" he let me kiss his dick.

"Yes" I breathed.

"Want another drink or something else?" Hans asked

"What's the something else?" I asked interested.

"Coke?" he answered looking at me.

"Oh I see" I replied trying not to act dumb. It's not like I've never tried it. I did in College with Maddy a few years ago. We had a fucking great time. I think we had an orgy that night.

"I don't know, is Monique having some?" I asked wondering where she was.

"Yeah, I think so, Karlos and her are in the bedroom." He looked at me for an answer.

"Ok just a little." I said as I thought what the hell.

"Can I put a white shirt on of yours if you have one?" I asked as I didn't want to be in towel the whole night. I didn't feel like putting on my lingerie.

"Sure, hang on." Hans disappeared and then returned with white shirt. I put it on only buttoning up a few buttons. I rolled up the sleeves and thanked him.

"Where is the bathroom?" I asked suddenly busting.

"Down the hall on your right" he replied smiling.

I half ran down the hall and found the bathroom and quickly did my business. I looked in the mirror to freshen up and I still looked pretty even though my hair was half wet and I was only wearing a white shirt. I came out and Hans was sitting on the couch. He had put on some tight boxers that showed his bulge. He was cutting some coke on a little mirror on the table

"Can I please have mine in a drink?" I asked sweetly.

"Sure honey" he replied with a cute smile. He made two up, one for me and one for Monique.

"Let's go and surprise them." he said cheekily

"Ok" I giggled.

Chapter Twenty-Six

I followed Hans up the hall to staircase that led up to a loft.

"We're coming up." Hans yelled out as he went up he stairs.

It was an amazing it had 4 double beds in a potbelly. In the middle, sofa's, a huge TV screen and a bar. Its own bathroom as well. Big windows that overlooked a lake that lights flickered around. Monique was lying on a sofa by the pot belly with only a fluffy animal print blanket, her hair ruffled. She looked like a wildcat that just feasted. Karlos looked pretty damn hot in his tight boxers which showed his huge bulge. He caught me looking at him and smiled at me. I blushed immediately.

"Drinks and more?" Hans announced.

Monique moved over for me to snuggle next to her. I climbed in and she kissed me tenderly on the lips. Her tongue propping for mine and I accepted her tongue. The Boys were just staring and smiling and then looking at each other with huge grins. Not only will they get to fuck them, they also might get girl on girl action. They sat back on their sofa and watched with hard on.

"I've missed you." she whispered in my ear.

"Me too" I whispered back.

"Are you alright?" she asked smiling. I knew what she meant.

"Yes" I breathed back.

"Do you want coke?" I looked at her

"Yes, if you do." she replied quietly.

"It's great with sex." she giggled

"I'm not sure." I said a little worried.

"It's ok I will look after you." she kissed me again and her hand unbuttoned my shirt to expose my breasts and she caressed them. Her head trailed down there to lick and tease me. The boys were enjoying the show. They were smoking a joint and were about to wank themselves.

"Girls have your drinks" Karlos urged with excitement.

We stopped kissing and Karlos handed our drinks to us. We drank our drink followed by a Jack Daniels and my body was feeling it. I had tingles all over. Monique was giving me a sexy look and I was feeling horny as well.

"I want to taste you." she whispered in my ear and she pinched my nipple as she said it.

Oh god my pussy was pulsating just thinking about it. She took the blanket off and my shirt. We were both naked. Our legs draped over each other. Her head went to my breasts where she teased me and then followed down to my pussy I opened my legs to receive her tongue. Hans stopped her and put coke on my clit and then told her to lick and suck it off. I lay there in anticipation my whole body surrendering for what was about to come. Hans put some on my clit and some on his tongue. Monique tongue went into my pussy and then on my clit where she sucked and licked. The feeling was amazing and I was in another world of lust.   Hans kissed me with the coke in his mouth and made me suck his tongue and take all the juices. I think I was having an orgasm in my mouth. I was floating and I remember his mouth was replaced by his throbbing cock and then another cock inside me. Monique was beside me sucking my breasts and sucking Hans with me. Then Hans put coke on Monique's clit for me to suck and Hans fucked me from behind. Karlos straddling Monique face for her to feast with coke on his knob. Oh my god it was a feast all round with so much desire and groaning of 4 people in ecstasy. We all came loudly and fell against one another. I was cradled in Monique pussy and I couldn't move. My body in another place.   I was still so horny and I knew I wanted more. I felt hands on my bum cheeks massaging me and then spreading my cheeks where I felt his tongue on my clit and hole. His finger going in and out.   I moved with his tongue and finger. His other hand pinching my nipples. I realized Monique had moved and then there was a man lying there instead. He was a blur he looked different from Hans and Karlos. He kissed my breasts and suckled on my nipples. I felt a huge penis entering me and thrusting upward. Oh I groaned as I felt hands pinching my nipples at the same time. His kissed my lips and I felt that taste of coke in his mouth. His tongue giving it to me. I then was lifted on to his cock and I felt another behind him. Yes, they're were definitely two men now. Should I be doing this my head was saying. But my body was betraying my thoughts and I was lost in ecstasy and lust. I opened my eyes to look at this man and he looked clearer now. He was darker than the others and he had brown eyes. I thought where did he come from.   He smiled at me and I smiled back. He thrusted his cock upward and held my hips to take him. I felt something cold around my bottom and then felt the massaging of a finger in my forbidden place. It felt very erotic and gentle. His finger was then replaced by his dick and he gently slid in and out. Mr brown eyes would thrust at the same time and I was in their control, I had lost all control. I was in their submission. Someone kissed my mouth and then it was a penis with coke on top for me to feast on. I sucked and licked and sucked like never before while the other two fucked me.   I was having three different orgasms at the same time. I was groaning and moving my body with them. Warm salty juice hit mouth first then my clitoral and pussy. It all exploded into one. I let a moan and my body went limp. I was molded into three bodies. A towel had been wiped on my face and I remember a drink was handed to me. I was pulled up into a sitting position. I looked around for Monique and she was on the other sofa's with three men I could make out.   I looked at my men around me who had just seduced me. Karlos was there and two others I was darker and one was blonde. Both cute and muscley. They smiled at me with beautiful white teeth. I grabbed the animal blanket and wrapped some around me. I felt a little shy now exposed to all these men.

"Are you cold honey?" the blonde one asked as he slithered up to me to cuddle.

His big arms wrapped me up and the warmth of his body was reassuring. I glanced over at Monique she was giving one of them a blow job while two were fucking her. She was moaning and
I felt for her. Go with it honey I said to myself. Let it take your body to another place. I smiled to myself and thought how naughty this all is. This is an orgy with total strangers.

"Would you like a hot spa?" the dark one said with a beautiful smile.

"Yes, actually that would be nice." I tried to get up but my body wouldn't respond.

The blonde one scrooped me up and carried me to the spa. He put me in. I lay back and let the hot steam sooth every inch of my body.   It was revitalizing and made me get tingles all over. Marcos was the dark one and Swen was the blonde. Monique had finished her sexual seduction and joined me in the spa.

"Hi Baby" she kissed me on the lips and kept there with her tongue looking for mine. Her hand under the water playing with my nipples. I let out a cry and she kissed me again to hush me up. The boys staring with wide horny eyes.

"Drinks girls?" Hans asked with a smile

"Yes, please 2 vodka sunsets" I replied smiling at him

"And not too strong" I added. Hans laughed.

We lay back and the bubbles of the spa were tantalizing. Monique was playing with my clit and I was slowly coming with her finger going in and out underwater with four, no wait is that 6 I can see as I was feeling a little bit exposed now and shy to let go in front of so many men. I didn't know who the other men were and I looked at them and they also were handsome. Big buffed and blonde.

Chapter Twenty-Seven

Drinks arrived and they were in coconuts with little umbrellas and a strawberry.

"Ladies your drinks" he handed us them.

"Oh cute" I said as I sipped my drink through a straw.

It tasted yummy and I wondered if Hans had put coke in it. It was delicious and before long we had two and on our   Third.   I needed to pee and I got out with the help of the New guy Swen who had a towel waiting, he handed it to me and I went and freshened up.

The drinks were now taking affect and I thought to myself   That I must slow down. I came out of the bathroom and the other 2 guys I hadn't met were in the downstairs bedroom.   The door was opened And I had to walk past and as I glanced back to the room They were lying on the bed naked waiting for me Beckoning me to come in.

I stopped and was intrigued when Swen came up behind me.   He pushed me gently into the room. I wasn't sure if I wanted to but I was turned on by these Strangers with no strings attached and with such hunky Bodies. Swen led me to the bed where I was put in the Middle.

"Hello I'm Luis and this is Anton pleased to meet you"? He said in a sexy voice.

"Hi I'm Tasmin" I said a little shy as I only had a towel On.

I shivered a bit and Anton put his around me and pulled Me close.

"Cuddle up close and I will keep you warm" he said warmly with a lovely smile and very nice eyes.

I took advantage of his offer and I snuggled into him. I was feeling vunderble and shy, I think the coke is Wearing off.

"Would you like some more pick me up"? Anton asked

"yes please a little bit" I replied thinking it might take Away my shyness.

Anton put some on his finger and told me to suck. I did and it was very seductive. He then kissed me And I felt hands all over me Another finger was put in my mouth with more Coke and I sucked again. His finger then replaced by his hot big dick. I sucked And teased him rolling my tongue around and over His knob. Tingles returned to my body and I was now Over any shyness.

Hands and fingers were everywhere and I was sucking While someone was fucking me from behind. I was moving with them all. They Were very gentle and swapped after a while. Two men entered me and I gave the odd one out a blow job. I was lost now in the rythem of everybodies bodies moving To a beat of ecasty.

We were all groaning now and our Orgasms collided together.
Moulded with two bodies I couldn't move. They all got up and helped me sit up and asked if I Wanted a shower. Luis carried me to the shower and held me as he   Washed me.   His erection straining into my back. He was nuzzling my neck and telling me how sexy I Was.

"I want you honey" he huskily said.

His hands caressing my nipples and his manhood throbbing Waiting for entry. He picked me up and let me forward and entered me swiftly. He pumped and pumped, ny body moving with his thrusts. He then withdrew and his finger was preparing me for Something else. He entered me slowly and gently and I Groaned with he did.   He pumped me and before long His groans were enter twined with mine.

"That's it honey keep going"? he would urge me on

He withdrew when he was finished and kissed my neck He left the shower and another man entered, this time It was Swen and he also was very aroused.   He took me To great heights of ecasty and then also made love to Me in my forbidden place.

"Beautiful Baby" he nuzzled my neck.

He came with a groan and held me tight as my knees Buckled beneath me. He kissed my neck and his arm was replaced by another. Anton was with me now and I could hardly stand up. He held me close and washed my body with the sponge. He dipped in to all my private places and then bent to Suckle my nipples. He turned me around to face the wall and bent me over to enter me. Once again I was lost in lust and I let him Take my body over the edge.

"That was beautiful honey" he whispered in my ear

When he had finished. I couldn't talk I just held him And let him dry me and wrap in a towel and carry me Back to bed.

"Have a rest and I will be back soon"? he kissed me

On the cheek but I think I was already gone. I must of slept for 2 hours and I woke up in a strange Bed. I looked around at my surroundings and then Remembered where I was. I got up and found a white teeshirt in the wardrobe and I put that on it was like a dress and my nipples still hard And horny sticked out.

I went to the bathroom and Freshened up. Put some toothpaste on my finger And did my teeth as best I could. I found my g/string on a chair in the hall, I don't know how it got there I thought to myself. I went out to the lounge room and Monique was Sitting on the sofa drinking coffee.

"Mmm that smells good"? I commented as I went to Sit next to her and we both kissed.

She put the animal blanket on me and we snuggled Together like two feline cats who were very contented. Anton brought us the coffee and I said I hope don't mind I I borrowed the teeshirt to wear. He smiled at me and said I would like to see that wet?

His eyes sparkling at me and I felt goosebumps go through Me. He was intoxicating and I was drawn to him. I smiled at him and he gave me a beautiful smile back. His eyes saying it all. I could melt in those eyes, he was So handsome and hot, I could jump on him now! Tasmin I scolded myself in my head do not get involved With anymore men!!! Youre in trouble as it is!!

"Be careful if you're cheeky I might throw you in the Spa" he said huskily looking at my breasts heaving

Up and down and my nipples hard and sticking out. My pussy pulsating at the seduction of his eyes and Words. Our eyes were locked together and I had to Look away to break the spell. He also felt a connection and smiled to himself. We all lay around on the sofa's and talked. They were

Perfect gentlemen who were all really easy to be around. We asked what they did here on the job and some were Carpenters and some were electricians and engineers. They told us they were building   a spinal care unit and Rehabilitan centre. Swen said it was a huge project And that they were half finished. No wonder theyre all buffed theyre hot tradies with big hands as well as other big things.

"Drink with spice girls"? Karlos asked from the bar.

We both looked at each other and nodded.

"Ok thanks" we both said

"I feel like doing something naughty? I said kissing Her lips.

"What"? she was excited her eyes lit up.

"Go to the bedroom and put on a teeshirt and g/sring And come back and we will do a wet dance together In front of all of them"? I giggled feeling very horny   About the seduction.

"Ok I"II be right back"? she kissed me a little too Long as it was attracting a lot of horny hot eyes.

She got up and excused herself and I got up and said

"We have a show for you so sit back and watch"?

I teased them with a jiggle and smile.

"I need some sexy music on please"? I added

I strolled over to the bar, Luis was there.

"Is it alright if the floor gets a little wet"? I asked Him trying not to giggle.

He smiled at me and said no problems and he would Mop the floor if it got too wet

"is there anything else you need"? he looked me straight In the eye. God he was hot too!

"Well um some water in 2 small buckets"? I looked at Him and he gave me a beautiful smile and gleamed his White teeth at me.

"No problem I'II get them now"and he was like my slave

Doing whatever I wanted. Mmm that's very seductive. He came back with what I wanted and some towels as Well.

"you might need these too"? he said sexily

I blushed and thanked him.

"You can thank me personally later"? he came in For the kiss.

His tongue took mine and tingles returned to my body. His hand holding my bum cheek and around my hip pulling Me into in.

"Cant wait for the show"? he pulled away from me.

"I've made you two little special drinks"? he pointed To the bar bench.

"thank you" I breathed.

Monique was beside me now and she grabbed my Hand.

"Are you alright"? she asked tenderly.

"yes but after this play we go home ok"? I said Looking into her eyes.

"yes" she breathed back.

We had our drinks and wow that felt better. My whole body tingling and feeling sexy.

"How will we do this"? Monique asked excitedly.

"Do a front dance, then back, then front   then pour water on ourselves"? I looked at her for her answer.

She nodded and she said lets tie up our shirts up

"Good idea" I agreed with her.

The boys pumped up the music and we looked at Each other to go. Our bodies moving to the same beat, seductedly and sexy. We then turned Around and did a bum dance. The boys were whistling And hooting at us. Monique and I were in another World and our bodies couldn't stop moving.

We stood with the buckets and moved to the music. We slowly poured water down our tops and saturated Our breasts. Putting the buckets down and then we Played with our breasts and teased them. Our tops wet and see through. Our tits were firm and our nipples were sticking out. The men were ya hooing us and yelling more, more, more.

We walked up to them, Monique starting at one end of The couch and me to the other. We let each of them tease and suck through our shirts With their hands trying to grab our hips to get us on Them. Well it wasn't long and my legs were lifted and I was lying across Three mens laps on my back. I couldn't move.

Monique was in the same situation. A finger entered my mouth and a soft voice told Me to suck. I obeyed. Then a tongue with more and I gave in to desire. Hands were everywhere. On my Breasts and pussy. Lips nipping at my legs and on my Nipples.

I was then lifted and carried away to a sofa where the boys Had joined together so it was like a massive big bed. Monique was there on one side and I was placed on the Other.   Our teeshirts were taken off and we lay there In g/strings. Anton, Karlos and Luis came up to me and Anton Kissed me on the lips his tongue searching for mine. His tongue dipped in white powder for me to lick. My legs were spread and I felt something cold and then Warm on my clit and somebodys tongue doing naughty Things to me.

Anton put his throbbing penis in my mouth and I accepted His gift.   I sucked and teased as I looked him in the eye. It was driving him wild and I kept seducing him until he Made me stop.

"You little wild witch"? he teased

"I'm having you first to teach you a lesson"?

He looked at the other two men. They nodded smiling and I started giggling.

"Oh you think this is funny"? Anton teased me with his Horny eyes.

"I'm definitely spanking you now"? he grabbed me And threw me on my back.

Oooh I liked this forceful, but gentle seduction. Karlos and Luis held my hands so I couldn't move. I shook and wriggled but they were too strong. My breasts heaving and my nipples sticking up wanting A man's touch. It was a game and we all knew it.I was their prey and Now they are going to feast. Anton teased me with his cock with more coke on it.

"Suck Baby Suck"? he said tenderly as he guided his throbbing cock towards my mouth.

I opened and had my own feast on this beautiful man. I sucked him hard and he knew my game.

He pulled out and said "Enough you sex goddess"

He bent his head to my pussy and his tongue entered. He did amazing things to me with his fingers as well. I had Karlos in my mouth now and Anton bringing me To a climax down. I think Luis was pinching my nipple And sucking it. That beautiful feeling starting happening and I groaned As Karlos urged me on sucking him. I sucked him hard and fast as I climaxed and he also climaxed in my mouth On and my face.

"Sorry" he spluttered and got up to get a towel.

He came back with a towel and a glass of water.

"Thanks" I grabbed the towel first then the water.

I cleaned myself up and then I was flipped on my Stomach with luis underneath me. Anton was gently Smacking my bum and teasing me with his finger.

"Oooh" I cried out as Luis sucked my tits and Anton Entered my pussy with his big dick.

Luis had a condom on as well ready to go. Anton then withdrew and Luis Lifted me on to his throbbing cock. He slid into and I Groaned and held his biceps for support.

"It's ok Baby"? he looked at me and thrusted upward.

I was lost and I went with it. Anton bent me over while Luis was inside me and then he entered my forbidden place Gently. I groaned and my whole body sank into their rhythm until I could feel no more. I was taken to the shower and washed. Anton held me tight while he washed me and then he left and Karlos Entered. I knew this would happen as he hadn't fucked me except in my mouth. He held me tightly and I was Facing him. He was a big man with big muscles.

He picked me up so I was straddling his hips and placed Me on his throbbing cock. He held my bum cheeks and My back was against the wall. He could hold me with one arm while the other supported Himself on the wall. He could thrust me deeply and I cried out at the pleasure.

"That's it honey take it Baby" he cooed in my ear.

I let go and went on a journey of lust and desire, my   Orgasm loud and exhausting. He had withdrawn before coming inside me as he didn't Have a condom on. He spurted his semen out and shook The rest out with his hand.

I clung to the wall with the water running down my Back. His arm supporting my weight so I wouldn't fall. He nuzzled my neck,

"That was beautiful baby you're so hot." he was Behind me and pushing into me with his hands sliding All over my body.

His Manhood coming back to life. He soaped me with the sponge and lathered around My pussy and bum.

"Honey I want you again." he nuzzled my neck as he said it. I knew what he wanted and I thought that will be the end Of me.

"I'II be gentle honey" he pinched my nipples and kissed My neck.

Oooh tingles I giggled to myself. He entered me slowly and gently and his finger was on My clit with his other inside my pussy while he took me in my place that lately was happening too much. I couldn't resist his strong arms holding me and his Groaning making me more aroused and wanting him.

I moved my hips with him and he took me over the edge. I cried out when my orgasms collided and he also let out a ragered groan. He had not withdrawn and was still inside my bum. I coaxed him out and I washed there again. My legs straining to keep up. Karlos helped me and then Picked me up and wrapped me in a huge towel and carried me to a bedroom and laid me under some covers.

I dozed off for a while and then woke and looked around me. I got up and a white shirt and my g/string were on the bed I put them on and went out to the lounge room. Everybody was dressed even Monique sitting around the Pot belly.

"Hi honey" Monique said with a smile from ear to ear.

I couldn't help but smile back she was so beautiful. I went to the bar and went to get a drink. Luis offered but I said I can get it.   I made a vodka sunrise for Monique and I and as I was putting the straws in, I saw a Business Card on the bar. It said Stefano's Swiss Constructions on it.

I picked up the card and read Stefano's name and Number. That was my Stefano and that was his phone no. My head starting spinning and I thought Holy Fuck. I've just fucked the whole crew of my lover's company. My heart was beating fast and my breathing was rapid. I felt sick and I was dizzy and then I collapsed.

Chapter Twenty-Eight

I woke up in a bed with Monique sitting beside me with a face washer on my forehead.

"Tasmin are you alright, can you hear me?" she was saying. I looked at her and she cradled me like a baby and rocked me.

"What happened?" I whispered

"You fainted." Monique said softly

"Oh, I did, when?" I asked

"You were at the bar and then you collapsed?" she replied stroking my hair.

The men all piled into the room to see how I was. Anton carrying a glass of water for me.

"How are you feeling?" he looked at me with his brown eyes.

"I feel better now" I said trying to sit up.

"Sit up slowly Baby." Anton helped me and put cushions behind my back.

"Sorry about that I don't usually pass out like that." I said trying not to look embarrassed.

"It's ok as long as you feel ok and don't need to go to the hospital." Luis said firmly.

"I'm fine honestly" I drank my water and went to get up.

The boys left Monique to help me dress. She had found my lace dress and she helped me put it on.

"Anton will drive us home." she said as she put her arm around me.

I nodded and let her lead me out to the lounge room. I kissed each one goodbye and thanked them for a great night. Anton led me to the door and out to the car. He helped me in the front seat and held the door for Monique. We drove off and I didn't see Stefano's car pull up when we left. Stefano knocked on the door and Swen answered with a smile.

"Hi ya Boss." he shook Stefano's hand firmly.

"Come in" he held the door for him to walk through.

The boys were all getting a drink and said hello to their boss and Luis asked what he would like to drink.

"A beer"? Stefano answered as he sat at the bar.

"What brings you out here." Marcos looked at him.

"I wanted to go over the plans for the accommodation houses." he said looking at Marcos.

"No problem I'II get them." Marco went to the study to get the plans.

Luis handed Stefano his drink and as he went to get it he noticed a red corset folded on the bar. He picked it up and smelt it. He knew that smell. He looked at Luis

"Yours or one of the others?" he asked with a smile.

"Ha Ha no its one of the women we had here tonight" He answered with a big grin.

"Nice"? said Stefano still looking at the corset.

"What were their names?" he enquired casually.

Swen overheard and said one was Monique and the other a hot sweet girl called Tasmin. Stefano nearly choked on his beer.

"Tasmin, you say?" he tried to keep calm.

"Very pretty girl is she?" he asked more questions.

He was fuming now visualizing Tasmin in her corset with all these men.

"Hot Hot Hot, they were both hot and horny." said Hans with a big grin on his face.

"I've missed all the fun." Stefano said

"Where are they now?" Stefano continued the interrogation.

"Anton took them home" replied Hans.

"Has Anton got his cell on him?" Stefan asked his face looked a little angry now.

"Yes, he does." answered Marco wondering why his boss is looking like a bull steaming.

"Ring him and ask him to bring the ladies back here." Stefano said with a smile.

"You want to have some fun Boss?" Luis asked

"Yeah I do, I want to have a lot of fun." he answered firmly.

Marcos said that Anton had got the message and was returning with the ladies even though he said that they were not happy about coming back.

"Why do we have to go back?" I asked Anton as we drove back to their house.

"I forgot something." he lied trying not to look at me.

We pulled up in the driveway and Anton said we had to get out of the car. A Black BMW was parked there. I looked at the car and I thought that looks like Stefano's car but it couldn't be, could it. We went inside and I entered the big room. Stefano was sitting at the bar he looked mad.

"Hello Tasmin I think this is yours." he threw my corset at me in disgust. I caught it and just stared at it; I couldn't look at him.

"Look at me Tasmin." he roared at me. I was shaking and I looked up into his eyes.

"Being having a good time have we?" he said roughly as he slid off his bar stool and came up beside me and grabbed me around my waist.

"Your fun has just stopped and you will be punished for this." he said firmly.

I was in shock and I couldn't say anything. I just stood there. I couldn't look at any of the men, they were silent as they didn't want to lose their jobs. No one would stand up to him, no one would dare.

"Say goodbye to your lovers?" he mocked me.

"I will talk to you all later." he said to the men firmly and half dragged me out with Monique following.

We got into his car, me in the front and Monique in the back. He drove fast and angry. I had never seen him this mad before, he was fluming, I was shit scared of him and what he was going to do. We got to Monique's and he made me pack my things.

"Is that everything?" he asked me

"Yes" I breathed.

"Goodbye Monique and thank you for looking after her." Stefano said to her. Monique hugged me and whispered in my ear.

"Call me anytime honey." she kissed me on the cheek.

I hugged her back and thanked her for everything.

"Let's go." Stefano grabbed my arm.

I was put back in the car and we sped off in silence except for the roar of the engine. We drove to Zurich where we were back at the penthouse. He took me upstairs with all my bags and opened the door and then locked it behind him.

"Go to the bedroom" he ordered.

I went to the bedroom and went to lay down. He came up behind me and grabbed me around my waist before I could lay down. He held me tightly and spun me around to look into my eyes.

"Did you enjoy your orgy with all those men?" he yelled at me.

"No, no, it wasn't like that." I said back to him trying to be calm.

"Did you fuck them all at once?" He asked in disgust.

He pushed me back and I fell onto the bed. I started crying and hid my head from him in the pillow. He pinned me down and his lips met mine brutal and rough.

"Is that how you like it?" he pulled up my dress. He sucked my nipples hard and I cried out in pain.

"What's the matter can't handle one man?" he was angry now. His hand in my g/string where he ripped it off.

He pulled his manhood out and spread my legs. He entered me with force and was trying to make a point of who's the boss and don't ever fuck with me again. He turned me over and put me on my knees. His cock entering my pussy hard and fast.

"Take it Baby, your naughty slut" he pumped me harder and harder.

I moaned with his roughness and I couldn't move he was holding me tightly and spanking me with his cock. He withdrew and then entered my forbidden place. This time though he was not gentle. He was angry with me and he was taking it out on me. I cried out again but he didn't listen.

"You liked it when they did it." he spat at me.

"Now you will like it when I do it" he laughed as he pumped more.

He slapped my bum cheek and it stung and then he plunged deeper into me. I was coming and I couldn't stop it, even though he was mad and angry I still wanted him and loved him. After he had finished his angry sex, he climbed off me and took a shower. I lay there and cried. I knew I had done the wrong thing but it was too late now I couldn't change what happened. He came out of the shower with just a towel on. God, he looked hot, his body muscled and lean. I looked at him and he caught my eye.

"What am I going to do with you?" he said as he strode towards me. He sat on the bed and began to lecture me. I knew it was coming.

"Tasmin you are mine and mine only. I do not wish to share you with any other men or my workers." He looked at me seriously.

"If I had known they work for you I would never would have gone there." I said quietly not wanting to look him in the eyes.

His hand pulled my chin up to look at me. His eyes boar into mine. Tears had started swelling and I tried to be strong. He wiped away the tears and then kissed me tenderly on the lips.

"I love you Baby forever." he said in between kissing.

"I need you honey" his arms wrapped around me.

"I love you too but I'm not ready to settle with one man yet." I said honestly. Not sure now if I should say it.

His face changed from beautiful to angry again. He kissed me again urgent and forceful.

"Why won't you give in to me?" he asked when we came up for breath.

"I want to give you the world." he nuzzled my neck and ear.

I couldn't talk my head spinning from all these decisions and I still hadn't told him about the horrible lady in the shop.

"Why did you leave the other day?" he asked gently.

I looked at him and I thought whatever I say it will hurt him. I had to be honest with him, no more lying.

"I went to the shops and an old lady was very rude to me and she told me to leave this country as I don't belong here. She called me horrible names and was very angry" I answered slowly and sadly.

"Oh honey." he held me close.

"You shouldn't listen to her or anyone it is none of her business."
he said quietly.

"So, I rang Monique whom I had met on the plane and picked me
up. I wasn't going out but she said we had to go out and cheer me up".
The boys approached us and I was only thinking of you".

I said looking at him into those beautiful eyes. Why can't I be
happy and content with one man? I thought to myself; Am I being
selfish?

He kissed me tenderly and gently, his tongue finding mine. His
hand already playing with my breasts and his manhood was straining out
of his towel. He kissed me all over and was gentle in every way. He made
passionate love to me and took me to another place of lust, desire and
love. This was the Stefano I knew and loved. I fell asleep in his arms and
woke early afternoon. I was exhausted and my body had enough drugs
and alcohol in me I needed to sleep. No more I said to myself.   No
More! I got up and went to the shower and got in. The water was
invigorating and refreshing. I didn't hear Stefano enter and felt his arms
around me as I washed my hair. I giggled as he was tickling me and I
was helpless as I was getting shampoo in my eyes. He helped me rinse it
off and gave me a hand towel to wipe my eyes.

"You took advantage of me then." I said cheekily

"I'm going to take advantage of you now." he said huskily as he
leaned in to kiss.

Oh my legs always give way when he kisses me, I clung to his
strong arms and shoulders. He picked me up to straddle his waist and he
slipped in his erection. He held me under my bum and thrusted up and
up. I had by back on the wall and he used that to support my weight on
his cock.

"Oh honey" he groaned. I was close now and his powerful thrusts
were taking me over the edge.

"I cried out his name" as I came.

Stefano groaning and breathing hard as he exploded into me. He did not withdraw and kept pumping until his juice was all gone. I clung to him until he lifted me off. He washed me again and then dried me and gave me the complimentary robe to wear.

"I think Madam this is yours." he smiled at me with those fuck me eyes.

I went out to the lounge and an afternoon snack had been laid out with freshly brewed coffee. I poured myself some and sat on the sofa and looked out the window. He had dressed in jeans and a tee shirt. He smelt good enough to eat.

"Why didn't you tell me you were building a spinal care and stroke unit?" I asked him as he sat down with his coffee and croissants.

"I didn't think you would be interested?" he looked at me.

"You're doing it because of your wife?" I asked gently.

"Yes, there is no facility for people like my wife and her condition." He answered

"Tasmin you are never to see those men again." He said sternly.

"Will they lose their jobs?" I asked worried.

"No not this time a warning will be given but if they try to see you then they will be fired" he said firmly.

"We will never talk of this again and you my love are going to become my mistress and mine only." he looked into my eyes.

"But I haven't decided yet." I stammered.

"Well, I have and my decision is final" he said more firmly now.

I knew I was fighting a losing battle; he was stubborn, determined and strong willed. I would not win this battle.

Chapter Twenty-Nine

We stayed in the Penthouse for two days until Stefano said we would be going away for a few days.

"Where?" I asked glad to get out.

"Paris?" he said excitedly.

"Paris? When and How?" I was jumping around for joy.

We are going to the French Chateau in the countryside where no one knows us" he replied as he kissed my lips. I kissed him back and I knew once again I was lost in his eyes and arms.

"Pack and I will be back in an hour." he kissed me again.

"Tasmin don't go anywhere promise me you will be here when I get back." he was worried about leaving me.

"I will be here I promise" I kissed him goodbye.

Stefano left and went to the job site where he called a meeting. The men sat there with solemn faces they knew they were in trouble.

"No one is to see or contact Tasmin again is that clear?" He said sternly to them all.

"This is a warning next time you will be fired." he said with no emotion.

The men all nodded and understood. They did not want to lose their jobs and none of them would stand up to Stefano and challenge him. Anton wasn't too sure about the whole situation. He liked Tasmin and was not going to be intimated by his Boss. I will find a way he thought to himself. I want to see her again; she is beautiful and a goddess. No woman had ever touched his heart and head before and he knew he needed to see her again.

Stefano left there and went home to pack and leave instructions to the Nurse to call him if there was an emergency. He was back in an hour like promised and Tasmin was packed and ready to go. A taxi arrived to take us to the airport. Our plane leaves in 1 hour and we will be there in an hour he said as we walked through the foyer.

"What about your car"? I asked

"My car is safe here"? he smiled warmly at me.

The driver had the door open and I climbed in followed By Stefano. The plane trip was quick and I hardly had time to snuggle into Stefano's shoulder to doze. He was working on his lap top and just kept kissing my head. Stefano had hired a Audi and we drove out of Paris towards the Chateau. We were greeted by Fran who had a big smile on her face.

"You both look wonderful"? she said her face beaming.

A porter took our bags and we were taken to our room. It was the room we had before and it was perfect. Stefano pulled me into his arms and kissed me longingly. His tongue found mine and he was taking my jacket off to get to my blouse. That came of too and then he unzipped my black mini and let it fall to the ground. I stood there in my lacey black bra and suspenders, stockings and lace knickers.

"Oh Baby" he carried me to the big bed.

His tongue and hands everywhere and before I knew it I was naked except for my suspenders and stockings.

"I'll leave them on"? he said huskily.

He laid me on my back and spread my legs. His tongue finding my sensitive spot and his finger going in and out.

"Oooh" I cried out.   I lay there and let him love me.

After our sexual encounter of lust and love we went to the shower. We made love again in the shower and I gave Stefano a blow job and gave him no mercy. He showed me no mercy as well. He wrapped me up in a big towel and took me back to bed. I snugggled in and he told me to rest before supper. We had a light snack on the plane but I wasn't hungry for food only for sex.

"Sleep my Angel" he whispered in my ear and kissed my cheek.

I fell asleep and dreamt of a lot of men all tugging at me and trying to have their way with me. They were all rough and strong and they pushed me around like I was a rag doll. I screamed when James face appeared and he was fucking me hard and smacking my bum at the same time.

"Tasmin wake up youre having a nightmare"? he was holding me when I opened my eyes.

I looked into them and I felt immediately safe. All these lovers are playing with my head and I don't know how to let go of them.

"I'ts alright Baby" he rocked me in his arms.

"I'm here I wont leave you" he kissed my top of my head.

I lay there safe and warm away from anyone or anything.

"Do you want to get up for a while"? he looked at me.

"Yes I would thank you" he pulled me up and and helped me stand.

"Are you alright"? he asked again holding my arm.

"Yes just a little shaky"? I answered getting my balance.

I went to the bathroom to freshen up. I got dressed in silk pants and a silk sleeveless top with buttons. I felt relaxed and calm now. I sat on the balcony with a wine and looked at the view, it was chilly but the air was cool and refreshing.

I went back inside and sat on the sofa. There was something on my mind that I had forgotten to do and it was troubling me and I couldn't remember what it was I was thinking to myself and then it hit me.   I hadn't filled my script for the pill!

"Oh my god I'm being having unprotected sex with how many men"? "shit" I was anxious now and trying to work

Out in my head who wore a condom and who didn't. Well I knew Stefano hasn't a couple of times. But was there anyone else?

"Are you alright Honey"? Stefano looked at me and commented I looked a little pale.

"I havent got my pill packet"? I looked at him worried.

He looked back at me and understood, he nodded and

Said " Baby it will alright you cant get pregnant that easily and quickly after the pill"? he said trying to reassure me.

"Yes I suppose youre right I will fill it when I get home next week, till then you will have to always wear a condom:? I said as a matter of fact kind of voice.

He pouted at me and wasn't happy about that.

"Well there are other ways to have sex so you cant get pregnant"? he said wickly.

I knew what he meant and I wasn't sure of just anal sex for the next week was what I wanted. He might but I didn't!!

"No you will agree to a condom or no sex"? I challenged him.

His eyebrow raised up and I thought Shit should I have said that.

"Baby when I want it I take it"? he challenged me back.

"You have to behave or I will scream"? I looked him square in the eye.

In one stride he was there his mouth and tongue devouring mine.

"Scream hey"? he kissed me again so I couldn't scream.

"I'll put something big in your mouth and I'm sure you won't be able to scream"? he laughed at me and then kissed me again, commanding and urgent.

My body betraying me again, my nipples hard and waiting for his touch. He lay me on the sofa and unbuttoned my blouse. I had a white see through bra on and his lips went to my nipples and sucked. I cried out and arched my back he lips now kissing and biting my nipples gently but enough to give me pleasure.

His other hand sliding my silk pants down to reveal my white see through knickers. His head trailed down there and he sucked me through my knickers and slipped his finger in to find my favorite sensitive spot.

He pulled my knickers off and lifted my bum and put my legs over his shoulders. He was about to take his prey and feast. He pounced and held me tight. I couldn't get out of his hold and he didn't show me any mercy. I climaxed and my hips moved with his mouth where he lapped up my juices like a lion licking his lips and making sucking noises.

He came up for air and kissed me. I could taste my sweetness on his tongue and mouth. I wanted some of that I thought to myself. I slid down and made him roll on his back. I pulled off his jeans his erection making it hard to do so, so Stefano helped me.

I unleashed his manhood and took him my mouth. I sucked him hard and teased him for more. He was mine now he had lost all control. I sucked harder and harder taking more of him in my mouth. His groans were of no use as I just sucked harder. I took him until he could take no more and he came loudly in my mouth and on my face.

"Mmm Salty now where's my Sweets"? I thought to myself as I lapped up what I could and then laughed.

"Men's juices are a good face mask"? I said as I spread semem on my face.

Stefano laughed too. I went to the bathroom to wash off my facial mask and I looked at myself in the mirror. Hes's a beautiful man takes him and be with him when you can I thought to myself. But I want a man to call my own, have his name and be his wife and mother of his children. The thoughts were going around my head. I want him. I can't live without him. I will be his Mistress. I will be his lover. My decision had been made. That was the end of it.

I freshened up and went back to the lounge room. My mind clearer now and I knew I had to tell him.

"I will be your Lover and Mistress if that what it takes to have you in my life" I said with all my heart.

Stefano grabbed my hand and kissed it.

"I love you Tasmin and I can't live without you and I will always treat you special" he kissed my lips to seal the deal.

I kissed him back and he held me close and his tongue met mine. I knew I loved this man who could not give me what I wanted.   To be his wife and not just his lover. He was pure addiction one I couldn't give up. He carried me to the bed and made passionate love to me.

We were entwined together and fell asleep; our breathing was as one. I woke early as the sun shone through the windows. Another beautiful day I thought.

Stefano was already awake and was lying there watching me.

"Good morning Princess" he said softly nuzzling my ear.

"Good morning my King" I cooed back.

We lay there and kissed. His erection full swing first thing in the morning. He lips trailing over my body and giving me pleasure. Lust and desire swept over me and once again I was lost in his big arms. We showered and dressed. Breakfast was waiting on the balcony.

"What shall we do today?" Stefano asked me.

"I'm fine to do whatever you want to do." I replied between bites of my toast.

"Let's take a drive." he said looking at me smiling.

We left after breakfast and drove through the country. It was very picturesque. We had lunch at a lovely café in a small town, the people were very friendly and had always a smile on their faces. We enjoyed the day and went back to a Chateau in the vineyards.

Fran had made us a beautiful dinner by candle light and it was very romantic. Stefano stood up and said "Sweets" and carried me to the sofa by the fire. He produced a small long box and handed it me. I graciously accepted his gift excited to see what was in it. It was a beautiful bracelet, purple amethyst and diamonds. It was exquisite. I took it out and he put it on my wrist.

"Thank you I love it" I kissed him and he lay me on my back.

"I have a surprise for you." he said with greedy eyes.

"More surprises?" I replied back excited.

"Go and put on something sexy and I'II meet you in the bedroom." he said huskily.

I did what he asked and put on my black peekaboos but this time I didn't bother with knickers or a g/string. I lay on the bed seductively and he came in with a tray of strawberries, champagne and a bottle of my chocolate baileys sauce.

"Oh when did you get that?" I asked spying the bottle.

"I always travel with one." he said grinning.

He poured the champagne and dipped a strawberry in it to soak up the alcohol. He then placed it near my lips and teased me. Only letting me have it after I had used my tongue to get it.

"You want more?" he asked smiling.

I nodded and held his gaze. He got the chocolate sauce and dripped it on my pussy. I let out a gasp and waited for the feast. First, he put some on his finger and spread it on my nipples. I lay back, my breasts ready for the kill. His lips were demanding but gentle, he sucked and teased he then trailed to my favorite spot and feasted like he hadn't eaten in days.

I was in bliss and my orgasm took me over the edge. Now it was my turn I thought when my senses came back. I rolled him on his back and straddled him making sure his huge cock would not enter me.

"Give it to me honey" he groaned.

"Not yet you must beg me to give it to you." I teased as my tongue circled his knob.

He took an intake of air and looked at me deep into my eyes, I had him and now I would show him no mercy. I dripped sauce over his knob and started to drip down.

"Oooh I had better clean that up."

I licked my lips looking at him. I licked and sucked his knob and then took him deeper in. He groaned and held my head wanting more. I would then slow it down again and tease him some more.

"You little witch." he said huskily

I continued my game knowing it was dangerous. It wasn't long until he was lost, groaning and thrusting his hips to meet my mouth and I took him further. The taste of Sweet and Salty hit my mouth and he withdrew and spurted the rest out into some tissues. I licked my lips like a wildcat after a feed and knew I had more to come. The excitement overwhelming me and I shivered in anticipation.

"Are you cold baby?" he pulled me underneath him.

He kissed me and our lips were hot and demanding. Our mouths tasted of Baileys and come and we both

Were content from our feed. My body awakening to his erection growing for round 2. Our bodies awake now and desire and lust took over, I cried out his name when I climaxed and clung to his shoulders. He groaned and pumped me harder and collapsed on top of me after his climax. I fell asleep and didn't wake when he got up to shower. I dreamt I was in a field of flowers and there was a young boy running through the grass. I was running after the child laughing. Sam was there and I waved to him and he waved back. The boy running up to Sam and he scooped him up. We were both laughing and hugging each other and when I woke it took me a few minutes to realize it was a dream. A strange dream.

The sun was coming up and the sunrise was beautiful. Stefano was asleep beside me and I crept quietly from the bed, grabbed my robe and went to the window. It was very pink and purple, the colors was brilliant. I didn't hear Stefano come up behind me and he wrapped his arms around me.

"There's going to be a storm"? He said in my ear.

"How do you know"? I asked as I looked at the beautiful sky and thought its gorgeous there's no storm.

"it's a Shepherds warning"? he answered as he nuzzled my neck. His hands around my breasts and teasing them.

"Come back to bed." he half carried me and we got back into bed and snuggled up.

"This is very nice, isn't it?" he asked me tenderly.

"Yes, it is its perfect" I looked up at him.

He kissed my lips and our tongues danced together. It was only 6am but I couldn't sleep and either could Stefano. Our hands were everywhere and we made passionate love as we watched the sunrise from our bed. I fell back to sleep and didn't wake until 9am. Stefano was already up and dressed. I came out to the lounge room where he was sitting with his laptop.

"Good morning my lady" he said with a big smile.

"You slept for ages sleepy head"

He held his arms for me to snuggle in. We hugged and kissed tenderly and then I went and had a shower. I came back out and breakfast was ready and waiting.

"Come on I'm starving and this time for food." he said with a big grin.

I laughed and sat down and joined him. The day had turned dark and there were big clouds and no sunshine.

"Told you there would be a storm." he looked and smiled.

We ate and watched the clouds roll in with thunder trembling in the background.

"Good day to stay inside." Stefano looked at me cheekily.

I laughed and thought the same. After breakfast we lounged around and watched a movie. It was midafternoon and Stefano ran the hot tub.

"Let's get drunk and have some fun." he said wickedly.

We drank some champagne and then a couple of shots and got into the hot tub. It was great, tingles all over my body. It soothed every part of me. Stefano came in and we more drinks and we lay back and giggled. His hands already caressing every inch of me under the water. I found what I was looking for and he let out a breath of air when I wrapped my hand around him. He lifted me up so he could suck and caress my breasts.

My hand would not let go of him and we both wanted more. He picked up and placed me on the fluffy towel beside the hot tub. He got out and he lay down on his back and prompted me to straddle his face while I could then feast on him. We took each other to lust land and could not turn back, our orgasms loud and releasing. Stefano helped me up and put me back in the Hot Tub. It was warm and inviting. We finished our drinks and got out and went back to bed. We once again explored each other's bodies like it was the first time and took each other to total ecstasy.

Every time feeling like it was the first. his must be love I thought to myself. We dozed for a while and then got up and showered. I knew it was dangerous to shower together but he wouldn't have it any other way.

"Come let me wash you." he purred in that sexy voice.

How could I resist. He washed me everywhere and took me everywhere gently and tenderly. My orgasms exploding together and my legs could not stand up anymore. He dried me and carried me back to bed where I stayed till dinner. I think I slept for a couple of hours and I got up and put on a silk nightie and silk robe. Did my hair and put a little makeup on. Dapped some perfume on and even got my stilettos on.

I gracefully walked out to the lounge room where Stefano was on the phone. He was talking German so I didn't understand him. He was talking softly and it sounded like he was talking to a woman. He smiled and winked at me when I entered and I sat down at the table where it was ready for dinner. I poured myself a wine and sat there and sipped it listening in on Stefano's conversation even though I couldn't understand it. He hung up and strode over to me.

"Hi Baby." he kissed me on the lips. He poured himself some wine.

"Who was that?" I asked innocently.

"That was the nurse from home." he replied

"Oh is everything alright?" I asked worried.

"Everything is fine but we will go back to Switzerland tomorrow afternoon" he answered as he poured another wine for himself and me.

"Ok whatever you want honey." I flashed my beautiful smile at him.

"Let's eat before I get distracted." he growled at me joking.

The night flew into the next day and then we were on the plane home. Stefano picked up his car from the airport and we started to drive back to our Chalet.

"Do you want to see my project?" he asked as he sped along the winding road.

"Yes, I would love to if that's ok." I answered smiling back.

We drove for 10 more minutes and arrived at a big construction site. It was huge. Men everywhere and trucks and machinery. We went to the site office and Stefano put a hard hat on my head.

"Safety rules." he said as I tried to take it off.

Marcos was in the office and he stood when we entered.

"Stefano, Tasmin" he spluttered

"How nice to see you." he shook Stefano's hand and mine.

"I thought I would show Tasmin my project." Stefano said

"Good I'm actually glad you're here I need some cheques signed and a couple of things approved." Marcos said as he went back to the desk.

"No problem I can do that." Stefano answered.

"Just be a minute honey." he turned to me and smiled.

Just as he said that Anton entered and stopped short when he saw me.

"Good morning boss, Tasmin" he said smiling at me.

"Ah Morning Anton would you show Tasmin around while I talk to Marcos?" he asked

"Yes, Sir I would be happy to." he replied trying not to smile again at me.

Anton turned to me. He grabbed a safety vest and held it to me to put on. I accepted his touch as he helped me put it on and tried not to notice the electricity between us.

"Come on I'll show you around." he stood aside so I could pass through the door.

I could smell him as I brushed past him. His eyes boar into mine and I knew what he was thinking. Tasmin, I scolded myself do not feel any feelings and do not look into his talking eyes. Anton took me to a big entrance and foyer. It was very impressive. He told me this was the main reception area. Workmen were everywhere doing their jobs. They all looked in our direction when we entered. I saw Swen talking to two men, he turned when he saw me and nodded at me. His smile said it all.

"It's nearly ready for painting" he said looking into my eyes.

"How are you Tasmin?" he asked quietly.

"I'm good thank you" I replied softly not wanting to look at him.

"I'm sorry about the other night it shouldn't off happened." I continued on.

"I'm not sorry at all you are a very beautiful woman." He looked at me and held my gaze. I started blushing and turned away.

"It was wrong and I am in love with Stefano."

"It can never happen again" I said quietly looking around so nobody could hear.

"I was hoping we could see each other again just us this time." he whispered under his breath.

"I can't, Stefano would kill me and probably you too."

I whispered back, not wanting to look at his eyes as my eyes were thinking of him as well. We had an attraction and he wanted more. Maybe I did too.

"So, what's down the hallway?" I asked trying to change the subject.

"Consulting rooms and treatment rooms" he replied.

He showed me the main building and then we went to Accommodation Houses.

"These are 24-hour care houses for the patients." He said as he took me through to the big lounge room.

"Nurse station is over there and there is a big kitchen going in there." he pointed to far end of the room.

"Wow this is amazing." I replied looking around.

"I'll show you the pool."

Anton grabbed my hand and led me to a huge room with a 25mtre heated pool. There were workers in there as well and Karlos was there with Hans. They both came up to me with big smiles.

"Hello Tasmin" they both said.

God, they looked hot. There's something about a man with a tool belt, the way it hangs on their hips hiding that huge bulge. I felt myself getting tingles just thinking of them standing there around me.

"Hello boys." I replied with a sweet smile.

I was blushing again and felt a little uncomfortable. Their eyes undressing me and their thoughts I could hear.

"What's next?" I asked Anton who also was giving me hot vibes.

"Uh Um the Gym and Rehabilitation House?" he said looking at me in a trance.

We said goodbye to the others who still had their tongues hanging out of their mouths and were very jealous of Anton giving me the grand tour. We entered a huge building and it ready for painting and carpet and all the equipment Anton was telling me. He went to another room off that and I followed.

"What's in here?" I asked as I walked into a large room.

"It's the staff room" Anton said as he turned to me.

He was very close and I could feel his whole sexual aura surrounding me. The gap closed in and his arms were pulling me in.

"Oh Tasmin I've missed seeing your beautiful face." He looked into my eyes.

"Anton don't, please, its wrong. Stefano and I are together now." I tried to push his arms off me.

He wasn't listening. His lips met mine and I tried to turn away. He held my head in his hands and his tongue prying my mouth open to accept him. He was too strong and my lips opened to receive his tongue. His hand going to my buttons on my shirt. My hand trying to stop him but he was too strong.

"I want you Baby again" he said huskily as he nuzzled my neck. His hand was inside my bra now and he was pinching my nipples gently.

"God, I want taste you." he pulled me tighter so I could feel his erection or was that his tool belt.

"Anton we mustn't."

I begged as his lips went to my aching nipples that were craving his touch. I let him suck them and tease them. My knees going weak and my body betraying me.

"Stop! Sop! Anton you must Stop." I begged him again. He finally released me.

"Ok, I'm sorry. I didn't mean to attack you but your so hot." he tried to compose himself.

I buttoned up my shirt trying to stop my hands from shaking. I looked at him seriously this time and I knew I had to be forceful and firm.

"Anton you will lose your job if you pursue me in any way." I said with a serious tone.

"Stefano will fire you and I don't want that"? I added

"I wish there could be another way as I really like you Tasmin."

He looked at me with big horny hot eyes. God don't look at him I thought to myself he is trying to seduce you. We heard Stefano calling out my name and it shook us out of our trance.

"Coming honey" I yelled out.

Thank God or I would have been coming in that room with Anton! I came out of the room and Stefano was standing there looking at me. I tried not to blush or let anything look suspicious. His eyes tore into mine and I looked back at him and smiled.

"This is fantastic you are very cleaver." I said praising him.

His arms opened for me to hug him. I buried my face in his chest so he couldn't see my eyes and my betrayal. I reached up and kissed him tenderly on the lips in front of Anton who was watching everything.

"It's great, isn't it? he replied back beaming.

"Anton is my foreman and he is very reliable and trustworthy" he said as he looked Anton in the eye. Anton looked back at him and replied

"Yes boss, I'm your man for the job" he said proudly.

"Good we understand each other then." Stefano looked him in the eye as if to question his loyalty to him.

"We certainly do" Anton answered with a smile Mmm that was awkward I thought.

"Let's go and have a drink." Stefano held my hand and led me to the entrance.

We walked along a walkway which Stefano said it would be covered with the lawns and gardens on that side of the path. He had thought of everything and I asked him when would it be open.

"In about 2 months I would think if there's no hiccups." he replied putting his arm around me. We went back into the office and no one was in there. He took off my vest and helmet.

"I could keep going." his fingers strayed at my buttons.

My nipples were sticking out from the material. His finger traced it and he bent to kiss my lips. His tongue searching for mine. His hand pushing my bum into his groin.

"Baby" I pulled away

"Let's go somewhere and be alone." I suggested with a wicked smile.

"Ok" he pulled me back for another kiss.

My knees were buckling and I thought he was going to throw me on the desk and have his way with me. We heard a cough at the door and Marcos and Anton were standing there trying not to look.

"Uh sorry Stefano we just need the plans for the plumbers."

Marcos asked trying not to look at my protruding nipples. I could feel Anton's gaze on me as well, I thought I was going to faint.

"Ah yes sorry we will be going now I will you leave you to it." he shook their hands and pulled me behind him.

"Bye" I said quietly as I struggled to keep up with Stefano.

He held the door for me to get in and we then sped away. The boys watched as we left with big smiles and big dreams. We drove up the road and turned off to a side dirt road. After pulling out of sight he turned the engine off. His hand pulling me in to kiss and his tongue urgent and hot. His other hand unbuttoning my shirt and his fingers going fast nearly breaking the buttons. He finally revealed my lace bra and peeled it up and bent down to tease me. His tongue and lips torturing me in the front seat.

He stopped and told me to get in the back. I got out of the front and got in the back. He climbed in the other passenger door. He made me lie down on the back seat and took my jeans off. Followed by my lacy knickers. He spread my legs and his finger found my sensitive spot. His lips trailing down my legs to join his finger. He licked and teased bringing me to climax in the back seat of an Audi. He then bent me on my knees and he entered from behind. Thrusting me and pounding me urgent and needing. His climax strong and loud as he pounded me harder and harder till he was spent. He had a condom this time as he didn't want the mess on the back seat. He discarded it in plastic bag and put it in a little bin on the backseat floor. He helped me out of the car and I got quickly dressed not wanting anyone to see us in this disarray.
We drove further down the road to a gorgeous Chalet for Coffee.

Stefano held my hand as he drove and had a big smile on his face. I knew I made him happy and he also made me happy. So, what was the problem, I thought to myself as we got out of the car. Why did I have feelings for other men? Why can't I let go? Why can't I be happy with one man? These thoughts were going through my head as we were seated by the window.

I gazed out in my own little world unaware of the waitress asking us what we wanted. Stefano ordered for us. The pretty blonde waitress not taking her eyes of Stefano and then she left to get our order.

"Are you ok Honey?" he asked me tenderly.

"Oh sorry" I snapped back to reality.

"I was just thinking how lucky and happy I am" I said looking into his come fuck me eyes.

"Me too" he answered looking into mine. He squeezed my hand across the table and smiled at me.

"It's all going to be wonderful for us." he said with love.

The waitress stopped our lips from touching as she approached the table. We both pulled back and behaved ourselves. She gave Stefano a little smile and you could see she was intrigued.

"Your coffee Sir."

She purred at him putting his cup in front of him and leaning in so he could take a good look at her cleavage beckoning his eyes. He just smiled and thanked her. I watched everything and thought what a flirt and in front of me. When she went to walk off, I said out loud so she could hear

"Oh baby I can't wait to have you alone." I teased him from across the table.

He pulled me in to kiss and our lips locked. The waitress came back with our open grilled sandwiches and could not take her eyes off Stefano.

"Your beautiful wife is very lucky to have such a charming man." She said her tongue licking her lips glancing at me and smiling.

"She is very lucky and so I am I" he replied back to her with a smile you could die for.

I think she came in her panties and she totttled off quickly.I laughed to see Stefano flirting with her, he had her in his spell.   It was quite amusing. I didn't care as I knew he was mine. If he asked her to take her top off she would have right there and then. He certainly had a way with women.

"What's funny"? he asked amused

"You"? I replied as I winked at him. "You had that waitress all tongue tied"? I said giggling.

"Yeh her tits nearly fell out in my coffee"? he winked back at me

We both giggled and then ate our lunch.We had a lovely afternoon chatting and looking out at the view.   The waitress came up again and asked sweetly if there was anything else she could get us.   Her eyes looking at him and then me.   I knew what she wanted, she wanted him on a platter.

"Thankyou the meal was very delicious and we are going now"?

He got up to get my jacket and help me into it. He gave her a generous tip and as he did, she slipped a piece of paper in his hand. She also said something to him In German and smiled sweetly. We got in the car and I said what was that all about. Stefano told me she gave him her number and also had said She did not mind if we had a 3 threesome as we were a Hot couple. I was a little shocked at how forward she was Stefano dismissed it saying it was normal for shared partners and threesomes in Europe. Well I knew that hello I just had an orgy with one woman and 6 men!!! God thank goodness he can't read mines.

"Do you want a threesome"? I asked him as we drove along.

"Maybe it would be interesting to see another woman seducing my woman"? he said with a wicked look in his eye.

"With her"? I asked a little intrigued.

"She was cute with big tits but not as cute as you"? he said smiling those warm and inviting eyes.

"I would do it if you wanted to, I would rather see you with another woman than with a man"? he said firmly.

"Only one cock in this harem"? he joked laughing.

"Have you been with another woman Tasmin"? he asked seriously this time.

"Yes" I said softly.

"Did you like it and was there a man as well"? he asked more question

"Yes there was"? I replied back wanting to yell yes yes I to yell yes yes I loved it.

"Then if you want to we could do it"? he asked a little excited.

"Is that what you want"? I said not really sure I could share him.

"It would be quite desirable only if you agree to it"? he   answered as he drove through a lovely town.

"Is that one of the conditions of being your Mistress"? I was afraid to ask.

He pulled over and stopped the engine.

"Tasmin there are no conditions except your faithfulness and commitment"? he said seriously.

"It would be appealing and quite hot to have you and another woman in my submission but its only if you want too"? he added with a smile.

He held my hand and his other hand tipped my chin up to meet his eyes. I was drawn to them and he looked deep into mine for an answer.

"I suppose it would be hot and very wicked to see you under our submission and not able to control it"? I said with a little smile.

"Oh is that right under your spell you little witch"?

I thought I would tie you both up and have my way with you both"? he said huskily making my body tingle all over his hands playing with my breasts and nipples.

"Honey not here someone will see us"? I tried to take his hands away.

He laughed and said I'm taking you home I'm hungry and he drove like a racing car driver to get back to the Chalet. We got there in record time thank god as Stefano had his hand in my crotch and one on the steering wheel I thought we were going to crash even though I was confident of his

Driving skills. He raced me up to our room and he chased me to the bed.

"Come here you little wildcat I'm hungry"?

He went to grab me and I ran around the side of the bed giggling.

"Oh, you want to play"?

He teased, his look said it all. He was a lion and his sleek muscular body moved slowly towards me ready to pounce. I giggled more and I had nowhere to run. I braced myself for the impact. His big arms grabbed me and flung me on the bed. His body coming down but he held his weight from squashing me.

"What are you going to do now sweetie pie"?

He kissed my neck. I tried to struggle but he was too strong. He held my hands with one hand while the other hand attacked me. I couldn't stop giggling as he tickled, teased and tormented me.

"Stop Stop I give in"?

I begged and giggled at the same time.

"You give in"?

He looked at me uncertain.

"Yes Yes"

I begged again. He released me and rolled to one side. I jumped up quickly and ran to the lounge room, he went to lunge for me but missed and I heard a groan as he hit his leg on the bed. I tried not to giggle again and ran to the sofa.

"Come here honey youre going pay for that you cheeky little wildcat"?

He was coming fast. No bump on the leg would stop him.
I giggled more and I knew I was playing with fire. He caught me in two strides and threw me over his shoulder in a fireman hold. He slapped my bottom gently but enough for me to cry out.

"Ouch put me down"? I tried to struggle free. He threw me down on the bed and told me to stay.

"Baby struggle all you like it just makes me hotter"?

He said huskily and losing patience. He came for me then pulling at my clothing and underwear. I was naked in no time and he was already down to Boxers. His erection jutting out and wanting attention. I laid back and waited with anticipation. My breasts heaving and wanting to be touched.He put a condom on the side table and lay beside me.

"Well that was fun"? he nibbled my nipple.

"Ooh honey"? I cried out when he bit it.

"That's for being a naughty girl and making me chase you"? He looked up and smiled with those come fuck me eyes. I giggled and he smiled back.

"Youre going to beg me for mercy"? he said sexily in that european voice.

I giggled again as his lips and tongue collided with my nipple. He took me then and brought my body to ecasty.He gave me no mercy and I gave in to his desires.We lay together wrapped in each other's arms and it felt right. Our lovemaking exhausting our bodies.We showered and got casually dressed and lay around and waited for dinner. We had Seafood Lingunie which was delicious. We drank a lovely crisp white wine which was delicious with the seafood.

The fire was lovely and we sat cuddled up in each other's arms and watched the flames dance. I was sleepy and I started to doze off. Stefano picked me up and carried me to bed.   He tucked me in and said he would be in soon. I fell into a deep sleep and this time I dreamt of a threesome with Stefano and this waitress.   It was a sensual dream and I woke up feeling horny. The day looked better than yesterday and the sun was shining.   Stefano was already up. Gee does this man ever sleep. He needs 5hours I need 8. We had a lovely breakfast and we talked about what our plans were. I was leaving in two days and I had to confirm my ticket.

"I will fly back with you if you like"? he asked me

"No its ok you need to be here"? I said gently and looked into his eyes reassuringly.

"Yes well I do but I need to be with you too"? he said sadly.

I hugged him then and tried not to think about leaving him again. I had to show him I could be strong so he would be strong also.

"I will be ok honestly you have to stay here and finish your amazing work"? I said looking deep into his eyes.

"You're right but I will miss you"? he kissed my lips and held me tight so it was decided I would be leaving in two days and Stefano would drive me to the airport. The phone rang and he went to answer it. He talked in german and it sounded serious.

He hung up the phone and said he had to go home there was some kind of emergency.

"What's wrong"? I was worried for him now.

"The doctor wouldn't say he just said to come home immediately"? he replied hugging me.

"I have to pack"? he got up and packed a small black bag.

"I will ring you when I know but I will be here in time to

Take you to the airport ok"? he said reassuringly.

He kissed me tenderly and held me close, he whispered in my ear and told me he loved me, and then he was gone. I sat on the sofa and watched him drive off down the road and felt a little sad. It will always be like this? I thought to myself. He will always be leaving to go home to her? I was jealous but sad because of her condition. I spent the day going for a walk around the village. It was energizing and the air was crisp and cool. The afternoon was setting in and I went into a restaurant for hot coffee and snaps. There was not many people in there and the lovely woma Seated me by the window. I ordered a coffee and snaps and she left to get it.

She brought over my drinks and smiled at me, I smiled back. I sat there and gazed out the window and thought about my life and what complications I had.   Nothing seemed easy. I ordered another snapps and it certainly warmed me up. I felt a little whoozy at first and thought I had better not   Have anymore. I thanked the lady and thought I would be   ok now to walk home. I was a little unsteady and had to hold on to the chair for support.

"Sit down Frauline"? she put me back on the chair.

Just as she done that the door tingle went and we both looked up and saw Anton standing there.

"Tasmin what are you doing here"? he asked with a smile on his face.

I looked at him in shock and was tongue tied. The lady talked in German to Anton and he nodded and then smiled at me.

Oh great I thought he thinks I'm drunk on two snapps!!

"Tasmin let me help you home"? he held his hand to mine.

The electricity between us was escatic. My heart was beating fast. His eyes boar into mine and I could feel his sexual aura overpowering me.

"Come I will look after you"?

He held my hand and led me to his car.He helped me in and asked where to.

I gave him directions to the Chalet and he drove there. He helped me out when we got there and I insisted I was ok and that I didn't want him to come up to my room as I didn't trust myself or him.Anton gave me his phone no. and said call me if you need me.

"Wheres Stefano"? he asked with curious eyes.

"He had to go somewhere he will be back later"? I lied as I didn't want him to know I was alone.

I thanked him and he was so close. He pulled me in to kiss me on the lips. His arms too strong and they held me against him. His lips brushing mine and his tongue teasing my lips to open.

Oh god please don't I thought I am weak and I will not be able to resist the temptation. I pushed him off and said goodbye and ran inside. Anton stood there and watched me confused and horny. I went to my room and it felt lonely. Fran had made me a   light dinner but I didn't feel like eating. The phone rang and it was the doctor from Stefano's Town.

"Hello" he said "is Stefano there"? he asked in English.

"No he left this morning to go home"? I replied.

"Is he not there yet"? I asked the Doctor.

"No he did not say he was coming"? replied the Doctor.

"Didn't someone ring and ask Stefano to come home straight away this morning"? I asked the Doctor.

"No no one did"? he replied a bit confused.

We hung up and I sat there to try to work out what was happening. Where was Stefano? Why did he tell me he was going home? Why did lie to me? I rang his cell and a woman answered.

"Hello is Stefano there please"? I asked in English hoping she would understand.

"Yes he is in the shower"? she replied cooley.

"Who is this"?   I asked a little too demanding.

"I am Dannielle Stefano's girlfriend"? she replied

"Who are you"? she asked me.

"No one special"? I replied lying.

"Ok who should I say is calling"? she asked politely.

"It doesn't matter goodbye" I hung up.

Shit what just happened. He has a girlfriend. Dannielle who the fuck was Dannielle?I was pissed now he is lying to me and cheating on me. I poured a large Jack Daniels and sat down and drank it. The phone rang and I answered it.

"Tasmin Baby did you just ring"? Stefano asked

"Yes and a Dannielle answered and she told me you were in the shower"? I said a little pissed off.

"That's the nurse she is just fooling around"? he said coolley.

"Where are you"? I asked him sweetly.

"I'm at home"? he answered confused.

"Ok" I replied knowing now he is lying to me.

"See you tomorrow honey love you" and he hung up.

Tears started to flow and I couldn't believe he would lie to me. Fuck Men they're all Bastards!! I sat on the sofa and complicated what to do I know I will ring Anton and he will come and get me. I rang Anton and he said he would come and get me and We would stay at another hotel for the night. I packed all my bags and left a note for Stefano.

"I have left and I am going to the airport by myself. I do not want to see you or talk to you again. You have betrayed our love and you have lied to me. I hope you and Dannielle will be very happy together"? I love you always Tasmin.

There was a knock at the door and Anton was there to take me away from all the lies. He took my bags and I followed him downstairs to his car.

"Where are we going"? I asked as he helped me in the car.

"I booked a hotel near the airport we will stay there'? he replied smiling at me.

We drove in silence I was still in shock of what Stefano was doing and I still couldn't believe it. He must have other Mistresses I thought. How could I be so stupid to think I was the only one? We arrived at the hotel and Anton got my suitcase out and my other bag. I followed him into the foyer and we checked in under a different name. Anton paid cash and they didn't want to see any ID. Anton said something in German, I recognized some words And I smiled at him when he smiled at me.

"Come honey let's get comfortable"? he led me to our room.

It wasn't the Penthouse but it was still a nice room. There was a knock at the door and a trolley was brought in with champagne, strawberries, cream and some other snacks. Anton tipped the waiter and closed the door and locked it. He pulled me into his arms and kissed my lips.

"I've been waiting all day for that"? he said as he came up for air.

"I might get changed and freshen up"? I said taking my suitcase to the bedroom.

I put on my Black peek a boos sexy corset and the whole lingerie. might as well seduce him as Stefano is busy seducing some bitch. I was angry now and I looked at myself in the mirror and thought what the hell. Stefano doesn't give a shit he's having a 'fucking great time' so I will also, even though I knew in the back of my mind. Stefano is there and I couldn't get him out of my head or heart. I do look hot I thought as I gazed at myself, Anton will love this and I will make him beg. I smiled to myself and thought how wicked I was. Wicked, hot and horny. Ready for the seduction. I put my Black silk robe on and tied the sash. I walked out to the lounge room and Anton had the Champagne already poured and waiting.

"Honey" he handed me a glass.

"You look gorgeous"? he said as he eyed me up and down and licking his lips. He grabbed the sash and untied it so it fell to the floor. He dipped a strawberry in cream and teased my lips to eat it. I teased it with my tongue and he couldn't take his eyes off me

"Beautiful" he whispered.

I dipped a strawberry in cream and teased his lips with it he ate it and grinned at me. His lips now on mine and the strawberry and cream tasted in my mouth. He nibbled my neck down to my breasts where they protruded out from the holes in my corset. He put cream on his finger and then put it on my nipples. He bent his head to suckle me and I lay back on the sofa and let him tease and seduce me. His head then went down to my sensitive spot and he pulled my g/string off and spread my legs. He put cream on his finger and then circled my clit. His tongue then followed. I lay there in bliss and let him take me over the edge.   My orgasm exploding in his mouth where he lapped up my juices and the cream.

"You sure taste good"? he grinned at me.

He held my hand and led me to the bedroom where he undressed and unleashed his weapon. His throbbing penis ready for me to tease. I put cream on my finger and circled his knob. He took a breath inward and waited for my mouth and tongue. I did not disappoint him and I made him come in my mouth with the taste of cream and come it was delicious. We drank some champagne and teased each other with strawberries and cream. He was ready for round 2 and he put a condom on and slowly entered me. God, he felt so good. He pumped me and our hips joined together and thrusted the same rhythm until we both climaxed and groaned. In the background my cell was ringing and I let it go to message bank. I'll check it later I thought. I lay there in Anton's arms and thought how different things happen. One minute I'm happy with Stefano and the next he is lying to me and with his lover bitch! Well two can play that game I thought to myself.

"What time's your flight tomorrow"? Anton asked as he stroked my hair.

"2pm so I have to be there around midday"? I said thinking of how I will get out of the country without Stefano finding out.

"Ok then we have to leave about 11am so we can get there on time" he replied we snuggled together and I fell asleep in his arms.

"I love you Tasmin and I would always treat you right"? he whispered in my ear but I was already asleep. We both woke around 7am and Anton was horny as ever. We made passionate lust together and then he led me to the shower. Anton soaped me all over and his hands were everywhere. His fingers slithered around my pussy and bum. He washed me and then entered me gentle but urgent. His finger circling my anus and tickling me. I moaned when his finger entered me and thrust the same rhythm as his penis in my vagina. He took me to total bliss and my knees buckled beneath me. He held me tight and then washed and dried me then carried me back to bed.

"That was incredible" Anton looked at me with those hot eyes.

"It was beautiful" I answered still in a dream.

We lay there and recovered and then got up and dressed and had breakfast. After breakfast I made sure I was packed and ready to go. My ticket would be waiting at the terminal and I would be flying first class again.

Stefano had arranged everything, yes, he wanted to keep me happy. Sonofabitch I thought to myself as I fixed my makeup and hair. Anton took my bags to the car when we were ready to leave. I got in the car and we sped up the Auto Barnto the Airport.

My cell rang again and I knew it was Stefano seeing where I was. I turned my phone off and sat back and took in the view.

"Tasmin I want to come to America to see you again"? he asked with a smile.

"I will ring you when I get home and we will talk about it then"? I answered not knowing if I could see Anton again.

Stefano will find out and he would lose his job for sure. We arrived at the Airport and Anton got my bags out of the car.

"I will walk you in" he said with a smile.

"No its ok I want to say goodbye here"? I said looking into his eyes. We kissed tenderly and he whispered in my ear.

"Goodbye my beautiful goddess"? he held me close.

"Goodbye Anton and thank you for everything"? I said as I held him back tightly.

I walked off with my trolley and left him standing there.I could not look back. I arrived at First class Gate and got my ticket and then went into the lounge area. I didn't see Stefano sitting there and I was surprised when I heard my name.

"Tasmin thank god I was worried about you"? he came up behind me.

"Where have you been"? he asked looking at me

"Where have you been I should ask you"? I said angrily.

"Who is Dannielle"? I added looking at him.

" and don't tell me she is the nurse because I know you're lying"? I said with a steady voice. He looked at me he knew he was defeated he could not lie.

"Ok I will tell you the truth"? he replied softly.

"I'm all ears"? I said patiently listening.

"Well Dannielle is a ex lover of mine and she needed my help with something"? he said truthfully.

"What does she look like"? I asked wanting to know every detail about her.

"She is tall blonde" he replied not wanting to tell me much.

Suddenly it hit me she was the woman you were talking to last time I was here in France wasn't she"? I asked raising my voice this time.

"Calm down its over now and it has been for some time"?

He answered looking into my eyes.

"That day she got in your car did you take her somewhere and fuck her"? I asked wanting to know the truth even though it might hurt.

"No, yes I did but that was the end"? he said quietly.

"I should have known this would happen you are an attractive man and obviously you have many women

Admirers"? I said trying to stay calm and talk softly.

"Yes I have but when I met you I only wanted you"? he tried to persuade me.

"I can't think straight anymore I'm so confused. I thought you loved me and that we were going to be so happy"? I spat at him as I was very angry.

He looked at me sadly and took my hand.

"Tasmin honey I love you and one day we will be together forever"? he said looking at me.

Tears were starting to swell in my eyes and I had to turn away. My boarding had been announced and I got up with my overnight bag and looked at him.

"I loved you and I trusted you and now I don't know if I can ever trust you again"? I said honestly not really wanting to let him go. I needed him, he was my obsession, my addiction and my strength.

"Goodbye Stefano" I went to hug him one last time. He held me tight until I had to go. "I love you and I will be over soon to work this out ok"? he held my face in his hands. He kissed me tenderly and then let me go. I walked through the security door and I didn't turn back. My tears were rolling down my face and I felt like I had just lost my best friend. Goodbye Stefano my love Goodbye forever I sat down in my seat and closed my eyes, I would have to forget the man I fell in love with. The man I could never have as my husband just my lover. I kept my eyes closed as we took off and tried not to think of him as it made me cry. My flight was long and tiring. I didn't want to talk to anyone and I sat there and looked out the window or dozed when I could.

I arrived in L.A. 10 hours later and I hailed a taxi and gave him my address. We pulled into my driveway and the censor lights went on. The taxi driver got out and helped me with my bags, I paid him and he drove off. I didn't hear footsteps behind me and a hand covered my mouth as I was unlocking the door. I was shoved inside and then the door was closed.

"Do the alarm"? A man's voice said behind me roughly and firm. I was shaking. was that James I wasn't sure. I did the alarm and then he tied a sash around my eyes so I couldn't see and then led to the lounge room. He switched on a lamp on the table as he dragged me past it to the sofa. He pushed me on my hands and knees on the sofa my face being pushed into the cushion and then took his hand away.

"James is that you"? I tried to turn my head around to see him through my blind fold. He pushed my head down into the sofa cushion and pulled at my silk pants. He then ripped my top from its buttons exposing my bra.

Oh god hes going to rape and suffocate me"? I tried to struggle and I couldn't move. He fingers plunged into me rough and brutal. His tougue Ploughing into my pussy and his teeth biting me.

I cried out and he got tissues and shoved them in mouth. I nearly gaged. I couldn't breathe. I tried to spit them out but he only put more in and kept his hand there. I was defeated. I was his captive. He had me in his control. I knew I had to give in. I heard him unleash his weapon and I knew it was over soon. He plunged into me with force and anger. His hands pinching my nipples and massaging my breasts hard and rough. I cried out through the tissues and tried again to struggle free. He slapped me hard then on my buttock and I again cried out in pain.

I couldn't take anymore. He ploughed deeper and harder and I knew he was close. God please let him finish and let me live.

I still thought in the back of my mind it was James' as he was about the same build and James is rough and urgent like this.

I heard him groan as his thrusting became faster and then he withdrew and spurt his semen on my back. He went limp against me.
I dared not move.   He then wiped me with some tissues and held me down still with one arm. He was strong. James was strong. I tried to spit out the tissues and talk

To my attacker. He pushed me down again into the cushion. His hand now preparing me for anal sex and I braced myself for what was to come.

I knew he would not be gentle and I knew I he would hurt me.

I started to cry and whimper, he shussed me and caressed my bum cheeks gently. I felt his penis wanting to gain entry and he gently eased himself into me. He wasn't brutal or rough just gentle and little thrusts. He caressed my breasts and pinched my nipples hard. He was turned on and I knew he wouldn't be gentle for long. His thrusts were more urgent now and going deeper. His other hand in my pussy also getting a little rough and faster. He pounded me then in and out hard and fast. He didn't say a word just his breathing loud and raggered.He groaned as he thrusted deeper and he then came loudly.

Thank God it was over. I lay there and didn't move. He kissed my back and neck and told me to stay like this for 20 seconds and not to move or he would hurt me. I felt him get off me and I went to move, I sharp pain hit my other bum cheek not one before and cried out in pain.

"I said don't move"? the voice said gruffly and angry. Was that James I thought to myself through my pain.

Tears rolled down my cheeks and I don't know how longI stayed there. I remembered hearing a click of the door and was too scared or paralyzed to move. I finally found the courage and got up to take my blindfold off and looked around me. I looked down at myself and my blouse was torn and my bra was also ripped.

There were little bite marks on my breasts, arms, legs and back and bum I gasped in horror as I inspected my wounds in the mirror.

"Shit was it James or was it someone else"? I wasn't sure but I knew it couldn't happen again.

I went and secured fort knox and thought maybe I might get a gun. Then I can blow his dick away. Should I report this? I thought no I didn't want the hassle or interrogation from the police or family.

No, I will have to handle it my way. I made a strong Jack Daniels and went upstairs and ran a bath.

The water soothed my sore bum cheeks and I cringed at the pain as the water did its magic. I washed my body and lay back against the bath.

My thoughts drifting about Stefano, Anton, Sam and this horrible man stalking me. It's time for a man to protect me from all of this, I thought as I sipped my drink. I cannot live alone for much longer I am venerable and lonely. But who should I pick and would I be happy just with that man. All these thoughts were spinning around in my head.

I love them all they have all touched my heart. I am addicted to each man differently. They're all gorgeous men with a lot to offer.

Except Stefano he cannot give me his name or fulltime life. Sam could give me a family and contentment. I think he would be a wonderful husband if I can't have Stefano.

But is that cheating on Sam if I 'm in love with another man? While I'm with Sam as my husband and lover.

I knew I would never forget Stefano in my head or heart if I picked another.

Oh God I'm so confused! Then there's Anton and he is very tempting. Gorgeous and Hot and would also make an excellent husband.

How can I pick I want them all! The phone rang and startled me from my thoughts.

I let the answering Machine get it and it was Sam.God he sounded good. I needed his strong arms around me. I started to cry and lay there listening to his voice. I'II be over in the morning hope to see you he said in a deep husky voice. He then hung up. I lay there and closed my eyes and thought of Sam, He was with me and holding me. His strong arms held me tight. Our lips met and we kissed passionately. His hands

Caressing me softly and gently. His touch was soothing and warm. I let my hand guide over my body as if it was his.   He was gentle and then his finger found my sensitive spot where he brought me to a gentle climax that was calm and soothing. I vilized Sam's hands and body and voice was with me.

I cried after my orgasm it was all too much. I got out of the bath and dried off. Put on my silk pjs and went to bed.

I didn't want any bad dreams and I was scared to close my eyes. My eyes were sore from crying and it wasn't long before they closed from exhaustion.

I woke in the morning and couldn't remember any bad dreams. My body ached when I went to get up. I heard Sam's truck pull up the driveway. I grabbed my satin robe and put on my slippers and slowly went down stairs to open the door.

I opened the door and there he stood. He smelt so manly and I was drawn to his scent. He embraced me with his big arms and gorgeous smile.

"How are you honey"? he asked tenderly and soft.

I clung to him and burst into tears.

"Oh Baby whats wrong"? he pulled me free to look at me in my eyes.

Our eyes met and I swear he could see the scared and pained look in my eyes. I looked up at him and the tears swelled again. He took me inside and sat me on the couch.

"Honey are you ok"? he cradled me in his arms.

I finally was able to speak.

"I'm ok now I was just a bit emotional"

"sorry" I spluttered out

"Are you sure you look pale"? he stroked my hair back from my face.

I sniffed and reached out for the tissue box beside the sofa and as I took a tissue it hit me again. I hadn't cleaned up from last night and there were tissues everywhere.

I started crying again and covered my face with my hands.

"Baby stop its ok I'm here now"? he rocked me in his strong

Arms and uncovered my face to kiss away my tears. He carried me upstairs and put me on the bed. I wasn't sure if he should see my body like this, he would sure to notice the bruises. Oh Shit, I tensed up as he reached to unbutton my top.

"Baby what's wrong I won't hurt you, I've missed you"?

He nuzzled my neck as his hand went to my nipple and gently squeezed. He felt so safe and his voice was gentle and tender. Hopefully he won't see the bruises on me.

His lips were sucking my nipple and his hand caressed the other nipple. He felt so good.   I was a little sore but I didn't show it. He was Sam my saviour and lover he would always be gentle with me.

His head came up for air and then kissed me tenderly on the lips. His tongue propabing for mine. I gave him what he wanted and our tongues danced together. He pulled away and went to undress me.

"Honey I've missed seeing your hot body"? he cooed ashe undid my buttons and took off my top. His hands stopped and I knew he was inspecting my wounds.

"What the Fuck"? he said and then looked at me.

Tears were rolling down my face and I was biting my lip. He then took off my pants and inspected me further. He rolled me over and took a deep sigh when he saw my red bum cheeks and the bitemarks. He turned me over gently on my back.

"What happened Tasmin"? he asked firmly and wanting an answer.

I couldn't talk. I was shaking and he took me in his arms and rocked me like a baby.

"Sshh   Sshh" he hushed.

After I calmed down, Sam got up and said he was calling the police. I grabbed his arm and begged him not to.

"Why not you can' let this man get away with this"? he angrily and firmly.

"Tasmin he has raped and beaten you"? Sam said alittle too loud and angry.

"No Sam I don't want it public"? I pleaded with him.

"Please just hold me safe"? I held my arms out to him.

He came to me then and lay down beside me and put the blanket on both of us.

"I will never leave you alone again"? Sam said softly in my ear.

I clung to his arms and I felt safe and warm. I could feel his erection and I wanted him. I wanted him to love me. I felt his manhood in my hands and proceeded to slowly arouse him further. His eyes searching mine when I looked into his. His lips met mine tenderly and passionately. He was soft and gentle.

"I will never hurt you baby and if anyone ever hurts you again I will kill them"? He said gently but firmly.

"I want you so bad"? he purred into my neck.

I was lost then his lips were sucking my nipples gently so He wouldn't hurt me. His other hand in my favorite spot being ever so gentle there too.

"Ok"? he looked deep into my eyes.

"Yes" I breathed.

His tongue trailed down to his fingers and he licked and teased me gently. My orgasm was silent but sweet. He entered me after he put on a condom and gently pounded me in and out. He was scared he was hurting me and would look at me for reassurance. I would smile and reassure him back.

"Oh Baby" he cried when his climax was close.

His breathing raggered and he was going faster now to complete his mission. I clung to him and moved with him and closed my eyes and knew this felt so right.   He loved me and I loved him. Our breathing became one and we clung to each other when our orgasms collided. Sam held me close and stroked my hair as I lay there in a dream. He then took me to the shower and washed me gently all over.   He then dried me and wrapped me in a fluffy robe and carried me back to bed.

"Stay here and I will make us a coffee"? Sam got off the bed and went downstairs. I lay there and felt safe and warm. My hero was here and he would look after me. Yes Sam was here and Stefano was not. My emotions were taking over my life and what I needed right now was a man here with me to comfort and protect me.

Where was Stefano when I needed him? I thought to myself at home with his Wife was my answer. Sam was reliable and loving He was certainly a very available and attractive man in every way.
My heart was torn between all my lovers (Addictions). Anton was also still on my mind he was hot and easy going and maybe he was the one.

Phillipe had not rung me and I knew he wanted an answer even though I had told him I didn't love him. I knew I deeply loved two men maybe three, I was narrowing my options down. I snapped out of my thoughts when Sam came back with coffee and chocolate biscuits He must of found them in my cupboard.

Mmm Sweet, hes thought of everything.

I smiled and he smiled back with those come fuck me eyes.

What a darling. My body responding with tingles all over.

We sat up in bed with my cushions behind our backs and drank our coffee and ate chocolate biscuits.

We laughed at each other's jokes and talked easily and happily.

Sam looked into my eyes and held my chin up to meet his strong gaze.

"I love you Tasmin you are beautiful"? he said tenderly.

His lips touched mine and we kissed passionately. His strong arms holding me close against his chest. He was comforting and warm. Sam's hands exploring my body as our tongues danced together. His erection was noticed and he tenderly made love to me asking me all the time if I was ok. He didn't want to hurt me. we showered and dressed then went downstairs to greet the garden and views. It was glorious, the sun was shining, the perfume of roses and a slight breeze. Sam pulled me into his arms.

"Honey I have to do some work or the boss will take it out on me"? he laughed with his sexy smile and eyes.

I laughed,

"Yeh you had better get to work and with no top"? I grinned at him. My eyes finding his and we were locked.

"I want to see sweat"? I added with a wicked smile and then licked my lips.

He was upon me then his lips crushing mine and yet so gentle.

Sam smacked my bottom gently and said in his husky voice

"Baby if youre not careful I will take you here on the patio"?

I clung to him and we kissed passionately again. I wanted him to take me here and now. He picked me up and carried me to the outdoor lounge, He lay me down and I just watched his every move. I was in a trance.

Lust and Desire taking control of my feelings and I felt so carefree and sexy lying there on the lounge.

Sam unbuttoned my top and exposed my bra, my breasts heaving up and down. He undid my bra and released my breasts and cupped them in his hands. It was a big handful. His fingers finding my nipples and gently pinching them. Our eyes locked together while he seduced me slowly and gently.

The anticipation was such a turn on and very seductive.His lips finding my nipples gently nipping and sucking, I arched my back and went with desire and pleasure My body wanting more and more. His tongue trailed down to my sensitive spot and Sam removed my jeans and knickers.

"You wont need these honey" he purred while his eyes were on my pussy now licking his lips as he was about to feast.

I lay there and looked at this gorgeous hunk. I am so lucky. He was about to take me over the edge and I couldn't help feel suddenly great amount of love lust and desire for this man. He certainly loved me. He was more than an addiction.

Sam teased and teased and made me beg him to stop

"Baby let go" he whispered to me when he knew I was close.

"Open your eyes honey so you can see me"? his husky voice raggered as he had a mouthful.

I opened my eyes and Sam's eyes were there while his tongue was doing amazing things His fingers exploring as well. I cried out when my orgasm exploded and Sam lapped me Up and then prepared himself for more. He entered me slowly and gently looking deep into my   Eyes to seek any sign of pain. I smiled at him and reassured him. I clung to his big arms and wrapped my legs around his bum while he pumped and thrusted to a explosive sensual Rythum.

His breathing was raggered and mine was no better. We came together, our bodies intertwined.

"Oh honey youre going to give me a heart attack"? he said when he finally got his breath back. I laughed and hugged him.

Sam withdrew and got up.   Removed the condom and dressed

"Drink"? he asked as I lay there exposed still looking at him with dreamy eyes.

"Yes please" "non alcoholic" I added with a sexy smile.

"Yes Mam" he winked at me and left.

I got up and dressed and then heard a noise from the bushes in the far corner. was it a bird? I thought to myself.

I put my flats on and wandered over towards the bushes.

I suddenly heard footsteps and I stopped short and froze. somebody was in the bushes and I suddenly felt vulnerable and scared.

"Who's there"? I yelled out loud hoping I would scare them.

I heard the bushes moving and then a flash of a black jacket and a car start up. I moved into the bush to see more and a white pickup truck took off quickly on the street. The windows were tinted and I couldn't see the number plate.

"Tasmin where are you"? I jumped when I heard Sam calling me.

"Coming" I yelled and half ran back to the house.

"What were you doing"? Sam looked at me.

"A bird was making a lot of noise in the bush so I went to see if it was ok"? I answered hoping he believed me.

I didn't see the point of telling him about James and his evil ways. Sam could get hurt, James is definitely a unstable person with big problems. I couldn't trust him.

Sam took my hand and led me to the patio. We sat there and enjoyed our non alcohol drinks and Sam even made biscuits and cheese.

Wow a girl sure could get used to this.

"Well beautiful boss woman I have to do a little bit of work"? he got up and then leant down and kissed me on the lips.

"Ok sweetie" I purred back at him.

Sam left to do some mowing and tidy up the hedge. I sat there and thought about what just happened in the bushes. was someone watching us. Did they see anything? Thoughts were going around my head.

I got up and went inside and got the binoculars and went down to the bushes. I crouched down in the cover of the bush and looked without the binoculars.You could see the patio and the lounge easily even though it seemed along way away. I then picked up the binoculars and looked and gasped when the view was clear and close.

Whoever it was they would have seen everything.

Shit Shit!! Now I was worried. I moved through the bush and could see where they had climbed the fence. The road is down from the bank easily accessible foranyone to climb.

I went back to the house and wondered what to do.I can't tell Sam he would go balistic. I would have to be more careful.

I went inside and tied up the kitchen. The phone rang and I answered it.

"Hello Baby" Stefano's voice was deep and husky.

"Hi Stefano" I whispered back.

"How are you"? he asked gently.

"I'm ok" I answered I didn't want to tell him that my lover was here comforting, protecting and fucking me.

"You don't sound ok"? he enquired again being gentle.

"I'm fine really you shouldn't worry" I replied trying to sound chirpy and happy.

"I do worry honey I miss you"? he said in a sexy voice.

"I miss you too" I whispered back,   my tears were now swelling up.

"Tasmin honey I love you and I want to make it up to you, I have been an idiot and stupid to let you go"? he said with compassion.

I didn't know what to say I just listened.

"Baby are you there"? he breathed into the phone.

I whispered back I'm here.

"I need to see you baby girl"?   his voice was urgent.

"I'm coming over in two weeks whether you like it or not"?

He said with firmness.

"Ok" I nodded at the same time holding the phone to my ear in a daze.

"Tasmin we need to talk and work out some things"? he said Calmly and softly.

"Yes" I breathed back.

"Ring me later so we can have some fun"? he asked sexily

"Ok" I replied still in a daze.

"I will talk to you later"? he asked again softly

"Love you" he hung up the phone.

I looked at the phone and couldn't believe he still wants me.   I said some nasty things and I wasn't sure I could trust him again.

I heard the mower stop and I snapped out of my daze.

Stefano would have to wait Sam was here and that was all that matters.

I went and got a cool drink for Sam and took it out to him.

"Thanks honey" he took the drink from me and winked.

Oooh I could melt into those come fuck me eyes.

I giggled and watched the sweat run down his back.

"Whats funny"? he asked with a cheeky smile

"nothing" I giggled again.

He grabbed me and pulled me in to his sweaty chest and arms.

"You want sweat I'll give you sweat"? he held me tightly and kissed my lips and preyed my mouth open to receive his tongue.

He smelt of grass, sweat and man.

I felt my knees buckle and I clung to him.

Sam felt my need and lifted me into his arms and carried me inside to the sofa.

"No No you need a shower"? I wriggled free.

I ran up the stairs with Sam right behind me smacking my bum gently.

I giggled and kept running to the bedroom.

He grabbed me and dragged me to the shower.

He stripped off my clothes nearly ripping the buttons on my top in frustration.

He peeled his jeans and boxers off and we entered the warm shower.

Sam washed me all over, his hands sliding up and down

My body.   I then did the same to him. After washing his body I let my hand cover his manhood which was standing
To attention.   God he was sexy and hot.

I went down on my knees and covered his knob with my mouth. I sucked and rolled my tongue around the top like I was devowing a lollie pop.

I then took more of him and sucked and teased as his hips were jerking to take more of him. He was close now and I gave him no mercy, I sucked him like a hoover.

Sam let out a groan and his juice squirted out over my face and breasts. Sam pulled me up and washed me and laughed.

"Told you to be careful"? he teased we kissed then and let the water flow over us.

"I want you in bed"? Sam said sexily

He dried me and wrapped me in a fluffy towel and then carried me to bed. Yep a girl sure could get used to this.

Once again Sam took me over the edge making sure I was comfortable and not in pain. He was so considerate.

"That was beautiful baby" he purred in my ear.

I was in a dream world my body was numb with love and my thoughts were of only Sam. Strong, reliable Sexy Sam. We lay together and listened to each other's heartbeat. We were very relaxed and didn't need to talk. After we both came back to earth, we got up and showered Sam wanting to take me again in the shower, I didn't argue. It was lunchtime and I fixed us some lunch and then we went out on the patio to enjoy food and each other's company. We had a lovely day and before Sam left he made love to me again.Telling me he would be back tomorrow night and that he would stay with me for awhile. I said it wasn't necessary and that I would be ok. He said he had made up his mind and that was the end of it.

I didn't argue and we kissed passionately and I clung to him, I didn't want him to go.

"I have to check on Mum and Dad and then I will be back"? he hugged me tight.

I watched him go and locked up Fort Knox I felt better then. I lit the fire and made a drink and sat down and watched the flames dance around.

I phoned Maddy and we chatted for a while.   We arranged to meet at our usual Café on Saturday for lunch.

Maddy said she would let Max know.

I then rang Stefano and we talked for a while until he was getting aroused on the phone.

"I need you"? he said huskily through the phone.

"I don't know about anything anymore"? I said all confused.

"It's going to be alright, I love you baby"? he said softly through the phone.

"Is it over between you and Danielle"? I asked

"Yes it is over she wanted to continue a relationship but Itold her I loved you and you only"? he replied

"oh I see" I answered still not sure of anything.

"I will be coming in two weeks and I want us to talk about everything and sort stuff out"? he asked tenderly.

"Alright I would like that and maybe we can talk about everything"? I replied feeling a little better now.

"Good Honey that's great, I can't wait to see you"? he purred into the phone.

"I miss you too"? I replied thinking that maybe we can work things out and that I still love this man.

He still was my obsession, my addiction. I didn't want to let him go.

"Honey I want you now"? Stefano purred huskily

"What do you want"? I asked cheekily

"I want you naked and hot"? he replied impatiently

"I want to feel you all over"? I purred back.

"Baby youre teasing me"? he replied huskily.

"Have you got a handful"? I asked wickedly

"Honey its huge and throbbing"? he replied in a deep voice.

"Baby I want to take you in my mouth and suck you hard"?
I answered feeling all hot and horny.

I knew Sam was still outside working so I had some time. I didn't think he should know what I'm doing inside having phone sex with my lover. I don't think he would understand.

"Baby you feel so good"? I purred through the phone.

"Oh honey give it to me"? he groaned back

"Baby my pussy is purring for you"? I cheekily replied

"I want to eat you"? he was close now.

"Give it to me honey you're so hot"? I urged him on

Stefano let out a groan and I knew I had completed my mission of lust over the phone.

"Feel better honey"? I asked laughing

"I'll feel better when I'm fucking you properly"? he slurred back.

"Baby I have to go now I will ring you tonight"? I said as

He asked for more.

"Ok Ok but I want more tonight"? he replied firmly

"I love you Tasmin" Stefano then hung up.

Sam came into the house then and snapped me out of my lustful thoughts, I was feeling rather randy after my sexual tease on the phone.

"Honey there you are I've been looking for you"? he asked

With those Come Fuck Me Eyes.

"Honey I was just doing some laundry"? I answered trying not to show my lie.

"Come here you little wild woman"? he grabbed me then and pulled me close into his strong arms.

Our lips met and our tongues collided and once again our bodies responded by wanting more.

"I want you Tasmin"? he whispered in my ear.

"I want you too"? I whispered back.

With those words Sam picked me up and carried me upstairs to the bedroom. He laid me on the bed and then begun to devow my clothing slowly, kissing me as he did. His lips stopping at my breasts to give them full attention. His other hand pulling down my silk pants and knickers. His finger found my sensitive spot and I laid there and let go.

"Honey youre wet"? he purred as his head went to join his finger.

Sam feasted on me and brought me to a climax. I arched my back up and could not control that beautiful feeling taking over my body. Sam was preparing himself and I lay there in anticipation. He entered me slowly and thrusted his manhood deeper into me. I groaned with pleasure and wrapped my legs around his bum and thrusted with him He was groaning now and I knew he was close. He pounded me harder and more urgent. Our breathing becoming one. His orgasm hit mine and we lay together in each other's arms until our bodies came back to normal.

"That was great Baby" Sam nuzzled my neck.

"Sure was" I replied feeling satisfied with my sexual release.

Sam had to leave soon and I lay there and watched him get dressed. What a hunk! What a body! What a man! I was still very confused, I love Stefano, but I love Sam.

"Are you checking me out"? Sam looked at me with those eyes.

"Yeh and I like what I see"? I replied with a smile.

"Is that so"? he winked at me.

I giggled and hid under the covers.

He jumped on the bed and found me under the covers and covered my lips with his.

"See you soon"? Sam said tenderly.

I got up and dressed when he went to go. I had to lock up Fort Knox, I still didn't feel safe. I watched Sam leave and a part of me was sad but another part of me was happy. I was a lucky girl, I have all these men who want to own me. But do I want to be owned by one man. I wasn't so sure. I ate a light meal and then showered and went to bed. Stefano rang and we again had incredible phone sex. I fell into a deep sleep with no bad dreams. I woke up early and got ready for work.   I knew Jaine' would be happy to have me back. I arrived at work early and eager.

Jaine' was there bubbly as ever.

"Tassy you look fantastic" she hugged me tight.

I didn't feel fantastic I felt confused, but happy to be back   at work.

"It's good to see you" I hugged her back.

After we chatted over coffee we set out to work. There were cakes to be made and flowers to be made also. We got through the day easily and quickly, all our jobs accomplished. We said our goodbyes and I headed home.

On the way I dropped in to see Jake at the Café .He wasn't there, the new lady told me he wasn't coming back and that he was setting up a new Café in New York. Well done Jake I thought to myself even though a small part of me missed him. I arrived home and made myself a Jack Daniels and sat on the patio and enjoyed the sunset. My garden looked amazing at night with fairy lights and solar lights everywhere. It was enchanting. I suddenly felt a cold chill down my back and shivered I felt like I was not alone. I have ran to the doors and went inside and locked up Fort Knox. I grabbed the phone and made a drink and went upstairs. I pushed my dresser up against my door and made myself a Prisoner in my bedroom. Shit I can't live like this I thought to myself. The phone rang and I jumped God I'm so on edge. Stefano's voice was comforting and made me cry.

Shit what's with all the emotions lately I thought as I   tried to control myself.

"Honey are you alright"? he said tenderly and gentle.

God I wished he was here.

"No not really"? I replied with a snob.

"What's wrong Baby"? he purred in his sexy voice.

"I'm a bit scared at home by myself at the moment"?

I answered back quietly, and waiting for his reaction.

"What do you mean scared"? he urged me on.

"I heard a noise and I'm a bit jumpy"? I replied

"so I'm in my bedroom and I locked and barricaded the   door"? I added.

"Tasmin ring the police and ask them to do a check"? he was firm now."

"No its ok honestly" I tried to sound convincing.

"Honey if you don't ring them I will"? he half yelled down the phone.

"Alright Alright I will ok"? I said back loudly.

"Baby I don't mean to upset you Shit I 'm booking a   flight I need to be there to protect you"? he was fuming

You could hear it in his voice.

"I might go and stay with Maddy"? I said feeling a bit better now.

"That's a good idea I would feel much happier if   youre safe with her" he answered in his deep voice.

"I miss you Baby"? he purred through the phone.

"We need bloody skype"? he added annoyed.

I giggled and he then laughed too.

"Honey I will talk to you all night and so you won't be alone ok"? he huskily said.

I wished he was with me. Shit why did Sam go I felt safe with him too and he lived closer.

"Baby I want to hear you come over the phone"? he purred I lay on the bed and got comfortable, getting my trust friend out of the drawer on Stefano's instructions.

"Oh honey let the vibrator be my fingers and cock"? he urged me on.

I lay there and buzzed away letting the tingling take over my body. It was beautiful and Stefano whispered sweet dirty talk to me telling me he was licking me all over and then fucking me Like a Wildman. I knew the Wildman had his cock in his hand and was getting his own release.My orgasm was a soothing release and I let go some of my tension. I felt better now.

"Thanks Baby that was beautiful and I needed that"? he said huskily through the phone.

I curled up with the phone to my ear and we talked for another hour. We did another round of hot phone sex and then I said I had to sleep.

"Love you honey and remember to sleep with the phone and I still think you should ring the police"? he had his serious voice now.

"Ok baby I will, love you too" and I quickly hung up.

Well he didn't like that and my phone rang 5secs later.

"Don't just hang up like that and leave me without a proper answer"? he still was firm.

God he was persistant. He wouldn't let go.

"Tasmin I want you to ring the police and ask them to do

A sweep please"? he said gently now.

"Ok I will I promise so I will hang up and ring them ok. I love you and I will ring you tomorrow"? I said gently and softly.

"Ok Baby I will talk to you tomorrow and I love and cant wait to see you"? he purred in my ear in that sexy deep voice.

"Goodnight honey" I purred back

"Goodnight my Princess" he cooed back and hung up.

I lay there and thought about my feelings for Stefano and then Sam. I loved them both. How could I decide. Maybe I will have to see them both without them knowing I thought thinking that's very deceitful. No I can't do that I will have to one way or the other decide who. Should I ring the police I got up and went to the windowand had a little peek I couldn't see anything and I couldn't see any cars near my drive.I went to the bathroom and got ready for bed. I curled up and hugged a pillow wishing it was either Sam or Stefano. I fell into a deep sleep and I'm sure my dreams were of those two hunks fighting over me and then the one that wins gets to fuck me.

I woke when my alarm went off and lay there for ten minutes and thought about my day ahead. I would ring Maddy before I left for work and organize my going there. I showered and dressed. I put on a black mini and the gorgeous silk blouse Stefano brought me in Zurich. Rang Maddy over breakfast which for me was yoghurt or   Toast and She said she would love the company and also   Asked if James had been hanging around and is that why I Need to leave. Maddy knew me so well I was an independent woman who has lived on her own quite safely for the past 7 to 8 years alone.

Have you rung the police she added firmly. Shit she wasn't going to let up either. Yes Yes I lied hoping it would keep her off my back.

I'II see you around 5 Maddy said as she hung up.

I grabbed my suitcase and packed a week's clothing and   things for work and play.

Locked up Fort Knox and drove to work I arrived at work in perfect time.   Jaine' was bubbly as ever.   We hugged each other and kissed on the cheeks.

"How are you Tassy I've missed you"? she squeezed me again.

"I'm good and its great to see you too" I squeezed her back.

"How is Jean-Paul"? I asked her when we separated.

"Not so good I'm afraid he has been seeing other women and I don't know how I feel about that"? she said alittle sadly.

"So we are having some time apart until he knows what he wants"? she added with a sigh.

"Oh sorry to hear that Jaine" I hugged her again and she sighed in my arms.

"I was enjoying our time together and I liked being pampered by a man and the sex of course"? she continued on.

"You can meet other men for companionship"? I said trying to cheer her up.

"Yes you are right I will keep my eyes open"? Quil laughed

"Qui Qui" I giggled.

"Well off to work we have a big week and lots to talk about and plan"? she said getting our aprons.

We baked and iced and made chocolate flowers. We made the usual cakes and we filled the cake cabinets with fresh cakes, croissants, chocolate and slices. Our day busy working and then drinking coffee and chatting about our week ahead.

The day went quickly and we both hugged and l left and Jaine' said she would stay and lock up. I drove to Maddy's unaware Jame's was watching me go.

James watched me drive off and then spotted Jaine still at the shop. Mmm I might get some afternoon cake he thought to himself. He went into the shop just as Jaine' was about to lock the door.

"Oh sorry sir I am closing now"? she looked at James and then remember him from the other day.

"Oh its you"? she said smiling.

James smiled back Shit she was a bit old for me but she had big tits and he sure liked big tits.

"Sorry I didn't know you were going to close and I was

Driving past and saw your lights on and remembered how delicious your cakes are"? he said gently flashing his smile.

Jaine' smiled back why not his young and cute no harm and opened the door further so he could enter.She then locked the door behind her. James smiled to himself.

"What would you like"? she purred at him in her French accent.

James was very turned on her voice and smiled sweetly at her.

"That chocolate cake I had last time was to die for"? he looked at her and then licked his lips. Jaine' blushed when he did this and thought how naughty

This man was flirting with her.   She also was a little turned on.   I mean she was attractive and she was upset over Jean-Paul. No harm in him flirting with me.

" in the back fridge you can come out here and eat one with coffee"? she looked at him thinking would he think she was a bit forward.

"I would love to"? he was so polite.

"I'm Jaine"? she offered her hand to him.

"Peter" he shook her hand and smiled. He followed her to the back and watched her arse swayIn her tight skirt licking his lips as he followed. She offered him a chair and he sat down. Jaine' got him his cake and coffee and sat down beside him and had some coffee.

James put some chocolate cake on the spoon and let his tongue seduce the chocolate as Jaine watched mesmerized.

"You are very attractive"? James purred at her.

She blushed and then James came in to kiss her. She obliged and was in his spell. His tongue devowing hers and Jaine' could not stop, her body betraying her making her feel very aroused. She had not had sex for weeks and she was very aroused by this stranger. James went to her blouse buttons but hesitated and looked into her eyes for approval.

"May I suck your nipples"? he asked greedily

"That's a bit forward"? Jaine' giggled looking at him.

"Have you got some cream I want cream on them"? he sounded like a spolit brat.

Jaine was shocked, her mouth was open, should she let this young man seduce her. She blushed and he nuzzled her neck whispering that his tongue could do magic things. Why the hell not I'm free and hes seems like a charming young man. Jaine went to the fridge and produced a bowl of cream. She put some in a smaller bowl and took it over to the bench.

"Have you somewhere more comfortable"? he asked as his eyes were looking at her greedily.

"Well yes a small room out the back with a lounge"? she said understanding why.

She led him out there and James thought how easy to get this Slut to fuck me, Oh wait till I tell Tasmin I fucked her boss. He smiled to himself. He told Jaine' to lie on the bed. He also told her he wanted to rip her clothing off as he has a fetish for that and would she mind.

Jaine' was in a spell she could see his bulge and she didn't care what he did as long as she got that with cream in her mouth. She nodded in her trance. James ripped her blouse down the middle and exposed her bra with big tits spilling out the top. His hands went to fondle them but not gently.

"Oooh Baby gently"? Jaine' purred at him

James took no notice of her he was going to be boss and make her beg. He unclipped her bra and took her blouse and bra off. Jaine's breasts were a eye full and Jame's was very aroused. He wanted to spert his sperm all over them. He got some cream on his finger and circled her nipple. His head then went down to suckle.   He licked and sucked hard and Jaine' screamed out to stop. But she wanted more and she liked this dominent man.She couldn't stop him. He put more cream on the other nipple and repeated the torture Making her whimper and beg him to stop and then beg him for more. Jaine's hand playing with his bulge through his pants until he unleashed his weapon and put cream on it for Jaine to feast Jaine obliged opening her mouth to receive and sucked obediently. James pinching her nipples and molding her big tits with his hands. He then got Jaine to straddle his face while she pobbed up and down on his cock. Putting more cream on as she sucked greedily.James licked and finger fucked her pussy until Jain started to beg to go faster and then she climaxed in hismouth. Jaine' sucked Jame's hard and fast and he couldn't control it anymore. He pulled out and spurted semen all over her tits and face. Jaine' laughed and said how naughty he was and that she should spank him.

Well James thought I'm the one going to spank you woman so you better watch what you say.   He was angry now. He told her to get up and clean her tits and then return back here on all fours. Jaine' was turned by this game and did exactly what he asked.

"Oooh yes Sir" she purred as she cleaned herself up.

She got on all fours and waited in anticipation of his next command. James prepared himself and ploughed into her roughly and hard.

"Who's the boss Baby"? he thrusted into her making her whimper with pleasure.

She had not had this much attention for a while since Jean-Paul left and Jean-Paul was not like this wild dominant lover which she quite liked as Jeanpaul was more submissive and lay there for her to do all the work. She went with it knowing it was very wicked.

Oh no one will know I will keep this a secret she thought as James continued his thrusts and pinching her nipples. James was enjoying this game and made her beg for more. He would gain her trust and then take her all the way next time. Oh yes there will be a next time. Jaine's orgasm was loud and James came soon after. He withdrew from her and then lent down and bit her on her bum cheek quite hard. Jaine screamed out in pain but James rubbed and kissed it

Better putting his finger inside her as he did it.

Oh my he wants more she thought as she winced from the pain but then received pleasure from his fingers.

What is his game she thought as she turned to look at him.

"That hurt Baby boy"? she looked at him with big eyes and a sexy look.

James leant in to kiss her and apologized for his roughness

"Sorry I got carried away I couldn't control myself youre so hot and horny"? he gave her a sweet smile and then kissed her again gently on the lips.

"Can I see you again for chocolate cake and coffee"? he asked ever so charming that any woman would have relented to.

"Yes I would like that but next time come to my flat"? she replied with a beautiful smile.

"That would be very nice thank you"? James had her in his spell.

Jaine and James left the room and Jaine opened the door for
James.
He leant down and kissed her tenderly

"Keep this our secret my hot love"? he whispered in her ear as he went to go through the door.

She nodded and closed the door and locked it. Oh my did that just happen she giggled to herself. That was very naughty but nice. She grabbed her bag put on security and went home with a   smile and hot dreams. I had got to Maddy's and she was there to greet me.

"Hi honey" she hugged me tightly.

"Hi beautiful girl" I hugged her back.

"Lets get you settled" she took me to my room.

"thanks for letting me stay" I said looking at her.

"What's going on Tasmin"? she was serious now.

"I'm lonely at home and I don't feel safe"? I tried to reassure her with a calm voice not really telling her I was raped by a stranger with a mask and I'm not sure if it was James or not.

"I'll be ok"? I hugged her.

"Ok lets relax and have a drink"? she grabbed my hand and led me to the bar.

"Lets have cocktails and get pissed"? she giggled.

"Ok" I replied just glad to feel safe with someone else.

Maddy made us some sex on the beach cocktails and they were yummy. We had two and were feeling it. She put some music on and we danced around the lounge room. We finally sat down and had another drink.

"Oh I havent told you yet Scott and Rick are dropping

By"? she said with a sexy smile.

"For dinner and sweets"? she laughed

"Why didn't you tell me I look like crap"? I suddenly wanted to go and get freshened up.

"When will they be here"? I asked

"Soon so lets go and get ready"? She grabbed my hand and we went into her bedroom.

"What will we wear"? she asked me.

"I don't know are we being seduced or are we seducing"? I asked not sure.

"Both"? she answered as she went through her wardrobe.

"Oh I'm not sure if I want to complicate my life with these men at the moment"? I said trying not to look at her sadly.

"Nonsense you need cheering up and whats better two hot men or a scrabble game"? she looked at me and smiled.

"Yeah she was right no point moping around and feeling sorry for myself" I thought.

I had rung Sam earlier and told him I was staying at Maddy's and that he should stay with his parents and that I would see him soon.   He was happy I was at Maddy's and said he would see me on the weekend.

So once again I was alone and feeling horny.

Maddy wanted me to wear a black lace top with a suspenders and a black mini. You could see my black bra underneath the lace it was very sexy. Maddy also chose a see through top with a black bra. Her long legs were gorgeous with a mini that barely covered her arse. We curled our hair and put make up on. Jewellery was our last item and stilettos.

Hot Hot Hot we looked at ourselves in the mirror. We looked good enough to eat! We giggled and went downstairs and prepared dinner. Entrée of seafood cocktail, Rack of Lamb, and Chocolate Mousse with Baileys. I did the entrée and put it in the fridge. Maddy had done the mousse and put it in wine glasses and in the fridge. We prepared string beans and a potatoe anna. We then set the table with candlesticks, flowers and MaddylLit the fire. There everything was done. We made fresh drinks and waited for the men to arrive. The doorbell chimed right on cue and Maddy got up and greeted our guests. I stood when they entered the room and their faces had big smiles on them.

"Tasmin how lovely to see you again" Rick embraced me hugging me tightly so I could feel his body against mine.

"Rick nice to see you too" I hugged him back.

Scott moved in then to hug me too and I obliged him also.

"Girls you both look hot and delicious tonight"? Scott licked his lips and winking at us both.

Well we both blushed and Maddy got their drinks and settled down on the sofa's to chat.

Rick and I sat on one and Maddy and Scott sat on the other.

Scott's eyes boar into my breasts and I could see what he was thinking.

Rick also was staring at Maddy's breasts showing through her top.

"Can we have a taste before dinner"? Rick asked me as he turned to me for a kiss.

His lips met mine and his tongue was there teasing mine. His hand went to my breast and pinched my nipple through the lace and bra. I looked over at Maddy and she was getting the same treatment. Rick's hand was going up my mini to my pussy which was starting pulstate. I let him enter me with his finger and he circled my clit and teased me some more. I then withdrew his finger and sucked it.

"You sure taste good Baby"? he said huskily, his eyes greedy with lust and desire.

He made me lie back and he pulled my g/string down and his head went to where his finger had been. He spread my legs and put his tongue and finger on my sensitive spot and feasted like a hungry lion. I could hear Maddy climaxing on the next couch and that made me go over the edge. I climaxed too and let that beautiful feeling take over my body.

"Well that was part of entrée' she said as she got up to get the real entrée.

I got up and helped her after putting back on my g and arranging my mini.

"God that was great"? Maddy said as I followed her into the kitchen.

"It was pretty good to start the night"? I agreed.

We took entrée to the table where the boys were seated with smiles. We ate with lots of yummy sounds as it was delicious. Main would be aleast half an hour so we got more drinks and went back to the sofa's.

The boys were randy as hell and their bulges were a real turn on. Maddy had got some tissues ready for our next feast. The boys unleashed their throbbing dicks for us to tease and suck. We obliged by going on our knees and teased the boys with our tongues and lips.

I took Rick hard and fast giving him no relief and showing him no mercy.

"You wildcat"? he hissed at me through gritted teeth.

He grabbed some tissues and quickly withdrew and spurt in into them. I looked up at him and smiled.

He looked at me and gave me a sexy look of dreamy eyes.

"Dinner is ready"? Maddy called out snapping us out of our thoughts.

Rick helped me up and kissed me on the lips.

"Baby that was great" he purred me.

We sat down to a delicious dinner and the boys kept praising us on our cooking skills. We cleared the table and made drinks and relaxed by the fire. The boys were still horny as anything and asked cheekily if we could do girl on girl action while they fucked us. We giggled and nodded saying how naughty and wicked they were. Maddy kissed me on the lips and then starting undressing me. The boys were in a trance. They couldn't keep their eyes off us. Maddy left my suspenders, stockings and stilettos on. She then caressed my breasts and sucked my nipples. I went along for the ride and let her take control. I then undressed her and did naughty things to her breasts. She then lay down and spread her legs for me to feast and tease. I went on all fours and licked and tickled her sensitive spot. Scott came behind me and gently entered me with little thrusts. His hands on my hips pulling me with him back and forth. Rick put his erection in Maddy's mouth and we all groaned loudly as our orgy had started.Lust and desire took us all over the edge and then we all swapped positions and the boys pumped us again.

After our sexual appetite was satisfied we had sweets down by the fire. We spoon fed the boys and they spoon fed us.It wasn't long before chocolate mousse was on our nipples for them to suckle. The boys prepared themselves for another round of lust and we all sucked chocolate mousse off each other's bodies. They then fucked us again and then we had two at once. We were all sticky from chocolate mousse we all went to the shower.

Rick and I went to mine and Scott and Maddy went to hers. There was no way we could fit 4 in the shower. Rick soaped me all over dipping in all my sensitive places. I knew he wanted more so I thought what the hell might as well. He circled my forbidden place with the sponge and then eased himself gently into me His other fingers inside my pussy.

I leant forward with my hands against the wall and let him take me over the edge. My orgasm exploded around me and my knees became weak. Rick came loudly and was very gentle the whole time making sure he wasn't too rough.

We washed again and then dried off and I put a fluffy robe on.Rick put his jeans on and his shirt open down the front. He had a great body and god he looked so hot.   I wanted to have him again.

We went out to the fire and I made some coffee. Maddy and Scott joined us soon after and we all laughed and chatted easily. I yawned and my eyelids were heavy I could hardly keep my eyes open .

"Come honey I will put you to bed"? Scott held his hand to mine.

Yeh sure I thought he wants more we are obviously swapping again. I kissed Rick goodnight and Maddy and took Scott's hand. He led me to my room and laid me on the bed

"Your'e gorgeous Baby"? he lay down beside me and traced my robe around my breasts.

He pulled the sash open and exposed my breasts to him. His finger circling my nipple and then the other one. My body betraying me once again. I let Scott make passionate love to me and once again he did. Not disappoint.My climax was incredible just like everyone before it. My body numb from our episode and I felt safe And content in his arms and fell asleep. I woke in the morning to my alarm and rolled over to Scott.

He was stirring and he gave me a beautiful good morning smile. He kissed me tenderly and we both got up and showered. Morning sex was the best and Scott once again took me to another place. We washed again and then I got dressed for work. Scott kissed me goodbye and said he was great to catch up And maybe he would see me later.I went downstairs and Rick was also getting ready to go. He kissed me goodbye and said it was a great night one he would remember. Maddy and I sat there with our coffee and toast and laughed about our wicked night. We left for work and didn't notice James sitting in his pickup truck down the road. He saw two men come out of the apartment and he was fuming.

"What the hell"? I'll teach her to play with fire.

I will see you soon Tasmin and this time you won't forget.   Soon my love we will be together. I arrived at work and Jaine' was bubbly as ever.

"Good morning Tassy" she chirped and then hugged me.

"Good morning Jaine' you're looking happy"? I hugged her back.

"Oh Tassy I feel wonderful" she beamed back.

I laughed and we both got to work.   Lots of baking and making icing flowers.

We sat down and had a coffee and made sandwiches.

"You are in good mood"? I looked at her.

"Iam happy and love is a wonderful thing"? she replied with a beautiful smile.

"Love what do you mean is Jean-Paul back on the scene"? I asked her with big eyes.

"Well no I met someone last night and he was very charming and was very attentive to my needs"? she replied with a big smile.

"Oh I see"? I answered not wanting to know all the details.

"Well if you're happy then I'm happy for you"? I added.

We got back to work and got everything ready for tomorrow.

"See you tomorrow"? Jaine' hugged me and I hugged her back.

I left and Jaine' said she wanted to stay and do a few more things.

Jaine' actually was hoping Peter would drop by and she was excited about the thought of his lustful ways.

She didn't have to wait long, there was a knock at the door and she half ran to answer it.

Peter (James) stood at the door with beautiful red roses and a big smile.

"Come in Come in"? she said sexily in her French accent.

Peter entered the shop and gave her the flowers.

"Thank you Peter there beautiful" she chirped happily.

He leant in to kiss her on the lips.   Jaine' obliged and let his tongue take control of her mouth.

Her body wanting his touch and he strained up against her with his erection.

"Lets go to my place"? she looked at him with big eyes.

"Sounds good to me"? he replied licking his lips.

Jaine' locked up and Peter followed her in his truck to her place.

Jaine' made a platter of anitpasto and wine and they sat there and drank and ate and laughed together.

Peter kissed her on her lips and his hands went to her blouse.

"You cant rip my clothes off again, I will run out of clothes if you keep doing that"? she looked at him and he nodded.

He thought to himself I must be gentle and gain her trust and then she would love me and do whatever I want.

He unbuttoned her Blouse and hesitated when he exposed her breasts. God they were big and round.   Her nipples erect and waiting to be suckled like a baby.

His lips went to her nipples and he sucked and teased her until he knew she was ready for fucking.

He unleashed his weapon and put a condom on and entered her gently. Jaine' was in bliss with her young lover.   She did what ever he said and when he asked to take her anally she did not refuse.

"Let me take you in the shower"? he purred in her ear.

She lead him to the shower and let him take her over the edge even though he was a little rough but her orgasm took over her body so she let him take her again and again.

After their lovemaking   Jaine' led him back to her bed where he whispered sweet words in her ear.

She fell asleep in his arms and woke early.   Peter had already gone but left a rose and a note on his pillow.

"See you soon my love"? he had written.

She picked up the rose and smelt it and then read the note. She hugged herself in glee and thought how lucky she was. She got ready for work and sang to herself as she did. Tasmin had a quiet night with Maddy and woke full of beans. She got ready for work and arrived just as Jaine' was unlocking the shop. The day went quickly and all the orders were nearly ready. One more day and they would be done.

"Goodnight Tassy"? Jaine' chirped happily hoping her secret lover would surprise her again.

"Goodnight Jaine'" I replied hugging her.

Gee she was awfully happy obviously her new friend was pleasing her. Good I thought she deserves to be happy.I left and drove home to Maddy's and got there quickly as I wanted to sit and have a Jack Daniels.

I decided to run a bath and relax, Maddy had left a message saying she was at a meeting and would probably be late would that be ok? I didn't mind as a Bath and Drink was all I wanted. I put some music on and I sank into the bath and didn't hear the back door being forced open. I hadn't put on the alarm but had locked the doors. I relaxed in the bath and let the bubbles smother my body.

I didn't hear the bathroom door open and James entered and stood there and watched, licking his lips. God she looked hot in the bath, he thought as his erection was growing in his pants. I opened my eyes and got the fright of my life.What the fuck! James was standing there, how did he get in.

"What are you doing here"? I yelled at him.

"I'm here to see you"? he replied huskily.

"Get the Fuck Out"? I yelled again.

"I don't think so"? James replied looking at her breasts that were visible now.

"You must leave or I will ring police"? I spat him angrily.

"What with this phone"? he said as he crushed my moblie on the bathroom floor.

I was scared now and looked around for a weapon. There was nothing I could use to defend myself. James was undressing and getting ready for his mission. His erection jutting upward ready for action. Shit I was trapped. I went to get up from the bath and he pushed me back down.

"I want you there"? he said firmly, and his eyes were boaring into mine.

"You're fucking mad"? I screamed at him.

"Maddy will be home any minute"? I warned him.

"Don't think so I think she is at a Meeting"? he said with a sly smile.

"How would you know that"? I asked with disgust.

"Tasmin I know everything my love"? he was naked now and he grabbed my arms and pulled me out of the bath and pushed me on the cold floor.

"I'm going to make love to you baby"? he purred at me holding my hands above my head.

His body crushing mine beneath him. I could not move I was once again his victim. He pushed his erection into me and ploughed deeper and deeper groaning as he did. His lips sucking my nipples roughly and I closed my eyes and thought about Sam or Stefano who once again was not there to protect me. He groaning was loud now and I knew he was close. He withdrew and spurted his horrible seed over my tits and belly. He then pulled me up and made me get back into the bath.

He washed me and then put me on all fours and I knew he wanted more.

Oh God will he ever let me go? I thought to myself.

He plunged into me and took me roughly and would bite my back and shoulders as he analing raped me.   His hands molding my breasts and pinching my nipples roughly and I tried to scream out in pain.

"No one will hear you Baby"? he cooed in my ear as he emptied himself on my back.

He washed me again and then pulled me up and out of the bath.

He put a towel around me and told me to stand still.

I was shaking all over and I begun to cry.

"SShh" he wrapped his arms around me.

"It's ok honey I love you"? James held me tight.

I stood there in his arms and didn't say anything. Nothing I say could make him go away and leave me alone.

"Come baby back to bed"? he led me to the bed and made me lie down.

James had washed himself and took his towel off to expose yet another erection.

Not more I thought I just want him gone.

James had no intention of leaving not yet anyway.

"Suck me Baby"? he purred into my ear.

"No I wont you pig"? I spat at him angrily.

"You will honey and you will enjoy it"? he answered back firmly. He wanted Tasmin's lips wrapped around his cock and sucking him like a wildcat.

I looked at him and he looked back and smiled.

"Baby do this and then I will go"? he said softly and gently.

I looked at him.   Could I trust him.

"I promise baby just suck me"? he held his huge cock in his hand ready for me to oblige.

"Ok but then you will go and leave me alone"? I asked shocked with myself for giving in.

"Yes I will"? he was anxious now he wanted her lips, and now.

I took his cock in my mouth and tried not to gagg.   I imagined it was Sam and let my mouth and tongue do the work.

"Oh Baby that feels so good"? James voice was raggered now.

"Keep going"? he urged me on.

I kept going and sucked hard and fast hoping this would be over soon.

He pulled my head off and spurted his semen into his towel.

Thank God now he will leave.

But James was more horny now and wanted to taste Tasmin and take her again.

"YOU PROMISED"? I yelled at him.

"Let me taste you baby and then I will go"? he licked his lips in anticipation.

"I want to make you come"? he purred on.

I lay there and knew I was defeated just get it over with and then he will go.

His fingers playing with my clit and then he bent down and begun to feast.

"That's it baby come for me"? he slurred through his mouth.

I did not want to come and he was making it very difficult to resist.

"Let go honey"? he was trying to make me orgasm.

"No No"? I yelled out

His fingers plunged into me and he finger fucked me while his tongue licked and teased my clit. I could feel myself coming and thought go with it and let him have what he wants. He knew I was close and he urged me on. Just as I was coming he plunged his cock into me and fucked me roughly while his hand played with my tits.

"That's it Baby give it to me"? he kept thrusting and plunging.

He was brutal and rough and did not stop. He lifted my legs over his shoulders and plunged deeper.

"I'm coming baby"? he huskily said as he withdrew and spurted into the towel.

Thank God it's over. James kissed me then all over my breasts and then my lips.

"Tell no one of this and I won't hurt any of your friends"? he stroked my hair as he said it.

I was numb and just nodded.

"Good girl"? he whispered in my ear.

James left and smiled to himself as he did. He would now go to Jaine's and give her a serve as well.   He was aroused and wanted to spend the night with Tasmin but that couldn't happen so he would have Jaine instead. I lay there and waited till I was sure he was gone. I suddenly felt nauseous and ran to the bathroom and threw up in the toliet. I then showered and scrubbed off James's scent. I went downstairs and made a hot chocolate and didn't feel like eating. Maddy arrived soon after and I told her I was tired and was going to bed. She hugged me and didn't suspect a thing.

"Sleep well honey"? she said.

I climbed into bed and thought about what had happened. I have to get him out of my life.   He was a monster and I hated him. I fell asleep crying. James arrived at Jaine's horny as hell. He wanted her to blow him first and he imagined it was Tasmin's lips and mouth.

"That's it honey take it all"? he urged his throbbing cock in her mouth and came in there Jaine spluttered and spat out the juices into some tissues.

"Peter next time give me some warning"? she purred at him.

Peter didn't care he wanted more and he was only thinking of Tasmin and not this French Whore. James took Jaine roughly and she didn't complain she just thought it was a game. James on the other hand thought he was fucking Tasmin and took out all his frustration on Jaine'. Jaine' once again fell asleep in his arms thinking this is very ecrotic and how she liked this man. I woke early and felt a little better.   Maddy was up and was preparing breakfast.

"Not for me"? I said as I saw pancakes and fruit.

"Why not you need to eat"? she replied looking at mc.

"Ok just one pancake and some fruit then"? I answered ignoring my stomach grumbling.

I ate slowly and sipped my coffee. We both left the same time and hugged each other as we left.

"Will we go out on Friday night"? she asked with a smile.

"If you want and maybe we should see what Max is doing"? I added smiling back at her.

"ok I will ring her later"? Maddy replied as she beeped her car to unlock it. I arrived at work and Jaine' was not there yet. I unlocked and started the coffee brewing. I heard the door bell tingle and Jaine' entered with a big smile on her face.

"Good Morning Tassy"? she beamed

"My you are glowing Jaine'"? I looked at her thinking this new man of hers is obviously doing her good.

"I slept in sorry I'm late"? she chirped

"That's ok you can be late anytime"? I laughed at her.

We grabbed a coffee and chatted about our work to be done. The day went quickly and before I knew it it was time to go home. Jaine' also was in a rush saying she wanted to purchase some lingere for her new lover. So I left and Jaine' went shopping for something sexy to wear for her lover and his wicked games. I arrived home and Maddy was already there.

"Hi honey"? she jumped up when she saw me and went to the bar.

"Want a drink"? she asked

"Yes please a vodka sunset"? I replied sitting down and taking my shoes off.

"Not too strong" I added. My tummy had been sensitive the last week and I found myself   feeling a little nauseas. I was due for my period so I put it down to my cycle. I also had to get the pill prescription filled but I knew I had been having protected sex so I wasn't worried about that.

"Are we going out tomorrow night"? Maddy asked me as she poured my drink.

"Do you want to and does Max"? I answered her as I curled up on the sofa.

"Max cant make it some family function but she said she would catch up next weekend"? Maddy said as she handed me my drink.

"Cheers" she clinked my glass.

"Cheers" I repeated smiling.

"Well it looks like you and me honey"? Maddy said as she sipped her drink.

"Ok if you want to"? I replied.

"Tas I also have to talk to you about something"? she said looking at me.

"What is it"? I asked her.

"Well Scott and I have been seeing each other for the past month and we are both fond of each other but he's not sure if he wants to settle down with one girl"? Maddy said looking at me.

"So we are going to see other people and then in a month we will make a decision"? she said looking at me to see what I thought.

"Ok that sounds a good idea at least give him the time to work out what he wants"? I agreed with her.

"So in the mean time I can still have a little fun"? she clapped her hands like a little girl in a candy shop.

"You're funny and naughty"? I clapped my hands with her.

"What about you Tas is there someone special"? she looked at me for an answer.

"Yes and no, sort of, I'm not sure"? I stumbled out.

"What do you mean not sure, yes or no"? she asked me looking at me with big eyes.

I can't lie to her she is my best friend and I love her dearly.

"Well actually I'm in love with two men one married and one not and I do not know which one to choose"?

There I said it. She looked at me with her mouth open and took a moment to think about it.

"ok well the single one would be the choice Yeh"? she asked me with curious eyes.

"Well you would think so but the married one is very special too so my decision is very hard to make"? I answered her firmly.

"Well let's go out and forget about these men with complications and just have some fun"? Maddy said looking at me for approval.

"Yes you're right lets forget and let loose"? I agreed with her.

"Ok that's settled where will we go"? Maddy asked me.

"You pick I'm happy to do what you think"? I replied getting up and making some more drinks.

Maddy got up and said let's order pizza and grabbed the menu. Our pizza was delivered and we sat down to pizza, drinks and a movie.

Half way through the movie I started yawning and nearly dozed off.

"Tas honey go to bed, we can watch this another night"? she got up to help me to bed.

"Ok I'm beat"? I accepted her hand and we walked arm in arm to my room.

"Goodnight sweetie"? she kissed me on the lips and hugged me.

"Goodnight honey"? I purred and hugged her back.

"Maddy thanks again for everything"? I said with my whole heart. She truly was my best friend.

"You're always welcome my sweetest friend" she purred Back at me.

I got into bed and fell asleep instantly. I woke in the morning after a good nights sleep. My mind was clearer and I had a busy day ahead. I had to buy a new phone thanks to the Maniac James My shower was soothing and refreshing, I dressed in a grey skirt and black silk blouse and black flats. Put my hair up and applied a little of makeup as I did look a little pale.Went downstairs where Maddy was already eating breakfast and had the coffee brewing.

"Good morning sunshine"? she chirped at me with a beautiful smile.

"Good morning sweetie" I chirped back.

"You look gorgeous in that outfit"? Maddy looked me up and down.

"Where did you buy that"? she added.

"Europe"? I said with a big smile.

"You know we should go to Europe together and have. A no strings attached holiday"? Maddy said with a big smile already dreaming of all those European Men everywhere.

I laughed and agreed smiling thinking of all the European men I've had.

"Well we'll see what happens"? I said smiling at her.

We both finished our breakfast and hurried out the door.

"See you tonight around 5"? Maddy said as she got in her car.

"Yes see you then"? I replied and got into my car.

I drove to work and didn't notice the white pickup truck around the corner watching and waiting.

Jaine' was as bubbly as ever and was singing when I came in.

"Morning Jaine'" I said smiling.

"Good Morning Tassy"? she beamed back at me.

Well she certainly is happy and cheerful I thought to myself. This man she has must be wonderful and full of love for her. I'm glad she deserves it and especially after Jean-Paul. Cheated on her. She deserves love and fun. I wonder if I will meet him ooh I hope so I thought. We got busy and decorated and boxed up the wedding cakes. Friday was a busy day as the Wedding customers picked up their cakes.   People came all day manly after lunch. Once the final cake had been picked up, Jaine' said go Tassy and have a good weekend.

"You have a good weekend too with your new man"? I winked at her.

"When will I meet him"? I added with a cheeky smile.

"Oh, one day"? she looked at me and blushed.

"Why are you blushing"? I asked looking at her worried.

"Well please don't tell anyone but he is a bit younger"? she said a little worried.

"Oh, how much younger"? I asked interested.

"I think around 15 years" she said softly.

"You little couger"? I said laughing.

"Oh Tassy you won't tell anyone will you"? she asked me again with a frown on her face.

"Jaine' it's your business and I'm happy if you're happy"?

I said gently and honestly.

"Thank you Tassy that means a lot to me, I am happy, he

Makes me happy. He gives me lots of attention" She said smiling.

I hugged her and she hugged me back.

I left and drove to Maddy's. I really wanted to go home and see my house. I really missed being there. I had to go home and think about more security. I won't be scared of living in my own home by anyone. Maddy was already home and looking gorgeous.She had on a Black mini dress with squinnes around the bust line and her long legs shot out from the small material. That covered her bum with stilettos on. She looked hot.

"OOh I better get ready then"? I wolf whistled her and winked.

"You're going to get eaten alive"? I said as I looked at her.

"Good I feel like being sweets and getting eaten"? she purred at me smiling.

"You cheeky sexy wildcat"? I purred at her sexily.

"Come here"? she outstretched her arms for me to come in.

I hugged her and she hugged me back.

Her hands were on my bum and I didn't mind until she went to slide her hand up my skirt.

"Cheeky" I slapped her bum gently and we both laughed.

"If we pick up tonight we can have an orgy and then I can

Play with you too"? she said as she looked at me.

I knew Maddy was more Bi than me I was happy with a man with a big cock and I knew she got off on watching me with men.We all have our own addictions when it comes to sex. Maddy has a fetish of sexual fantasy with men and women   In a wild orgy. So I don't mind along as she is happy and I must say we have had some pretty amazing sexual episodes with men together

"What will I wear"? I asked her as she poured some drinks.

"Anything you look hot in anything"? she chirped from the bar.

I went to my room and had a quick shower got dressed in a black corset, stockings, lace knickers, a black mini with a red silk blouse which was very revealing in the cleavage.

Silletttos and some jewelry and red lipstick. I wore my hair down and lightly curled it. I looked at myself in the mirror and thought how hot I looked. I grabbed a red sequinned clutch bag and a jacket as it gets cool later at night.

"See I told you anything looks hot on you"? Maddy remarked with a smile.

"Thanks" I replied laughing.

"I've rung a taxi and we are going to that new club"?

Maddy said as got up to get her bag.

"Sounds good from what I've heard from some customers"? I replied

The taxi beeped and we headed out the door.

We both climbed in the back seat and Maddy gave instructions to where we were going.

"No problem miss should take about 15mins depending on traffic" he flashed a sweet smile.

Maddy smiled back and the taxi driver was in heaven. Maddy had that impact on men they melted at the sight of her. She was gorgeous and she deserved the very best of   everything. She would make a great wife and mother to some lucky man. We arrived at the club and Maddy paid the fare.

"Thankyou Miss"? he said smiling and looking at this Beauty before him.

Maddy smiled back and gave her hair a little flick. The taxi driver who would have been around 40 will certainly have hot wet dreams tonight. The club was pumping Maddy suggested we get something light to eat first. I just followed and watched all the men staring in our direction. Maddy was certainly an eye opener. A waiter got us a table booth and some menus.

"MMmm what's on the Menu"? she asked me with a big smile.

I looked at her she wasn't looking at the menu she was checking out all the potentual victims.

"Maddy food Menu not men Menu"? I giggled at her.

Maddy giggled back.

We ordered light and some wine and sat back and chatted.

"Where do you see yourself in 5 years"? Maddy asked me

"Oh God Maddy I don't know but I would hope I am married and having kids"? I answered honestly.

"Yes me too I have been thinking about babies for awhile
My mum reckons its because she had babies young so I have that feeling as well"? Maddy said.

"You would make a great mum honey"? I purred at her

"You would too"? she purred back.

Our drinks arrived and soon after our pasta and salad.

We only ordered entrée size.

I didn't realise how hungry I was. And enjoyed every mouthful.

The wine was a Mascato and it was delicious.

We went through to the bar lounge after dinner and found a table near the dance floor.

Maddy was checking out various men as potential victims.

"Those two over there by the end of the bar"? she said quietly as she sipped her wine.

I waited a few minutes then casually gazed in that direction. There was two men both very attractive sitting chatting. One of the men gazed back in my direction and I quickly turned away.

Shit he was cute and he saw me checking him out.I started to giggle and Maddy said theyre coming over. Get a hold of yourself I said to myself and took a deep breath.

"Hello Ladies" a charming deep voice said.

He was tall, blonde, and muscley. Mmm just my type I thought.

"Hello" Maddy answered with her sweet voice and smile.

"Hello" I stammered. Fuck I felt myself blushing.

"I'm Evan and this is Will" he said with a cute smile.

"I'm Maddy and this is Tasmin" Maddy replied her smile gorgeous and sexy.

"Would you like to join us"? she asked as I said nothing just smiled at them.

"We would love to"? Evan said with a smile and sat down Next to me.   Will sat next to Maddy.

They had Irish accents and were quite funny to listen too. We all chatted easily and they told us about their home back in Ireland.   They were here on a holiday and were making their way to California. They were interesting and very charming in every way.

"Dance Ladies"? Evan stood up to take my hand.

Will also stood up and it was hard not to resist these two cheeky Irish Lads. Maddy and I both accepted and smiled. Evan drew me into his arms and swayed with me to the beat. I could feel his heart beat and the scent of his cologne was intoxicating. My knees went weak and my body. Why does my body betray me like this when it comes to men. I clung in his strong arms and felt his hand caressing my back.We drew apart and I looked up into his eyes.   His eyes boar into mine and I knew

I was lost. He gave me the most beautiful smile with white teeth and my body melted.

"Youre very attractive and hot"? Evan said in a Irish husky voice.

His lips found mine and it was soft and tender.Just enough to tease and want more. The song finished and we kept dancing still holding each other close.

"I want you beautiful girl"? he whispered in my ear.

Tingles went through my body and I looked up at him and smiled.

"You'll have to be a good boy then wont you"? I cheekily replied.

"I'll do anything you ask or want of me"? he huskily answered looking deep into my eyes

My body pulsating to his touch and I knew the seduction

Was already happening.   I had him my submission I only had to clink my fingers and he would be at my beck and call.   I also was weak to his advances.

We returned to the table where Maddy and Will were giggling like old friends.

"Drinks"? Will had already ordered and they were waiting for us at the table.

"Thankyou" I flashed a sweet smile in his direction.

"Cheers" we all clinked glasses.

Maddy asked if the boys wanted to join us for cocktails at her place and they were eager to leave when it was settled.

Evan hailed a taxi and we piled into it with Maddy Evan and I in the back and Will in the front.

Evan put his arms around both of us and smiled his gorgeous smile.

"Well I have the luck of the Irish"? he said as he squeezed our shoulders.

He then leaned towards my lips and kissed me passionately. Then he kissed Maddy passionately.

"Very Nice" he said as he nuzzled our necks.

Maddy and I both giggled as he was tickling our necks.

"Do you mind if we all share"? Evan asked us both.

"No not at all"? replied Maddy as her hand went to his   bulge.

He kissed me again while Maddy played with his erection through his pants.

"Ok guys wait for me"? Will said from the front seat.

The taxi driver also getting a good look at the action in the seat wishing it was him getting some action with these hot
Girls.

"Lucky guys"? he exclaimed to Will who was smiling and thinking about what was going to happen when they get to Maddys'.

"Yeah" replied Will in a daze.

"Need some help"? the taxi driver asked
With big horny eyes.

"I think we will be ok thanks anyway"? Will looked at him

With a Thanks but no thanks kinda of face.   Will thought the taxi driver was a lot older than all of them so he didn't think the girls would want an older man to join them. Like I don't want to share these hot beauties only with my mate.

Evan was fondling Madddys' breast and kissing me longingly and tenderly. His tongue playing with mine and whispering now and then wait till I get you home. His hand then went to my nipple through my dress which was aching to be touched by his hand and tongue.

"Where here"? Will announced as the taxi pulled up outside Maddys.

Thank God I thought I was going to come in the back seat. The taxi driver gave us a big grin and didn't want to leave.

"Sure you boys can handle it"? he slurred raggered licking his lips as he said it.

He had greedy eyes and was hungry for pussy. He had not feasted for a week and it was killing him.

"Thanks where fine" Evan said firmly and shut the door.

The taxi driver gave us one last look up and down especially us girls and thought to himself he would love to fuck these two beauties. Oh well now I know where they live, Mmm I might call back another time he smiled to himself as he drove off. The boys couldn't wait to get us inside. Grabbing us around our waists and pulling us inside.

"Drinks"? Maddy asked as we went into the lounge room.

"Yes Please" we all chorused.

I jumped my cell rang and I got my bag and looked at it.

It was Stefano and I had 3 missed calls from him. I excused myself to the bathroom and went to the loo and rang him back.

"Hi honey" I said as Stefano answered the phone.

"You've missed my calls" he said not happy.

"Sorry baby I went out to dinner with Maddy" I tried to sound normal and not tipsy.

"Have you been drinking"? he asked firmly shit he could still hear it in my voice.

"A little" I lied a small lie.

"Who's there with you"? he asked not quite believing me.

"No one just Maddy and I"? I lied again.

"Oh ok" he said sounding relieved.

Good he believes me. I took a breath and asked how everything was going.

"Good the project is opening next week and Anna is a little better" he said

"So that's why I'm ringing to tell you I can't come for aleast 2-3 weeks"? he said with a sad voice.

"Oh why not I thought you said you would be here soon"? I said a little confused.

"I have to settle Anna into her new room at the clinic and then I can come"? he tried to reassure me.

"Oh alright you have to do what you have to do"? I said a little too matter of factly.

"What's that meant to mean"? he snapped at me.

"Nothing I mean nothing, I miss you that's all and we havent discussed anything yet so I guess that means we can see other people"? I was pushing my luck now.

"What the fuck do you mean"? he bellowed down the phone.

"Tasmin you are mine and mine only do you hear me"? he yelled through the phone.

"Well I'm sure youre seeing someone so why cant I"? I challenged him as I was feeling alittle frisky now and thought well hes over there and I'm here so why not?

"Wait till I see you, you disabedent little wildcat"? he purred at me angrily.

"What are you going to do big boy"? I echoed back at him.

"Make you pay for that remark for one"? he bellowed at me through the phone. I had to hold my phone away from my ear as it hurt when he yelled at me and also cursing me in German.

"I have to go now sweetie" I said sweetly smiling to myself

"No Baby don't hang up"? he voice a bit softer this time.

"I love you and want you"? he said softly and gently.

"I miss you too but youre not here are you"? I tried to be gentle.

"Ok Ok I can see we will keep fighting about this so lets sleep on it and I will talk to you tomorrow when you have a clearer head"? he finally said knowing he had lost that battle, for now.

As I freshened up a knock at the door startled me and I opened it to Evan standing there looking very hot indeed.

"Baby I thought you had fallen in"? he laughed at me

I laughed back and he grabbed me around my waist and pulled me in to his arms. His hard chest on mine and his breath on my face wanting access to my tongue.I gave him what he wanted and his hands were all over my body. He pulled up my dress and put his hands under my bum cheeks and lifted me up to lean against the vanity. His hand sliding into my g/string to gain access to my favorite spot. He did not disappoint. His other hand pulling down my dress below my breasts to reveal a gorgeous black corset. My breasts heaving and spilling out the top. He murmured something like gorgeous and his lips sought out my nipples. He licked and sucked like a hungry lion and I arched my back as lust succumbed my body. He teased me with his tongue and nipped me every time his finger thrust into my pussy deeper and then withdrawing and then circling on my clit. It was Bliss. Pure passionate pleasurable uninhibited sensual bliss!! My orgasm came and I grabbed his shoulders as he head was between my legs and his lips, tongue and finger was bringing me over the edge. Evan held me there against the vanity while he pulled his jeans and jocks down where his weapon was unleashed. He produced a condom and slid it on his huge erection and then slid gently but firmly into me.

"Baby take that you sexy wild gyspy"? he groaned as he plunged deeper into me.

I clung around his neck and he picked up my bum cheeks and held me firm and fucked me like a Jack rabbit. God it was great. He was groaning and plunging and I was lost in his thrusts of ecasty and lust. He was coming now and the sound of his sexual ecrotic groans made me come and we both exploded together. He lay against me and then withdrew and cleaned himself up. I checked him out as he was standing there half naked and with a huge dick still needing attention.

"Baby let me"? I took cloth and wiped his penis.

I then bent down and swirled my tongue around his knob.

I cleaned it with my tongue and looked up at him with big sexy eyes and licked my lips.

"That's very nice honey"? he purred at me stroking my hair and urging me on.

I sucked him hard and tickled his balls with my tongue, he leant back against the vanity and gave in to my submission.

"Oh honey easy youre gonna wear it"? tried to pull me off.

I knew I was playing with fire I sucked till I knew he was about to blow and then plunged his throbbing spurting cock into the towel.

"Aaahh" he groaned huskily.

I licked my lips and smiled at him sweetly and seductedly.

"MMMmm that was yummy"? I said cheekily.

"Gorgeous baby just fucking hot god dam hot"? he replie huskily and sexy.

He pulled me in for a cuddle and kiss. He was very sweet and definitely easy to be with.

"Lets get a drink"? Evan held the door for me.

We went out to the lounge room and Maddy and Will had just finished their sexual eposide.

"Drinks guys"? Evan asked them smiling.

They both nodded and we sat down and had some drinks and nibbles that Maddy had whipped up.
"Do you both want to swap"? Will asked us both with excitement.

Maddy and I looked at each other and both smiled and agreed. I sat down next to Will and his big arms engulfed me. He was cute too and easily drawn into his puppy dog eyes that were full of excitement and intrigue. His lips met mine and his tongue was searching for mine. I gave in to him and let him devow my mouth and tongue. His hand pulling up my dress where he slid his hand up to my pussy wanting to gain entry.

I sat up and pulled my dress over my head to reveal my corset, suspenders and g/string. I kept my stockings and stilettos on as I felt hot and sexy. He made me lay back on the sofa and he spread my legs. His hands started at my breasts and he traced around them to where he pinched each nipple. He then trailed down my navel to my g/string

And he slipped his finger in.

OOOhh!!! That felt so good. I watched him and he looked into my eyes as his finger did the searching.

He then bent his head to nuzzle my breasts and nip at my corset. I unbuttoned the top few buttons and my boobs spilled out.

His tongue instantly found my nipples and started torturing me and also with his finger doing amazing things to my vagina and clit.

After he feasted and suckled my breasts his head proceeded down to my favorite spot. He pulled off my g/string and came in for the kill.

He was hungry and he gave me no mercy. When he was content and knew I was ready for fucking he undressed and sheathed himself.

"Baby" he groaned as he entered me gently. He also was a big boy. He picked up my bottom and plunged deeper into me. I moved with his hips and we danced the most beautiful dance. Our bodies entwined together our breathing raggered and loud. My orgasm came crashing down inside me and Will also groaned loudly and let out a husky groan.

He lay on me holding his own weight until our breathing   returned to normal.

"That was sensational"? he whispered softly in my ear.

I nodded and agreed with a big smile. We got cleaned up and then dressed.

"Drink honey"? he asked in a cute Irish accent.

"yes please a vodka sunset" I replied as I got up to go to the bathroom.

I went down the hall and past Maddys' bedroom where I could hear a lot of groaning.

The door was open and I saw that Maddy was getting a real serve while on her knees.

She saw me as I went to walk past and called me in the room.

"Tasmin help me with this man   hes' going to give me a heart attack"? she said trying to get her breath.

I giggled and went up to the bed and kissed her on the lips.

"Take it Baby"? I said in sexy voice.

I pinched her nipples as he pounded her and she groaned with excasty. He withdrew and grabbed me and put me on all fours next to Maddy.

"You want to be spanked too"? he said jokingly.

He hitched up my dress and pulled my g off. His finger plunging into me to get me ready.

"OOOhh" I purred as his cock entered me.

"Now you take it"? said Maddy with a giggle.

He held on to my hips and thrust deeper into me.

"Baby youre so wet"? he said huskily as his other hand played with Maddys' Bum.

Will appeared at the door looking very amused.

"Wondered where you got too"? he said with a smile.

He came into the room and kissed Maddy on the lips and then me. His hands went to my nipples and he gently pinched them

"You want two of us Baby"? Will asked as I groaned.

Will sheathed his hard on and then lay down on his back. He pulled me on top and slid into me. I groaned with pleasure. He pulled Maddy over to his face to straddle it   while she faced me. Evan was preparing my forbidden place with his finger and some lubricant.

He then entered me gently while Will pumped me up and down. Hands were everywhere and my body went with the rhythm of two men taking me at once. My orgasm came loudly and my whole body shuddered around me. Maddy also was coming and Will gave her no mercy. The boys were still frisky and had not come yet must be the alcohol they wanted more. They put fresh condoms on and then it was Maddys' turn to have two men at once.

Maddy sat on Evan while Will came from behind. Evan pulled me on his face and he feasted like a wolf. My body still numb from before but still could take more pleasure. We all groaned as our orgasms hit us and lay still till the boys removed themselves and cleaned themselves up.

"Wow" Evan said catching his breath.

"That was Hot"? Will agreed.

I was exhausted so was Maddy and we all agreed to call it a night. the boys wanted to stay the night and we didn't object Evan came to my room and Will to hers.

"Shower"? I asked Evan who was following me like a lost puppy.

"Sounds good"? he replied stripping off.

I peeled my dress off then my corset and everything else. I entered the shower the water was soothing and invigorating.   Evan soaped me all over and I did the same to him. His hands straying at my breasts longer and then dipping down to my pussy and bum. Evan's erection was in full swing again.   Is there no stopping this Irish Stud Muffin I laughed to myself.

"You want more"? I enquired with a cheeky smile.

"Always want more"? he looked at me with a sexy smile.

"Come here honey" his arms engulfed me in a bear hug.

His hands sliding all over me and were between my legs before I knew it. I had my back to him and his erection was straining into me. He bent me over and entered my vagina gently.

"You feel so good without a condom on"? he huskily said.

"Well be careful and pull out" I said firmly trying to stay in control as my body was betraying me once again. He pumped away and I thrust into his thrusts. His arms around me holding me caressing me. His finger went into my forbidden place and his dick replaced his finger. Gently and slowly he slid in and out. I groaned as his thrusts became more and his finger giving me a clitoral orgasm at the same time. It was total bliss. I was lost. I cried out when my orgasms collided. Evan held me tightly and supported my weight when my knees gave way. He had withdrawn and had spurted over my back.He washed me again and himself and then helped me   Dry off and get into bed.

I grabbed a silk nightie from my drawer with Evan holding my side.

"I don't think you'll be needing that"? he said wickedly.

I grinned at him and still put my black silk short nightie on.

"But then again you look mighty hot in that number"? he licked his lips like a lion about to pounce on his prey.

He scooped me up in his strong arms and carried me to the bed. He lay me under the covers and kissed my lip gently and tenderly.

"You are a beautiful woman Tasman   a man could get used to you"? he said passionately.

Looking deep into my eyes he continued on,

"You have touched my heart and soul I hope one day we meet again"? he said with big puppy dog eyes.

"Yes it has been a wonderful and sensual experience with you but I'm not sure if I can see you again"? I looked at him and tried to be honest and gentle.

"Why not are you attached"? he asked looking back at me.

"Well sort of"? I said softly.

"Ok I see well if it doesn't work out with this other man give me a call ok"? he held my chin up so our eyes would meet.

"Tasmin baby have you a secret what is troubling you"?

He was reading my mind.   He was so intuned with my thoughts I couldn't believe it.   Especially as it was a man.

I thought only women had telepathy with each other.

"Tell me and I will help you see things clearly"? he said as he lay beside me.

I looked at this man with big beautiful eyes full of desire and intrigue.

Could I tell this man my problems? Should I tell him everything? Evan lay there watching me and waiting.I decided there was no harm in telling Evan about my life, Problems or were they Addictions.I started from the start telling him about Stefano the lover who wanted me to be his mistress. Then I told him about Sam the ever supportive and sensitive lover and then I went further and told him about James the Rapist and Stalker.

"Tasmin you must go to the police and tell them about him and what he has done"? Evan looked at me seriously.

"I cant I let him in my home and I was drunk so it was consensual sex"? I replied looking at him with tears in my eyes. He pulled me in to his strong big arms and rocked me like a baby.

"Sshh" he purred at me stroking my hair tenderly.

He lifted my chin to meet his eyes and then his lips met mine.

He kissed me passionately and tenderly. His tongue gently propping mine teasing and urging me on. His hand already inside my nightie caressing my breasts.

"I could look after you and take you away from all your problems"? he whispered in my ear as he nuzzled my neck.

"How could you do that"? I said quietly looking at him.

"Well for one we'll start by making love to you and take you to a place of pleasure and lust"? he slurred as his head bent down to suckle my nipples. I giggled as he tickled me and teased me.Oohh my he sure knows how to get my attention.I gave in to his advances and before long we were dancing together our breathing became one.Our orgasms collided together and we lay together feeling very content after our sexual interlude.

"Well what do you say will you let me take you away from all your troubles"? he said once he came back down to earth.

"It's ok I will be alright"? I replied thinking I cant give up Stefano, Sam, or any of my lovers yet.   James yes I could give him up hes a pyhco maniac. One I could live without.

"Baby if you ever need me I will come running"? Evan said so tenderly and softly.

"You and I could make a good life together"? he continued on.

"Youre so sweet"? I answered with a smile.

He smiled back and his eyes were shining with love and affection.

He kissed me again and then picked me up and carried me to the shower.

Once again he made passionate love to me and to me over the edge.

I cried out his name when I climaxed and he held me tight.

We washed again and then dried off and got dressed.

We went to the kitchen smelt the freshly brewed coffee and pancakes.

"MMmm smells great Maddy"? I hugged her and asked how her night was.

"Just great and yours"? she replied giggling.

"Perfect" I answered flashing a smile at Evan.

He smiled back and we were both thinking the same thing.

Hot hot no strings attached hot sex!

We all enjoyed our breakfast and then it was time to for the boys to go.

The boys didn't want to leave saying we would love to repeat last nights sexual romp.

It was Sunday and we weren't doing anything special so Maddy and I agreed that they could stay another day and night.

We all went for a walk after breakfast down to the park by the lake. It was beautiful and the sun was shining and we made our way down to the lake to feed the ducks.

Maddy like always comes prepared with stale bread.

We fed the ducks and then lay on the grass and let the sunshine warm our bodies.

Evan lay beside me and then kissed me gently.

"This is beautiful and with two gorgeous women"? he slurred as his hand went under my top for access to my breasts.

"naughty boy hands off"? I slapped his hand gently away.

"Wait till I get you home"? he said cheekily as his eyes were dancing in the sunshine.

Will also was getting frisky with Maddy and we all agreed it was time to go home and deal with our horny bodies and thoughts.

We all half run from the park home giggling all the way.

The boys were eager as we were and we didn't realise how much these boys were teasing us with their sexy eyes and bodies.

Maddy and I both wanted more, yes more hot sex!!

James was in his truck parked down the road and saw everything.

"What the hell"? he bellowed in his head. Who are these two bastards and what are they doing with my Tasmin.

That Maddy is a bad influence and maybe I will have to teach her a lesson as well.

Mmm he thought that could be interesting, she is very hot and she does have big tits as well.

Mmmm I sure like big tits James thought to himself as his hand went to his bulge which was growing in his pants.

He pulled it out and imagined it was Tasmin and Maddy sucking him and pulling him hard.

He came into his hankichief but still was not content, he wanted more.

I will show those girls whose Boss and not to fuck with him,

He was serious and Tasmin would be his one way or another.

He decided to go to Jaine's and have his way with her and take out his frustrations on her, she would have to do she was not Tasmin but he could imagine it was Tasmin he was fucking and loving him.

So James went to Jaine's and she was so excited that he was here with her.

"Close your eyes baby I have a surprise for you"? she said in a sexy French accent.

She came back in the room and told him to open his eyes.

"Surprise"? Jaine said delightedly.

James looked at her with big eyes.

She had on a sexy black corset and the whole lingere.

Her tits were spilling out the top and he licked his lips thinking how much he wanted to suck them and hard.

He took her roughly and urgent making her suck him first

And then he took her vaginally and then anally.   She cried out his name when she climaxed and he held her tightly and kept pumping her till he came.

"Oh Peter that was beautiful and very ecrotic"? she purred at him.

"yeah great Baby just great"? he said as he cleaned himself up.

"I want more honey"? Jaine' purred at him sexily.

"You want more you slut"? James said roughly

"Peter don't call me that"? she was upset with him now.

"Sorry baby I mean you are my beautiful horny Slut"? he replied a little more gently now.

"oohh I see you like calling me names"? Jaine' thought it was a game.

I will play along she thought to herself.

"Have you got a dildo"? James asked her with big eyes.

"Well yes I have but since being with you I havent needed it"? she said confused.

"Get it"? James replied firmly.

Jaine' went and retrived her toy and gave it to James.

"Lie on your back and I will fuck you with this"? he said   with a big smile.

"Ok" Jaine' obeyed his command.

Jaine lay there in anticipation and spread her legs to receive her toy.

James was going to punish her for wanting more.

How dare she ask for more? He thought as he pinched her nipples hard.

Jaine' yelled out in pain and then James would suck them better.

Jaine liked this game and went along with it. James took full advantage of her and her body. She wasn't Tasmin but she would have to do for now. Maddy and I played with the boys all day and night it was Orgasmic bliss and we swapped partners and also had both at the same time. It was late and we were all tired so we all retired for bed.

Evan wanted to stay with me the night and Will was happy to stay with Maddy so it was agreed and we all said our

Goodnights and retired to our rooms.

Evan and I showered and once again he took me to great heights of ecasty.

Yes I could keep him as a Lover he was very attractive and attentive.   But should I commit to another man with all these complications with all my other lovers?   All these thoughts running around my head. I thought I would just sleep on it and see what happens.

We slept together in each other's arms and in the morning I woke to Evan nuzzling my neck and a good morning erection.

Oh shit what the hell might as well enjoy this while it lasts.

We made passionate love and then I showered this time by myself as I had to get ready for work.

I got dressed and Evan was already dressed and looking very hot lying on the bed.

"Come here honey"? he purred at me.

I looked at him and laughed,

"No time for that"? I said cheekily.

He jumped up then and in two strides he was holding me close.

"I will miss your sweet smile and of course hot body"? he said as he nuzzled my neck.

I giggled as he tickled my neck

"I will miss you too"? I said truthfully.

"Then we will meet up when I get back from my trip"? he asked with big puppy dog eyes.

"Yes ok we will see each again"? I replied smiling at him.

He was happy now and kissed me tenderly and gently.

"Goodbye for now my beautiful goddess I will see you when I get back"? he kissed me again.

We both went to the kitchen and Maddy was there with coffee and fruit and toast waiting.

"Good morning you two"? she said looking up from the   table.

"Good morning Maddy Will"? we both said at the same time.

Will flashed his big smile and we sat down and had coffee and breakfast.

It was time to go and I said I could drop the boys off but they insisted that they would walk back to their hostel.

"Ok are you sure"? I asked them both

"Yes we need to work off breakfast"? Evan smiled his gorgeous smile.

"Ok take care of yourselves and we will see you when you

Get back"? I said as I drove off.

They both waved and started walking up the road.James was sitting there watching everything. so they are leaving but who are they.   He was curious. He started his engine and drove up beside them. He pushed the electric window down and smiled at them both.

"Hi where are you headed"? James asked politely.

"Down town to the hostel"? Will replied

"You want a lift"? James was being very nice.

Will and Evan looked at each other and nodded.

"So stayed out of town for the night"? James enquired.

"Yeah we had dates with two hot chicks"? Will answered smiling.

"Nice girls were they"? James was trying to get information out of them.

"Yeah very hot and gorgeous"? Will added with a grin

Evan just nodded as he was dreaming about Tasmin and her lips.

"Whats up Evan"? Will asked him when he saw him smiling to himself.

"Oh nothing Will just thinking"? Evan replied smiling back at him. "Hes in love"? Will went on

"In love"? James laughed outloud

"with who"? he added.

"This girl he met and now he wants her as his wife"? Will said with a cheeky grin.

"His wife well that's quick"? James said curious which one he meant.

"Whats her name"? James kept prying.

"Arrh Tasmin she's so cute"? Will said licking his lips as if he was tasting her.

"Did you have them both"? James was interested now.

"Yeah Man we had both and they both tasted very sweet if

you know what I mean"? Will couldn't keep his thoughts to

himself.

"Lucky guys two at once you say"? James was fuming inside.

"Yeah two at once and all night"? Will was excited now he couldn't keep his mouth shut.

"is that so"? James was vilizing Tasmin and Maddy being mauled by these two animals.

Disgusting he thought.

"How about a drink"? James asked them both as they approached their hostel.

"Yeh mate that would be ok but can we meet later in the pub"? Will said with a big smile.

"Ok but I want to hear more about your night with those hot naughty girls"? James couldn't wait till later he wanted to know everything now and this man Will was easy to get

Information out of.   The other one didn't say much he looked like his was in a dream world.

It was arranged that later that day they would meet up and have a few pints at the local pub just near the hostel.

James had told them he was interested in going to Ireland and would like to know more about their interesting country.

"No worries we can give you some knowledge of our town and whats good to see there"? Will said Evan nodded and they parted ways.

"That was easy"? thought James as he was planning a exciting evening. Yes this would be great he thought to himself smiling proudly.

I arrived at work and Jaine' was bubbly as ever.

"Hi Tassy what a wonderful day"? she chirped happily.

"Well hello to you"? I smiled back at her.

"Had a good evening"? I asked not wanting to pry.

"Yes I did it was different but very naughty"? she said shyly.

"What do you mean"? I asked slowly I didn't want to know all the details.

"Well this is very personal but Tassy you are my closet friend and I need to confide in someone"? she purred in her French Accent.

"What is it Jaine'"? I was intrigued now I had to know what was on her mind.

"Tassy you know I'm seeing this young man"? she said looking at me.

I was making coffee and I sat down and handed her a cup.

"Yes go on"? I urged her.

"Well he likes kinky sex and sometimes a little rough"? she said slowly and quietly.

"Oh" I replied not knowing what to say.

"I thought it's a game but he really enjoys it and hes quite

Rough and aggressive"? she continued on.

" I really like him but I'm not sure if I like the rough sex though its not like its all the time"? she added   she looked at me for my answer.

"Have you told him how you feel"? I asked her

"no I think I would loose him"? she said sadly.

"Jaine' you have to be honest with him, if he likes being with you he will understand your feelings"? I told her firmly but gently.

"Yes Yes Tassy you are right I will talk to him when I see him and tell him I don't like it"? she felt better now for sharing her little secret.

We both hugged and then struck into work.

The day went quickly and Jaine' said go and she would lock up.

I was tired after my energetic weekend so I hugged her and said goodbye.

James was outside the shop in his pick up truck watching Tasmin get into her car and drive away.   I'll deal with you later he thought.

Jaine' heard the tingle of the shop bell and went to see who it was yelling as she went " Were' closed"

She stopped when she saw Peter standing there with white roses and a box with a big white ribbon around it.

"Peter I wasn't expecting you"? Jaine' smiled at him warmly.

"Honey these are for you"? he handed Jaine' the flowers and box.

"Oh you shouldn't have"? she accepted the gifts and felt escatic once again for this man.

She opened the box and their inside was a red corset with holes where the nipples should be and some knickers with a slit in the crutch.

"OOooh my" she exclaimed as she held them up.

"Theyre very naughty"? she inspected the holes and slit with big open eyes.

"Why don't you lock the door and then put them on to show me how hot you will look"? he purred at her as she flung her arms around his neck and thanked him.

Jaine' locked the door and took her exciting lingere out the back and got changed.   Her nipples sticking out of the corset holes and her pussy exposed where the slit was.

James came out the back when she called to say she was ready.

"Oh honey" he purred his horny eyes on her nipples that were sticking out ready for his torture.

He pulled her in and kissed her lips tenderly and then went to suckle her.

Jaine cried out when he sucked hard but there was no deneying it she did enjoy it.   She wanted more.

He took her to the sofa and lay her on her back. His head suckled her nipples again until his head trailed down to where his finger was inspecting the slit in her knickers.

His tongue followed his finger and Jaine' lay there and let her young lover do naughty things to her.

James was so horny and he couldn't wait for a blow job he wanted her now.

The red corset with the peek a boos was the same as Tasmins'. When he saw it in a magazine from France he sent away for it straight away. He had to have it.

One day Tasmin will wear it for him and him only.

James entered her firmly and pumped hard and fast. Slapping Jaine'
on her buttocks and making her scream out. That turned him on more
and every time she whimpered in pain he pounded her more and deeply.

"Take that you French Slut"? he slurred at her.

Jaine' didn't like when he called her that but she did like his gifts
and of course his big dick.

James withdrew and spurt his semen on her tummy and all over her
corset.

"Peter look what you've done"? she was not happy he had made a
mess on her new lingere.

James handed her a hand towel and she cleaned herself up.

"There good as new"? James said as his arms went around her
waist. He kissed her on her cheek and said that he had to go but would
see her later at her place if that was alright.

"yes that would be alright I will see you then"? she said as he kept
nuzzling her neck.

"Come home with me now"? she said as she knew he wanted more.

"I have to do something first but I wont take long and if youre good
I will love you again so have that corset on Ok"? he said looking into her
eyes.

"Yes I will" she breathed.

James left as he had a appointment with two Irish lads who needed
punishing after what they had done with his Tasmin.

James met the Irish men at the pub who were already downing
pints.

"Sit down and I will get the next round"? Will said as he got up.

"So all recovered from last night"? James said to Evan.

"yes it was quite a night"? Evan replied.

"Which one did you like the best"? James wanted to know everything.

Evan who had had a few pints was not shy at telling James that Tasmin was very hot and willing.

"I would love to see her again and do it all again"? he said as he drank his beer.

James looked at him and smiled and nodded in agreeance.

Will arrived back at the table with another round of drinks and they all cheered.

James got the next round and they were getting quite drunk. James who was pacing himself and was able to decive them by not drinking as much as them. They all talked about their Country and James listened and looked interested in what they were saying. They kept drinking and then James said do they smoke and would they like a joint outside. The boys who were drunk now agreed that that would be good and they all went down to the river by the pub.

I arrived home and Maddy was already there.

"Hi ya" I said as she smiled at me.

"Hi wow the weekend was great wasn't it"? she replied smiling her beautiful smile.

"Sure was Evan wanted to take me away forever"? I said

"really he was very nice and so was Will"? she grinned at me.

There was no denying it those two Irish men had left an impression. One I would like to do again and again. We made drinks and sat down to a peaceful night of light dinner and a movie.

Little did we know we would never see them again as somewhere near the river two Irish tourists were lying slient with their throats slit. James arrived at Jaine's impatient and a little drunk. Jaine' answered her door to her lover and he looked her over and was very happy she was wearing her new corset he had brought her. He couldn't wait to fuck her she would help him with his frustration. Jaine sucked and teased James's Cock until he could take no more.

"Enough" he growled and he flipped her on her stomach.

He took her roughly and fast, Jaine whimpers were ignored only making more aroused. He took her anally and her whimpers made him mad and he would slap her bum cheeks hard telling her she is a very naughty girl that needed punishing All the while he was imagining it was Tasmin he was fucking and punishing. He came loudly and didn't withdraw this time leaving his seed inside her.

"Peter that was a little rough"? she said softly as he removed himself from her.

"Sorry I missed you and I couldn't control myself"? he said in a gentle voice not like the one before.

Jaine' who was a very lonely woman accepted his apology and let James take her again this time he was more gentle with her.   She decided he was having a bad day and that she could handle a little roughness from time to time.

Once again she was lost in his charms.

The week went quickly and Jaine' and I got all our orders done finishing early Friday as everybody had picked up their orders.

"What are you doing this weekend Tassy"? Jaine' asked.

"I'm having a quiet one"? I replied giving her a hug.

"What about you"? I asked her giving her a sweet look.

"Oh I don't know I'll see what happens"? she answered with a smile.

"How is your lover is everything alright now"? I asked wanting to know if she had talked to him.

"All sorted out he brought me some naughty lingere and I must say I have never seen anything like it"? she said

"What is it like"? I asked

"Its red and it has holes for the nipples and the knickers have a slit in them very naughty indeed"? she replied blushing as she said it.

"It sounds rather wicked"? I said as I looked at her

"Anyway he likes it and our lovemaking is very good"? she added with a smile.

"Well enjoy Jaine' you deserve that"? I said as I hugged her again and left.

That corset sounds like my one or very similar I thought as I drove back to Maddys'.

They must be available everywhere I thought as I dimissed any more about it.

Maddy was seeing Scott tonight and was getting ready for the seduction.

"You look hot honey"? I remarked as I eyed her up and down.

"I'm meeting Scott at that bar and I'm hoping he has missed me too"? she said as she applied lip gloss.

"Go for it Girl"? I said as she got her bag and kissed me on my cheek.

"I might be late and maybe Scott will come home with me"? she said smiling.

"Do you mind Tas if he comes and brings a friend"? she added with a wicked smile.

"I don't care as long as hes not a dickhead"? I replied thinking I will have a quiet night in.

Maddys' taxi arrived and it was the taxi from the other night.   He looked at Maddy and licked his lips.   God she looked hot and sweet enough to eat.

Maddy didn't recognise him from the other night and was unaware of his greedy horny eyes watching her.

He nodded when he got his instructions to where to go.

He decided to take a side road and Maddy asked him where he was going.

"I just have to take a pee"? he said as he checked her out.

"Well just hurry up I'm meeting someone and I don't wont to be late"? she said impatiently.

The taxi pulled over to a side road, it was dark and no one was around. Should he be so bold and approach her. Yes he thought to himself she was hot and ready for him to take.

He got out and pretended to do a pee and thought about his next move.

He approached the back door and opened it and got in.

"What are you doing"? Maddy exclaimed as he was sitting very close to her.

"Baby you don't remember me do you"? he purred as he took in her scent making him very aroused.

"I don't know you at all"? Maddy looked at him confused.

He put his hand on her bare leg and trailed it up to her thigh.

"Very nice"? he breathed

"Stop it you brut get out and drive"? she commanded slapping his hand away.

"I will honey after you and I have some fun"? he slurred as

His eyes were checking out her big perky breasts.   God he wanted to suck those tits till they hurt.

"What do you mean fun I want you to drive me to town"?

she repeated again firmly.   She was worried now, how dare he touch her.   He was old enough to be her father.   She wasn't at all attracted to him.   Mind you if it had been a   younger hunk Maddy might have considered being seduced in the back seat of a taxi.   She got her phone out and began to dial. He grabbed it and threw it out the window.

"What are you doing let me go"? she was getting scared now.

"Baby just let me taste you and then I will take you to town"? he huskily said licking his lips.

"No No you pig get out"? Maddy was yelling now.

He put his hand across her mouth and with the other hand held her hands tightly so she couldn't move.

He knew he was playing with fire but he could not stop now and he would have to finish the job,   he could not back out his cock was throbbing in his pants and he had to have pussy. Maddy was terrified and knew she was in trouble.

"What do you want"? she tried to say through his hand.

"I want you baby"? he said as he tried to fondle her breasts.

" if I give you what you want you will not hurt me"? she was crying now.

"Honey I don't wont to hurt you I want to pleasure you and give you whats in my pants its hot and throbbing"? he said gently.

"But if you scream or try to resist then I will hurt you"? he said then in a deep voice.

Maddy looked at him. He was older but not bad looking and he was big and muscley.

"I will give you what you want along as you don't hurt me"? she said still a little scared.

"I wont hurt you baby come here"? he said as he tried to kiss her on the lips.

His tongue searching for entry and finally Maddy gave in to him. His hand pulling down her dress to reveal a black lacey bra and nipples firm and ready for him. He pinched her gently and then went to suckle her.Maddy decided not to fight this man, he was big and he could hurt me she thought. She tried to imagine it was Scott sucking her. His other finger was in her panties and he withdrew and then sucked it.

"Mmm you sure taste good baby"? he purred in her ear.

He lay her down and removed her knickers and bent his   head to feast.Maddy lay there and let him do his mission.   She lay still and rigid.

"Relax honey"? he purred deeply from her pussy.

"Come for me honey I want your sweet juice"? he cooed   to her.

Maddy wasn't sure if she could give this man her orgasm as she didn't think she could come for him. She didn't like him so how could she climax.

He kept urging her on and before Maddy knew it her body betrayed her thoughts and she was coming in his mouth. He sucked up her juices and when he had finally had enough he came up for air.

"There I gave you what you want now take me to town"? She said impatiently and angry.

"Not yet my pretty"? he unzipped his pants and unleashed   his huge manhood for her to pleasure.

"No I wont"? she yelled at him.

He slapped her then across her face and told her she would do as she was told, he was not in the mood for games.

Maddy gave in and gave him a blow job trying not gage when he forced more in her mouth.

"Oh Baby your sweet lips are like silk"? he groaned at her just before he was going to blow he pulled out of her mouth and slowed down the pace.

"Honey whats the rush I'm not finished yet"? he pulled her up and rolled her on her knees.

Maddy braced herself she knew he would be rough and hard. She was not wrong he took her everywhere and came inside her when he had finished. He kissed her back and fondledher breasts from behind. Maddy just wanted it over and started to cry.

"Oh sweet baby girl don't cry you enjoyed it just like I did"? he said huskily.

She didn't say anything.

"If you tell the police I took advantage of you I will come and get you and your friend, remember I know where you   live"? he said firmly and quite nasty.

Maddy looked at him and knew he was serious.

She nodded and then he got out of the back seat.

Maddy retrieved her knickers and rearranged her clothing she was very shaken up and couldn't believe a taxi driver would take advantage of her. The driver got her phone and handed it to her and warnedher again of the consequences of telling anyone.

She nodded at him she did not want to look at him.

He got in the front and proceeded to drive to town.

Maddy rang Scott and told him she was running late. the taxi driver watching her every move.   He was content for now he had got some pussy and that would have to do though he knew he wanted more, and maybe he would take more at another time.   He knew where she lived and he also wanted to taste her friend.   Yes there would be another time, he smiled to himself.

Maddy looked at herself in her compact mirror.

She did her lip gloss and tried to fix her hair which looked liked she had been put through a hurriacane.

They arrived at her destination and she went to pay him and he said no charge as your pussy was payment.

He smiled at her and licked his lips,

"remember what I said or I will come and get you and your friend"? he said quietly as he didn't want anyone to hear him.

Maddy nodded and got out, she couldn't let Scott see her like his.

She went straight to the Ladies and looked at herself in the mirror.She had a red mark on her cheek so she applied some blusher to cover it up. Bastard she thought to herself.

She went out to the bar and Scott was waiting there with his friend Nick whom Maddy had not met.

He was very charming and he was waiting for his date to arrive. It wasn't long before a gorgeous girl with long black hair with long legs and big boobs arrived at their table.

"Hi baby"? Nick purred at her as she kissed his cheek.

Nick introduced us even though I had the feeling Scott

Already knew her.   Maddy could veal the sexual aura around her and the way Scott looked at her she knew he had fucked her.   Oh well I've been having a fucking good time as well Maddy thought to herself.

She had come from the Philliphens on a working Visa and she loved living in America.

She spoke perfect English and was studying law here.

Our meals arrived and we all chatted while we ate.

After eating and refreshing in the ladies, Tina wanted to dance and so did I. The boys wanted to watch and have a beer.   Tina led Maddy to the dance floor and they both danced a sexy salsa together.   They looked hot and sexy.   One tall Blonde and One tall long haired black beauty.

They had the attention of a lot of men and even some women.   The boys watched as a few men approached them for a dance.   Finally they stepped in and took possesion of their prey.   Mens eyes looking envious at them.   Nick and Scott couldn't wait to get us out of the club with all the horny eyes.

They would have started a riot.

I lay on the sofa and drank my drink watching the fire dance around.

My cell rang and I knew it was Stefeno.

We talked easily and he didn't yell at me and was very gentle.

"I miss you baby" he purred into the phone.

"I miss you too" I replied.

We ended up having phone sex and it was short and sweet.

Stefano seemed content and we talked for another hour.

"I should be there soon honey"? he purred into the phone.

"I hope so I miss you so much"? I answered sadly.

We hung up and I sat there with another drink and stoked the fire.

I heard a car door and some giggling and footsteps at the door.

Maddy entered followed by Scott and two people I didn't know.

Lucky I wasn't in my Pjs, I was in my silk pants and a white silk top which was a little seethrough showing my black bra.

We were all introduced and Maddy got drinks.

Nick and Tina were very easy to talk to and we all got on well. Scott was very affectionate towards me and I didn't want to get too close as I knew Maddy was attracted to him.   Maddy came and sat down beside Scott and me.

"Cheers" we all clinked.

"Lets put some music on" Said Tina looking at Maddy.

Maddy put some music on and we all danced to a salsa tune.   It had a sexy beat and Tina and Nick and I did a dance together while Scott and Maddy clung to each other.

More drinks were handed around and before long we were dancing again and this time Nick pulled me close and felt my bum through my pants.

I looked up at him he was very attractive, brown hair, and gorgeous green eyes.   He smiled at me and whirled me around and then back into his arms.

Tina didn't mind she came up into Nicks arms when he opened them for her.

He kissed her tenderly and then he kissed me tenderly.

Then Tina touched my face and came in to kiss me.

Her lips were soft and gentle.   I gave her my tongue and she gently played with it with her tongue.   I felt tingles go down my body it was very sensual and sexy.

Nick enjoyed seeing two women making out and he whispered in my ear and said do you want to have fun with Tina and I.

I looked at Tina and she smiled and took my hand.

"Its ok we are adults and you are very sexy"? she purred to me.

I looked over at Maddy who was pashing Scott and he was fondling her back and bum.   She came up for air and then they excused themselves, Maddy winking at me when she left the room.

"Ok lets have some fun"? I said to Nick and Tina.

"Lets go to your bedroom"? asked Tina holding my hand.

I took them both to my room and we lay on the bed, Nick was in the middle.

"What's this"? Tina picked up the Sweet Obsession,baileys, chocolate sauce that was sitting on my dresser.

She was reading the label and looked at me and smiled.

"Very wicked sauce to be eaten with your lover" She smiled again sweetly and said we will have to try this.

She opened the bottle and smelt the contents.

"Umm" she had a wicked look in her eyes.

Nick undressed and   unleashed his manhood that was standing to attention.

"OOhh Nick youre a big boy"? Tina exclaimed as if it was   the first time she saw his dick.

Tina unbuttoned my top and took it off.   She then traced with her finger around my breasts and then pinched my nipples.

Again I felt tingles through my body.   I was attracted by this woman and she was beautiful.

Tina unclipped my bra and took it off.   Keeping her eyes on me the whole time. She got the sauce and dripped it on my nipples She bent her head to lick and suck my breasts and I groaned in pleasure.

"Its so delicious" she exclaimed when she went to put more on my nipples to feast.

Nick had his cock in his hand waiting for our mouths.

Tina stopped teasing my breasts and smiled at me.

"You are very beautiful"? she said sweetly licking her lips.

She then put the sauce on Nick's knob and let it dribble down.

Nick waiting in anticipation for those sweet lips to suck him.
Tina and I then bent down and teased and tortured Nick and gave him no mercy.

We lapped up the Baileys Sex Sauce like wildcats on heat.

Nick groaning and telling us both to slow down or he'll give us more than just Baileys!!

Tina made me suck Nick some more this time on my knees

She put more sauce on Nick who insisted Youre playing with fire. I took it slow and teased his cock licking the sauce up and down his shaft

Tina came around behind me and pulled my pants off and then my knickers.

I felt some sticky sauce around my hole and her finger entered me and then her tongue.   Oh God it felt amazing.   Her tongue was like silk and very experienced.

She knew how to give pleasure to a women.

I teased and tortured Nicks Cock while she seduced myclit with her tongue. We were all groaning in excasty and lust.

I felt my climax coming and I groaned more as she finger fucked me.

"That's good Baby you taste so good"? she urged me on.

I was lost then her tongue and finger doing amazing things to me, it took me over the edge.

Nick was about to blow and he pulled out of my mouth just in time and spurted his juice into a hand towel I had given him earlier. When I came back down to earth after my shattering orgasm,

I helped Tina take off her clothes.

She had a gorgeous body very petite and big boobs which Ithink must be fake. Tina wanted me to play with her so I obliged her with my tongue and lips, putting some sexy sauce on her nipples first.   I sucked her fake tits which were quite nice for fake ones, I actually have never seen fake tits before so this was a new experience.

She lay on her back and I trailed my tongue down to her pussy which was waiting in anticipation throbbing and pulsating. I dribbled some love potion on her pussy.She breathed in looking at me with big eyes. I did not disapoint her I finger fucked her while my tongue flicked and teased her clit.

Nick had a come back to life and had sheathed himself ready for round two. He came from behind and gently eased himself   into me.   I groaned as he thrusted and pumped me, trying hard to concentrate on Tina and not Nick who was fucking me stupid.   Tina climaxed and groaned and I kept thrusting with Nick as he was making me orgasm. My groans were loud and Nick came with me groaning and thrusting as he pounded and pumped like a lion on heat. We all collapsed on each other and when we got our breaths back we all had a laugh and hugged each other.

"That was great girls" Nick grinned from ear to ear.

Tina agreed but said she wanted more.

"Give me a minute honey and then I will fuck you too"?

 Nick purred in Tina's ear.

"How about I get drinks"? I asked them both as they were kissing.

"Thank you yes"? they agreed

I got up and slipped my g on and a silk robe and went to the bathroom to freshen up.   I had sticky sauce all over my face.

After freshening up I went to the lounge to make drinks.

Maddy and Scott were there and had big smiles on their   faces.

"Hi honey" Maddy said as she saw me.

"Hi both of you" I replied

"Do you both want a drink"? I asked them both.

"Yes please" they both said at the same time.

I made drinks for everyone and then took Nick and Tina's drinks to them.

"Thanks honey" they said.

"I'm going back out to the lounge so I will leave you two to have some more fun together"? I said as I could see they were both ready for round 3.

"You could stay and join us again? Tina asked sweetly.

"Its ok you guys have some time together"? I replied back

"ok baby we'll see you later"? Nick answered with a big smile as Tina was licking   his erection with love sauce   dribbling down.

I went back out to the lounge and got my drink and sat down beside Maddy and Scott.

"You want to join us honey baby"? Maddy asked me sweetly

"love to" I replied sipping my drink.

We sculled down our drinks and then Maddy undid my sash and slid her hand in to feel my breasts.

"Your boobs are so sticky"? she purred at me.

I giggled had forgot to clean them.

"What's funny"? she giggled back at me.

"We had Baileys love sauce and I forgot to clean them, Sorry" I giggled back at her.

Maddy laughed and said how wicked I had been. Maddy nuzzled my neck and then bent down to suckle my nipples gently.

She looked up at me with those gorgeous come fuck me eyes and said how delicious and sweet I taste.

Oh god that felt so good.   Tingles were going through my body and once again it betrayed me. Scott guided me to his throbbing cock and I accepted it into my mouth.

Maddy lay me on my back and went down to my favorite   place and did sensual things to me.

Scott held me head as I sucked him hard and teased his knob like it was a all day sucker.

He groaned when I rolled my tongue around and around.

"You little hussy"? he purred at me as his cock slid in and

out of my mouth. I looked up at him with big eyes that said come fuck me,   His hot eyes melted in mine and I was in lust.

Maddy was a expert at bringing a woman to climax and I let go when she kept urging me on.

Scott also was close but pulled out to save it for fucking. After Maddy had feasted Scott lay on the carpet and   coaxed me on top of him. He had sheathed himself and   was ready for pounding.

Maddy straddled his face and was facing me giving me   beautiful smiles.

She played with my tits as I bounced up and down on Scott.

He plunged into me and thrust me up and down.

I groaned as his manhood took me deeper and deeper.

"Take it Baby Girl take all of him"? Maddy whispered to   me and then kissed me on the lips.

Nick and Tina came in to the lounge room and watched the   whole show.

They were aroused and wanted to play as well.

Nick took Maddy off Scott's face and made her go on her knees.

He protected himself and came at her from behind. Tina playing with Maddy and My tits and clit while the men fucked us.

She pushed me forward and put Scott's cock in my forbidden place, I groaned when he entered me and then

Tina finger fucked me from behind teasing my clit as well.

I was coming now and I could not stop that beautiful feeling of ecasty.   Scott also groaned he was close too.

Tina moved towards Maddy and Nick also had started to enter Maddy's forbidden place.   Tina played with Maddy's pussy and clit as Nick gently fucked her arse.

Maddy was groaning and her orgasm was loud like Nick'sand it really was a sensual explosion around us.

After we all came back down to earth Maddy got drinks we sat and laughed.

"Well that was fantastic"? Nick said with a big grin on his face.

"Sure was"? Scott agreed.

The girls and I nodded and smiled.

Yes it was a pleasurable and sensual experience. The night was getting late nearly 2am and I started yawning.

"I might retire if that's ok"? I said as I got up and retrived   my silk robe and g/string.

I said my goodnights and went to my room. I quickly showered and put on my silk Pjs.

Climbed into bed and snuggled in.   I thought about our night and realized that I was the odd one out.   I didn't   really mind as it was kind of nice to be spoiled   by a man and a woman.

My dreams were of Stefano yelling at me and calling me a slut. I remember running away down the road and a car came along and I got in.   I looked at the driver it was

James and he was smiling at me.   I was smiling back. In the back seat were a lot of men some I recognized and some I didn't.

I woke with a start.   How could that be, why would I smile at James.   No it doesn't make sense.   I love Stefano not James.   Those men in the back seat what were they doing there. I lay there and couldn't get back to sleep. I tossed and turned But couldn't sleep.   My head confused and spinning round and round with so many emotions. It gave me a headache. I got up and went to the bathroom and took some pain relief.I drank 2 glasses of water and lay back on my bed. After 15 minutes I felt better and snuggled into my coversAand dozed.

It was about 6am and I couldn't hear anybody up yet. I heard the sound of footsteps near my door and then heard a quiet tap tap.

"Come in"? I called out softly.

Nick entered the room only in his black boxers he looked hot and horny.

"Hope you don't mind me coming in"? he asked in asexy husky voice. His eyes looking wild and hungry.

He was Lion on a early morning feed.

"No not at all I actually cant sleep"? I replied softly.

I opened the covers for him to come in and in two strides he was beside me. We snuggled together and I asked if Tina minds him being here.

"No not at all you do realize she is very Bi and enjoys Men

But I think she prefers Women"? he said with a cheeky grin.

"After last night I can see you love a Man's touch"? he was close to my face now.   His lips teasing me and tempting me.

I licked my lips and didn't take my eyes off him.

"You know Tina thinks youre hot and I'm sure she wants to play with you again"? He said as his hand went to my buttons on my silk pj top.

"She is gorgeous and hot, I can see why men and women are attracted to her"? I said as I watched his lips move.

He had undone my buttons and he slid my top off me. My breasts heaving and aching to be touched.His finger touched each one gently and then he went back and pinched each one.

My eyes boar into his and we were talking with our thoughts. No words were needed.   His lips now upon mine and his tongue devouring my tongue.

 His hands teasing my nipples until I could take no more.I needed him to suck them better. He read my thoughts and suckled gently and passionately.
 My hand was in his boxers feeling his throbbing erection. He slipped off his boxers and made me go in a sixty-nine position so I was straddling his face.

He pulled off my silk pants and G/string and started teasing my clit with his finger and then his tongue.

I had my own mission.   His hot cock now in my mouth sliding up and down.   I took as much as I could and teased and rolled my tongue around his knob and down his shaft.

Nick was doing amazing things with his tongue also and my orgasm was not far away.

The way he slid his finger in and out with his tongue was sending me over the edge.

I bobbed up and down reaching out for the box of tissues beside the bed on the table and grabbed a handful.   Nick thrusting his hips upward for me to take more.   We were both groaning with lust and ecasty. Our orgasms taking over our bodies until we melted into one.

Our breathing raggered and loud.   Nick's chest heaving up and down while I lay numb from my explosion.

"Shower honey"? Nick rolled me off him and then rolled himself on top of me.

His lips crushing mine and his tongue probing for entry.

God morning orgasms were the best.   I was horny and my body was wanting more.

We got up and went to my bathroom.   The water was soothing and invigorating.

We soaped each other, Nick dipping the sponge around my pussy and into my bum cheeks.

His hands sliding all over my body.   It felt amazing.

He turned me towards the wall and bent be forward and then entered my purring pussy.   His cock hot and ready plunging deeper into me.   He held my hips and thrust me back and forth.

He pumped me until I could feel his need, and then he withdrew and spurted on my back.

He washed me again and then nuzzled my neck while his hands were around my breasts squeezing my nipples.

I wanted more I was so on heat lust and greed had taken over my body.

God what is wrong with me.   Can I not be satisfied with what we just did.

I turned to look into his eyes and he hugged me with his big arms.

He then picked me up and I wrapped my legs around his hips and he leant me on the wall for support.

"You want more Baby"? he asked huskily

"Yes" I breathed.

"Give me a minute baby I will love you again"? he purred in my ear.

I could feel his manhood coming back to life.

His finger was playing with my forbidden hole. He soaped me around there to get me ready.

He gently eased himself into me. Gently he did little thrusts and slowly went up and down. His finger in my pussy and his thumb circling my clit. God he was good, 3 things at once, That's what I call a Talented Man.

I groaned when he went deeper and he was very gentle

His finger teasing my clit and pussy it was taking me to another place.

His lips nipped at my nipples and I lost control.

My orgasm complete now and I let out a raggered cry.

Nick also coming, he quickly withdrawed and spurt his seed out.

His groans colliding with mine.

We clung to each other for a few minutes and then washed again and Nick wrapped me in a towel and carried me back to bed.   I snuggled in and Nick joined me too.

"That was great Tasmin very very nice to meet you and spending time with you"? he said as I lay my head on his chest..

"A man could get Addicted to good loving like that"? he said tenderly.

I laughed and thought shit I'm a no strings attached girl

Not wanting any commitment just hot sex! With a hot guy.! I felt a little sleepy now and my eyes closed and I snuggled into Nick's chest.

He also must of dozed off as we both woke 2 hours later to the sounds of everyone in the kitchen.

"Wake up sleepy head"? he kissed my head.

I dazed at him dreamily and sat up in bed.

We were both naked and I looked around for my robe.

"I'll get it honey"? Nick jumped up and grabbed it off the back of the chair.

"Thanks" I smiled at him as he handed it to me.

I tied my sash and found my pj silk long pants.   Nick grabbed me before I went to open the door.

He untied the sash and let my breasts spill out.

His head went down and gave each one last suck and nibble.

"OOhh Baby"?I cried out softly.

"Just wanted one last taste honey"? he grinned at me.

I grinned back at him and he gave my bum a little squeeze.

"Maybe we can see each again"? he asked when I went to open the door.

"Maybe"? I replied thinking I would love to but can I fit you in my life.

" I'll organize it with Scott and Maddy"? he said insistently.

"Ok we can meet up another weekend"? I gave in as my weakness is Men and he sure had a magic Aura about him.

We went to the kitchen and everybody was there eating

Breakfast and drinking coffee.

"Good morning you too"? Maddy said as she smiled at me.

Scott was grinning from ear to ear.

Tina also had a wicked smile on her face, they all obviously knew what we were doing.

I blushed and poured Nick and myself a coffee.

I handed it to him and he gave me a beautiful smile.

I blushed again and tried to look away.

We all enjoyed breakfast and then Nick said he had to go and do some things before working tomorrow.

Tina asked if she could stay for awhile and we said that would be ok.

She looked at me with a sweet smile and I felt tingles go through my body.   She had a beautiful aura about her too.

Nick kissed Tina and Maddy goodbye and shook Scott's hand.

I showed Nick out and he pulled me into his arms to give me one last kiss.

"Thanks for the great time, I would like to see you again"? he purred in my ear.

He kissed me tenderly and then left.

James was in the street and could see this strange man leaving Maddy's and kissing his Tasmin.

He did not like this one bit at all.

"What the fuck"? he bellowed in his head.

She still doesn't understand that she is mine and mine only.

I will have to show her again? He thought to himself.

He watched as Tasmin went back inside.   God she looked good. Hot and horny.   He wanted her but he would have to wait.   He decided to go to Jaine's and have his way with her.   At least that would ease some of the tension he was feeling.

I went back inside and everybody was relaxing in the lounge.

Scott and Maddy   looked very cosy on the sofa.

"I might shower and get dressed"? I said as I eyed them.

"Can I join you"? Tina asked sweetly.

"Sure" I replied with a cheeky smile.

We went to my bedroom and as soon as I closed the door she was at my side.

Her lips were upon mine and wanting my tongue.

Her hand pulled my sash loose and my breasts were exposed to her hands and tongue.

God it felt good.   Her sweet lips teasing my nipples and her other hand trying to pull down my pants.

She led me to the bed and lay me down.   I was in a trance.

I let her take control and watched her every move.

I was naked now on the bed and she undressed also to reveal her perky big breasts and petite body.

She wanted to feast and I didn't stop her.

"You taste so sweet Tasmin"? she purred through her tongue.

I was in bliss she was doing incredible things with her tongue and it felt great.

"Have you a dildo"? she asked

"Yes" I breathed back.

I got my friend out of the drawer and gave it to her.

"I want to fuck you"? she said in a sexy voice.

There was a knock at the door and Scott and Maddy were at the door.

"Want some company"? Scott asked us both.

Tina nodded and they entered.

Scott lay on the bed and asked me to blow him while Maddy straddled his face.

Tina wanted to fuck me with the dildo while I sucked Scott.

I bobbed up and down on Scott's cock while he teased Maddy with his tongue.

Tina played with my clit some more until I was ready.

She pounded me with the love toy and before we knew it we were all coming together.

Tina was excited at seeing us all climax,   she was waiting for her turn.

She wanted me to do the same to her so I washed the dildo and proceeded to fuck her.

She asked Maddy to straddle her face as she still wanted pussy juice.

Maddy didn't mind at all she liked all this female attention.

Scott was getting ready for round 2 and while I was on my knees giving it to Tina he came at me from behind and gently entered me.

"Oh honey you feel so good"? he huskily said.

Tina was close now and she thrust with me and the dildo.

Maddy wanted the dildo after her so we said we would do her after Tina.

Scott was pounding me and I pounded Tina.

We were all groaning now and my orgasm collided with theirs.

Scott got up and washed the dildo for Maddy's turn.

Tina wanted to fuck her and Maddy wanted me to straddle her face.

Scott wanted to fuck Tina's arse and she did not argue.

Once again our loud groans took over the bedroom.

We lay there together getting our breaths back.

"Shower time"? Tina said as she got up pulling my hand to come with her.

"You girls go Maddy and I want to play again"? Scott said passionately looking at Maddy who was still horny.

Tina and I went into the shower and Tina brought the dildo with her to wash.

She soaped me all over and washed the dildo ready for use.

I let her wash me and then she got the dildo and buzzed around my clit with it.

Oh my she was an expert at this.

I groaned when she entered me and thrust and buzzed inside me.

She pinched my nipples hard and I cried out in pleasure.

My orgasm came and left my knees weak.

"Youre a real turn on Tasmin"? Tina purred to me.

"You are too Tina"? I replied softly still trying to stand up without my knees shaking.

Tina washed the dildo and it my turn to return the sexual favour.

Tina groaned and moved her hips as I thrust the toy into her pussy. I pinched her fake tits and before long she was

Climaxing, her orgasm loud and releasing.   We both washed and dried off and then went back out to the bedroom.

I got dressed in jeans and a silk top and flats.

Tina also got dressed in her clothes from last night.

"Coffee"? I asked her when she was dressed.

"love one" she replied.

We went out to the kitchen and Maddy and Scott were already there drinking freshly brewed coffee.

I poured Tina and I a coffee and then we went out to Patio and sat in the sunshine. We sat there and enjoyed each others company and chatted. The day was getting late in the afternoon and

Tina had to go and Maddy rang a taxi. Scott said he would drive her but Maddy insisted that Scott was not ready toleave yet.

I suspected Maddy was jealous of Tina and didn't want Scott alone with her. I can understand why she was a gorgeous and very sensual, sexy woman.

The Taxi came and Tina said goodbye to us all.

"Would love to see you again just us"? Tina whispered in my ear as she hugged me.

"I'd like that"? I answered quietly back.

Tina climbed in the back seat and gave the driver instructions where to go.

The driver sat there with horny eyes he answered the call when he heard the address. Yes he wanted that fare and with all the trimmings.

He checked out the pretty girl standing there and licked his lips, she was hot, but where was the other one with long blonde hair. He had not forgotten the blonde and wanted more of that.

He drove away and checked out the black haired beauty in the back. She was hot and those tits were very appealing.

He was aroused and knew he would have to wank later to relieve himself. He did not dare approach this one she looked like she would put a fight. No he would pick his time with those two beauties and hopefully soon.
He licked his lips as he drove and his horny eyes one on the road and one on her tits.

Maddy, Scott and I were all very tired after our orgy. It was a great weekend one I would not forget.

It was time for Scott to go and we said goodbye with big smiles and hugs.

"Great weekend girls we must do it again"? he said in a husky deep voice.

I left Maddy to say goodbye alone and went inside and started to make a light dinner.

Maddy joined me some time later and I smiled at her and she smiled back.

"Hes so cute"? Maddy exclaimed when she saw me.

"I can see youre smitten"? I laughed at her.

"Yes well there is a sexual attraction and he would make a perfect husband"? she replied still daydreaming.

We ate dinner and then I said I'm having a early one.

Maddy said she would do the same.

I went to my room and rang Stefano and a lady answered his cell.

"Hello Stefano's cell"? she purred into the phone.

I was shocked who was this lady and where was Stefano.

I hung up quickly and sat there pissed off.

Ten minutes later Stefano rang and I answered it not knowing how to react.

"Hi honey"? he purred into the phone.

"who was that lady"? I asked him firmly and a little angry.

"Oh that was the maid"? "I was in the shower"? he answered. God he was liar and not a good one.

"Really why would the maid answer your phone"? I asked

With a nasty tone.

"Tasmin you don't think I would do the maid"? he asked me.

"Why not you do everybody else"? I yelled into the phone.

I regretted my words when they came out but it was too late, I said them and now I would have to eat my words.

I felt guilty inside as I wasn't excately faithfull to him either.

"Baby that's not fair I miss you and I need you"? he purred into the phone.

"I don't give a fuck anymore"? "You do what you have to do"? I replied thinking to myself is that what I want.

"Honey I love you don't be like that"? he was getting very insistent now, I could hear it in his voice.

"No I've heard enough excuses if you love me you would be here with me"? I was crying now.

"Baby girl I will be there soon you just have to be patient"? he tried to reassure me.

"I'm sick of being patient and waiting for you"? I cried into the phone.

"Baby please wait for me I will be there as soon as I can"? he was losing control now.

"That's what you always say I'll be there soon"? I chanted back at him.

"Tasmin please honey don't be like that, I can hear youre upset but honestly youre reading the situation wrong"? he trying to make it right.

"I've heard enough shit for one night I'm going and I don't   want to talk to you again"? there I said it even though I didn't mean it.

"Baby youre tired and upset please sleep on it and I will talk to you tomorrow when youre clear headed"? he said gently.

"No I wont change my mind I love you but its too late, I cant wait any longer for you, it is over Stefano forever"? I cried as I spat out the words.

"Baby I love you and I will be there with you soon"? he tried to promise something he knew was a lie.

He couldn't argue anymore he knew Tasmin was determined to disabey him and do what she wanted.

"I love you honey please give me more time"? he pleaded one more time with her.

I listened to his voice but didn't answer and then I hung up and cried.

Is it really over? The thoughts went over and over in my head. NO I can't let him go he was my addiction my lover and my life.

Maddy had heard me crying and tapped on my door.

"Tas are you alright"? she opened my door and came in.

"Oh honey whats wrong"? she came to my side.

I was crying and couldn't get any words out.

"Its Stefano hes with another woman and its over"? I spitted out between sobs.

"Oh honey it will be ok he loves you and nothing will stand in his way"? she tried to comfort me.

She rocked me in her arms and I felt a little better.

"how about a hot drink before bed"? she asked gently.

"Thanks that would be nice"? I replied looking at her.

She smiled back at me and I smiled back.

Maddy had this way of making me feel better and she only had to smile and flash her beautiful eyes full of love.

Maddy went to the kitchen and put the kettle on. The taxi driver had finished his shift and was horny as hell.

He couldn't stop thinking of those two sluts and as he was in their area decided to stop by and surprise them with his

Throbbing cock which needed attention. He pulled into the street and looked at the house. Yes the lights were on and he made his way to the door. He knocked and stood there wondering who will answer it.

Maddy heard the knock and thought it must be Scott coming over to surprise her.   A little tingle went through her body just thinking of him. She rushed to the door thinking Scott must want more of me

And thought this must be love if he makes me feel like this.

She answered the door with a smile and was surprised and shocked to see the taxi driver from the other day standing there.

"What do you want"? she spluttered out trying to close the door.

"You my lovely"? he came in and grabbed her before she could protest.

He covered her mouth and closed the door with his foot.

Maddy tried to struggle free but he only held her tighter.

"Wheres your friend"? he whispered in her ear.

"Shes not home"? she tried to say through his hand.

"If you scream I will hurt your pretty face"? he said firmly

Maddy tried to struggle free and he laughed and said that it only made him more hot to see her struggle.

"Wheres your room"? he asked huskily

Maddy pointed to the end bedroom and he dragged her there easily. She was light as a feather and could not fight his strong arms.

I lay in my bed waiting for Maddy and I thought I heard a noise.   I got up and called out for Maddy who didn't answer.

I went into the kitchen and the kettle clicked off it had boiled.

She must be in her room, I thought as I got down two cups from the cupboard.

I didn't hear anyone behind me just felt a strong arm around me and a hand across my mouth.   I froze with fear.

Was it James I wasn't sure and I didn't say a word.

"Youre very pretty baby girl? A man's voice was near my ear.   I tried to struggle but he was too strong.

That's not James I thought to myself.

His hand was feeling my breast and squeezing my nipple.

"Baby youre so hot"? he purred again near my ear.

I tried to turn around and see my attacker.   He held me tighter so I couldn't turn.

"Where's Maddy"? I tried to say

"Your friend is waiting for you"? he said huskily.

He dragged me to Maddy's room and I saw her lying on her bed.
I looked at her and realized she was tied up to the bed posts.

"Tasmin"? she yelled at me.

"Oh Maddy are you alright"? I asked her trying to keep calm.

He dragged me to the bed and tied me beside Maddy.

He had got her silk scarves that were hanging on her chair and used
them to tie us up.

"Who is this man"? I asked Maddy when he left us alone for a
minute.

"it's the taxi driver from the other night"? she replied worried now
what is going to happen.

"What taxi driver"? I replied confused.

"The one who brought us and Evan and Will home"? she answered
looking at me.

"Why is he here"? I asked again confused wondering why

a taxi driver would be so bold to attack us.

"The other night when I met Scott he picked me up and he attacked
me and had his way with me in the back seat"? she whispered to me when
he came back in the room.

"He raped and attacked you"? I whispered back watching every
move this man was doing.

"yes" she breathed back scared trying to touch my tied hand with
hers.

"Why didn't you tell me"? I asked her quietly

"I was so scared and he threatened me if I told anyone"? she whispered back to me.

He had got our cells and house phone and had put them on the floor and stomped on them.

Great now I have to buy another phone, I thought to myself as he turned and smiled at both of us.

"What do you want"? I finally asked this man

"You and your friend naked"? he said as he approached us.

He ripped Maddy's top down the middle and her breasts spilled out.

She screamed at him and called him a creep.

He slapped her then across her face and told her to behave or he will hurt me.

Maddy shut up then she did not want her best friend hurt.

He then ripped my top down the middle and licked his lips when he saw my breasts.

"Very very nice girls we are going to have fun"? he slurred as he eyed his beauties and their big boobs.

"You wont get away with this"? I yelled at him

"Oh wont I"? he came in for a feel and Maddy and I were helpless.

He sucked our boobs and slobbered over them with his tongue. He was rough and pinched our nipples and bit them making us scream in pain. He was aroused and liked seeing these sluts in his submission and control. He wanted to spurt his seed over their breasts and faces.

But that can wait he thought to himself with a horny grin.

He pulled his manhood out and put it near Maddy's mouth for her to receive.

"No I wont'? she screamed at him.   He hit her again and told her to do as she was told.

"Maddy it will ok just go along with it"? I whispered to her.

She looked at me and nodded.   I knew we would be ok if we didn't fight this man.

Maddy opened her mouth and he made her suck him.

He pinched my nipples hard and I tried not to scream.

"Youre next baby girl"? he huskily said as he looked at me.

He pulled out when he was close, he wanted to take his time and not blow everywhere just yet.

He pulled my pants off and smiled when he saw my black lacey knickers.

His head went down there and his teeth tugged at my knickers until he tore them.

He was a animal.

I tried to kick him but it only made it worse.   He held my legs down and then he slipped is finger in and started fucking me.

His tongue circling my clit and his fingers going in and out.

"You taste so sweet"? he slurred through his tongue.

I closed my eyes and tried to imagine it was one of my lovers and not this horrible man.

"Come for me my pretty"? he purred as his finger went deeper.

"NO I WONT!!!" I replied angrily

Well that was not appreciated and he slapped me hard on my leg thigh.

I cried out in pain.

"Do it"? he commanded again.

I cried and Maddy spat at him.

"You pig"? she screamed at him.

He was mad now but he didn't like having to hit them.

He never had to hit women before but somehow now it was a turn on, watching them beg in pain.   They were under his control.

"Girls behave and I wont hurt you"? he said again as he sheathed himself ready for action.

He untied Maddy and put her between my legs on her knees holding her arms behind her back.

"Lick her pussy"? he said loudly and rough.

Maddy obeyed and started licking and teasing me with her tongue.

He came behind her and entered her roughly.   He grabbed her hips and thrust deeper and deeper.

"Take that Baby Take my big cock"? he slapped her bum cheeks as he said it.

"Keep licking her"? he urged her on as he pounded and thrust into Maddy making her whimper.

I lay there and could do nothing.   I felt so sorry for Maddy but I knew I would be next.

He climaxed and groaned when his release was happening.

"Good Girl"? he kissed Maddy's back as he withdrew.

"Don't move and stay there"? he ordered her.   Maddy dared not move she did not want another slap as that hurt.

Her arms hurt from him holding her and she kept silent.

She lay with her head on my tummy and cried softly.

"Ssshh" I tried to comfort her.

"Its ok honey it will be over soon"? I cooed her.

Well I spoke too soon.   He tied Maddy back up beside me and then untied me and pulled me down to Maddy's   pussy.

"On your knees"? he commanded.

I obeyed hoping this would be over soon.

He sheathed himself again thank god he was doing that.

He made me lick Maddy while he pounded me from behind holding my arms behind me.

He withdrew and then entered my forbidden place.

"Oh Baby you feel so good"? he breathing was raggered.

I closed my eyes and tried not to scream when he ploughed deeper in me.

He was rough just like James and I hated him.   He was a pig and a brut.

He slapped my bum cheek hard and I cried out in pain.

"You like that don't you"? he groaned at me.

He was fucking my arse hard and rough and I knew he was close.

Please God let it be over.

He let out a groan and I knew he was finished.

He collapsed on my back and I could feel his sweat on my back. I felt sick and I thought I was going to throw up.

I held back my sickness and thought about Sam or Stefano.

Where were they when I needed them.

I choked back my nausea and tears.

He got up off my back and then retied me next to Maddy.

He went into the shower and then came back and untied

Maddy and dragged her to the bathroom.

He was having fun now and he was going to take her in the shower and rough.

He took her anally and this time did not wear a condom.

Maddy was screaming for him to stop.

Her screaming just made him more aroused and he pumped her harder and left his seed inside her.

Maddy's knees were weak and she couldn't stand after her or deal.

He carried her back to bed and retied her hands tightly.

He untied me and dragged me to the bathroom.

"Let us go you pig"? I spat at him.

He dragged me into the shower and held me close.

"If you struggle I will hurt you do you understand"? he was getting pissed off now.

I nodded, get it over with I thought rather than he hurt me

I will imagine it is someone else, God please give me strength.

"Wash me all over"? he commanded but this time a little more nicer.

I obeyed him and soaped him all over.

I thought if I pounched him in the balls would that take him down. I was terrified I would not have the strength to do it.

"Now blow me like you love me"? he had his hands on my Head.

He could snap my neck at any moment I thought as I closed my eyes and took him in my mouth.

I tried not to gag and get it over with.

"That's it baby suck it better"? he purred at me still holding one hand on my head and one mauling my breasts.

I sucked him hard and decided to suck the hardest I've ever sucked. I would torture him the only way I know how.

"You wildcat I'm going to fuck you honey everywhere"?

"I know your little game, you'll be punished for this"?

He groaned at me as I knew he was close.

He held me head as he spirted his semen in my mouth and then withdrew and spurted more on my face.

I tried not to gage or throw up.   Keep it together Tasmin I thought to myself.

I cleaned my face and gargled some water he pulled me up and pulled me in to kiss him.

"Kiss me like you love me"? he looked into my eyes.

They were greeny grey and were very lonely eyes.   Sad   eyes. He bent his head and his lips crushed mine. His tongue probing for entry.

"Give me your tongue and if you bite me I will bite you.

Your nipple and then the other"? he was serious now.

His eyes and wicked evil grin were frightening.

I was shaking and he put me under the water more.

"That better baby don't wont you to get cold"? he was gentler now.

He kissed me again probing for my tongue and telling me to do it and love him.

His lips left mine and went to my nipples where he sucked and gently nipped at them.

I tensed every time he did that thinking any moment he's going to bite one off.

He then turned me around and bent me over and thrust his

Cock into me. He held my hips with one and the other around my neck.

"Oh honey you feel so good"? he purred deeply

I closed my eyes and wished I was in a field in France with Stefano.

He was rough and urgent.

He then turned the shower off and pushed me out on to   the floor.

He put a towel on the floor and put me on all fours.

He was behind me and he put both hands on each breast and pinched my nipples.

"Spread your sweet cheeks honey" he commanded in adeep voice. Oh God he was not going to stop this torture I had to visilize it was Stefano or Sam playing this game with me.

I did what he asked and he spat in my forbidden hole. His finger circling and getting me ready.

He was pinching my nipples hard and I cried out in pain.

He eased into me thank god, and was gentle and not too forceful. I was surprised but still scared. Let it be over soon. He started to go faster and deeper. I groaned and whimpered. That only made him slap me on my bum hard and I would cry out again.

I could hear Maddy screaming from the bedroom yelling   for him to take her instead.

He would yell back soon my pretty it will be your turn to scream and beg.

Was there no stopping this Mad man.

He was close now and he withdrew and turned me over and tried to put his horrible penis in my mouth.

"Suck it you slut"? he angrily said to me.

"I wont" I screamed back.

He slapped me hard across my face and told me to open my mouth.

"Do it now"? he commanded roughly.

I did what he said and his penis spat its horrible seed into my mouth. I had to hold back my nausea.

"Baby that's so good" he said as he pulled his penis in my mouth.

"You like that honey"? he purred at me as his orgasm took over his body.   He was still in his dreamland of lust and

I struck then he was straddling my face and my hands were free. I punched his balls hard and then pushed him back so I could quickly get up. He groaned in pain but not enough to knock him over and he caught my leg as I was about to stand up.

It caught me off balance and I fell against the vanity hitting my head and landing on the floor unconscious.

The man looked at me and leant down and felt my pulse.

Yes she was breathing.

Shame he thought I was having so much fun with her.

He was in pain from the punch to his balls and he cringed

when he went to walk.

Bitch he thought she deserved that!!

He left her lying there and went back out to the bedroom and Maddy looked at him terrified.

"Where's Tasmin"? she asked angrily.

"Shes ok"? he purred at her.

He raped Maddy   over and over making her scream and beg to stop.   She was defeated and could not fight anymore.

He was enjoying this and thought he would stay here for a while no rush he thought.   He could work late tomorrow.

Maddy was sobbing on the bed and he tried to comfort her.

"Don't cry honey were going to have some more fun"? he stroked her face.

He got up and went to the bathroom and got a face washer and wrung it out.

He looked at the beautiful girl lying on the floor naked.

She looked so peaceful and he was a little aroused.

He wanted to fuck her like that.   No I had better not.

She will wake soon and then I will play with her.

He went back to Maddy and washed her face and body with the face washer.

Maddy lay still and watched him wash her.

He then untied her when she lay silent and numb.

He lay beside her and felt her breasts and trailed down to her bum.

"Youre so beautiful Baby"? he purred in her ear.

His erection pushing into her side.

"I want you to love me"? he whispered to her.

She looked at him and nodded.   She could not fight anymore. She was broken and her will had been take from her.

He lay on his back and coaxed her on top of him.

His cock sliding into her and he held her bum cheeks and thrust her up and down.

His hands going to her breasts and Maddy kept bouncing on top of him.

"That's it baby give it to me"? he urged her on. His hips grinding upward as she went up and down.

He was groaning in excasty and Maddy groaned in disgust and hatred.

She would play his game and wait for the right time.

"Honey that was beautiful" he kissed her breasts and then withdrew and got off the bed to clean up.

He was very content with his feed and wondered what to do with them when he was finished.

I'll stay and keep fucking them he thought to himself.

They will give in and beg him for more.   Yes that's a good plan he thought smiling.

He got up and left Maddy lying there curled in a ball.

She's not going anywhere he thought

He checked Tasmin on the bathroom floor, she was still breathing.

As he reentered the bedroom he didn't see Maddy standing behind the door.

He felt a hard whack across his head it caught him off balance and he fell against the sideboard hitting the side of his head. That would be the last thing he ever felt again.

Maddy was shaking and didn't know what to do.

She looked at the man he was lying still.   Blood was trickling out of his head.

She bent down and checked him her hand shaking.

She couldn't find a pulse.

She went into the bathroom and saw Tasmin lying on the floor.

"Tasmin can you hear me"? she bent down and felt her pulse.

Thank God she was breathing.

Maddy put a blanket on Tasmin and then quickly dressed.

The man on the floor had not moved.

He was dead.

Maddy was sure of it.

Maddy retrieved the phones but they were of no use.

She ran down the road to the nearest house and knocked on the door.

A woman answered and Maddy flung into her arms.

"Help, help me"? was all Maddy could say.

"Whats wrong sweet girl"? the older lady said.

"I need your phone"? Maddy spilled out frantically.

Maddy rang the police and an ambulance.

The older woman came back with Maddy to her house.

"Oh my god"? was all she could say when she saw the man lying there in a pool of blood.

The lady went into the bathroom and checked Tasmin.

"She's alive"? she said as Maddy who was white as a ghost.

They heard the sirens and the lady went to door to greet them.

"In here"? she ushered them towards Maddy's room.

Maddy was sitting beside Tasmin looking pale and shaking.

She was in shock.

The ambulance men entered the bathroom and one took

  Maddy and put a blanket around her.

Maddy watched as the ambulance men got me ready for transport.

"We need to get her to hospital quickly, he was saying to the other ambo.

They took Tasmin out in a stretcher and took her to hospital.

Maddy was also taken there but in a police car.

The taxi drivers body was covered with a sheet and left there for the coroner to arrive.

Maddy was interviewed about what had happened and she told them they had been raped and held captive by this maniac taxi driver. She also told them he raped her in his Taxi last weekend and that he knew where she lived.

She told them she hit him over the head with a wooden candlestick and that he had fell and hit the sideboard.

She was shaking and starting to sob uncontrollably. My friend Tasmin lying on the floor dying she was saying over and over.

She was hysterical now and the police were told to leave so they could sedate her.

Maddy fell into a deep sleep.   Her body was bruised and battered. The hospital were also worried about her mental state as she has gone through a terrible ordeal.

Tasmin was in a deep coma, her body also told the tell tale signs of assault and battery.

Police were stationed outside our rooms as no one was allowed in.

Tasmin's parents were rung as they are next of Kin.

They rushed to the hospital and waited patiently for news of their daughter who was in Intensive Care.

They were told briefly of what had happened and Tasmin's

Mother was in shock to hear what her daughter and friend had been through.

Tasmin's Father worried about his little girl.

He was also angry with himself for not protecting her enough. How could this happen.

They rang Jaine' and let her know what has happened.

"Oh my heavens"? she exclaimed worried and concerned.

They said they would let her know if there was any change with my condition.

Tasmin's Parents waited at the hospital for 10 hours, they were exhausted.

The nurse came and saw them and told them to go home and get some rest and that they would ring if there was any change.

Tasmin's Father took Tasmin's Mother home, she was tired,and distraught.

Her baby girl was injured and not out of the woods yet.

The doctor's were very concerned saying the next 24 hours were critical.

Jaine' was so upset to hear Tasmin was in hospital.

Peter came over and she told him what had happened to her best friend.

"She was attacked you say"? Peter looked at her very concerned.

"You will stay with me tonight"? Jaine' looked at Peter for understanding.

"Of course, of course I'II stay" he held her in his arms and rocked her.

He was actually very horny that's why he came to her house.

He would have to be gentle and kind to her so she'll love me, he thought to himself.

"Come let me take you to bed so you can lie down"? heheld her and led her to her room

Jaine was sobbing softly and muttered away in French to herself.

"Here baby lie down and I will take your mind of everything"? he coaxed her to the bed.

Jaine' lay down and Peter lay next to her.

He tried to console her slowly and gently.   He didn't want to scare her and not want sex   He was horny as hell

And had been thinking about Tasmin and how he would show her he loved her and she loved him. He was ploting a plan for them to be together forever. He also had masturbated to Tasmin's photo picturing her naked and

Hot sucking him hard and loving.

He now needed more and Jaine' will have to do.   He actually enjoyed her company and of course the sex.

But he knew deep down he would have to end it soon.

He kissed her tenderly on the lips and wiped away her tears with his tongue.

She smiled at him and he kissed her again a little more urgent this time his hand caressing her breast gently.

"Peter I don't think I am in the mood"? she said as she pulled away from him.

"Honey don't be like that I can relax you and help you sleep better"? he tried to talk calm and gentle.   Stroking

 her face and looking deep into her eyes.

She was lost then he took her breath away.

He took it slow and gentle.   He liked it rough but this time   he tried very hard to be gentle.

He sucked her big big nipples like a newborn needing milk.

His tongue trailing down to her lace knickers with the silt.

"Mmm did you wear these to work"? he grinned at her licking his lips.

"Yes I did I felt a little naughty though"? she smiled back at him and he knew he had her in the palm of his hand.

His finger found entry and he gently played with her clit and then dipping his finger inside her.

He continued this game until Jaine' needed his tongue there.

He spread her legs and he came between them.   He picked up her hips and bum and thrust his tongue through the slit inside her.

Jaine' groaned in pleasure and his finger also went inside.

He thrust his finger in and out while his other finger circled and teased her clit.

It was driving Jaine' wild.   She jerked her hips and pussy into his mouth more and he feasted like a lion who hadn't eaten in a week.

Her orgasm came in his mouth and lapped up the juices and then grinned at her licking his lips.

She lay there fully submissed, waiting for the hot throbbing cock. She wanted it and now.

She didn't have to wait long, Peter unleashing his weapon, hot and throbbing for attention.

Jaine's lips found his erection and she licked and sucked like it was a lollypop.

Peter groaned with pleasure, yes he was enjoying this softer side. He didn't want to blow in her mouth so just as

He was about to come he pulled her gently off him and plunged his cock into some tissues.

She looked up at him with big eyes and was still in his submission.

"Give me a minute baby and I will give you more"?

"If youre a good girl"? he teased.

Jaine' lay there and Peter went and got drinks to quench their thirst.

They would need it for the next round.

He handed Jaine's wine to her and they clinked glasses

"To your friend Tasmin I hope she is ok"? he said gently and trying to be compassionate.

"Thankyou Peter that's really nice of you"? she smiled and sipped her wine.

The wine relaxed her and Peter was very supportive she liked this side of him.

He kissed her and then went to her nipples which were very sexy and appealing

He made sure he was gentle using his tongue instead of his teeth.

His finger finding her slit and sliding in.

"Baby youre wet for me"? he purred in her breasts.

His erection straining against her.   He spread her legs and left her knickers on.   He entered her in her slit and pumped her gently.

She groaned with pleasure and dug her nails into his back.

He pulled out and turned her gently on her knees.

"You like it like this baby I will be gentle"? he kissed her bum cheeks.

He slid his finger in and then pulled her knickers off.

He spread her cheeks and gently eased into her pussy.

He was tempted to take her anally but told himself no, she was in no state for rough sex.

He held her hips and thrust her gently but urgent.

He held her breasts in his hands and gently squeezed her nipples to give a little more pleasure.

He was pumping her now and his thrusts were becoming more deeper and he was close.   His breathing becoming rapid and raggered.

"Give it to me baby"? he thrusted hard and fast.

He could not hold back now he couldn't be gentle. He needed to explode.

His orgasm was met with hers and they lay side by side for a while until they came back down to earth.

Jaine' lay content and sleepy.   He covered her with the covers and kissed her cheek.

He got up and went to the shower.   He washed his penis and as he did he thought of Tasmin and masturbated to an imaginary hand and her sweet lips upon him.

Maddy woke from her sedation and wanted to know about Tasmin and her condition.

The nurse said the doctor would be in soon and would talk to her.

Maddy lay back in bed with Tea and sandwiches.

She went over the events of the last 24 hours. My god weare lucky to be alive.

Tears starting flowing as she thought if her best friend lying in Intensive Care.

The doctor came around and told Maddy that Tasmin is on the critical list.   We have to wait another 24 hours and then the swelling of the brain should be shrinking.

We will know more then.

Maddy curled into a ball and fell back asleep.   Her pillow wet from her tears.

Scott had gone to Maddy's after work and surprised to see the police tape and a police officer there.

"What's going on"? Scott asked the police man worried.

"Are you family"? he asked Scott.

"No I'm Maddy's boyfriend"? Scott was impatient now.

"What's happened to Maddy"? Scott asked a little more stressed now.

"I'm sorry sir you have to go to the hospital and get information there"? The police man said.

Scott got into the car and drove to the hospital and rushed in to enquire about Maddy.

The nurse told him to wait while she talked to the doctor in charge.

Scott sat there impatiently tapping his foot and then pacing around the waiting room.

The doctor finally came and he explained to Scott what had

Happened to Maddy and Tasmin.

Scott just listened with his mouth open in shock.

"Can I see her"? he asked quietly, a tear had rolled down his face he was angry at himself that he was not there to protect her.

The doctor led Scott to Maddy's room.   Scott went in and sat in the chair by the bed.   Maddy had her eyes closed and was sleeping. He touched her hand and she opened her eyes in fear and then realized it was Scott and she started to cry.

"Oh sweet baby I'm so sorry I wasn't there to protect you"? he cried into her hair.

"Scott I'm going to be ok its Tasmin I'm worried about"?

Maddy said through sniffles.

Scott lay beside her and she rested her head against his chest.   His big arms around her.

He stroked her hair and promised for forever to keep her safe.

The next day Jaine' wanted to go to the hospital and see how Tasmin was.

"Peter could you take me please"? she asked him.

"I I suppose so if you want me to"? he said not sure if it was a good idea they were both seen together.

"Ok then let's go"? she grabbed her bag and they locked her door and left.

They arrived at the hospital and were told of no change to Tasmin's condition.   Jaine wanted to wait for a while and

Peter said he would wait with her.

The nurse said that Jaine' could see Tasmin through the glass for one moment and Jaine said she needed Peter to help her as she was very upset and needed support.

The nurse agreed but only for a moment.

Jaine' and Peter were led to the glass wall outside Tasmin's room.

Jaine gasped when she saw Tasmin lying there with a big bandage around her head and tubes going in and out of

Tasmin's body. The beeping sound of her heart beat and   lots of other monitors.

She clung to Peter who was close to tears seeing his

 Tasmin in this state. Oh god she could die, I could loose her. forever.

Don't die my love I need you, stay with me and I will love you forever, I will never let anyone hurt you again, the thoughts were going around in his head.

I was dreaming I was in a field somewhere in France. The wind was in my face and I was running and laughing.

Stefano was chasing me and then he caught me and wrestled me to the ground.

We made passionate love there in the field of wildflowers in the sunshine.

I opened my eyes and I saw Jaine' standing there crying and beside her was a man.   I looked at him and he looked at me.

I looked deeper and my feeling of love turned to fear.

He looked like James.

I tried to focus but it became burley and I drifted back into unconscious.

Jaine' was surprised and shocked to see Tasmin's eyes open,

It was only for a few seconds but they had opened.

"Nurse Nurse she opened her eyes"? Jaine' was excited now. James also was surprised to see Tasmin's eyes open and looking at him. Did she recognise me he thought to himself.

The doctor was sent for and they checked Tasmin over.

"That is very good and positive she might be coming out of it soon"?   He said with a small smile.

"Go home and leave your number at the desk and we will ring you if she wakes fully"? he added as he headed off with a clipboard ready for the next patient.

Jaine' felt better then and Peter held her hand as he walked proudly beside her. They had got a couple of stares, as this was the first time they had been out in public together.

He took her home and made passionate love to her.

Making her beg for his big erection that was in need of   her lips and pussy. He was dreaming it was Tasmin sucking him and he hoped one day soon it would be. He was gentle and had to restrain himself from being too rough. Later he thought to himself. Later when Tasmin is better.

The next morning Tasmin's mother was sitting in the chair beside her bed.

The doctor said that talking out loud might trigger off   sensors in her brain and she might respond and wake.

Tasmin's mother talked for hours until she exhausted herself.

Tasmin's father came into the room and took over. Go to   the café and get a coffee and fresh air he had said to her.

He sat beside his baby girl and told her about his weekend at the golf country club and that he had got a hole in one.

Tasmin could hear talking and people calling out her name.

Her eyes weighed heavy and she could not open them.

Her hand twitched and she heard more voices.

She knew she had to open her eyes but something stopped

her doing it.   She moved her mouth to say something and more voices were in the room.

She finally opened her eyes, her vision very blurry.

"Tasmin its mum can you hear me"? I heard a voice say.

I turned to where I heard the voice and my mother's face was a little clearer now.

I tried to move my hand towards her face,

"Mummy" I cried weakly.

There was a lot of voices and people moving around the bed.

The doctor spoke and his voice was clear. I turned towards

him and listened while he talked to me.

"Tasmin you are in hospital, you hurt your head but you will be ok now, you need rest"? he said as a light flashed in my eyes.

I tried to nod but my head hurt and I tried to raise my hand to it but couldn't.

I fell back asleep and didn't wake for another 5 hours.

The doctor explained that this is normal after Brain and head injury, and that it would just take time for me to heal.

A lot of rest and sleep he had said.

My parents kissed me goodbye and went home for some rest. They would return tomorrow.

The nurse rang Jaine' and told her I would be moved to a room out of Intensive Care.

"Oh thank God" she had said to the nurse.

"that's great Jaine' she is doing better"? Peter put his arm around her and kissed her gently on the lips.

Maddy was also told that Tasmin was going to be moved to another room and that she could see her later.

Maddy smiled and thanked the nurse for the great news.

She lay there and thanked God for listening to her prayers.

I was moved to another room and with every hour I was focusing more of what was around me.

I kept asking that I wanted to see Maddy and that could they arrange that.   The nurse finally brought Maddy to my room in a wheelchair.

"Oh Tas thank god youre ok"? she hugged me gently.

We were allowed to stay together for 15 minutes and then the nurse came and got Maddy and took her back to her room.

We blew kisses in the air at each other.

I was exhausted from her visit, Maddy had told me quickly what had happened and how she hit him over the head and killed him. I lay there and tried to remember what had

happened and could remember little bits of pieces.

I remember a horrible man raping us and was very rough but I couldn't remember anything else.

I fell asleep from exhaustion, I couldn't keep my eyes open any longer.

My parents visited me later that afternoon and I could see the pain in their eyes when they looked at me.

"It's ok I'm going to be ok"? I reassured them with a smile.

Our visits were short as 20 mins of keeping my eyes open was long enough. They kissed my cheek and said they would see me tomorrow.

I slept till dinner and ate very little.

Jaine' visited after dinner, the nurse telling her it had to be

Short as I needed rest.   Jaine' said ok she would just be a minute.

I smiled when Jaine' entered my room with beautiful flowers and a card.

"Hello sweetie" she purred softly to me.

"Youre looking better everyday"? she said cheerfully.

I knew she wanted me to tell her everything that happened but I honestly couldn't remember everything and in which order.

She didn't press me for information but said just get better,

I miss you and so does the shop.

Oh god the shop, how was she coping. Well that I knew she would be able to cope she was a better chef than me.

I looked at Jaine' and suddenly had a flash of James standing next to her, they were behind glass.

"What's wrong Tassy have you pain"? she panicked when she saw my face of   fear and got the nurse straight away.

I couldn't talk and I was confused. Jaine was told to leave and they sedated me lightly so I would sleep.

My dreams were confusing.   I dreamt Jaine' and James were kissing and laughing at me through the glass.

Stefano was calling my name Where are you my Tasmin, And the nurse talking to me as well.

"Tasmin Tasmin wake up I need to take your blood pressure"? she gently said.

I woke up and sleepily gave my arm to the nurse.

I don't remember anything else.   I woke in the morning to the smell of breakfast and realized I was hungry.

I ate a little more today and felt better.

My head seemed clearer and I wasn't getting dizzy every time I sat up.

The doctor came in and smiled at me sitting up in bed having toast and tea.

"Good to see you eating"? he commented   with a lovely bed side manner.

"How are you feeling Tasmin"? he looked at my chart

"Better everyday"? I said with a smile.

"Tasmin I need to talk to you"? he sounded serious now.

I nodded and just looked at him.

"Tasmin when you came in we did some tests and we have results of those"? he said looking at me

"Yep" I answered not really understanding what he fussing about.

"Tasmin all the tests look normal except one"? he said

"Ok which one"? I asked as he had my attention now.

"Youre Pregnant"? he replied looking at me for my reaction.

"I'm what"? I said "Did you say pregnant"? I repeated with my mouth open.

"Yes Tasmin I think very early stage"? he said

"Oh" I wasn't prepared for this.

"I'll leave you to process this and I will be back later to talk to you"? he said kindly and gently.

I lay there in shock and thought about what the doctor had said.

Shit how could I be.   I have been careful. All these thoughts went around my head.

Oh My God who is the father.

I tried to calculate my last period and when, and who.

My head started to hurt and I closed my eyes to sleep.

I dreamt of all my lovers tugging at me and saying that they are the father of my baby.

I woke when the nurse was checking my obs.

"Would you like a cuppa"? she asked as she put my chart at the end of the bed.

"Yes thank you" I replied trying to smile.

She came back with a cuppa and some biscuits.

"There you are honey just relax and rest"? she smiled at me and left the room.

I looked around at my surroundings.

Beautiful flowers everywhere.   Well-wishing cards as well.

I wondered if Stefano knew what happened and why haven't I heard from him.

I started to cry quietly and all these thoughts going around my head.

I'm going to have a baby, the thought going round in my mind.

I was crying but also smiling.

Suddenly I thought of the baby and what I had been doing the last 8 weeks of my life.

I've been drinking and also I had some coke.

Shit what if the baby is not healthy.   I felt very guilty now of what I might have done.

My world was spinning out of control and I didn't know what to do.

Was this baby Stefano's.

Would he be happy and be with me and his child.

No he wouldn't he would never leave his wife.   I would be his part time lover "Mistress".

What if its Sam's it could be.   What should I do.

I decided to ask the doctor later about the chances of the baby being affected.

What am I to do, I thought.

Do I want a baby now in my life, is it time.

A horrible thought crossed my mind, what if the baby is James.

The thought made me sick and I didn't want to think about it any longer.

I knew in my heart I hoped the baby was Sam's as that would be the best outcome.

I loved Sam but I loved Stefano as well.

I fell asleep confused and upset.

It was some hours later when the doctor came by to talk to me.

I told the doctor my personal fears and what I had done.

"Its ok we will do some tests but at this stage I don't think you have anything to worry about, you're young and fit"?

He reassured me with a big smile.

He had also said they can do DNA tests once the baby is born. So that was clear to me now. I knew what I had to do.

I wont tell anyone about this until I'm sure what to do about my lovers and which one would I choose.

Deep down I knew it was Stefano's baby as he was the only one who loved me unprotected for that week.   It must be him.

Should I tell him, not yet I thought.

Anyway where is he? He should be here not over there.

I he loved me he should be with me.

Just as I lay there and thought about my problem, Sam came to the door.

"Hi Beautiful"? he stood there with pink roses in his hand and a gorgeous smile on his face.

His eyes were sad and he looked at me worried and concerned.

"Hi" I said softly from my bed.

God I must look a sight I thought.

"Honey are you alright"? he came beside the bed.

I think he was too scared to touch me as I looked very fragile with tubes hanging out of me and my head still in a bandage.

I had black eyes and I knew I looked terrible.

"Baby girl"? he whispered to me with a tear in his eye.

"I should have been there to protect you and Maddy"? he said softly.

"You weren't to know its going to be ok"? I tried to reassure him.

My tears were now rolling down my cheeks.

Sam wiped them away softly with a tissue.

"Tasmin I love you and I cant bear to be without you"? he purred in my ear.   He kissed my cheek gently and sat in the chair beside me.

"When can I take you home"? he asked looking into my eyes.

"Home"? I asked "which home"? I asked again.

"Your home and I will be there right beside you"? he replied with a smile.

"I will never leave you alone again"? he added holding my hand.

I looked at him and smiled, he was so reliable and supportive.

Just what a girl needs, especially me.

His eyes danced with mine and we didn't have to talk.

He stroked my hand gently and I drifted back to sleep.

Sam wasn't there when I woke up and my Father was sitting in the chair reading his book.

"Hello sleepy head"? he smiled at me.

"Hi daddy" I whispered.

He helped me drink some water and then sat me up slowly so I could have a cup of tea.

"Wheres Mum"? I asked.

"She will be in soon" and she is fine"? he added.

The nurse did my obs and got me a cuppa and sandwiches.

She brought them back and said I need to keep up my strength now. I thanked her and caught her eye and told   with eye contact not to say anything about being pregnant in front of my father.

She nodded and I think she understood.

Mum arrived at the door with fresh flowers and some bananas and grapes.

"Hi honey" she cooed to me with a big smile.

"My you are looking much better today"? she added happily.

I looked at my parents, I was so lucky, will they be ok about   me having a baby. No don't tell them yet, not until I'm showing.   I didn't really know when that would be.   I must get a book about pregnancy I thought to myself.

They left after Mum fussed about and Dad could see I was getting tired.

I wanted to see Maddy and I asked the nurse if I could.

"Have a sleep and then I will bring Maddy in for dinner so you can eat together"? she said

"Would you like that"? she added smiling even though I could see the sadness in her eyes. She must know   everything.   I knew only a few nurses and doctors were told   of our rape and torture.   But the look on her face, I could tell she was informed.

"Thank you I would love that"? I said as I snuggled down and closed my eyes.

I slept for 2 hours and woke about 5pm. Dinner would be soon. Mine was light soup and sandwiches and maybe a dessert.   My appetite was returning slowly.

Maddy appeared at my door but this time not in a wheelchair.

"Maddy" I squealed

"Tas my beautiful friend" she came in and hugged me gently.

"God I've missed you" she kissed my lips softly.

"I"ve missed you too" I answered trying not to cry.

We chatted about how we were feeling but didn't talk about what had happened.

"Sam came in before and he wants to live with me"? I said to Maddy.

"Oh Tas he's really nice"? she said looking at me.

I wanted to tell Maddy about my pregnancy but thought I would wait a while.

We ate our light dinner and it was really nice to be together again.

The nurse came in and said would I like to move into Maddy's room with her.

Would I what I exclaimed excitedly.

So it was arranged and my bed was wheeled into Maddy's room and we both sat up in bed with huge smiles.

"But you both need to get some rest ok"? the head nurse said firmly

"Or I will have to separate you"? she gave a little smile. The doctor had said it would be a good healing process for   both of them after all the trauma they had been through.

I smiled back and assured her we would rest.

We both fell asleep and didn't wake until morning, I didn't even wake when the nurse checked my obs.

Breakfast arrived and this time we had porridge.   Toast and coffee.

Maddy and I sat up in bed and said this was great we were together.

After Breakfast Maddy got up and showered. I was jealous I couldn't wait for the feel of water on m body.

Bed sponging was not much fun.

I asked the nurse when can I shower.

She answered soon Tasmin let your body heal and in about a week you should be able to walk and shower with assistance.

Thank goodness I needed to walk and go to the bathroom myself. A week too long I will try in two or three days I thought.

After Maddy showered and dressed in light clothes for lounging around in the chair or in bed.

She told me she was allowed to go home in a couple of   days. She also said she was terrified to go home and that

Scott knew this and he suggested she moved in with him.

"I'm going to sell the apartment I cant go back there after

knowing a man died and I killed him"? she splurrted out and then she started crying.

"Oh honey come here"? I stretched my arm out to her and she came and lay down beside me.

She nestled in my arm and lay her head on my chest.

"SShh" I tried to comfort her.

The nurse came in and didn't like Maddy lying in my arms.

"Maddy please get in your own bed"? she instructed and helped her to her bed.

Maddy and I giggled like school girls and the nurse gave us both a stern look.

"Sorry" I said to her and she nodded and smiled.

She left us to get ready for sleep and we lay there in our own beds and chatted. Maddy was doing most of the chatting and I fell asleep to the sound of her beautiful voice.

Maddy looked over at me and I was in a deep sleep and smiled to herself. God Tasmin you are beautiful and I love you so much. Thank God you are going to be ok.

She lay there and watched the television quietly and then the news caught her attention.

Two faces appeared on the news, they looked very familiar

She thought to herself.

She looked closer and realized they looked like Evan and will.

She was listening to their reporter and what he was saying.

Two Irish Tourists found dead near river, the reporter was saying.

Maddy couldn't believe it. It couldn't be them. NO NO they can't be dead.

Maddy was distressed now and started to cry.   The nurse came in and asked her what was wrong.

She just kept mumbling over and over they can't be dead.

The nurse got the doctor and he came and said to sedate her to the nurse.

Maddy was sedated and I was unaware of what was happening, I was in a deep sleep.

I dreamt I was in a garden and I was there in a beautiful dress.   It was someone's wedding and there were

People sitting down on white chairs. Flowers everywhere and a big white Marquee on the lawn with

fairy lights around it. I was walking with my Dad who's wedding was it, was it mine.

Sam was there but he didn't smile at me. He looked mad and turned away when our eyes met.

I remember searching for Stefano's face in the crowd and could not see him anywhere.

As we all approached the Alter a man was standing there his back to me.   It was Stefano and he turned around.

His face was smiling and he looked so handsome. I was looking into his eyes and suddenly they became a blur and his face changed into James. I started sceaming and pulling away from my father.   He was saying its alright

Darling this is your husband to be. he said as he held his grip on my arm.

"No daddy no I hate him" I was screaming and daddy pulled me up to the alter and handed me over to James

"She's all yours now" he had said

James had me in a tight grip and I remember screaming and hitting him.

I can't marry him he is evil.

I started screaming somebody help me I don't love him.

Maddy Maddy I was screaming but she said it's ok he loves you. No No I kept saying.

I saw Jaine' sitting there and she was crying. She looked at me with big sad eyes. I looked at her and she didn't smile at me.

Jaine' Jaine' help me I don't love him, I was screaming at her. She looked at me and said nothing.

I looked at Sam and he didn't come to my rescue. He was laughing and everybody was laughing. I was screaming uncontrollably and James had this evil look in his eye.

You will be mine soon and you will have to obey your husband, he laughed at me.

I'd rather die than be your wife I screamed at him James just laughed at me.

My head was whirling around and around and I think then I passed out. A beeping sound was in my head and I remember voices near me. Am I dreaming I wasn't sure? My eyes were open and I was floating and I looked down and saw a girl in the bed. She looked so peaceful and beautiful. Who is she.

What were all the people doing. I heard my name being called. I recognized this name. A bright light was pulling me in. Tasmin I heard a voice through the light.

Evan and Will were floating like an Angels, they looked beautiful and handsome. What were they doing here.

I reached out and Evan touched my hand. come with me he sang softly. I was confused why was Evan calling me.

His eyes full of love and life. His hand still reaching out for mine.

Evan, Evan I need you help me, I was saying Tasmin come with me let go Evan was softly saying.

I wanted to go with him but something was pulling me back. All these voices were calling my name come back to us they were saying.

I looked down at the girl and suddenly it hit me. I know who that girl is

That girl is me.